PENGUIN  CLA

THE ASPERN PAPERS AND OTHER TALES

SERIES ADVISOR: PHILIP HORNE

HENRY JAMES was born in 1843 in Washington Place, New York, of Scottish and Irish ancestry. His father was a prominent theologian and philosopher and his elder brother, William, also became famous as a philosopher. James attended schools in New York and later in London, Paris and Geneva, before briefly entering the Law School at Harvard in 1862. In 1864 he began to contribute reviews and short stories to American journals. He visited Europe twice as an adult before moving to Paris in 1875, where he met Flaubert, Turgenev and other literary figures. However, after a year he moved to London, where he met with such success in society that he confessed to accepting 107 invitations in the winter of 1878–9 alone. In 1898 he left London and went to live at Lamb House, Rye, Sussex. Henry James became a naturalized British citizen in 1915, and was awarded the Order of Merit in 1916, shortly before his death in February of that year.

In addition to many short stories, plays, books of criticism, biography and autobiography, and much travel writing, he wrote some twenty novels, the first of which, *Watch and Ward*, appeared serially in the *Atlantic Monthly* in 1871. His novella 'Daisy Miller' (1878) established him as a literary figure on both sides of the Atlantic. Other novels include *Roderick Hudson* (1875), *The American* (1877), *The Europeans* (1878), *Washington Square* (1880), *The Portrait of a Lady* (1881), *The Bostonians* (1886), *The Princess Casamassima* (1886), *The Tragic Muse* (1890), *The Spoils of Poynton* (1897), *What Maisie Knew* (1897), *The Awkward Age* (1899), *The Wings of the Dove* (1902), *The Ambassadors* (1903) and *The Golden Bowl* (1904).

MICHAEL GORRA is Mary Augusta Jordan Professor of English at Smith College and the author of *Portrait of a Novel: Henry James and the Making of an American Masterpiece* (2012), a finalist for both the Pulitzer Prize and the James Tait Black Memorial Prize in biography. His earlier books include *The English Novel at*

Mid-Century; After Empire: Scott, Naipaul, Rushdie; and The Bells in Their Silence: Travels through Germany, along with, as editor, The Portable Conrad and the Norton Critical Edition of William Faulkner's As I Lay Dying. He lives in Northampton, Massachusetts.

PHILIP HORNE is a Professor of English at University College London. He is the author of Henry James and Revision: The New York Edition (1990); editor of Henry James: A Life in Letters (1999); and co-editor of Thorold Dickinson: A World of Film (2008). He has also edited Henry James, A London Life & The Reverberator; and for Penguin, Henry James, The Tragic Muse and The Portrait of a Lady, and Charles Dickens, Oliver Twist. He has written articles on Henry James, and on a wide range of other subjects, including telephones and literature, zombies and consumer culture, the films of Powell and Pressburger and Martin Scorsese, the texts of Emily Dickinson, the criticism of F. R. Leavis, poetic allusion in Victorian fiction, and Bob Dylan and the Mississippi Blues. He is a General Editor of the Cambridge University Press edition of the Complete Fiction of Henry James.

PENGUIN CLASSICS

Published by the Penguin Group
Penguin Books Ltd, 80 Strand, London WC2R ORL, England
Penguin Group (USA) Inc., 375 Hudson Street, New York, New York 10014, USA
Penguin Group (Canada), 90 Eglinton Avenue East, Suite 700, Toronto, Ontario, Canada M4P 2Y3
(a division of Pearson Penguin Canada Inc.)
Penguin Ireland, 25 St Stephen's Green, Dublin 2, Ireland (a division of Penguin Books Ltd)
Penguin Group (Australia), 707 Collins Street, Melbourne, Victoria 3008, Australia
(a division of Pearson Australia Group Pty Ltd)
Penguin Books India Pvt Ltd, 11 Community Centre, Panchsheel Park, New Delhi – 110 017, India
Penguin Group (NZ), 67 Apollo Drive, Rosedale, Auckland 0632, New Zealand
(a division of Pearson New Zealand Ltd)
Penguin Books (South Africa) (Pty) Ltd, Block D, Rosebank Office Park,
181 Jan Smuts Avenue, Parktown North, Gauteng 2193, South Africa

Penguin Books Ltd, Registered Offices: 80 Strand, London WC2R ORL, England

www.penguin.com

This edition first published in Penguin Classics 2014

015

Introduction and editorial material © Michael Gorra, 2014
Chronology copyright © Philip Horne, 2008
All rights reserved

The moral right of the editors has been asserted

Set in 10.25/12.25pt Postscript Adobe Sabon
Typeset by Jouve (UK), Milton Keynes
Printed in Great Britain by Clays Ltd, Elcograf S.p.A.

ISBN: 978-0-141-38979-0

www.greenpenguin.co.uk

Penguin Books is committed to a sustainable
future for our business, our readers and our planet.
This book is made from Forest Stewardship
Council™ certified paper.

Contents

Chronology

1843 *15 April*: Henry James born at 21 Washington Place in New York City, second of five children of Henry James (1811–82), speculative theologian and social thinker, whose strict entrepreneur father had amassed wealth estimated at $3 million, one of the top ten American fortunes of his time, and his wife Mary (1810–82), daughter of James Walsh, a New York cotton merchant of Scottish origin.

1843–5 Accompanies parents to Paris and London.

1845–7 James family returns to USA and settles in Albany, New York.

1847–55 Family settles in New York City; HJ taught by tutors and in private schools.

1855–8 Family travels in Europe: Geneva, London, Paris, Boulogne-sur-Mer. Returns to USA and settles in Newport, Rhode Island.

1859–60 Family in Europe again: HJ attends scientific school, then the Academy (later the University) in Geneva. Learns German in Bonn.

September 1860: Family returns to Newport. HJ makes friends with future critic T. S. Perry (who records that HJ 'was continually writing stories, mainly of a romantic kind') and artist John La Farge.

1861–3 Injures his back helping to extinguish a fire in Newport and is exempted from military service in American Civil War (1861–5).

Autumn 1862: Enters Harvard Law School for a term. Begins to send stories to magazines.

1864 *February*: First short story, 'A Tragedy of Error', published anonymously in *Continental Monthly*.

> *May*: Family moves to 13 Ashburton Place, Boston, Massachusetts.

> *October*: Unsigned review published in *North American Review*.

1865 *March*: First signed tale, 'The Story of a Year', appears in *Atlantic Monthly*. HJ's criticism published in first number of the *Nation* (New York).

1866–8 Continues reviewing and writing stories.

> *Summer 1866*: W. D. Howells, novelist, critic and influential editor, becomes a friend.

> *November 1866*: Family moves to 20 Quincy Street, beside Harvard Yard, in Cambridge, Massachusetts.

1869 Travels for his health to England, where he meets John Ruskin, William Morris, Charles Darwin and George Eliot; also visits Switzerland and Italy.

1870 *March*: Death in USA of his much-loved cousin Minny Temple.

> *May*: HJ, still unwell, is reluctantly back in Cambridge.

1871 *August–December*: First short novel, *Watch and Ward*, serialized in *Atlantic Monthly*.

1872–4 Accompanies invalid sister Alice and aunt Catherine Walsh ('Aunt Kate') to Europe in May. Writes travel pieces for the *Nation*. Between October 1872 and September 1874 spends periods of time in Paris, Rome, Switzerland, Homburg and Italy without his family.

> *Spring 1874*: Begins first long novel, *Roderick Hudson*, in Florence.

> *September 1874*: Returns to USA.

1875 *January*: Publishes *A Passionate Pilgrim, and Other Tales*, his first work to appear in book form. It is followed by *Transatlantic Sketches* (travel pieces) and then by *Roderick Hudson* in November. Spends six months in New York City (111 East 25th Street), then three in Cambridge.

> *11 November*: Arrives at 29 rue de Luxembourg, Paris, as correspondent for the *New York Tribune*.

> *December*: Begins new novel, *The American*.

1876 Meets Gustave Flaubert, Ivan Turgenev, Edmond de Goncourt, Alphonse Daudet, Guy de Maupassant and Émile Zola.

December: Moves to London and settles at 3 Bolton Street, just off Piccadilly.

1877 Visits Paris, Florence and Rome.

May: *The American* is published.

1878 Meets William Gladstone, Alfred Tennyson and Robert Browning.

February: Collection of essays, *French Poets and Novelists*, is the first book HJ publishes in London.

July: Novella 'Daisy Miller' serialized in *The Cornhill Magazine*; in November *Harper's* publish it in the USA, establishing HJ's reputation on both sides of the Atlantic.

September: Publishes novel *The Europeans*.

1879 *December*: Publishes novel *Confidence* and *Hawthorne* (critical study).

1880 *December*: Publishes novel *Washington Square*.

1881 *October*: Returns to USA; visits Cambridge.

November: Publishes novel *The Portrait of a Lady*.

1882 *January*: Death of mother. Visits New York and Washington, DC.

May: Travels back to England but returns to USA on death of father in December.

1883 *Summer*: Returns to London.

November: Fourteen-volume collected edition of fiction published by Macmillan.

December: Publishes *Portraits of Places* (travel writings).

1884 Sister Alice moves to London and settles near HJ.

September: Publishes *A Little Tour in France* (travel writings) and *Tales of Three Cities*; his important artistic statement 'The Art of Fiction' appears in *Longman's Magazine*. Becomes a friend of R. L. Stevenson and Edmund Gosse. Writes to his American friend Grace Norton: 'I shall never marry ... I am both happy enough and miserable enough, as it is.'

1885–6 Publishes two serial novels, *The Bostonians* and *The Princess Casamassima*.

6 March 1886: Moves into flat at 34 de Vere Gardens.

1887 *Spring and summer*: Visits Florence and Venice. Continues friendship (begun in 1880) with American novelist Constance Fenimore Woolson.

1888 Publishes novel *The Reverberator*, novella 'The Aspern Papers' and *Partial Portraits* (criticism).

1889 Collection of tales *A London Life* published.

1890 Novel *The Tragic Muse* published.

1891 HJ's dramatization of *The American* has a short run in the provinces and London.

1892 *February*: Publishes *The Lesson of the Master* (story collection).

   March: Death of Alice James in London.

1893 Three volumes of tales published: *The Real Thing* (March), *The Private Life* (June), *The Wheel of Time* (September).

1894 Deaths of Constance Fenimore Woolson and R. L. Stevenson.

1895 *5 January*: Play *Guy Domville* is greeted by boos and applause on its premiere at St James's Theatre; HJ abandons playwriting for many years. Visits Ireland. Takes up cycling.

   May: Publishes a volume of tales, *Terminations*.

1896 Publishes novel *The Other House* and a volume of tales, *Embarrassments* (June).

1897 Two novels, *The Spoils of Poynton* and *What Maisie Knew*, published.

   February: Starts dictating, due to wrist problems.

   September: Takes lease on Lamb House, Rye, Sussex.

1898 *June*: Moves into Lamb House. Sussex neighbours include the writers Joseph Conrad, H. G. Wells and Ford Madox Hueffer (Ford).

   August: Publishes *In the Cage* (short novel).

   October: 'The Turn of the Screw', ghost story included in *The Two Magics*, proves his most popular work since 'Daisy Miller'.

1899 *April*: Novel *The Awkward Age* published.

   August: Buys the freehold of Lamb House.

1900 Shaves off his beard.

   August: Publishes collection of tales *The Soft Side*. Friendship with American novelist Edith Wharton develops.

1901 *February*: Publishes novel *The Sacred Fount*.

1902 *August*: Publishes novel *The Wings of the Dove*.

1903 *February*: Publishes collection of tales *The Better Sort*.

September: Publishes novel *The Ambassadors*.

October: Publishes biography *William Wetmore Story and his Friends*.

1904 *August*: Sails to USA, his first visit for twenty-one years. Travels to New England, New York, Philadelphia, Washington, the South, St Louis, Chicago, Los Angeles and San Francisco.

November: Publishes novel *The Golden Bowl*.

1905 *January*: Is President Theodore Roosevelt's guest at the White House. Elected to the American Academy of Arts and Letters.

July: Back in Lamb House, begins revising works for the New York Edition of *The Novels and Tales of Henry James*.

October: Publishes *English Hours* (travel essays).

1906–8 Selects, arranges, writes prefaces and has illustrations made for New York Edition (published 1907–9, twenty-four volumes).

1907 *January*: Publishes *The American Scene* (travel essays).

1908 *March*: Play *The High Bid* produced at Edinburgh.

1909 *October*: Publishes *Italian Hours* (travel essays). Health problems.

1910 *August*: Travels to USA with brother William, who dies a week after their return.

October: Publishes *The Finer Grain* (tales).

1911 *August*: Returns to England.

October: Publishes *The Outcry* (novel adapted from play). Begins work on autobiography.

1912 *June*: Receives honorary doctorate from Oxford University.

October: Takes flat at 21 Carlyle Mansions, Cheyne Walk, Chelsea; suffers from shingles.

1913 *March*: Publishes *A Small Boy and Others* (first volume of autobiography). Portrait painted by John Singer Sargent for seventieth birthday.

1914 *March*: Publishes *Notes of a Son and Brother* (second volume of autobiography).

August: Outbreak of First World War; HJ becomes passionately engaged with the British cause and helps Belgian refugees and wounded soldiers.

October: Publishes *Notes on Novelists*.

1915 Is made honorary president of the American Volunteer Motor Ambulance Corps.

July: Becomes a British citizen. Writes essays about the war (collected in *Within the Rim* (1919)) and the Preface to *Letters from America* (1916) by the poet Rupert Brooke, who had died the previous year.

2 December: Suffers a stroke.

1916 Awarded the Order of Merit in New Year Honours.

28 February: Dies. After his funeral in Chelsea Old Church, his ashes are smuggled back to America by sister-in-law and buried in the family plot in Cambridge.

Philip Horne, 2008

Introduction

*First-time readers should be aware that details of
the plots are revealed in this Introduction.*

On 2 January 1888 Henry James sat in his South Kensington
apartment over a letter to his old friend, fellow-novelist and
former editor William Dean Howells. The two had known
each other since the mid-1860s, when as young men they had
walked at night through the streets of Cambridge, Massachusetts, miles of endless talk in which the art of fiction seemed to
fuse itself with the sense of their own futures. Howells was then
an assistant at the *Atlantic Monthly*, and had got the magazine
to take some of James's first stories. A few years later, and by
then its editor, he would serialize his friend's early novels, culmin-
ating with the 1880–81 publication of *The Portrait of a Lady*.
But James hadn't repeated the success of that first masterpiece,
and instead of continuing to write about the adventures of
Americans in Europe, he had turned to a pair of novels about
social questions, one of them wholly American in its cast of
characters, and the other almost exclusively European. *The
Bostonians* had taken up what he called a 'peculiar point of our
social life . . . the situation of women . . . the agitation on their
behalf',[1] while *The Princess Casamassima* examined the world
of anarchist cells. Together they constituted his response to the
naturalism of the contemporary French novel and, above all, to
the work of Émile Zola, whose seriousness of purpose James
admired but whose social determinism he found limiting. Their
reviews had, however, been mixed and their sales weak, and in
writing to Howells James claimed that he felt himself to be:

> staggering a good deal under the mysterious and (to me) inexplicable
> injury wrought – apparently – upon my situation by my two last

> novels ... from which I expected so much and derived so little. They have reduced the desire, and the demand, for my productions to zero – as I judge from the fact that though I have for a good while past been writing a number of good short things, I remain irremediably unpublished. Editors keep them back, for months and years, as if they were ashamed of them.[2]

Nor was it only his ego that suffered. He was starting to need the money. James always made more from magazine sales than from books, but though the editors of *Harper's* and the *Century* had bought those 'good short things' they hadn't yet paid for them; in 1887 he had taken in only $1,320, or just under £270, less than at any time since his apprentice days. In other ways, though, that year had been one of his best. He had spent its first half in Italy, in Florence and Venice, and once back in England had enjoyed a productive autumn on the start of a new novel. He believed that he was working well, and knew he was overstating his own desperation: as he went on to predict to Howells, 'very likely ... all my buried prose will kick off its various tombstones at once',[3] and find itself reborn on the printed pages of one monthly or another. As indeed it did, for in 1888 James published a short novel, *The Reverberator*, along with seven tales, two of them included in this volume, and banked over $8,000, or more than £1,600.

Still, this letter to Howells points to something more than a temporary struggle. *The Bostonians* and *The Princess Casamassima* are problem novels in the way that Shakespeare's *Measure for Measure* is a problem play. They ask questions so intractable that they do not quite resolve into form, books endlessly discussable and yet forever uncomfortable. And now James was at work on a third such novel. *The Tragic Muse* depicts its characters as variously engaged in painting, Parliament and the theatre. It's a book about the conflict between social expectation and individual fulfilment, about the choice of a vocation and, above all, about the shape and nature of an artistic career. Yet while it has its admirers, myself among them, few would argue that it's among James's most successful works. Its issues were precisely the ones that most absorbed him at the end of the 1880s, but he offered his richest account of them in a series of exceptionally brilliant stories from that period about the lives of writers and artists.

'The Aspern Papers' and 'The Real Thing', 'The Lesson of the Master' and 'The Middle Years': these are among the finest of James's 112 completed tales. He had long ago accepted and in fact welcomed his own expatriation. The question of America's relation to the Old World continued to interest but no longer preoccupied him, and he took up a new set of concerns instead, ones that now seemed to press in more immediately personal ways. He was a settled bachelor and had taken a different path from Henry St George, the uxorious title figure of 'The Lesson of the Master', but he still felt the ghost of an alternative life, and drew on it in that urbane comedy. He was in his own middle years when he wrote 'The Middle Years', a story about a dying novelist who's only just begun to glimpse his own potential, the splendid 'last manner' of which he now believes himself capable.

These fables of the creative life are at once wholly ironic and utterly transparent in defining the perplexities of James's own situation. What's the connection between art and life – not only between the artist's work and family responsibilities, but also between the act of representation and the thing represented? Does biography have a legitimate purpose, or do its prying investigations inevitably stand as a kind of crime, a form of violation? Is fiction an amusement or a fine art, the product of an intellectual calling, of some deliberate intention beyond the desire to amuse? What is the artist's relation to the marketplace – and then again to his own sense of ambition and career? I put all this as a series of rhetorical questions because these tales themselves are rhetorical questions. James comes to no definitive answers, and when taken as a whole these stories make no single statement. Instead they offer a series of parables and problems, a complex of issues that he never tired of examining, but to which he was especially drawn in the years when he saw his own career in crisis.

That crisis would continue. *The Tragic Muse* didn't earn back its modest advance, and in the first half of the 1890s

James turned away from the novel and instead put his energy into an attempt to make his fortune as a playwright. Several of the stories in this volume were written in the midst of that experiment – a trial that would utterly fail. Yet the skills he learned in the theatre – his heightened sense of the possibilities of dialogue and his increased ability to block a scene, to handle his characters' exits and entrances – would show themselves when he came back to the long form, and shape such late masterpieces as *The Ambassadors* and *The Golden Bowl*. 'Try to be one of the people on whom nothing is lost': such was the advice he gave to young writers in his 1884 'The Art of Fiction'.[4] He took it.

James's tales about writers and artists stand as one of the main groupings in the large body of his short fiction; other clusters include his ghost stories, 'The Turn of the Screw' above all, or his account of Americans abroad in such works as 'Daisy Miller'. These subjects were the ones to which he returned most often, and he wrote more stories about the artistic life than one volume can comfortably hold; tales such as 'The Next Time', about a writer's writer who dreams of composing a trashy best-seller, or 'The Real Right Thing', in which a biographer is chased away by the ghost of his subject. The seven pieces reprinted in this volume, however, are probably the most provocative and enduring, a loose group published between 1884 and 1896, and most of which use London or its near environs as a setting. For James was also a great writer about London. He had a shrewd eye for the social complexion of this street or that square, and his understanding of the capital went far beyond the Mayfair or Marylebone pavements with which he is most associated. He knew its forgotten corners and its sweaty crowds, the smell of gin and gas-lights, the clatter of its telegraph keys and the mud of its horse-fouled streets. But above all he knew its gossip, and some of the pieces in this book owe their origins to that gossip, a moment of chatter that James then recorded in his notebook. He got the idea for 'The Author of *Beltraffio*' from one friend, the critic Edmund Gosse;

another, the artist George du Maurier, gave him the anecdote
that became 'The Real Thing'.

James began to keep a notebook in 1878, not a diary but
a book of professional memoranda, and filled it with bits of
suggestive table talk, preliminary sketches for his stories and
novels, and sometimes even lists of potential names. Here's one
of his earliest entries, from 22 January 1879:

> I heard some time ago, that Anthony Trollope had a theory that a
> boy might be brought up to be a novelist as to any other trade. He
> brought up – or attempted to bring up – his own son on this prin-
> ciple, and the young man became a sheep-farmer, in Australia.
> The other day Miss Thackeray (Mrs Ritchie) said to me that she
> and her husband meant to bring up their little daughter in that
> way. It hereupon occurred to me (as it has occurred before) that
> one might make a little story upon this. A literary lady (a poor
> novelist) – or a poor literary man either – (this to be determined) –
> gives out to the narrator that this is their intention with regard to
> their little son or daughter. After this the narrator meets the parent
> and child at intervals, about the world, for several years – the
> child's peculiar education being supposed to be coming on. At last
> when the child is grown, there is another glimpse; the intended
> novelist has embraced some extremely prosaic situation, which is
> a comment – a satire – upon the high parental views.[5]

In the end it was a literary lady with both a daughter *and* a son,
and the story emerged in 1892 as 'Greville Fane'. By then it was
a much more complicated piece, and in a later notebook entry,
this one from 1889, James thinks his way through the 'little
story', canvassing a set of narrative possibilities and refining his
sense of its situation. 'There must be an *action*,' he writes, and
the scenario then appears to come to him immediately, right
down to the daughter's marriage 'on the edge of good society'.
The children think their mother's work is dreadful, but are
happy enough to live on it, and 'the thing had much best be
told by a witness of her life – a friend – a critic, a journalist,
etc.' By the end of his notes James has decided to call the story

after the poor woman's pen-name – 'some rather smart *man's* name'[6] – and in fact the version he's sketched in a few rapid moments is remarkably like the finished piece. Characters, structure, point of view: he snaps his fingers and they are all of them in place. All he now has to do is write it.

James performs such tricks on almost every page of his notebooks, seizing on some alternatives and rejecting others, deciding what in a given anecdote either can or cannot be used, and seeming to conjure a masterpiece out of nothing at all. Each story in this volume has an entry in those notebooks, some initial nubbin of an idea, and taken together they offer a sense of his methods that's at odds with our usual understanding of his work. Late in his career James prepared a collected edition – the New York Edition – in which he revised his earlier fiction to bring it in line with his later style. To each book he added a preface, and in the one he wrote for *The Portrait of a Lady*, he remembered a conversation in Paris with Ivan Turgenev, in which the Russian told him that his own work almost always began 'with the vision of some person or persons, who hovered before him . . . interesting him and appealing to him just as they were and by what they were'.[7]

Turgenev began, that is, with character, and the process of writing involved discovering their 'right relations, those that would most bring them out',[8] that would reveal a given character's essence. James himself had worked that way in *The Portrait of a Lady*, extrapolating as Turgenev did from a real person, his dead cousin Minnie Temple, and then searching for the incidents that would best show her. The notebooks, however, suggest that his usual practice in his shorter fiction was exactly the opposite. For all his reference to his fellow-novelists, 'Greville Fane' started not so much with a character as with an idea, a proposition or a dramatic situation, for which he had to invent the people who would let him explore it; and so it is in most of his tales, in those of London life or Americans abroad as much as in those about writers.

Let's look for an example at James's notes for 'The Figure in the Carpet'. The story's title has become a catchphrase that for better or probably worse now defines the act of criticism, of tracing the patterns in a given artist's work; patterns that the story suggests are hiding in plain sight. James's plans for this cryptic tale are unusually detailed, and predicated on his refusal to reveal the nature of that figure. He imagines a novelist, whom he would eventually call Hugh Vereker, who claims that his books contain 'a very beautiful and valuable, very interesting and remunerative *secret*, or latent intention, for those who read them with a right intelligence – who see *into* them, as it were'. The critic to whom he says this has not, however, seen anything like that at all, and wants to know what he's missing. But James won't allow the writer to tell him, to tell anyone, and so begins a tale in which interpretation and obsession are as one. The secret meaning of Vereker's fiction seems constantly to recede before us, and as James plots the story out he sees that he'll need three deaths, and three young critics, along with the novelist himself and an ingénue in order to make it all work.

In his first long notebook entry, however, none of these characters has a name, and the two who matter most are simply called 'the novelist' and 'the critic' – a pair of utterly generic types. James will of course particularize the people he needs for this game (Vereker is a particular success), and yet nobody remembers 'The Figure in the Carpet' because of its characters, or very much minds when he starts to kill them off. The drama doesn't belong to them but rather to James himself, to the play of his own ingenious mind. We read the story for what it says about the nature of fiction and the nature of criticism alike. We read for its ideas, for the frustration and thrill of never knowing the shape of that figure, and wondering all the while whether or not James's own work might possess a hidden pattern of its own. He puts a case, he sketches a proof, and is master enough to invent a plot and characters that will allow him to mask the tale's essentially didactic nature.

That description makes 'The Figure in the Carpet' sound rather cold and abstract; and so perhaps it is. Two of the tales in this volume do, however, owe their origins to something other and more than James's attempt to explore the terms of his own profession. One is 'The Aspern Papers' itself. The other is 'The

Author of *Beltraffio*', whose '*donnée*' grew out of a conversation with Edmund Gosse that James recorded in a notebook entry for 26 March 1884. The two friends had been talking over a third writer, a historian of the Italian Renaissance named John Addington Symonds, touching on his 'somewhat hysterical aestheticism', and also on his tubercular lungs, which had exiled him to the cold dry air of the Alps. But the worst of it, Gosse said, was that 'poor S.'s wife was in no sort of sympathy with what he wrote; disapproving of its tone, thinking his books immoral'. James saw the drama immediately, and imagined an intimate quarrel between a novelist he called Mark Ambient and his spouse: 'between the narrow, cold, Calvinistic wife . . . and the husband, impregnated – even to morbidness – with the spirit of Italy, the love of beauty . . . made extravagant and perverse, by the sense of his wife's disapproval'. He decided to use one of the novelist's admirers as the narrator, a young American who tries to patch things up by persuading Mrs Ambient to read her husband's new book. The results would be 'gruesome'.[9]

They were far more gruesome, in fact, than anything in the Symondses' actual marriage, but the family did see the tale as a portrait, and scandalous; and all the more so for those who knew the secret of Mrs Symonds's disapproval. James himself professed ignorance, and wrote Gosse to beg for enlightenment – just what *had* he divined about 'the innermost cause of J.A.S.'s discomfort'?[10] Even a postcard would help, so long as its wording was 'covert'. Yet both that word and the tone of the letter as a whole are so coy that it's hard to believe he didn't already know about Symonds's homosexuality.

Almost nobody today doubts the direction of James's own sexual leanings. His deepest erotic longings were for men, and at a certain point in his life he came to understand that. The precise date of that point has, however, proved impossible to fix, and nobody knows if he ever acted upon a physical desire. He burned most of the letters he received, asked other people to burn his, and his stories often depend on the things that the characters cannot quite manage to say to each other. Given that sexual preference, however, it's crucial to stress that

James's decision to remain unmarried was indeed a decision, one that was by no means inevitable and that he made despite the pressure of his family and friends. For them, in fact, the injunctions against marriage in 'The Lesson of the Master' might have seemed like an explanation. That story suggested a necessary choice between the perfection of the life or the work. Marriage was an expense and a distraction that could ruin a writer's career, and the tale allowed several generations of James's critics to see him as wed to his art alone.

But Symonds had made a different choice – had married in the hopes that it might change him. It didn't. In Venice the historian enjoyed a long affair with his gondolier, and in recent years he has become an important figure in our developing understanding of Victorian sexuality. At his death in 1893 Symonds left behind a frank memoir, unpublished until 1984, and two privately printed books. *A Problem in Greek Ethics* (1883) examined same-sex relations in the ancient world that he took as a model, and was circulating from hand to hand in London by the time James wrote 'The Author of *Beltraffio*'. The second, *A Problem in Modern Ethics* (1891), provided both a rigorous account of the state of medical knowledge and a refutation of popular prejudice; only fifty copies were printed, but Gosse had one and James read it almost immediately. He found the book impressive, and admired Symonds's bravery. Yet while his sympathy is clear, so too is his sense that he himself will not be joining any 'band of the emulous'.[11]

Reading 'The Author of *Beltraffio*' in conjunction with Symonds's own work does not, I think, tell us much about the facts of James's biography. But it can help us chart the shape of his mind. We never learn just what Mark Ambient's books are like. James gives us no quotations, no plot summaries, no details. There's an obvious dramatic reason for that: how could any novel be so wicked, any knowledge so dangerous, as Mrs Ambient believes it to be? Better to tantalize us with the thought of what *might* be there, and James teases us in similar ways in almost all of his stories about writers. The narrator of 'The Aspern Papers' never gets to read those eponymous letters, 'The Death of the Lion' concerns a manuscript that goes missing and in 'The Figure in the Carpet', as I've already suggested, the interpretative code of Hugh Vereker's work remains forever unrevealed. Nor are these puzzles limited to the stories James wrote about other artists. He refuses to tell us the source of Chad Newsome's wealth in *The Ambassadors*, and never lets us know if the ghosts in 'The Turn of the Screw' are really there.

The French critic Tzvetan Todorov has suggested that such lacunae are themselves the figure in James's own carpet, that his stories are 'always based on the *quest for an absolute and absent cause*'.[12] They depend on the unspoken. In 'The Beast in the Jungle' the life-determining secret of James's character John Marcher is the simple fact that he has one. It is there, and yet not; has shape but no substance. We call such haunting things 'uncanny', a term that Freud defines as the name for everything that 'ought to have remained hidden and secret, and yet comes to light'.[13] Except with James that light throws shadows, a chiaroscuro in which secrets are sensed but not shown. In 'The Private Life' he imagines a great writer with a literally divided self, a man with two bodies. One of them goes about in public, he dines and talks and is jolly. The other stays shut inside his chamber – where he works. Only in the late 'Jolly Corner' does the hidden step into sight, when Spencer Brydon finds himself staring at a ghostly figure who seems to be his own disfigured double, a figure at once like him and not, the same and yet different. Such a persistent pattern of the imagination runs deep, so deep that we should hesitate in giving it a name. But I think we must – must define it as James's sense of his own buried life, though even then we should pause before limiting it either to or by the word 'closet'.

That term does, admittedly, work for 'The Author of *Beltraffio*', a story that seems itself in the closet – the story, and not just its subject. The stakes for which its characters play go beyond the morality of books alone, and their urgency appears inexplicable in terms of the tale on its own. Its absent cause isn't Ambient's work but rather Symonds's own sexuality, and perhaps James's too; the story depends for its power upon its reticence, its inability to step forth and speak, to tell us what it means. What happens in the story itself – the tortured marriage, the unreliable young narrator – is bad enough, but the meanings that cluster around it are what give the tale its extraordinary poignancy, and its power.

'The Aspern Papers' presents an even more layered case. James spent the winter of 1886–7 in Florence, and on 12 January 1887 recorded a 'curious thing' in his notebook, an anecdote about Claire Clairmont, the last survivor of the circle around Byron and Shelley. She had been Mary Shelley's stepsister and Byron's mistress, the mother of his daughter Allegra, and had survived into old age, dying at eighty in 1879. In her last years she lived with a middle-aged niece in Florence; poor, and yet sitting on a treasure, a trove of letters and other memorabilia. Then an American appeared, a Salem-born sea captain and collector named Silsbee. He asked to rent a few rooms in her house, but what he really wanted were the letters, and he hoped 'that the old lady in view of her great age and failing condition would die while he was there, so that he might then put his hand upon the documents, which she hugged close in life'.[14] And so it passed – except that Silsbee didn't get the papers.

In writing James switched the scene from Florence to Venice. The change masked the tale's origins in the chitchat of a small expatriate community, and Venice did have more associations with Byron in particular. There were other reasons too. In an essay, James had already described the city as 'the most beautiful of tombs'[15] – a relic, as is his character Juliana Bordereau, the aged mistress of the long-dead American poet Jeffrey Aspern. Venice had lived on after its own end, a crypt in which all kinds of things might be buried, and it now seemed a place for secrets, in which it was easy to get lost, and maybe even to lose yourself. So he put his character there, a woman living 'in obscurity, on very small means, unvisited, unapproachable, in a dilapidated old palace'. James's syntax in describing her seems here to twist and to turn, a prose that serves, with all its commas and pauses, to evoke Venice's own world of dead ends: a city of hidden spaces, in which the very stones themselves can become the creatures of duplicity.

James wrote the story in the first person and made his narrator both a collector, like Silsbee, and an editor too, a 'publishing scoundrel' obsessed with Aspern's poetry and life. We never learn his name – neither his real name nor the false one he uses with Miss Bordereau – and yet it's too easy to describe him as unreliable. He's instead someone who believes he has scruples, a man given to elaborate justifications of his own desires. He persuades the shrivelled Juliana to rent him some rooms on the upper floor of her house on 'an out-of-the-way canal'; she herself lives on the *piano nobile* below with her niece, Tita, who is fifty-ish, unworldly and plain. At first the narrator isn't even sure that Aspern's papers survive, but once he knows that they do, he must face the question of how far he will go to get them. For the drama, James writes, lies 'in some price that the man has to pay – that the old woman – or the survivor – sets upon the papers. His hesitations – his struggle – for he really would give almost anything.'[16] Almost. But Silsbee had his limits, and this editor does too.

So much for the tale's origins. James sent it to the *Atlantic Monthly* from Venice, to which he had moved on from the Tuscan capital at the end of May 1887. Yet his living arrangements in Florence that spring present a further complication. One of his closest friends was a writer named Constance Fenimore Woolson, whom he had first met in Florence in 1880, and who had published a series of superb local-colour stories about both the Great Lakes region and the American South. She believed that in James's work she had found her 'true country, my real home',[17] and she too had expatriated herself, alternating between England and Italy, while claiming always to dream of her native New York State. The full history of their relationship and of her 1894 suicide lies beyond the purview of this introduction. Suffice it to say that Woolson saw herself as forever cut off from the life she craved, a woman who couldn't have the things she wanted. And perhaps among them was Henry James himself. He clearly enjoyed their conversations, but their relations were founded on silence, on what in their period remained unspoken; and he did not introduce her to his London world, where their friendship would not have passed without comment.

They did have mutual friends in Florence, however, and that year she leased the Villa Brichieri-Colombi on the hill of Bellosguardo, south of the Arno; the house sits a few hundred yards from the Villa Castellani, on which James had modelled Gilbert Osmond's home in *The Portrait of a Lady*. Woolson herself lived on the *piano nobile*, with its terrace and view, and offered James an apartment on the floor below. We know little of their lives in that building. Presumably they shared the servants, but we don't know how often they also shared a table. None of James's letters from the period refers to the woman upstairs, and yet it was in her house that he worked on 'The Aspern Papers'. Only a naïve critic would insist on a strictly autobiographical reading of the tale, would draw a clear connection between the story's narrator and its author. But it seems equally naïve to see no connection at all; each of them a tenant in a large Italian house, and each an object of fascination to the middle-aged spinster on the neighbouring floor.

James himself, however, would tell a very different story about 'The Aspern Papers', and one that finally owes little to his source in the life of Claire Clairmont. In his New York Edition preface he notes the thrill with which he discovered that this last survivor of the Romantic period had 'overlapped' with his own adult life, and yet he didn't actually wish he had met her. What intrigued him was the thought that he *could* have. 'I delight,' he wrote, in the 'palpable imaginable *visitable* past – in the nearer distances and the clearer mysteries', of a world that one might reach as by the long stretch of a mental arm. That to him was the most 'fragrant' history of all, and yet it wasn't the past of Byron and Shelley that stirred him. It was instead that of people like himself, the traces of his own American predecessors. Writing in an age when the United States was fast becoming a world power, James found himself fascinated by what in the story itself he called 'the early movements of my countrymen as visitors to Europe'. He belonged to a generation that had gone well supplied with guidebooks and photographs and letters of introduction, those 'conveniences [that] have annihilated surprise'. His elders had no such luxuries, and

James recognized that his own easy cosmopolitanism depended on the fact that they had cut the road before him.

They had made his world, his work – had made *him* – possible. He saw them with a filial piety, and in writing allowed himself to stretch back two full generations and more, to imagine a great poet of the 1820s who was yet not an English poet, to summon the shade of a non-existent American bard who

> ... at a period when our native land was nude and crude and provincial, when the famous 'atmosphere' it is supposed to lack was not even missed, when literature was lonely there and art and form almost impossible ... had found means to live and write like one of the first; to be free and general and not at all afraid; to feel, understand and express everything.

That description belongs as much to James himself as it does to the tale's far more duplicitous narrator, and in many ways it offers an account of his own ambition, of an artist who had come to the Old World as a pupil, and was now among its masters. Of course Aspern himself remains but a name. The tale provides neither a line of his poetry nor a scrap from his mythical letters, and the early days of American literature offer us no such worldly figure, not even the Nathaniel Hawthorne whom James saw as his own particular precursor. Nevertheless we believe in him, and believe too, if only from the spirit and rage of the aged Juliana, that he was a more vital figure than her scoundrel of a lodger. We don't have Jeffrey Aspern, but we do have 'The Aspern Papers', with its serene and troubled Venetian setting, the comedy of its narrator's discomfiture and the tragedy of the Bordereaus' long afterlife. This tale about the 'responsibilities of an editor' tells us of the tension between art and life and of the odd revenge they take upon each other. Yet it is also a kind of ghost story, and then too an examination of what remained James's greatest subject, the relation between the America of his birth and the Europe in which he made his career. It stands as the *summa* of his short fiction.

*

'The Aspern Papers' was one of the 'good short things' waiting to kick off its editorial tombstone at the start of 1888; Howells's successor at the *Atlantic*, Thomas Bailey Aldrich, had had it since the previous June but held it back until that March, when it began its three-month run. There is more, much more, that I might say about it, but I'll end by looking instead at another story James published that year. I have already mentioned 'The Lesson of the Master', a tale for which James's notebook contains only a few brief sentences of preparation. A mutual friend had suggested that the French novelist Alphonse Daudet would never have bothered to write his memoirs 'if he hadn't married', if his family's financial demands hadn't led him 'to produce promiscuously and cheaply'.[18] James accordingly makes the older novelist he calls Henry St George present himself as a warning to a promising young colleague named Paul Overt. The 'Master' believes that he was once a good writer, but he hasn't fulfilled his promise and now never will. For he has lost himself in the pursuit of 'false gods . . . The idols of the market – money and luxury . . . placing one's children and dressing one's wife'. He doesn't precisely complain, but he does want Overt to know that the family he loves has killed the artist in him. His wife manages his career, and each day shuts him up in his study to produce page after best-selling page. She even once made him burn a bad book; that is, an unprofitable good one.

Don't be like me – don't live in the knowledge that you haven't done your best. Don't marry. St George doesn't demand that Overt live in poverty; James's characters are as free of that Romantic illusion as he was. He does, however, suggest that no serious writer can possibly earn enough to support a family in bourgeois comfort. As such, the tale seems to pose a distinction, if not precisely between art and life, then at least between artistic and commercial success; and if commerce is necessary to live . . . well, then don't. The writer ought to stand outside the realm of material concerns and appetites. Yet no story by Henry James is quite so simple, and anyone reading 'The Lesson of the Master' quickly realizes that the truth of St George's claim depends entirely upon the particular man and the particular woman. It depends upon their individual temperaments and

7. Henry James, 'Preface' to *The Portrait of a Lady*, in *Literary Criticism: French Writers, Other European Writers, The Prefaces to the New York Edition* (New York: The Library of America, 1984), p. 1072.

8. Ibid.

9. *Notebooks* 25.

10. Letter to Edmund Gosse, 9 June 1884, *Henry James: A Life in Letters*, ed. Philip Horne (New York: Viking Penguin, 1999), p. 157.

11. Letter to Edmund Gosse, 7 January 1898, *Selected Letters of Henry James to Edmund Gosse, 1882–1915*, ed. Rayburn S. Moore (Baton Rouge and London: Louisiana State University Press, 1988), p. 90.

12. Tzvetan Todorov, *The Poetics of Prose* (1971), trans. Richard Howard (Ithaca: Cornell University Press, 1977), p. 145 (italics in the original).

13. Sigmund Freud, 'The Uncanny' (1919), trans. Alix Strachey, in *Collected Papers*, vol. IV (London: Hogarth Press, 1925), p. 376.

14. *Notebooks* 33. See Appendix: Henry James on 'The Aspern Papers', from his Notebooks and the Preface to the New York Edition.

15. Henry James, 'The Grand Canal', in *Italian Hours* (1909), ed. John Auchard (Harmondsworth: Penguin, 1992), p. 33.

16. *Notebooks* 34.

17. Letter from Constance Fenimore Woolson, 7 May 1883, *Henry James: Letters*, ed. Edel, vol. III, p. 551.

18. *Notebooks* 43.

19. Letter to Hendrik Andersen, 25 November 1906, *Dearly Beloved Friends: Henry James's Letters to Younger Men*, ed. Susan E. Gunter and Steven H. Jobe (Ann Arbor: University of Michigan Press, 2001), p. 61 (italics in original).

Further Reading

Those interested in learning more about James's short fiction should begin with his notebooks and prefaces. See *The Complete Notebooks of Henry James*, ed. Leon Edel and Lyall H. Powers (New York and Oxford: Oxford University Press, 1987) and Henry James, *Literary Criticism: French Writers, Other European Writers, The Prefaces to the New York Edition* (New York: Library of America, 1984). Critical editions of each are now (2014) in progress for a set of James's collected fiction to be published by Cambridge University Press. James's letters of different periods and to different correspondents are available in a variety of editions. The University of Nebraska Press is producing a complete run of his 10,000 surviving letters, under the editorship of Pierre A. Walker and Greg W. Zacharias, but there are many volumes to go before they reach the years in which he produced the stories in this book; in the meantime, readers should consult Volume III of *Henry James: Letters*, ed. Leon Edel (Cambridge, MA: The Belknap Press, 1980). Edel's five-volume biography (1953–72) remains the standard life; but see also my *Portrait of a Novel: Henry James and the Making of an American Masterpiece* (New York: Liveright, 2012).

The critical literature on James is rich and ever-changing. Most of it inevitably concerns his novels rather than his short fiction, but a useful reference book to the tales is Christina E. Albers's *A Reader's Guide to the Short Stories of Henry James* (New York: G. K. Hall, 1997). For more recent accounts, the *Henry James Review*, published three times a year by the Johns Hopkins University Press, regularly features articles on his tales; a trawl through its electronically available back issues is probably the best way to get a sense of current thought about a given story. Tzvetan Todorov's essays on James in *The Poetics of Prose* (1971), trans. Richard Howard (Ithaca: Cornell University Press, 1977) have been instrumental in shaping my own thinking about these works. See also Millicent Bell's chapter on 'The Aspern Papers' in *Meaning in Henry James* (Cambridge, MA: Harvard University Press, 1991). Michael Anesko's *'Friction with the Market': Henry James and the Profession of Authorship* (Oxford: Oxford University Press, 1986) offers a seminal reading of James the working writer; see too Jonathan L. Freedman, *Professions of Taste: Henry James, British Aestheticism and Commodity Culture* (Palo Alto: Stanford University Press, 1990). Amy Tucker's *The Illustration of the Master: Henry James and the Magazine Revolution* (Palo Alto: Stanford University Press, 2010) provides a rich account of James's relations with the medium in which these tales were first published.

Two invaluable but very different reference guides offer expert help. Eric Haralson and Kendall Johnson's *Critical Companion to Henry James* (New York: Facts on File, 2009) contains a brief entry for each work along with a summary of current scholarship. *Henry James in Context*, ed. David McWhirter (Cambridge and New York: Cambridge University Press, 2010) is organized thematically, and includes over forty essays by leading scholars on topics ranging from 'Law' to 'Things' and 'Time' along with more familiar subjects such as 'Psychology' and 'Victorian England'.

MG, 2014

A Note on the Texts

In 'The Middle Years,' James describes his protagonist, the novelist Dencombe, as a 'fingerer of style; the last thing he ever arrived at was a form final for himself'. He invariably finds himself making corrections in the books he's already published, and cannot bear to reread his own work without a pen or a pencil in his hand. James knew what he was writing about – he gave the character his own habits. The stories in this book all had their initial publication in English or American magazines, and James's invariable practice was then to revise them for book publication, normally by working directly on his proof sheets. Many of these revisions were minor. He changed some wording, made certain to preserve English rather than American spelling and lightened the punctuation that the magazine's house style had dictated.

Late in his career he made far more substantial revisions for the New York Edition of his work (1907–9). James thought of that edition as 'selective as well as collective', one meant to preserve what he believed to be his most important novels and tales. He added a preface to each novel or collection, and tried to bring the style of his earlier work in line with that of his later. All the stories in this volume were included in the New York Edition, though James's changes to them were small in comparison to the wholesale rewriting that he did on such early novels as *The American* or *The Portrait of a Lady*. He cut some commas and inserted more contractions; he sometimes avoided repetition by substituting a recondite word for an ordinary one.

The changes were small for a couple of reasons at least. These tales are the product of James's maturity – he simply saw less that he had to fix. But the process of revision was also an exhausting one, and he reworked these stories after completing a hard job on the edition's early volumes. Nevertheless I have chosen here to stay with the first book versions of these works. With *The Portrait of a Lady* I prefer the New York Edition; it deepens the novel's shadows, and its language has an extra degree of metaphorical richness. But those changes do slow its pace, and that's not desirable in these shorter pieces, which depend to some degree on speed and compression. The difference is but a hair – and yet it remains appreciable. Moreover James was always sensitive to the charge that his work was more elliptical than it needed to be, and some of his late changes worked to overemphasize his meaning. The original last line of 'The Aspern Papers', which I have preserved here, is just a bit more cryptic, and more interesting, than its revision, which I've included in the Notes. An additional benefit to keeping the first version of that tale lies in the name of one of its major characters. 'Miss Tita' is a shade more exotic and estranging than the New York Edition's 'Miss Tina'.

Readers interested in these questions should consult Philip Horne's masterly *Henry James and Revision* (Oxford: Clarendon Press, 1990).

Since the stories come from various sources and are somewhat inconsistent in spelling and punctuation, these have been standardized throughout this volume. In addition some errors, mostly the printers', have been corrected by reference to earlier and later texts; some minor adjustments have been made to punctuation, including the substitution of n-rule dashes for m-rule except for broken-off speech and sentences; in the Appendix, the Preface to the New York Edition of 'The Aspern Papers' has contractions opened up by James (e.g. could n't) and these are closed up (couldn't). Single quotation marks replace double ones, and for a single word or phrase in quotation marks, the closing mark is placed before a comma or full stop; and 'ise' spellings have been standardized throughout as 'ize', in accordance with Penguin Classics style. There has been no attempt to regularize James's use of italics for foreign words and expressions.

'The Author of *Beltraffio*' ran in the *English Illustrated Magazine* (June–July 1884) and became the title story in an 1885 collection (Boston: James R. Osgood) from which this volume's text is taken. A revised version appears in Vol. XVI of the New York Edition (New York: Scribners, 1909).

'The Aspern Papers' was serialized in the *Atlantic Monthly* (March–May 1888) and was then collected in *The Aspern Papers, Louisa Pallant, The Modern Warning* (London and New York: Macmillan, 1888). Its revision is in Vol. XII (1908) of the New York Edition.

'The Lesson of the Master' appeared in the *Universal Review* (July–August 1888) and was collected in *The Lesson of the Master* (London and New York: Macmillan, 1892). The New York Edition includes it in Vol. XV (1908).

'The Real Thing' was first published in *Black and White* (16 April 1892) and became the title story in an 1893 collection, *The Real Thing and Other Tales* (New York and London: Macmillan, 1893). It appeared in Vol. XVIII of the New York Edition (1909).

'Greville Fane' ran in the *Illustrated London News* (17, 24 September 1892); the text here is from *The Real Thing and Other Tales*. It is included in Vol. XVI of the New York Edition.

'The Middle Years' came out in *Scribner's Magazine* (May 1893); the text here is from its book publication in *Terminations* (London: Heinemann, 1895). It appears in Vol. XVI of the New York Edition.

'The Figure in the Carpet' was serialized in *Cosmopolis* (January–February 1896), and had its first book publication in *Embarrassments* (London: Heinemann, 1896). It is included in Vol. XV of the New York Edition.

MG, 2014

The Aspern Papers
and Other Tales

THE AUTHOR OF
BELTRAFFIO

Much as I wished to see him, I had kept my letter of introduction for three weeks in my pocket-book. I was nervous and timid about meeting him – conscious of youth and ignorance, convinced that he was tormented by strangers, and especially by my country-people, and not exempt from the suspicion that he had the irritability as well as the brilliancy of genius. Moreover, the pleasure, if it should occur (for I could scarcely believe it was really at hand), would be so great that I wished to think of it in advance, to feel that it was in my pocket, not to mix it with satisfactions more superficial and usual. In the little game of new sensations that I was playing with my ingenuous mind, I wished to keep my visit to the author of *Beltraffio*[1] as a trump-card. It was three years after the publication of that fascinating work, which I had read over five times, and which now, with my riper judgment, I admire on the whole as much as ever. This will give you about the date of my first visit (of any duration) to England; for you will not have forgotten the commotion – I may even say the scandal – produced by Mark Ambient's[2] masterpiece. It was the most complete presentation that had yet been made of the gospel of art; it was a kind of æsthetic war-cry. People had endeavoured to sail nearer to 'truth' in the cut of their sleeves and the shape of their sideboards; but there had not as yet been, among English novels, such an example of beauty of execution and value of subject. Nothing had been done in that line from the point of view of art for art.[3] This was my own point of view, I may mention, when I was twenty-five; whether it is altered now I won't take upon myself to say – especially as the discerning reader will be able to

judge for himself. I had been in England a twelvemonth before
the time to which I began by alluding, and had learned then that
Mr Ambient was in distant lands – was making a considerable
tour in the East. So there was nothing to do but to keep my letter till I should be in London again. It was of little use to me to
hear that his wife had not left England and, with her little boy,
their only child, was spending the period of her husband's
absence – a good many months – at a small place they had down
in Surrey. They had a house in London which was let. All this I
learned, and also that Mrs Ambient was charming (my friend,
the American poet, from whom I had my introduction, had
never seen her, his relations with the great man being only epis-
tolary); but she was not, after all, though she had lived so near
the rose, the author of *Beltraffio*, and I did not go down into Surrey to call on her. I went to the Continent, spent the following
winter in Italy, and returned to London in May. My visit to Italy
opened my eyes to a good many things, but to nothing more
than the beauty of certain pages in the works of Mark Ambient.
I had every one of his productions in my portmanteau – they are
not, as you know, very numerous, but he had preluded to *Beltraffio* by some exquisite things – and I used to read them over in
the evening at the inn. I used to say to myself that the man who
drew those characters and wrote that style understood what he
saw and knew what he was doing. This is my only reason for
mentioning my winter in Italy. He had been there much in former years, and he was saturated with what painters call the
'feeling' of that classic land. He expressed the charm of the old
hill-cities of Tuscany, the look of certain lonely grass-grown
places which, in the past, had echoed with life; he understood
the great artists, he understood the spirit of the Renaissance, he
understood everything. The scene of one of his earlier novels
was laid in Rome, the scene of another in Florence, and I moved
through these cities in company with the figures whom Mark
Ambient had set so firmly upon their feet. This is why I was now
so much happier even than before in the prospect of making his
acquaintance.

At last, when I had dallied with this privilege long enough, I
despatched to him the missive of the American poet. He had

already gone out of town; he shrank from the rigour of the
London season,[4] and it was his habit to migrate on the first of
June. Moreover, I had heard that this year he was hard at work
on a new book, into which some of his impressions of the East
were to be wrought, so that he desired nothing so much as
quiet days. This knowledge, however, did not prevent me – *cet
âge est sans pitié*[5] – from sending with my friend's letter a note
of my own, in which I asked Mr Ambient's leave to come down
and see him for an hour or two, on a day to be designated by
himself. My proposal was accompanied with a very frank
expression of my sentiments, and the effect of the whole pro-
jectile was to elicit from the great man the kindest possible
invitation. He would be delighted to see me, especially if I
should turn up on the following Saturday and could remain till
the Monday morning. We would take a walk over the Surrey
commons, and I should tell him all about the other great man,
the one in America. He indicated to me the best train, and it
may be imagined whether on the Saturday afternoon I was
punctual at Waterloo.[6] He carried his benevolence to the point
of coming to meet me at the little station at which I was to
alight, and my heart beat very fast as I saw his handsome face,
surmounted with a soft wide-awake,[7] and which I knew by a
photograph long since enshrined upon my mantelshelf, scan-
ning the carriage-windows as the train rolled up. He recognized
me as infallibly as I had recognized him; he appeared to know
by instinct how a young American of an æsthetic turn would
look when much divided between eagerness and modesty. He
took me by the hand, and smiled at me, and said, 'You must
be – a – *you*, I think!' and asked if I should mind going on foot
to his house, which would take but a few minutes. I remember
thinking it a piece of extraordinary affability that he should
give directions about the conveyance of my bag, and feeling
altogether very happy and rosy, in fact quite transported, when
he laid his hand on my shoulder as we came out of the station.
I surveyed him, askance, as we walked together; I had already –
I had indeed instantly – seen that he was a delightful creature.
His face is so well known that I needn't describe it; he looked
to me at once an English gentleman and a man of genius, and I

thought that a happy combination. There was just a little of the
Bohemian in his appearance; you would easily have guessed
that he belonged to the guild of artists and men of letters. He
was addicted to velvet jackets, to cigarettes, to loose shirt-
collars, to looking a little dishevelled.[8] His features, which
were fine but not perfectly regular, are fairly enough represented in his portraits; but no portrait that I have seen gives any
idea of his expression. There were so many things in it, and
they chased each other in and out of his face. I have seen people
who were grave and gay in quick alternation; but Mark Ambient was grave and gay at one and the same moment. There
were other strange oppositions and contradictions in his
slightly faded and fatigued countenance. He seemed both
young and old, both anxious and indifferent. He had evidently
had an active past, which inspired one with curiosity, and yet it
was impossible not to be more curious still about his future. He
was just enough above middle height to be spoken of as tall,
and rather lean and long in the flank. He had the friendliest,
frankest manner possible, and yet I could see that he was shy. He
was thirty-eight years old at the time *Beltraffio* was published.[9]
He asked me about his friend in America, about the length of
my stay in England, about the last news in London and the
people I had seen there; and I remember looking for the signs
of genius in the very form of his questions – and thinking I
found it. I liked his voice. There was genius in his house, too, I
thought, when we got there; there was imagination in the car-
pets and curtains, in the pictures and books, in the garden
behind it, where certain old brown walls were muffled in creepers that appeared to me to have been copied from a masterpiece
of one of the pre-Raphaelites.[10] That was the way many things
struck me at that time, in England; as if they were reproduc-
tions of something that existed primarily in art or literature. It
was not the picture, the poem, the fictive page, that seemed to
me a copy; these things were the originals, and the life of happy
and distinguished people was fashioned in their image. Mark
Ambient called his house a cottage, and I perceived afterwards
that he was right; for if it had not been a cottage it must have
been a villa, and a villa, in England at least, was not a place in

which one could fancy him at home. But it was, to my vision, a
cottage glorified and translated; it was a palace of art, on a
slightly reduced scale – it was an old English demesne. It nes-
tled under a cluster of magnificent beeches, it had little creaking
lattices that opened out of, or into, pendent mats of ivy, and
gables, and old red tiles, as well as a general aspect of being
painted in water-colours and inhabited by people whose lives
would go on in chapters and volumes. The lawn seemed to me
of extraordinary extent, the garden-walls of incalculable height,
the whole air of the place delightfully still, and private, and
proper to itself. 'My wife must be somewhere about,' Mark
Ambient said, as we went in. 'We shall find her perhaps; we
have got about an hour before dinner. She may be in the garden. I will show you my little place.'

We passed through the house, and into the grounds, as I
should have called them, which extended into the rear. They
covered but three or four acres, but, like the house, they were
very old and crooked, and full of traces of long habitation,
with inequalities of level and little steps – mossy and cracked
were these – which connected the different parts with each
other. The limits of the place, cleverly dissimulated, were muffled in the deepest verdure. They made, as I remember, a kind
of curtain at the farther end, in one of the folds of which, as it
were, we presently perceived, from afar, a little group. 'Ah,
there she is!' said Mark Ambient; 'and she has got the boy.' He
made this last remark in a tone slightly different from any in
which he yet had spoken. I was not fully aware of it at the time,
but it lingered in my ear and I afterwards understood it.

'Is it your son?' I inquired, feeling the question not to be
brilliant.

'Yes, my only child. He is always in his mother's pocket. She
coddles him too much.' It came back to me afterwards, too – the
manner in which he spoke these words. They were not petulant;
they expressed rather a sudden coldness, a kind of mechanical
submission. We went a few steps further, and then he stopped
short, and called the boy, beckoning to him repeatedly.

'Dolcino,[11] come and see your daddy!' There was something
in the way he stood still and waited that made me think he did

it for a purpose. Mrs Ambient had her arm round the child's waist, and he was leaning against her knee; but though he looked up at the sound of his father's voice, she gave no sign of releasing him. A lady, apparently a neighbour, was seated near her, and before them was a garden-table, on which a tea-service had been placed.

Mark Ambient called again, and Dolcino struggled in the maternal embrace, but he was too tightly held, and after two or three fruitless efforts he suddenly turned round and buried his head deep in his mother's lap. There was a certain awkwardness in the scene; I thought it rather odd that Mrs Ambient should pay so little attention to her husband. But I would not for the world have betrayed my thought, and, to conceal it, I observed that it must be such a pleasant thing to have tea in the garden. 'Ah, she won't let him come!' said Mark Ambient, with a sigh; and we went our way till we reached the two ladies. He mentioned my name to his wife, and I noticed that he addressed her as 'My dear', very genially, without any trace of resentment at her detention of the child. The quickness of the transition made me vaguely ask myself whether he were henpecked – a shocking conjecture, which I instantly dismissed. Mrs Ambient was quite such a wife as I should have expected him to have; slim and fair, with a long neck and pretty eyes and an air of great refinement. She was a little cold, and a little shy; but she was very sweet, and she had a certain look of race, justified by my afterwards learning that she was 'connected' with two or three great families. I have seen poets married to women of whom it was difficult to conceive that they should gratify the poetic fancy – women with dull faces and glutinous minds, who were none the less, however, excellent wives. But there was no obvious incongruity in Mark Ambient's union. Mrs Ambient, delicate and quiet, in a white dress, with her beautiful child at her side, was worthy of the author of a work so distinguished as *Beltraffio*. Round her neck she wore a black velvet ribbon, of which the long ends, tied behind, hung down her back, and to which, in front, was attached a miniature portrait of her little boy. Her smooth, shining hair was confined in a net. She gave me a very pleasant greeting, and Dolcino – I thought this little name of endearment delightful – took advantage of her getting up to slip away from her and go to his father, who said nothing to him, but simply seized him and held him high in his arms for a moment, kissing him several times. I had lost no time in observing that the child, who was not more than seven years old, was extraordinarily beautiful. He had the face of an angel – the eyes, the hair, the more than mortal bloom, the smile of innocence. There was something touching, almost alarming, in his beauty, which seemed to be composed of elements too fine and pure for the breath of this world. When I spoke to him, and he came and held out his hand and smiled at me, I felt a sudden pity for him, as if he had been an orphan, or a changeling, or stamped with some social stigma. It was impossible to be, in fact, more exempt from these misfortunes, and yet, as one kissed him, it was hard to keep from murmuring 'Poor little devil!' though why one should have applied this epithet to a living cherub is more than I can say. Afterwards, indeed, I knew a little better; I simply discovered that he was too charming to live, wondering at the same time that his parents should not have perceived it, and should not be in proportionate grief and despair. For myself, I had no doubt of his evanescence, having already noticed that there is a kind of charm which is like a death-warrant. The lady who had been sitting with Mrs Ambient was a jolly, ruddy personage, dressed in velveteen and rather limp feathers, whom I guessed to be the vicar's wife – our hostess did not introduce me – and who immediately began to talk to Ambient about chrysanthemums. This was a safe subject, and yet there was a certain surprise for me in seeing the author of *Beltraffio* even in such superficial communion with the Church of England. His writings implied so much detachment from that institution, expressed a view of life so profane, as it were, so independent, and so little likely, in general, to be thought edifying, that I should have expected to find him an object of horror to vicars and their ladies – of horror repaid on his own part by good-natured but brilliant mockery. This proves how little I knew as yet of the English people and their extraordinary talent for keeping up their forms, as well as of some of the mysteries of Mark Ambient's hearth and home. I found afterwards that he had, in his study, between smiles and cigar-smoke, some wonderful comparisons for his clerical neighbours; but meanwhile the chrysanthemums were a source of harmony, for he and the vicaress were equally fond of them, and I was surprised at the knowledge they exhibited of this interesting plant. The lady's visit, however, had presumably already been long, and she presently got up, saying she must go, and kissed Mrs Ambient. Mark started to walk with her to the gate of the grounds, holding Dolcino by the hand.

'Stay with me, my darling,' Mrs Ambient said to the boy, who was wandering away with his father.

Mark Ambient paid no attention to the summons, but Dolcino turned round and looked with eyes of shy entreaty at his mother. 'Can't I go with papa?'

'Not when I ask you to stay with me.'

'But please don't ask me, mamma,' said the child, in his little clear, new voice.

'I must ask you when I want you. Come to me, my darling.' And Mrs Ambient, who had seated herself again, held out her long, slender hands.

Her husband stopped, with his back turned to her, but without releasing the child. He was still talking to the vicaress, but this good lady, I think, had lost the thread of her attention. She looked at Mrs Ambient and at Dolcino, and then she looked at me, smiling very hard, in an extremely fixed, cheerful manner.

'Papa,' said the child, 'mamma wants me not to go with you.'

'He's very tired – he has run about all day. He ought to be quiet till he goes to bed. Otherwise he won't sleep.' These declarations fell successively and gravely from Mrs Ambient's lips.

Her husband, still without turning round, bent over the boy and looked at him in silence. The vicaress gave a genial, irrelevant laugh, and observed that he was a precious little pet. 'Let him choose,' said Mark Ambient. 'My dear little boy, will you go with me or will you stay with your mother?'

'Oh, it's a shame!' cried the vicar's lady, with increased hilarity.

'Papa, I don't think I can choose,' the child answered, making his voice very low and confidential. 'But I have been a great deal with mamma to-day,' he added in a moment.

'And very little with papa! My dear fellow, I think you have chosen!' And Mark Ambient walked off with his son, accompanied by re-echoing but inarticulate comments from my fellow-visitor.

His wife had seated herself again, and her fixed eyes, bent upon the ground, expressed for a few moments so much mute agitation that I felt as if almost any remark from my own lips would be a false note. But Mrs Ambient quickly recovered herself, and said to me civilly enough that she hoped I didn't mind having had to walk from the station. I reassured her on this point, and she went on, 'We have got a thing that might have gone for you, but my husband wouldn't order it.'

'That gave me the pleasure of a walk with him,' I rejoined.

She was silent a minute, and then she said, 'I believe the Americans walk very little.'

'Yes, we always run,' I answered, laughingly.

She looked at me seriously, and I began to perceive a certain coldness in her pretty eyes. 'I suppose your distances are so great.'

'Yes; but we break our marches! I can't tell you what a pleasure it is for me to find myself here,' I added. 'I have the greatest admiration for Mr Ambient.'

'He will like that. He likes being admired.'

'He must have a very happy life, then. He has many worshippers.'

'Oh yes, I have seen some of them,' said Mrs Ambient, looking away, very far from me, rather as if such a vision were before her at the moment. Something in her tone seemed to indicate that the vision was scarcely edifying, and I guessed very quickly that she was not in sympathy with the author of *Beltraffio*. I thought the fact strange, but, somehow, in the glow of my own enthusiasm, I didn't think it important; it only made me wish to be rather explicit about that enthusiasm.

'For me, you know,' I remarked, 'he is quite the greatest of living writers.'

'Of course I can't judge. Of course he's very clever,' said Mrs Ambient, smiling a little.

'He's magnificent, Mrs Ambient! There are pages in each of

his books that have a perfection that classes them with the greatest things. Therefore, for me to see him in this familiar way – in his habit as he lives – and to find, apparently, the man as delightful as the artist, I can't tell you how much too good to be true it seems, and how great a privilege I think it.' I knew that I was gushing, but I couldn't help it, and what I said was a good deal less than what I felt. I was by no means sure that I should dare to say even so much as this to Ambient himself, and there was a kind of rapture in speaking it out to his wife, which was not affected by the fact that, as a wife, she appeared peculiar. She listened to me with her face grave again, and with her lips a little compressed, as if there were no doubt, of course, that her husband was remarkable, but at the same time she had heard all this before and couldn't be expected to be particularly interested in it. There was even in her manner an intimation that I was rather young, and that people usually got over that sort of thing. 'I assure you that for me this is a red-letter day,' I added.

She made no response, until after a pause, looking round her, she said abruptly, though gently, 'We are very much afraid about the fruit this year.'

My eyes wandered to the mossy, mottled, garden-walls, where plum-trees and pear-trees, flattened and fastened upon the rusty bricks, looked like crucified figures with many arms. 'Doesn't it promise well?' I inquired.

'No, the trees look very dull. We had such late frosts.'

Then there was another pause. Mrs Ambient kept her eyes fixed on the opposite end of the grounds, as if she were watching for her husband's return with the child. 'Is Mr Ambient fond of gardening?' it occurred to me to inquire, irresistibly impelled as I felt myself, moreover, to bring the conversation constantly back to him.

'He is very fond of plums,' said his wife.

'Ah, well then, I hope your crop will be better than you fear. It's a lovely old place,' I continued. 'The whole character of it is that of certain places that he describes. Your house is like one of his pictures.'

'It's a pleasant little place. There are hundreds like it.'

'Oh, it has got his tone,' I said laughing, and insisting on my point the more that Mrs Ambient appeared to see in my appreciation of her simple establishment a sign of limited experience.

It was evident that I insisted too much. 'His tone?' she repeated, with a quick look at me and a slightly heightened colour.

'Surely he has a tone, Mrs Ambient.'

'Oh yes, he has indeed! But I don't in the least consider that I am living in one of his books; I shouldn't care for that, at all,' she went on, with a smile which had in some degree the effect of converting my slightly sharp protest into a joke deficient in point. 'I am afraid I am not very literary,' said Mrs Ambient. 'And I am not artistic.'

'I am very sure you are not stupid nor *bornée*,'[12] I ventured to reply, with the accompaniment of feeling immediately afterwards that I had been both familiar and patronizing. My only consolation was in the reflection that it was she, and not I, who had begun it. She had brought her idiosyncrasies into the discussion.

'Well, whatever I am, I am very different from my husband. If you like him, you won't like me. You needn't say anything. Your liking me isn't in the least necessary.'

'Don't defy me!' I exclaimed.

She looked as if she had not heard me, which was the best thing she could do; and we sat some time without further speech. Mrs Ambient had evidently the enviable English quality of being able to be silent without being restless. But at last she spoke; she asked me if there seemed to be many people in town. I gave her what satisfaction I could on this point, and we talked a little about London and of some pictures it presented at that time of the year. At the end of this I came back, irrepressibly, to Mark Ambient.

'Doesn't he like to be there now? I suppose he doesn't find the proper quiet for his work. I should think his things had been written, for the most part, in a very still place. They suggest a great stillness, following on a kind of tumult – don't you think so? I suppose London is a tremendous place to collect impressions, but a refuge like this, in the country, must be much better for working them up. Does he get many of his

impressions[13] in London, do you think?' I proceeded from
point to point, in this malign inquiry, simply because my hostess, who probably thought me a very pushing and talkative
young man, gave me time; for when I paused – I have not represented my pauses – she simply continued to let her eyes
wander, and, with her long fair fingers, played with the medal-
lion on her neck. When I stopped altogether, however, she was
obliged to say something, and what she said was that she had
not the least idea where her husband got his impressions. This
made me think her, for a moment, positively disagreeable; delicate and proper and rather aristocratically dry as she sat there.
But I must either have lost the impression a moment later, or
been goaded by it to further aggression, for I remember asking
her whether Mr Ambient was in a good vein of work, and
when we might look for the appearance of the book on which
he was engaged. I have every reason now to know that she
thought me an odious person.

She gave a strange, small laugh as she said, 'I'm afraid you
think I know a great deal more about my husband's work than
I do. I haven't the least idea what he is doing,' she added presently, in a slightly different, that is, a more explanatory, tone;
as if she recognized in some degree the enormity of her confession. 'I don't read what he writes!'

She did not succeed (and would not, even had she tried much
harder) in making it seem to me anything less than monstrous.
I stared at her, and I think I blushed. 'Don't you admire his
genius? Don't you admire *Beltraffio*?'

She hesitated a moment, and I wondered what she could
possibly say. She did not speak – I could see – the first words
that rose to her lips; she repeated what she had said a few minutes before. 'Oh, of course he's very clever!' And with this she
got up; her husband and little boy had reappeared. Mrs Ambient left me and went to meet them; she stopped and had a few
words with her husband, which I did not hear, and which
ended in her taking the child by the hand and returning to the
house with him. Her husband joined me in a moment, looking,
I thought, the least bit conscious and constrained, and said that
if I would come in with him he would show me my room. In

looking back upon these first moments of my visit to him, I find
it important to avoid the error of appearing to have understood
his situation from the first, and to have seen in him the signs of
things which I learnt only afterwards. This later knowledge
throws a backward light, and makes me forget that at least on
the occasion of which I am speaking now (I mean that first
afternoon), Mark Ambient struck me as a fortunate man.
Allowing for this, I think he was rather silent and irresponsive
as we walked back to the house – though I remember well the
answer he made to a remark of mine in relation to his child.

'That's an extraordinary little boy of yours,' I said. 'I have
never seen such a child.'

'Why do you call him extraordinary?'

'He's so beautiful – so fascinating. He's like a little work
of art.'

He turned quickly, grasping my arm an instant. 'Oh, don't
call him that, or you'll – you'll—!' And in his hesitation he
broke off, suddenly, laughing at my surprise. But immediately
afterwards he added, 'You will make his little future very difficult.'

I declared that I wouldn't for the world take any liberties
with his little future – it seemed to me to hang by threads of
such delicacy. I should only be highly interested in watching it.
'You Americans are very sharp,' said Ambient. 'You notice
more things than we do.'

'Ah, if you want visitors who are not struck with you, you
shouldn't ask me down here!'

He showed me my room, a little bower of chintz, with open
windows where the light was green, and before he left me he
said irrelevantly, 'As for my little boy, you know, we shall
probably kill him between us, before we have done with him!'
And he made this assertion as if he really believed it, without
any appearance of jest, with his fine, near-sighted, expressive
eyes looking straight into mine.

'Do you mean by spoiling him?'

'No – by fighting for him!'

'You had better give him to me to keep for you,' I said. 'Let
me remove the apple of discord.'[14]

I laughed, of course, but he had the air of being perfectly serious. 'It would be quite the best thing we could do. I should be quite ready to do it.'

'I am greatly obliged to you for your confidence.'

Mark Ambient lingered there, with his hands in his pockets. I felt, within a few moments, as if I had, morally speaking, taken several steps nearer to him. He looked weary, just as he faced me then, looked preoccupied, and as if there were something one might do for him. I was terribly conscious of the limits of my own ability, but I wondered what such a service might be – feeling at bottom, however, that the only thing I could do for him was to like him. I suppose he guessed this, and was grateful for what was in my mind; for he went on presently, 'I haven't the advantage of being an American. But I also notice a little, and I have an idea that – a—' here he smiled and laid his hand on my shoulder, 'that even apart from your nationality, you are not destitute of intelligence! I have only known you half an hour, but – a—' And here he hesitated again. 'You are very young, after all.'

'But you may treat me as if I could understand you!' I said; and before he left me to dress for dinner he had virtually given me a promise that he would.

When I went down into the drawing-room – I was very punctual – I found that neither my hostess nor my host had appeared. A lady rose from a sofa, however, and inclined her head as I rather surprisedly gazed at her. 'I daresay you don't know me,' she said, with a modern laugh. 'I am Mark Ambient's sister.' Whereupon I shook hands with her – saluting her very low. Her laugh was modern – by which I mean that it consisted of the vocal agitation which, between people who meet in drawing-rooms, serves as the solvent of social mysteries, the medium of transitions; but her appearance was – what shall I call it? – mediæval. She was pale and angular, with a long, thin face, inhabited by sad, dark eyes, and black hair intertwined with golden fillets and curious chains. She wore a faded velvet robe, which clung to her when she moved, fashioned, as to the neck and sleeves, like the garments of old Venetians and Florentines. She looked pictorial and melancholy, and was so perfect an image of a type[15] which I – in my ignorance – supposed to be extinct, that while she rose before me I was almost as much startled as if I had seen a ghost. I afterwards perceived that Miss Ambient was not incapable of deriving pleasure from the effect she produced, and I think this sentiment had something to do with her sinking again into her seat, with her long, lean, but not ungraceful arms locked together in an archaic manner on her knees, and her mournful eyes addressing themselves to me with an intentness which was an earnest of what they were destined subsequently to inflict upon me. She was a singular, self-conscious, artificial creature, and I never, subsequently, more than half penetrated her motives and mysteries. Of one thing I am sure, however: that they were considerably less extraordinary than her appearance announced. Miss Ambient was a restless, yearning spinster, consumed with the love of Michael-Angelesque attitudes and mystical robes; but I am pretty sure she had not in her nature those depths of unutterable thought which, when you first knew her, seemed to look out from her eyes and to prompt her complicated gestures. Those features, in especial, had a misleading eloquence; they rested upon you with a far-off dimness, an air of obstructed sympathy, which was certainly not always a key to the spirit of their owner; and I suspect that a young lady could not really have been so dejected and disillusioned as Miss Ambient looked, without having committed a crime for which she was consumed with remorse or parted with a hope which she could not sanely have entertained. She had, I believe, the usual allowance of vulgar impulses; she wished to be looked at, she wished to be married, she wished to be thought original. It costs me something to speak in this irreverent manner of Mark Ambient's sister, but I shall have still more disagreeable things to say before I have finished my little anecdote, and moreover – I confess it – I owe the young lady a sort of grudge. Putting aside the curious cast of her face, she had no natural aptitude for an artistic development – she had little real intelligence. But her affectations rubbed off on her brother's renown, and as there were plenty of people who disapproved of him totally, they could easily point to his sister as a person formed by his influence. It was quite possible to regard her as a warning, and she had done him but little good with the world at large. He was the original, and she was the inevitable imitation. I think he was scarcely aware of the impression she produced – beyond having a general idea that she made up very well as a Rossetti;[16] he was used to her, and he was sorry for her – wishing she would marry and observing that she didn't. Doubtless I take her too seriously, for she did me no harm – though I am bound to add that I feel I can only half account for her. She was not so mystical as she looked, but she was a strange, indirect, uncomfortable, embarrassing woman. My story will give the reader at best so very small a knot to untie that I need not hope to excite his curiosity by delaying to remark that Mrs Ambient hated her sister-in-law. This I only found out afterwards, when I found out some other things. But I mention it at once, for I shall perhaps not seem to count too much on having enlisted the imagination of the reader if I say that he will already have guessed it. Mrs Ambient was a person of conscience, and she endeavoured to behave properly to her kinswoman, who spent a month with her twice a year; but it required no great insight to discover that the two ladies were made of a very different paste, and that the usual feminine hypocrisies must have cost them, on either side, much more than the usual effort. Mrs Ambient, smooth-haired, thin-lipped, perpetually fresh, must have regarded her crumpled and dishevelled visitor as a very stale joke; she herself was not a Rossetti, but a Gainsborough or a Lawrence,[17] and she had in her appearance no elements more romantic than a cold, ladylike candour, and a well-starched muslin dress. It was in a garment, and with an expression, of this kind, that she made her entrance, after I had exchanged a few words with Miss Ambient. Her husband presently followed her, and there being no other company we went to dinner. The impression I received from that repast is present to me still. There were elements of oddity in my companions, but they were vague and latent, and didn't interfere with my delight. It came mainly, of course, from Ambient's talk, which was the most brilliant and interesting I had ever heard. I know not whether he laid himself out to dazzle a rather juvenile pilgrim from over the sea; but it matters little, for it was very easy for him to shine. He was almost better as a talker than as a writer; that is, if the extraordinary finish of his written prose be really, as some people have maintained, a fault. There was such a kindness in him, however, that I have no doubt it gave him ideas to see me sit open-mouthed, as I suppose I did. Not so the two ladies, who not only were very nearly dumb from beginning to the end of the meal, but who had not the air of being struck with such an exhibition of wit and knowledge. Mrs Ambient, placid and detached, met neither my eye nor her husband's; she attended to her dinner, watched the servants, arranged the puckers in her dress, exchanged at wide intervals a remark with her sister-in-law, and while she slowly rubbed her white hands, between the courses, looked out of the window at the first signs of twilight – the long June day allowing us to dine without candles. Miss Ambient appeared to give little direct heed to her brother's discourse; but, on the other hand, she was much engaged in watching its effect upon me. Her lustreless pupils continued to attach themselves to my countenance, and it was only her air of belonging to another century that kept them from being importunate. She seemed to look at me across the ages, and the interval of time diminished the realism of the performance. It was as if she knew in a general way that her brother must be talking very well, but she herself was so rich in ideas that she had no need to pick them up, and was at liberty to see what would become of a young American when subjected to a high æsthetic temperature. The temperature was æsthetic, certainly, but it was less so than I could have desired, for I was unsuccessful in certain little attempts to make Mark Ambient talk about himself. I tried to put him on the ground of his own writings, but he slipped through my fingers every time and shifted the saddle to one of his contemporaries. He talked about Balzac and Browning,[18] and what was being done in foreign countries, and about his recent tour in the East, and the extraordinary forms of life that one saw in that part of the world. I perceived that he had reasons for not wishing to descant upon literature, and suffered him without protest to deliver himself on certain social topics, which he treated with extraordinary humour and with constant revelations of that power of ironical portraiture of which his books are full. He had a great deal to say about London, as London appears to the observer who doesn't fear the accusation of cynicism, during the high-pressure time – from April to July – of its peculiarities. He flashed his faculty of making the fanciful real and the real fanciful over the perfunctory pleasures and desperate exertions of so many of his compatriots, among whom there were evidently not a few types for which he had little love. London bored him, and he made capital sport of it; his only allusion, that I can remember, to his own work was his saying that he meant some day to write an immense grotesque epic of London society. Miss Ambient's perpetual gaze seemed to say to me, 'Do you perceive how artistic we are? frankly now, is it possible to be more artistic than this? You surely won't deny that we are remarkable.' I was irritated by her use of the plural pronoun, for she had no right to pair herself with her brother; and moreover, of course, I could not see my way to include Mrs Ambient. But there was no doubt that (for that matter) they were all remarkable, and, with all allowances, I had never heard anything so artistic. Mark Ambient's conversation seemed to play over the whole field of knowledge and taste; it made me feel that this at last was real talk, that this was distinction, culture, experience.

After the ladies had left us he took me into his study, to smoke, and here I led him on to gossip freely enough about himself. I was bent upon proving to him that I was worthy to listen to him, upon repaying him (for what he had said to me before dinner) by showing him how perfectly I understood. He liked to talk, he liked to defend his ideas (not that I attacked them), he liked a little perhaps – it was a pardonable weakness – to astonish the youthful mind and to feel its admiration and sympathy. I confess that my own youthful mind was considerably astonished at some of his speeches; he startled me and he made me wince. He could not help forgetting, or rather he couldn't know, how little personal contact I had had with the school in which he was master; and he promoted me at a jump, as it were, to the study of its innermost mysteries. My trepidations, however, were delightful; they were just what I had hoped for, and their only fault was that they passed away too quickly, for I found that, as regards most things, I very soon seized Mark Ambient's point of view. It was the point of view of the artist to whom every manifestation of human energy was a thrilling spectacle, and who felt for ever the desire to resolve his experience of life into a literary form. On this matter of the passion for form – the attempt at perfection, the quest for which was to his mind the real search for the holy grail, he said the most interesting, the most inspiring things. He mixed with them a thousand illustrations from his own life, from other lives that he had known, from history and fiction, and, above all, from the annals of the time that was dear to him beyond all periods – the Italian *cinque-cento*.[19] I saw that in his books he had only said half of his thought, and what he had kept back – from motives that I deplored when I learnt them later – was the richer part. It was his fortune to shock a great many people, but there was not a grain of bravado in his pages (I have always maintained it, though often contradicted), and at bottom the poor fellow, an artist to his finger-tips, and regarding a failure of completeness as a crime, had an extreme dread of scandal. There are people who regret that having gone so far he did not go further; but I regret nothing (putting aside two or three of the motives I just mentioned), for he arrived at perfection, and I don't see how you can go beyond that. The hours I spent in his study – this first one and the few that followed it; they were not, after all, so numerous – seem to glow, as I look back on them, with a tone which is partly that of the brown old room, rich, under the shaded candlelight where we sat and smoked, with the dusky, delicate bindings of valuable books; partly that of his voice, of which I still catch the echo, charged with the images that came at his command. When we went back to the drawing-room we found Miss Ambient alone in possession of it; and she informed us that her sister-in-law had a quarter of an hour before been called by the nurse to see Dolcino, who appeared to be a little feverish.

'Feverish! how in the world does he come to be feverish?' Ambient asked. 'He was perfectly well this afternoon.'

'Beatrice says you walked him about too much – you almost killed him.'

'Beatrice must be very happy – she has an opportunity to triumph!' Mark Ambient said, with a laugh of which the bitterness was just perceptible.

'Surely not if the child is ill,' I ventured to remark, by way of pleading for Mrs Ambient.

'My dear fellow, you are not married – you don't know the nature of wives!' my host exclaimed.

'Possibly not; but I know the nature of mothers.'

'Beatrice is perfect as a mother,' said Miss Ambient, with a tremendous sigh and her fingers interlaced on her embroidered knees.

'I shall go up and see the child,' her brother went on. 'Do you suppose he's asleep?'

'Beatrice won't let you see him, Mark,' said the young lady, looking at me, though she addressed our companion.

'Do you call that being perfect as a mother?' Ambient inquired.

'Yes, from her point of view.'

'Damn her point of view!' cried the author of *Beltraffio*. And he left the room; after which we heard him ascend the stairs.

I sat there for some ten minutes with Miss Ambient, and we, naturally, had some conversation, which was begun, I think, by my asking her what the point of view of her sister-in-law could be.

'Oh, it's so very odd,' she said. 'But we are so very odd, altogether. Don't you find us so? We have lived so much abroad. Have you people like us in America?'

'You are not all alike, surely; so that I don't think I understand your question. We have no one like your brother – I may go so far as that.'

'You have probably more persons like his wife,' said Miss Ambient, smiling.

'I can tell you that better when you have told me about her point of view.'

'Oh yes – oh yes. Well, she doesn't like his ideas. She doesn't like them for the little boy. She thinks them undesirable.'

Being quite fresh from the contemplation of some of Mark

Ambient's *arcana*, I was particularly in a position to appreciate this announcement. But the effect of it was to make me (after staring a moment) burst into laughter, which I instantly checked when I remembered that there was a sick child above.

'What has that infant to do with ideas?' I asked. 'Surely, he can't tell one from another. Has he read his father's novels?'

'He's very precocious and very sensitive, and his mother thinks she can't begin to guard him too early.' Miss Ambient's head drooped a little to one side, and her eyes fixed themselves on futurity. Then, suddenly, there was a strange alteration in her face; she gave a smile that was more joyless than her gravity – a conscious, insincere smile, and added, 'When one has children, it's a great responsibility – what one writes.'

'Children are terrible critics,' I answered. 'I am rather glad I haven't got any.'

'Do you also write then? And in the same style as my brother? And do you like that style? And do people appreciate it in America? I don't write, but I think I feel.' To these and various other inquiries and remarks the young lady treated me, till we heard her brother's step in the hall again and Mark Ambient reappeared. He looked flushed and serious, and I supposed that he had seen something to alarm him in the condition of his child. His sister apparently had another idea; she gazed at him a moment as if he were a burning ship on the horizon, and simply murmured – 'Poor old Mark!'

'I hope you are not anxious,' I said.

'No, but I am disappointed. She won't let me in. She has locked the door, and I'm afraid to make a noise.' I suppose there might have been something ridiculous in a confession of this kind, but I liked my new friend so much that for me it didn't detract from his dignity. 'She tells me – from behind the door – that she will let me know if he is worse.'

'It's very good of her,' said Miss Ambient.

I had exchanged a glance with Mark in which it is possible that he read that my pity for him was untinged with contempt – though I know not why he should have cared; and as, presently, his sister got up and took her bedroom candlestick, he proposed that we should go back to his study. We sat there till after

midnight; he put himself into his slippers, into an old velvet
jacket, lighted an ancient pipe, and talked considerably less than
he had done before. There were longish pauses in our communion, but they only made me feel that we had advanced in
intimacy. They helped me, too, to understand my friend's personal situation, and to perceive that it was by no means the
happiest possible. When his face was quiet, it was vaguely troubled; it seemed to me to show that for him, too, life was a
struggle, as it has been for many other men of genius. At last I
prepared to leave him, and then, to my ineffable joy, he gave me
some of the sheets of his forthcoming book – it was not finished,
but he had indulged in the luxury, so dear to writers of deliberation, of having it 'set up', from chapter to chapter, as he
advanced – he gave me, I say, the early pages, the *prémices*,[20] as
the French have it, of this new fruit of his imagination, to take
to my room and look over at my leisure. I was just quitting him
when the door of his study was noiselessly pushed open, and
Mrs Ambient stood before us. She looked at us a moment, with
her candle in her hand, and then she said to her husband that as
she supposed he had not gone to bed she had come down to tell
him that Dolcino was more quiet and would probably be better
in the morning. Mark Ambient made no reply; he simply slipped
past her, in the doorway, as if he were afraid she would seize
him in his passage, and bounded upstairs, to judge for himself
of his child's condition. Mrs Ambient looked slightly discom-
fited, and for a moment I thought she was going to give chase to
her husband. But she resigned herself, with a sigh, while her
eyes wandered over the lamp-lit room, where various books, at
which I had been looking, were pulled out of their places on the
shelves, and the fumes of tobacco seemed to hang in mid-air. I
bade her good-night, and then, without intention, by a kind of
fatality, the perversity which had already made me insist unduly
on talking with her about her husband's achievements, I alluded
to the precious proof-sheets with which Ambient had entrusted
me, and which I was nursing there under my arm. 'It is the
opening chapters of his new book,' I said. 'Fancy my satisfaction at being allowed to carry them to my room!'

She turned away, leaving me to take my candlestick from the

table in the hall; but before we separated, thinking it apparently a good occasion to let me know once for all – since I was beginning, it would seem, to be quite 'thick' with my host – that there was no fitness in my appealing to her for sympathy in such a case; before we separated, I say, she remarked to me, with her quick, round, well-bred utterance, 'I daresay you attribute to me ideas that I haven't got. I don't take that sort of interest in my husband's proof-sheets. I consider his writings most objectionable!'

II

I had some curious conversation the next morning with Miss Ambient, whom I found strolling in the garden before breakfast. The whole place looked as fresh and trim, amid the twitter of the birds, as if, an hour before, the housemaids had been turned into it with their dustpans and feather-brushes. I almost hesitated to light a cigarette, and was doubly startled when, in the act of doing so, I suddenly perceived the sister of my host, who had, in any case, something of the oddity of an apparition, standing before me. She might have been posing for her photograph. Her sad-coloured robe arranged itself in serpentine folds at her feet; her hands locked themselves listlessly together in front; and her chin rested upon a *cinque-cento* ruff. The first thing I did, after bidding her good morning, was to ask her for news of her little nephew – to express the hope that she had heard he was better. She was able to gratify this hope, and spoke as if we might expect to see him during the day. We walked through the shrubberies together, and she gave me a great deal of information about her brother's *ménage*, which offered me an opportunity to mention to her that his wife had told me, the night before, that she thought his productions objectionable.

'She doesn't usually come out with that so soon!' Miss Ambient exclaimed, in answer to this piece of gossip.

'Poor lady, she saw that I am a fanatic.'

'Yes, she won't like you for that. But you mustn't mind, if the rest of us like you! Beatrice thinks a work of art ought to

have a "purpose".[21] But she's a charming woman – don't you
think her charming? – she's such a type of the lady.'

'She's very beautiful,' I answered; while I reflected that though
it was true, apparently, that Mark Ambient was mismated, it
was also perceptible that his sister was perfidious. She told me
that her brother and his wife had no other difference but this
one, that she thought his writings immoral and his influence pernicious. It was a fixed idea; she was afraid of these things for the
child. I answered that it was not a trifle – a woman's regarding
her husband's mind as a well of corruption; and she looked quite
struck with the novelty of my remark. 'But there hasn't been any
of the sort of trouble that there so often is among married
people,' she said. 'I suppose you can judge for yourself that Beatrice isn't at all – well, whatever they call it when a woman
misbehaves herself. And Mark doesn't make love to other
people, either. I assure you he doesn't! All the same, of course,
from her point of view, you know, she has a dread of my brother's influence on the child – on the formation of his character, of
his principles. It is as if it were a subtle poison, or a contagion,
or something that would rub off on Dolcino when his father
kisses him or holds him on his knee. If she could, she would prevent Mark from ever touching him. Every one knows it; visitors
see it for themselves; so there is no harm in my telling you. Isn't
it excessively odd? It comes from Beatrice's being so religious,
and so tremendously moral, and all that. And then, of course, we
mustn't forget,' my companion added, unexpectedly, 'that some
of Mark's ideas are – well, really – rather queer!'

I reflected, as we went into the house, where we found Ambient unfolding the *Observer*[22] at the breakfast-table, that none
of them were probably quite so queer as his sister. Mrs Ambient did not appear at breakfast, being rather tired with her
ministrations, during the night, to Dolcino. Her husband mentioned, however, that she was hoping to go to church. I
afterwards learned that she did go, but I may as well announce
without delay that he and I did not accompany her. It was
while the church-bell was murmuring in the distance that the
author of *Beltraffio* led me forth for the ramble he had spoken
of in his note. I will not attempt to say where we went, or to

describe what we saw. We kept to the fields and copses and commons, and breathed the same sweet air as the nibbling donkeys and the browsing sheep, whose woolliness seemed to me, in those early days of my acquaintance with English objects, but a part of the general texture of the small, dense landscape, which looked as if the harvest were gathered by the shears. Everything was full of expression for Mark Ambient's visitor – from the big, bandy-legged geese, whose whiteness was a 'note', amid all the tones of green, as they wandered beside a neat little oval pool, the foreground of a thatched and white-washed inn, with a grassy approach and a pictorial sign – from these humble wayside animals to the crests of high woods which let a gable or a pinnacle peep here and there, and looked, even at a distance, like trees of good company, conscious of an individual profile. I admired the hedgerows, I plucked the faint-hued heather, and I was for ever stopping to say how charming I thought the thread-like footpaths across the fields, which wandered, in a diagonal of finer grain, from one smooth stile to another. Mark Ambient was abundantly good-natured, and was as much entertained with my observations as I was with the literary allusions of the landscape. We sat and smoked upon stiles, broaching paradoxes in the decent English air; we took short cuts across a park or two, where the bracken was deep, and my companion nodded to the old woman at the gate; we skirted rank covers, which rustled here and there as we passed, and we stretched ourselves at last on a heathery hillside where, if the sun was not too hot, neither was the earth too cold, and where the country lay beneath us in a rich blue mist. Of course I had already told Ambient what I thought of his new novel, having the previous night read every word of the opening chapters before I went to bed.

'I am not without hope of being able to make it my best,' he said, as I went back to the subject, while we turned up our heels to the sky. 'At least the people who dislike my prose – and there are a great many of them, I believe – will dislike this work most.' This was the first time I had heard him allude to the people who couldn't read him – a class which is supposed always to sit heavy upon the consciousness of the man of letters. A man organized for literature, as Mark Ambient was, must certainly have had the normal proportion of sensitiveness, of irritability; the artistic *ego*, capable in some cases of such monstrous development, must have been, in his composition, sufficiently erect and definite. I will not therefore go so far as to say that he never thought of his detractors, or that he had any illusions with regard to the number of his admirers (he could never so far have deceived himself as to believe he was popular); but I may at least affirm that adverse criticism, as I had occasion to perceive later, ruffled him visibly but little, that he had an air of thinking it quite natural he should be offensive to many minds, and that he very seldom talked about the newspapers – which, by the way, were always very stupid in regard to the author of *Beltraffio*. Of course he may have thought about them – the newspapers – night and day; the only point I wish to make is that he didn't show it; while, at the same time, he didn't strike one as a man who was on his guard. I may add that, as regards his hope of making the work on which he was then engaged the best of his books, it was only partly carried out. That place belongs, incontestably, to *Beltraffio*, in spite of the beauty of certain parts of its successor. I am pretty sure, however, that he had, at the moment of which I speak, no sense of failure; he was in love with his idea, which was indeed magnificent, and though for him, as (I suppose) for every artist, the act of execution had in it as much torment as joy, he saw his work growing a little every day and filling out the largest plan he had yet conceived. 'I want to be truer than I have ever been,' he said, settling himself on his back, with his hands clasped behind his head; 'I want to give an impression of life itself. No, you may say what you will, I have always arranged things too much, always smoothed them down and rounded them off and tucked them in – done everything to them that life doesn't do. I have been a slave to the old superstitions.'

'You a slave, my dear Mark Ambient? You have the freest imagination of our day!'

'All the more shame to me to have done some of the things I have! The reconciliation of the two women in *Ginistrella*,[23] for instance – which could never really have taken place. That sort of thing is ignoble; I blush when I think of it! This new affair must be a golden vessel, filled with the purest distillation of the actual; and oh, how it bothers me, the shaping of the vase – the hammering of the metal! I have to hammer it so fine, so smooth; I don't do more than an inch or two a day. And all the while I have to be so careful not to let a drop of the liquor escape! When I see the kind of things that Life does, I despair of ever catching her peculiar trick. She has an impudence, Life! If one risked a fiftieth part of the effects she risks! It takes ever so long to believe it. You don't know yet, my dear fellow. It isn't till one has been watching Life for forty years that one finds out half of what she's up to! Therefore one's earlier things must inevitably contain a mass of rot. And with what one sees, on one side, with its tongue in its cheek, defying one to be real enough, and on the other the *bonnes gens* rolling up their eyes at one's cynicism, the situation has elements of the ludicrous which the artist himself is doubtless in a position to appreciate better than any one else. Of course one mustn't bother about the *bonnes gens*,'[24] Mark Ambient went on, while my thoughts reverted to his ladylike wife, as interpreted by his remarkable sister.

'To sink your shaft deep, and polish the plate through which people look into it – that's what your work consists of,' I remember remarking.

'Ah, polishing one's plate – that is the torment of execution!' he exclaimed, jerking himself up and sitting forward. 'The effort to arrive at a surface – if you think a surface necessary – some people don't, happily for them! My dear fellow, if you could see the surface I dream of – as compared with the one with which I have to content myself. Life is really too short for art – one hasn't time to make one's shell ideally hard.[25] Firm and bright – firm and bright! – the devilish thing has a way, sometimes, of being bright without being firm. When I rap it with my knuckles it doesn't give the right sound. There are horrible little flabby spots where I have taken the second-best word, because I couldn't for the life of me think of the best.[26] If you knew how stupid I am sometimes! They look to me now like pimples and ulcers on the brow of beauty!'

'That's very bad – very bad,' I said, as gravely as I could.

'Very bad? It's the highest social offence I know; it ought – it absolutely ought – I'm quite serious – to be capital. If I knew I should be hanged else, I should manage to find the best word.[27] The people who couldn't – some of them don't know it when they see it – would shut their inkstands, and we shouldn't be deluged by this flood of rubbish!'

I will not attempt to repeat everything that passed between us or to explain just how it was that, every moment I spent in his company, Mark Ambient revealed to me more and more that he looked at all things from the standpoint of the artist, felt all life as literary material. There are people who will tell me that this is a poor way of feeling it, and I am not concerned to defend my statement – having space merely to remark that there is something to be said for any interest which makes a man feel so much. If Mark Ambient did really, as I suggested above, have imaginative contact with 'all life', I, for my part, envy him his *arrière-pensée*.[28] At any rate it was through the receipt of this impression of him that by the time we returned I had acquired the feeling of intimacy I have noted. Before we got up for the homeward stretch he alluded to his wife's having once – or perhaps more than once – asked him whether he should like Dolcino to read *Beltraffio*. I think he was unconscious at the moment of all that this conveyed to me – as well, doubtless, of my extreme curiosity to hear what he had replied. He had said that he hoped very much Dolcino would read all his works – when he was twenty; he should like him to know what his father had done. Before twenty it would be useless – he wouldn't understand them.

'And meanwhile do you propose to hide them – to lock them up in a drawer?' Mrs Ambient had inquired.

'Oh no; we must simply tell him that they are not intended for small boys. If you bring him up properly, after that he won't touch them.'

To this Mrs Ambient had made answer that it would be very awkward when he was about fifteen, and I asked her husband if it was his opinion in general, then, that young people should not read novels.

'Good ones – certainly not!' said my companion. I suppose I

had had other views, for I remember saying that, for myself, I was not sure it was bad for them – if the novels were 'good' enough. 'Bad for *them*, I don't say so much!' Ambient exclaimed. 'But very bad, I am afraid, for the novel.'[29] That oblique, accidental allusion to his wife's attitude was followed by a franker style of reference as we walked home. 'The difference between us is simply the opposition between two distinct ways of looking at the world, which have never succeeded in getting on together, or making any kind of common ménage, since the beginning of time. They have borne all sorts of names, and my wife would tell you it's the difference between Christian and Pagan. I may be a pagan, but I don't like the name – it sounds sectarian. She thinks me, at any rate, no better than an ancient Greek. It's the difference between making the most of life and making the least – so that you'll get another better one in some other time and place. Will it be a sin to make the most of that one too, I wonder? and shall we have to be bribed off in the future state, as well as in the present? Perhaps I care too much for beauty – I don't know; I delight in it, I adore it, I think of it continually, I try to produce it, to reproduce it. My wife holds that we shouldn't think too much about it. She's always afraid of that – always on her guard. I don't know what she has got on her back! And she's so pretty, too, herself! Don't you think she's lovely? She was, at any rate, when I married her. At that time I wasn't aware of that difference I speak of – I thought it all came to the same thing: in the end, as they say. Well, perhaps it will in the end. I don't know what the end will be. Moreover, I care for seeing things as they are; that's the way I try to show them in my novels. But you mustn't talk to Mrs Ambient about things as they are. She has a mortal dread of things as they are.'

'She's afraid of them for Dolcino,' I said: surprised a moment afterwards at being in a position – thanks to Miss Ambient – to be so explanatory; and surprised even now that Mark shouldn't have shown visibly that he wondered what the deuce I knew about it. But he didn't; he simply exclaimed, with a tenderness that touched me –

'Ah, nothing shall ever hurt *him*!' He told me more about his wife before we arrived at the gate of his house, and if it be thought that he was querulous, I am afraid I must admit that he had some of the foibles as well as the gifts of the artistic temperament; adding, however, instantly, that hitherto, to the best of my belief, he had very rarely complained. 'She thinks me immoral – that's the long and short of it,' he said, as we paused outside a moment, and his hand rested on one of the bars of his gate; while his conscious, expressive, perceptive eyes – the eyes of a foreigner, I had begun to account them, much more than of the usual Englishman – viewing me now evidently as quite a familiar friend, took part in the declaration. 'It's very strange, when one thinks it all over, and there's a grand comicality in it which I should like to bring out. She is a very nice woman, extraordinarily well behaved, upright, and clever, and with a tremendous lot of good sense about a good many matters. Yet her conception of a novel – she has explained it to me once or twice, and she doesn't do it badly, as exposition – is a thing so false that it makes me blush. It is a thing so hollow, so dishonest, so lying, in which life is so blinked and blinded, so dodged and disfigured, that it makes my ears burn. It's two different ways of looking at the whole affair,' he repeated, pushing open the gate. 'And they are irreconcilable!' he added with a sigh. We went forward to the house, but on the walk, half way to the door, he stopped, and said to me, 'If you are going into this kind of thing, there's a fact you should know beforehand; it may save you some disappointment. There's a hatred of art – there's a hatred of literature!' I looked up at the charming house, with its genial colour and crookedness, and I answered with a smile that those evil passions might exist, but that I should never have expected to find them there. 'Oh, it doesn't matter, after all,' he said, laughing; which I was glad to hear, for I was reproaching myself with having excited him.

If I had, his excitement soon passed off, for at lunch he was delightful; strangely delightful, considering that the difference between himself and his wife was, as he had said, irreconcilable. He had the art, by his manner, by his smile, by his natural kindliness, of reducing the importance of it in the common concerns of life, and Mrs Ambient, I must add, lent herself to this transaction with a very good grace. I watched her, at table, for further illustrations of that fixed idea of which Miss Ambient had spoken to me; for in the light of the united revelations of her sister-in-law and her husband, she had come to seem to me a very singular personage. I am obliged to say that the signs of a fanatical temperament were not more striking in my hostess than before; it was only after a while that her air of incorruptible conformity, her tapering, monosyllabic correctness, began to appear to be themselves a cold, thin flame. Certainly, at first, she looked like a woman with as few passions as possible; but if she had a passion at all, it would be that of Philistinism. She might have been, for there are guardian-spirits, I suppose, of all great principles – the angel of propriety. Mark Ambient, apparently, ten years before, had simply perceived that she was an angel, without asking himself of what. He had been quite right in calling my attention to her beauty. In looking for the reason why he should have married her, I saw, more than before, that she was, physically speaking, a wonderfully cultivated human plant – that she must have given him many ideas and images. It was impossible to be more pencilled, more garden-like, more delicately tinted and petalled.

If I had had it in my heart to think Ambient a little of a hypocrite for appearing to forget at table everything he had said to me during our walk, I should instantly have cancelled such a judgment on reflecting that the good news his wife was able to give him about their little boy was reason enough for his sudden air of happiness. It may have come partly, too, from a certain remorse at having complained to me of the fair lady who sat there – a desire to show me that he was after all not so miserable. Dolcino continued to be much better, and he had been promised he should come downstairs after he had had his dinner. As soon as we had risen from our own meal Ambient slipped away, evidently for the purpose of going to his child; and no sooner had I observed this than I became aware that his wife had simultaneously vanished. It happened that Miss Ambient and I, both at the same moment, saw the tail of her dress whisk out of a doorway – which led the young lady to smile at me, as if I now knew all the secrets of the place. I passed with her into the garden, and we sat down on a dear old bench which rested against the west wall of the house. It was a perfect spot for the middle period of a Sunday in June, and its felicity seemed to come partly from an antique sun-dial which, rising in front of us and forming the centre of a small, intricate parterre, measured the moments ever so slowly, and made them safe for leisure and talk. The garden bloomed in the suffused afternoon, the tall beeches stood still for an example, and, behind and above us, a rose-tree of many seasons, clinging to the faded grain of the brick, expressed the whole character of the scene in a familiar, exquisite smell. It seemed to me a place for genius to have every sanction, and not to encounter challenges and checks. Miss Ambient asked me if I had enjoyed my walk with her brother, and whether we had talked of many things.

'Well, of most things,' I said, smiling, though I remembered that we had not talked of Miss Ambient.

'And don't you think some of his theories are very peculiar?'

'Oh, I guess I agree with them all.' I was very particular, for Miss Ambient's entertainment, to guess.

'Do you think art is everything?' she inquired in a moment.

'In art, of course I do!'

'And do you think beauty is everything?'

'I don't know about its being everything. But it's very delightful.'

'Of course it is difficult for a woman to know how far to go,' said my companion. 'I adore everything that gives a charm to life. I am intensely sensitive to form. But sometimes I draw back – don't you see what I mean? – I don't quite see where I shall be landed. I only want to be quiet, after all,' Miss Ambient continued, in a tone of stifled yearning which seemed to indicate that she had not yet arrived at her desire. 'And one must be good, at any rate, must not one?' she inquired, with a cadence apparently intended for an assurance that my answer would settle this recondite question for her. It was difficult for me to make it very original, and I am afraid I repaid her confidence with an unblushing platitude. I remember, moreover, appending to it an inquiry, equally destitute of freshness, and still more wanting perhaps in tact, as to whether she did not mean to go to church, as that was an obvious way of being good. She replied that she had performed this duty in the morning, and that for her, on Sunday afternoon, supreme virtue consisted in answering the week's letters. Then suddenly, without transition, she said to me, 'It's quite a mistake about Dolcino being better. I have seen him, and he's not at all right.'

'Surely his mother would know, wouldn't she?' I suggested.

She appeared for a moment to be counting the leaves on one of the great beeches. 'As regards most matters, one can easily say what, in a given situation, my sister-in-law would do. But as regards this one, there are strange elements at work.'

'Strange elements? Do you mean in the constitution of the child?'

'No, I mean in my sister-in-law's feelings.'

'Elements of affection, of course; elements of anxiety. Why do you call them strange?'

She repeated my words. 'Elements of affection, elements of anxiety. She is very anxious.'

Miss Ambient made me vaguely uneasy – she almost frightened me, and I wished she would go and write her letters. 'His father will have seen him now,' I said, 'and if he is not satisfied he will send for the doctor.'

'The doctor ought to have been here this morning. He lives only two miles away.'

I reflected that all this was very possibly only a part of the general tragedy of Miss Ambient's view of things; but I asked her why she hadn't urged such a necessity upon her sister-in-law. She answered me with a smile of extraordinary significance, and told me that I must have very little idea of what her relations with Beatrice were; but I must do her the justice to add that she went on to make herself a little more comprehensible by saying that it was quite reason enough for her sister not to be alarmed that Mark would be sure to be. He was always nervous about the child, and as they were predestined by nature to take opposite views, the only thing for Beatrice was to cultivate a false optimism. If Mark were not there, she would not be at all easy. I remembered what he had said to me about their dealings with Dolcino – that between them they would put an end to him; but I did not repeat this to Miss Ambient: the less so that just then her brother emerged from the house, carrying his child in his arms. Close behind him moved his wife, grave and pale; the boy's face was turned over Ambient's shoulder, towards his mother. We got up to receive the group, and as they came near us Dolcino turned round. I caught, on his enchanting little countenance, a smile of recognition, and for the moment would have been quite content with it. Miss Ambient, however, received another impression, and I make haste to say that her quick sensibility, in which there was something maternal, argues that in spite of her affectations there was a strain of kindness in her. 'It won't do at all – it won't do at all,' she said to me under her breath. 'I shall speak to Mark about the doctor.'

The child was rather white, but the main difference I saw in him was that he was even more beautiful than the day before. He had been dressed in his festal garments – a velvet suit and a crimson sash – and he looked like a little invalid prince, too young to know condescension, and smiling familiarly on his subjects.

'Put him down, Mark, he's not comfortable,' Mrs Ambient said.

'Should you like to stand on your feet, my boy?' his father asked.

'Oh yes; I'm remarkably well,' said the child.

Mark placed him on the ground; he had shining, pointed slippers, with enormous bows. 'Are you happy now, Mr Ambient?'

'Oh yes, I am particularly happy,' Dolcino replied. The words were scarcely out of his mouth when his mother caught him up, and in a moment, holding him on her knees, she took her place on the bench where Miss Ambient and I had been sitting. This young lady said something to her brother, in consequence of which the two wandered away into the garden together. I remained with Mrs Ambient; but as a servant had brought out a couple of chairs I was not obliged to seat myself beside her. Our conversation was not animated, and I, for my part, felt there would be a kind of hypocrisy in my trying to make myself agreeable to Mrs Ambient. I didn't dislike her – I rather admired her; but I was aware that I differed from her inexpressibly. Then I suspected, what I afterwards definitely knew and have already intimated, that the poor lady had taken a dislike to me; and this of course was not encouraging. She thought me an obtrusive and even depraved young man, whom a perverse Providence had dropped upon their quiet lawn to flatter her husband's worst tendencies. She did me the honour to say to Miss Ambient, who repeated the speech, that she didn't know when she had seen her husband take such a fancy to a visitor; and she measured, apparently, my evil influence by Mark's appreciation of my society. I had a consciousness, not yet acute, but quite sufficient, of all this; but I must say that if it chilled my flow of small-talk, it didn't prevent me from thinking that the beautiful mother and beautiful child, interlaced there against their background of roses, made a picture such as I perhaps should not soon see again. I was free, I supposed, to go into the house and write letters, to sit in the drawing-room, to repair to my own apartment and take a nap; but the only use I made of my freedom was to linger still in my chair and say to myself that the light hand of Sir Joshua[30] might have painted Mark Ambient's wife and son. I found myself looking perpetually at Dolcino, and Dolcino looked back at me, and that was enough to detain me. When he looked at me he smiled, and I felt it was an absolute impossibility to abandon a child who was smiling at one like that. His eyes never wandered; they attached themselves to mine, as if among all the small incipient things of his nature there was a desire to say something to me. If I could have taken him upon my own knee he perhaps would have managed to say it; but it would have been far too delicate a matter to ask his mother to give him up, and it has remained a constant regret for me that on that Sunday afternoon I did not, even for a moment, hold Dolcino in my arms. He had said that he felt remarkably well, and that he was especially happy; but though he may have been happy, with his charming head pillowed on his mother's breast and his little crimson silk legs depending from her lap, I did not think he looked well. He made no attempt to walk about; he was content to swing his legs softly and strike one as languid and angelic.

Mark came back to us with his sister; and Miss Ambient, making some remark about having to attend to her correspondence, passed into the house. Mark came and stood in front of his wife, looking down at the child, who immediately took hold of his hand, keeping it while he remained. 'I think Allingham ought to see him,' Ambient said; 'I think I will walk over and fetch him.'

'That's Gwendolen's idea, I suppose,' Mrs Ambient replied, very sweetly.

'It's not such an out-of-the-way idea, when one's child is ill.'

'I'm not ill, papa; I'm much better now,' Dolcino remarked.

'Is that the truth, or are you only saying it to be agreeable? You have a great idea of being agreeable, you know.'

The boy seemed to meditate on this distinction, this imputation, for a moment; then his exaggerated eyes, which had wandered, caught my own as I watched him. 'Do *you* think me agreeable?' he inquired, with the candour of his age and with a smile that made his father turn round to me, laughing, and ask, mutely, with a glance, 'Isn't he adorable?'

'Then why don't you hop about, if you feel so lusty?' Ambient went on, while the boy swung his hand.

'Because mamma is holding me close!'

'Oh yes; I know how mamma holds you when I come near!' Ambient exclaimed, looking at his wife.

She turned her charming eyes up to him, without deprecation or concession, and after a moment she said, 'You can go for Allingham if you like. I think myself it would be better. You ought to drive.'

'She says that to get me away,' Ambient remarked to me, laughing; after which he started for the doctor's.

I remained there with Mrs Ambient, though our conversation had more pauses than speeches. The boy's little fixed white face seemed, as before, to plead with me to stay, and after a while it produced still another effect, a very curious one, which I shall find it difficult to express. Of course I expose myself to the charge of attempting to give fantastic reasons for an act which may have been simply the fruit of a native want of discretion; and indeed the traceable consequences of that perversity were too lamentable to leave me any desire to trifle with the question. All I can say is that I acted in perfect good faith, and that Dolcino's friendly little gaze gradually kindled the spark of my inspiration. What helped it to glow were the other influences – the silent, suggestive garden-nook, the perfect opportunity (if it was not an opportunity for that, it was an opportunity for nothing), and the plea that I speak of, which issued from the child's eyes and seemed to make him say, 'The mother that bore me and that presses me here to her bosom – sympathetic little organism that I am – has really the kind of sensibility which she has been represented to you as lacking; if you only look for it patiently and respectfully. How is it possible that she shouldn't have it? how is it possible that *I* should have so much of it (for I am quite full of it, dear strange gentleman), if it were not also in some degree in her? I am my father's child, but I am also my mother's, and I am sorry for the difference between them!' So it shaped itself before me, the vision of reconciling Mrs Ambient with her husband, of putting an end to their great disagreement. The project was absurd, of course, for had I not had his word for it – spoken with all the bitterness of experience – that the gulf that divided them was well-nigh bottomless? Nevertheless, a quarter of an hour after Mark had left us, I said to his wife that I couldn't get over what she told me the night before about her thinking her husband's writings 'objectionable'. I had been so very sorry to hear it, had thought of it constantly, and wondered whether it were not possible to make her change her mind. Mrs Ambient gave me rather a cold stare – she seemed to be recommending me to mind my own business. I wish I had taken this mute counsel, but I did not. I went on to remark that it seemed an immense pity so much that was beautiful should be lost upon her.

'Nothing is lost upon me,' said Mrs Ambient. 'I know they are very beautiful.'

'Don't you like papa's books?' Dolcino asked, addressing his mother, but still looking at me. Then he added to me, 'Won't you read them to me, American gentleman?'

'I would rather tell you some stories of my own,' I said. 'I know some that are very interesting.'

'When will you tell them – to-morrow?'

'To-morrow, with pleasure, if that suits you.'

Mrs Ambient was silent at this. Her husband, during our walk, had asked me to remain another day; my promise to her son was an implication that I had consented; and it is not probable that the prospect was agreeable to her. This ought, doubtless, to have made me more careful as to what I said next; but all I can say is that it didn't. I presently observed that just after leaving her, the evening before, and after hearing her apply to her husband's writings the epithet I had already quoted, I had, on going up to my room, sat down to the perusal of those sheets of his new book which he had been so good as to lend me. I had sat entranced till nearly three in the morning – I had read them twice over. 'You say you haven't looked at them. I think it's such a pity you shouldn't. Do let me beg you to take them up. They are so very remarkable. I'm sure they will convert you. They place him in – really – such a dazzling light. All that is best in him is there. I have no doubt it's a great liberty, my saying all this; but excuse me, and *do* read them!'

'Do read them, mamma!' Dolcino repeated. 'Do read them!'

She bent her head and closed his lips with a kiss. 'Of course I know he has worked immensely over them,' she said; and after this she made no remark, but sat there looking thoughtful, with her eyes on the ground. The tone of these last words was such as to leave me no spirit for further aggression, and after expressing a fear that her husband had not found the doctor at home, I got up and took a turn about the grounds. When I came back ten minutes later, she was still in her place, watching her boy, who had fallen asleep in her lap. As I drew near she put her finger to her lips, and a moment afterwards she rose, holding the child, and murmured something about its being better that he should go upstairs. I offered to carry him, and held out my hands to take him; but she thanked me and turned away, with the child seated on her arm, his head on her shoulder. 'I am very strong,' she said, as she passed into the house, and her slim, flexible figure bent backwards with the filial weight. So I never touched Dolcino.

I betook myself to Ambient's study, delighted to have a quiet hour to look over his books by myself. The windows were open into the garden, the sunny stillness, the mild light of the English summer, filled the room, without quite chasing away the rich, dusky air which was a part of its charm, and which abode in the serried shelves where old morocco exhaled the fragrance of curious learning, and in the brighter intervals where medals and prints and miniatures were suspended upon a surface of faded stuff. The place had both colour and quiet; I thought it a perfect room for work, and went so far as to say to myself that if it were mine, to sit and scribble in, there was no knowing but that I might learn to write as well as the author of *Beltraffio*. This distinguished man did not turn up, and I rummaged freely among his treasures. At last I took down a book that detained me a while, and seated myself in a fine old leather chair, by the window, to turn it over. I had been occupied in this way for half an hour – a good part of the afternoon had waned – when I became conscious of another presence in the room, and, look- ing up from my quarto, saw that Mrs Ambient, having pushed open the door in the same noiseless way that marked – or disguised – her entrance the night before, had advanced across the threshold. On seeing me she stopped; she had not, I think, expected to find me. But her hesitation was only of a moment; she came straight to her husband's writing-table, as if she were looking for something. I got up and asked her if I could help her. She glanced about an instant, and then put her hand upon a roll of papers which I recognized, as I had placed it in that spot in the morning, on coming down from my room.

'Is this the new book?' she asked, holding it up.

'The very sheets, with precious annotations.'

'I mean to take your advice.' And she tucked the little bundle under her arm. I congratulated her cordially, and ventured to make of my triumph, as I presumed to call it, a subject of pleas- antry. But she was perfectly grave, and turned away from me, as she had presented herself, without a smile; after which I settled down to my quarto again, with the reflection that Mrs Ambient was a queer woman. My triumph, too, suddenly seemed to me rather vain. A woman who couldn't smile in the right place would never understand Mark Ambient. He came in at last in person, having brought the doctor back with him. 'He was away from home,' Mark said, 'and I went after him – to where he was supposed to be. He had left the place, and I followed him to two or three others, which accounts for my delay.' He was now with Mrs Ambient, looking at the child, and was to see Mark again before leaving the house. My host noticed, at the end of ten minutes, that the proof-sheets of his new book had been removed from the table, and when I told him, in reply to his question as to what I knew about them, that Mrs Ambient had carried them off to read, he turned almost pale for an instant with surprise. 'What has suddenly made her so curious?' he exclaimed; and I was obliged to tell him that I was at the bottom of the mystery. I had had it on my conscience to assure her that she really ought to know of what her husband was capable. 'Of what I am capable? *Elle ne s'en doute que trop!*'[31] said Ambient, with a laugh; but he took my meddling very good-naturedly, and contented himself with adding that he was very much afraid she would burn up the sheets, with his emendations, of which he had no duplicate. The doctor paid a long visit in the nursery, and before he came down I retired to my own quarters, where I remained till dinner-time. On entering the drawing-room at this hour I found Miss Ambient in possession, as she had been the evening before.

'I was right about Dolcino,' she said as soon as she saw me, with a strange little air of triumph. 'He is really very ill.'

'Very ill! Why, when I last saw him, at four o'clock, he was in fairly good form.'

'There has been a change for the worse – very sudden and rapid – and when the doctor got here he found diphtheritic symptoms. He ought to have been called, as I knew, in the morning, and the child oughtn't to have been brought into the garden.'

'My dear lady, he was very happy there,' I answered, much appalled.

'He would be happy anywhere. I have no doubt he is happy now, with his poor little throat in a state—' She dropped her voice as her brother came in, and Mark let us know that, as a matter of course, Mrs Ambient would not appear. It was true that Dolcino had developed diphtheritic symptoms, but he was quiet for the present, and his mother was earnestly watching him. She was a perfect nurse, Mark said, and the doctor was coming back at ten o'clock. Our dinner was not very gay; Ambient was anxious and alarmed, and his sister irritated me by her constant tacit assumption, conveyed in the very way she nibbled her bread and sipped her wine, of having 'told me so'. I had had no disposition to deny anything she told me, and I could not see that her satisfaction in being justified by the event made poor Dolcino's throat any better. The truth is that, as the sequel proved, Miss Ambient had some of the qualities of the sibyl, and had therefore, perhaps, a right to the sibylline contortions. Her brother was so preoccupied that I felt my presence to be an indiscretion, and was sorry I had promised to remain over the morrow. I said to Mark that, evidently, I had better leave them in the morning; to which he replied that, on the contrary, if he was to pass the next days in the fidgets my company would be an extreme relief to him. The fidgets had already begun for him, poor fellow, and as we sat in his study with our cigars, after dinner, he wandered to the door whenever he heard the sound of the doctor's wheels. Miss Ambient, who shared this apartment with us, gave me at such moments significant glances; she had gone upstairs before rejoining us, to ask after the child. His mother and his nurse gave a tolerable account of him; but Miss Ambient found his fever high and his symptoms very grave. The doctor came at ten o'clock, and I went to bed after hearing from Mark that he saw no present cause for alarm. He had made every provision for the night, and was to return early in the morning.

I quitted my room at eight o'clock the next day, and as I came downstairs saw, through the open door of the house, Mrs Ambient standing at the front gate of the grounds, in colloquy with the physician. She wore a white dressing-gown, but her shining hair was carefully tucked away in its net, and in the freshness of the morning, after a night of watching, she looked as much 'the type of the lady' as her sister-in-law had described her. Her appearance, I suppose, ought to have reassured me; but I was still nervous and uneasy, so that I shrank from meeting her with the necessary question about Dolcino. None the

less, however, was I impatient to learn how the morning found
him; and, as Mrs Ambient had not seen me, I passed into the
grounds by a roundabout way, and, stopping at a further gate,
hailed the doctor just as he was driving away. Mrs Ambient
had returned to the house before he got into his gig.

'Excuse me – but, as a friend of the family, I should like very
much to hear about the little boy.'

The doctor, who was a stout, sharp man, looked at me from
head to foot, and then he said, 'I'm sorry to say I haven't
seen him.'

'Haven't seen him?'

'Mrs Ambient came down to meet me as I alighted, and told
me that he was sleeping so soundly, after a restless night, that
she didn't wish him disturbed. I assured her I wouldn't disturb
him, but she said he was quite safe now and she could look
after him herself.

'Thank you very much. Are you coming back?'

'No, sir; I'll be hanged if I come back!' exclaimed Dr Allingham, who was evidently very angry. And he started his horse
again with the whip.

I wandered back into the garden, and five minutes later Miss
Ambient came forth from the house to greet me. She explained
that breakfast would not be served for some time, and that she
wished to catch the doctor before he went away. I informed her
that this functionary had come and departed, and I repeated to
her what he had told me about his dismissal. This made Miss
Ambient very serious – very serious indeed – and she sank into
a bench, with dilated eyes, hugging her elbows with crossed
arms. She indulged in many ejaculations, she confessed herself
infinitely perplexed, and she finally told me what her own last
news of her nephew had been. She had sat up very late – after
me, after Mark – and before going to bed had knocked at the
door of the child's room, which was opened to her by the nurse.
This good woman had admitted her, and she had found Dolcino quiet, but flushed and 'unnatural', with his mother sitting
beside his bed. 'She held his hand in one of hers,' said Miss
Ambient, 'and in the other – what do you think? – the
proof-sheets of Mark's new book! She was reading them there,

intently: did you ever hear of anything so extraordinary? Such a very odd time to be reading an author whom she never could abide!' In her agitation Miss Ambient was guilty of this vulgarism of speech, and I was so impressed by her narrative that it was only in recalling her words later that I noticed the lapse. Mrs Ambient had looked up from her reading with her finger on her lips – I recognized the gesture she had addressed to me in the afternoon – and, though the nurse was about to go to rest, had not encouraged her sister-in-law to relieve her of any part of her vigil. But certainly, then, Dolcino's condition was far from reassuring – his poor little breathing was most painful; and what change could have taken place in him in those few hours that would justify Beatrice in denying the physician access to him? This was the moral of Miss Ambient's anecdote – the moral for herself at least. The moral for me, rather, was that it *was* a very singular time for Mrs Ambient to be going into a novelist she had never appreciated and who had simply happened to be recommended to her by a young American she disliked. I thought of her sitting there in the sick-chamber in the still hours of the night, after the nurse had left her, turning over those pages of genius and wrestling with their magical influence.

I must relate very briefly the circumstances of the rest of my visit to Mark Ambient – it lasted but a few hours longer – and devote but three words to my later acquaintance with him. That lasted five years – till his death – and was full of interest, of satisfaction, and, I may add, of sadness. The main thing to be said with regard to it is, that I had a secret from him. I believe he never suspected it, though of this I am not absolutely sure. If he did, the line he had taken, the line of absolute negation of the matter to himself, shows an immense effort of the will. I may tell my secret now, giving it for what it is worth, now that Mark Ambient has gone, that he has begun to be alluded to as one of the famous early dead, and that his wife does not survive him; now, too, that Miss Ambient, whom I also saw at intervals during the years that followed, has, with her embroideries and her attitudes, her necromantic glances and strange intuitions, retired to a Sisterhood, where, as I am told, she is deeply immured and quite lost to the world.

Mark came into breakfast after his sister and I had for some time been seated there. He shook hands with me in silence, kissed his sister, opened his letters and newspapers, and pretended to drink his coffee. But I could see that these movements were mechanical, and I was little surprised when, suddenly he pushed away everything that was before him, and with his head in his hands and his elbows on the table, sat staring strangely at the cloth.

'What is the matter *fratello mio*?'[32] Miss Ambient inquired, peeping from behind the urn.

He answered nothing, but got up with a certain violence and strode to the window. We rose to our feet, his sister and I, by a common impulse, exchanging a glance of some alarm, while he stared for a moment into the garden. 'In heaven's name, what has got possession of Beatrice?' he cried at last, turning round with an almost haggard face. And he looked from one of us to the other; the appeal was addressed to me as well as to his sister.

Miss Ambient gave a shrug. 'My poor Mark, Beatrice is always – Beatrice!'

'She has locked herself up with the boy – bolted and barred the door – she refuses to let me come near him!' Ambient went on.

'She refused to let the doctor see him an hour ago!' Miss Ambient remarked, with intention, as they say on the stage.

'Refused to let the doctor see him? By heaven, I'll smash in the door!' And Mark brought his fist down upon the table, so that all the breakfast-service rang.

I begged Miss Ambient to go up and try to have speech of her sister-in-law, and I drew Mark out into the garden. 'You're exceedingly nervous, and Mrs Ambient is probably right,' I said to him. 'Women know – women should be supreme in such a situation. Trust a mother – a devoted mother, my dear friend!' With such words as these I tried to soothe and comfort him, and, marvellous to relate, I succeeded, with the help of many cigarettes, in making him walk about the garden and talk, or listen at least to my own ingenious chatter, for nearly an hour. At the end of this time Miss Ambient returned to us, with a very rapid step, holding her hand to her heart.

'Go for the doctor, Mark; go for the doctor this moment!'

'Is he dying – has she killed him?' poor Ambient cried, flinging away his cigarette.

'I don't know what she has done! But she's frightened, and now she wants the doctor.'

'He told me he would be hanged if he came back,' I felt myself obliged to announce.

'Precisely – therefore Mark himself must go for him, and not a messenger. You must see him and tell him it's to save your child. The trap has been ordered – it's ready.'

'To save him? I'll save him, please God!' Ambient cried, bounding with his great strides across the lawn.

As soon as he had gone I felt that I ought to have volunteered in his place, and I said as much to Miss Ambient; but she checked me by grasping my arm quickly, while we heard the wheels of the dog-cart[33] rattle away from the gate. 'He's off – he's off – and now I can think! To get him away – while I think – while I think!'

'While you think of what, Miss Ambient?'

'Of the unspeakable thing that has happened under this roof!'

Her manner was habitually that of such a prophetess of ill that my first impulse was to believe I must allow here for a great exaggeration. But in a moment I saw that her emotion was real. 'Dolcino *is* dying then – he is dead?'

'It's too late to save him. His mother has let him die! I tell you that, because you are sympathetic, because you have imagination,' Miss Ambient was good enough to add, interrupting my expression of horror. 'That's why you had the idea of making her read Mark's new book!'

'What has that to do with it? I don't understand you – your accusation is monstrous.'

'I see it all – I'm not stupid,' Miss Ambient went on, heedless of the harshness of my tone. 'It was the book that finished her – it was that decided her!'

'Decided her? Do you mean she has murdered her child?' I demanded, trembling at my own words.

'She sacrificed him – she determined to do nothing to make

him live. Why else did she lock herself up – why else did she
turn away the doctor? The book gave her a horror, she determined to rescue him – to prevent him from ever being touched.
He had a crisis at two o'clock in the morning. I know this from
the nurse, who had left her then, but whom, for a short time,
she called back. Dolcino got much worse, but she insisted on
the nurse's going back to bed, and after that she was alone with
him for hours.'

'Do you pretend that she has no pity – that she's insane?'

'She held him in her arms – she pressed him to her breast,
not to see him; but she gave him no remedies – she did nothing
the doctor ordered. Everything is there, untouched. She has
had the honesty not even to throw the drugs away!'

I dropped upon the nearest bench, overcome with wonder
and agitation: quite as much at Miss Ambient's terrible lucidity
as at the charge she made against her sister-in-law. There was
an amazing coherency in her story, and it was dreadful to me
to see myself figuring in it as so proximate a cause. 'You are a
very strange woman, and you say strange things.'

'You think it necessary to protest – but you are quite ready
to believe me. You have received an impression of my
sister-in-law, you have guessed of what she is capable.'

I do not feel bound to say what concession on this point I
made to Miss Ambient, who went on to relate to me that within
the last half-hour Beatrice had had a revulsion; that she was
tremendously frightened at what she had done; that her fright
itself betrayed her; and that she would now give heaven and
earth to save the child. 'Let us hope she will!' I said, looking at
my watch and trying to time poor Ambient; whereupon my
companion repeated, in a singular tone, 'Let us hope so!' When
I asked her if she herself could do nothing, and whether she
ought not to be with her sister-in-law, she replied, 'You had
better go and judge; she is like a wounded tigress!' I never saw
Mrs Ambient till six months after this, and therefore cannot
pretend to have verified the comparison. At the latter period
she was again the type of the lady. 'She'll be nicer to him after
this,' I remember Miss Ambient saying, in response to some
quick outburst (on my part) of compassion for her brother.

Although I had been in the house but thirty-six hours this young lady had treated me with extraordinary confidence, and there was therefore a certain demand which, as an intimate, I might make of her. I extracted from her a pledge that she would never say to her brother what she had just said to me; she would leave him to form his own theory of his wife's conduct. She agreed with me that there was misery enough in the house without her contributing a new anguish, and that Mrs Ambient's proceedings might be explained, to her husband's mind, by the extravagance of a jealous devotion. Poor Mark came back with the doctor much sooner than we could have hoped, but we knew, five minutes afterward, that they arrived too late. Poor little Dolcino was more exquisitely beautiful in death than he had been in life. Mrs Ambient's grief was frantic; she lost her head and said strange things. As for Mark's – but I will not speak of that. *Basta*,[34] as he used to say. Miss Ambient kept her secret – I have already had occasion to say that she had her good points – but it rankled in her conscience like a guilty participation, and, I imagine, had something to do with her retiring ultimately to a Sisterhood. And, *à propos* of consciences, the reader is now in a position to judge of my compunction for my effort to convert Mrs Ambient. I ought to mention that the death of her child in some degree converted her. When the new book came out – it was long delayed – she read it over as a whole, and her husband told me that a few months before her death – she failed rapidly after losing her son, sank into a consumption, and faded away at Mentone[35] – during those few supreme weeks she even dipped into *Beltraffio*.

THE ASPERN PAPERS

I had taken Mrs Prest into my confidence; in truth without her I should have made but little advance, for the fruitful idea in the whole business dropped from her friendly lips. It was she who invented the short cut, who severed the Gordian knot.[1] It is not supposed to be the nature of women to rise as a general thing to the largest and most liberal view – I mean of a practical scheme; but it has struck me that they sometimes throw off a bold conception – such as a man would not have risen to – with singular serenity. 'Simply ask them to take you in on the footing of a lodger' – I don't think that unaided I should have risen to that. I was beating about the bush, trying to be ingenious, wondering by what combination of arts I might become an acquaintance, when she offered this happy suggestion that the way to become an acquaintance was first to become an inmate. Her actual knowledge of the Misses Bordereau was scarcely larger than mine, and indeed I had brought with me from England some definite facts which were new to her. Their name had been mixed up ages before with one of the greatest names of the century, and they lived now in Venice in obscurity, on very small means, unvisited, unapproachable, in a dilapidated old palace on an out-of-the-way canal: this was the substance of my friend's impression of them. She herself had been established in Venice for fifteen years and had done a great deal of good there; but the circle of her benevolence did not include the two shy, mysterious and, as it was somehow supposed, scarcely respectable Americans (they were believed to have lost in their long exile all national quality, besides having had, as their name implied, some French strain in their origin), who asked no favours and desired no attention. In the early years of her residence she had made an attempt to see them, but this had been successful only as regards the little one, as Mrs Prest called the niece; though in reality as I afterwards learned she was considerably the bigger of the two. She had heard Miss Bordereau was ill and had a suspicion that she was in want; and she had gone to the house to offer assistance, so that if there were suffering (and American suffering), she should at least not have it on her conscience. The 'little one' received her in the great cold, tarnished Venetian *sala*, the central hall of the house, paved with marble and roofed with dim cross-beams, and did not even ask her to sit down. This was not encouraging for me, who wished to sit so fast, and I remarked as much to Mrs Prest. She however replied with profundity, 'Ah, but there's all the difference: I went to confer a favour and you will go to ask one. If they are proud you will be on the right side.' And she offered to show me their house to begin with – to row me thither in her gondola. I let her know that I had already been to look at it half a dozen times; but I accepted her invitation, for it charmed me to hover about the place. I had made my way to it the day after my arrival in Venice (it had been described to me in advance by the friend in England to whom I owed definite information as to their possession of the papers), and I had besieged it with my eyes while I considered my plan of campaign. Jeffrey Aspern had never been in it that I knew of; but some note of his voice seemed to abide there by a roundabout implication, a faint reverberation.

Mrs Prest knew nothing about the papers, but she was interested in my curiosity, as she was always interested in the joys and sorrows of her friends. As we went, however, in her gondola, gliding there under the sociable hood with the bright Venetian picture framed on either side by the movable window, I could see that she was amused by my infatuation, the way my interest in the papers had become a fixed idea. 'One would think you expected to find in them the answer to the riddle of the universe,' she said; and I denied the impeachment only by replying that if I had to choose between that precious solution and a bundle of Jeffrey Aspern's letters I knew indeed which would appear to me the greater boon. She pretended to

make light of his genius and I took no pains to defend him. One
doesn't defend one's god: one's god is in himself a defence.
Besides, to-day, after his long comparative obscuration, he
hangs high in the heaven of our literature, for all the world to
see; he is a part of the light by which we walk. The most I said
was that he was no doubt not a woman's poet: to which she
rejoined aptly enough that he had been at least Miss Bordereau's. The strange thing had been for me to discover in
England that she was still alive: it was as if I had been told
Mrs Siddons was, or Queen Caroline, or the famous Lady
Hamilton, for it seemed to me that she belonged to a generation as extinct.[2] 'Why, she must be tremendously old – at least
a hundred,' I had said; but on coming to consider dates I saw
that it was not strictly necessary that she should have exceeded
by very much the common span. None the less she was very far
advanced in life and her relations with Jeffrey Aspern had
occurred in her early womanhood. 'That is her excuse,' said
Mrs Prest, half sententiously and yet also somewhat as if she
were ashamed of making a speech so little in the real tone of
Venice. As if a woman needed an excuse for having loved the
divine poet! He had been not only one of the most brilliant
minds of his day (and in those years, when the century was
young, there were, as every one knows, many), but one of the
most genial men and one of the handsomest.

The niece, according to Mrs Prest, was not so old, and she
risked the conjecture that she was only a grand-niece. This was
possible; I had nothing but my share in the very limited knowledge of my English fellow-worshipper John Cumnor, who had
never seen the couple. The world, as I say, had recognized Jeffrey Aspern, but Cumnor and I had recognized him most. The
multitude, to-day, flocked to his temple, but of that temple he
and I regarded ourselves as the ministers. We held, justly, as I
think, that we had done more for his memory than any one
else, and we had done it by opening lights into his life. He had
nothing to fear from us because he had nothing to fear from the
truth, which alone at such a distance of time we could be interested in establishing. His early death had been the only dark
spot in his life, unless the papers in Miss Bordereau's hands

should perversely bring out others. There had been an impression about 1825 that he had 'treated her badly', just as there had been an impression that he had 'served', as the London populace says, several other ladies in the same way. Each of these cases Cumnor and I had been able to investigate, and we had never failed to acquit him conscientiously of shabby behaviour. I judged him perhaps more indulgently than my friend; certainly, at any rate, it appeared to me that no man could have walked straighter in the given circumstances. These were almost always awkward. Half the women of his time, to speak liberally, had flung themselves at his head, and out of this pernicious fashion many complications, some of them grave, had not failed to arise. He was not a woman's poet, as I had said to Mrs Prest, in the modern phase of his reputation; but the situation had been different when the man's own voice was mingled with his song. That voice, by every testimony, was one of the sweetest ever heard. 'Orpheus and the Mænads!'[3] was the exclamation that rose to my lips when I first turned over his correspondence. Almost all the Mænads were unreasonable and many of them insupportable; it struck me in short that he was kinder, more considerate than, in his place (if I could imagine myself in such a place!) I should have been.

It was certainly strange beyond all strangeness, and I shall not take up space with attempting to explain it, that whereas in all these other lines of research we had to deal with phantoms and dust, the mere echoes of echoes, the one living source of information that had lingered on into our time had been unheeded by us. Every one of Aspern's contemporaries had, according to our belief, passed away; we had not been able to look into a single pair of eyes into which his had looked or to feel a transmitted contact in any aged hand that his had touched. Most dead of all did poor Miss Bordereau appear, and yet she alone had survived. We exhausted in the course of months our wonder that we had not found her out sooner, and the substance of our explanation was that she had kept so quiet. The poor lady on the whole had had reason for doing so. But it was a revelation to us that it was possible to keep so quiet as that in the latter half of the nineteenth century – the age of newspapers and telegrams and photographs and interviewers. And she had taken no great trouble about it either: she had not hidden herself away in an undiscoverable hole; she had boldly settled down in a city of exhibition. The only secret of her safety that we could perceive was that Venice contained so many curiosities that were greater than she. And then accident had somehow favoured her, as was shown for example in the fact that Mrs Prest had never happened to mention her to me, though I had spent three weeks in Venice – under her nose, as it were – five years before. Mrs Prest had not mentioned this much to any one; she appeared almost to have forgotten she was there. Of course she had not the responsibilities of an editor. It was no explanation of the old woman's having eluded us to say that she lived abroad, for our researches had again and again taken us (not only by correspondence but by personal inquiry) to France, to Germany, to Italy, in which countries, not counting his important stay in England, so many of the too few years of Aspern's career were spent. We were glad to think at least that in all our publishings (some people consider I believe that we have overdone them), we had only touched in passing and in the most discreet manner on Miss Bordereau's connection. Oddly enough, even if we had had the material (and we often wondered what had become of it), it would have been the most difficult episode to handle.

The gondola stopped, the old palace[4] was there; it was a house of the class which in Venice carries even in extreme dilapidation the dignified name. 'How charming! It's grey and pink!' my companion exclaimed; and that is the most comprehensive description of it. It was not particularly old, only two or three centuries; and it had an air not so much of decay as of quiet discouragement, as if it had rather missed its career. But its wide front, with a stone balcony from end to end of the *piano nobile* or most important floor, was architectural enough, with the aid of various pilasters and arches; and the stucco with which in the intervals it had long ago been endued was rosy in the April afternoon. It overlooked a clean, melancholy, unfrequented canal, which had a narrow *riva* or convenient footway on either side. 'I don't know why – there are no brick gables,' said Mrs Prest, 'but this corner has seemed to me before more Dutch than Italian, more like Amsterdam than like Venice. It's perversely clean, for reasons of its own; and though you can pass on foot scarcely any one ever thinks of doing so. It has the air of a Protestant Sunday. Perhaps the people are afraid of the Misses Bordereau. I daresay they have the reputation of witches.'

I forget what answer I made to this – I was given up to two other reflections. The first of these was that if the old lady lived in such a big, imposing house she could not be in any sort of misery and therefore would not be tempted by a chance to let a couple of rooms. I expressed this idea to Mrs Prest, who gave me a very logical reply. 'If she didn't live in a big house how could it be a question of her having rooms to spare? If she were not amply lodged herself you would lack ground to approach her. Besides, a big house here, and especially in this *quartier perdu*,[5] proves nothing at all: it is perfectly compatible with a state of penury. Dilapidated old palazzi, if you will go out of the way for them, are to be had for five shillings a year. And as for the people who live in them – no, until you have explored Venice socially as much as I have you can form no idea of their domestic desolation. They live on nothing, for they have nothing to live on.' The other idea that had come into my head was connected with a high blank wall which appeared to confine an expanse of ground on one side of the house. Blank I call it, but it was figured over with the patches that please a painter, repaired breaches, crumblings of plaster, extrusions of brick that had turned pink with time; and a few thin trees, with the poles of certain rickety trellises, were visible over the top. The place was a garden and apparently it belonged to the house. It suddenly occurred to me that if it did belong to the house I had my pretext.

I sat looking out on all this with Mrs Prest (it was covered with the golden glow of Venice) from the shade of our *felze*,[6] and she asked me if I would go in then, while she waited for me, or come back another time. At first I could not decide – it was doubtless very weak of me. I wanted still to think I *might* get a footing, and I was afraid to meet failure, for it would leave me, as I remarked to my companion, without another arrow for my bow. 'Why not another?' she inquired, as I sat there hesitating and thinking it over; and she wished to know why even now and before taking the trouble of becoming an inmate (which might be wretchedly uncomfortable after all, even if it succeeded), I had not the resource of simply offering them a sum of money down. In that way I might obtain the documents without bad nights.

'Dearest lady,' I exclaimed, 'excuse the impatience of my tone when I suggest that you must have forgotten the very fact (surely I communicated it to you) which pushed me to throw myself upon your ingenuity. The old woman won't have the documents spoken of; they are personal, delicate, intimate, and she hasn't modern notions, God bless her! If I should sound that note first I should certainly spoil the game. I can arrive at the papers only by putting her off her guard, and I can put her off her guard only by ingratiating diplomatic practices. Hypocrisy, duplicity are my only chance. I am sorry for it, but for Jeffrey Aspern's sake I would do worse still. First I must take tea with her; then tackle the main job.' And I told over what had happened to John Cumnor when he wrote to her. No notice whatever had been taken of his first letter, and the second had been answered very sharply, in six lines, by the niece. 'Miss Bordereau requested her to say that she could not imagine what he meant by troubling them. They had none of Mr Aspern's papers, and if they had should never think of showing them to any one on any account whatever. She didn't know what he was talking about and begged he would let her alone.' I certainly did not want to be met that way.

'Well,' said Mrs Prest, after a moment, provokingly, 'perhaps after all they haven't any of his things. If they deny it flat how are you sure?'

'John Cumnor is sure, and it would take me long to tell you how his conviction, or his very strong presumption – strong enough to stand against the old lady's not unnatural fib – has built itself up. Besides, he makes much of the internal evidence of the niece's letter.'

'The internal evidence?'

'Her calling him "Mr Aspern".'

'I don't see what that proves.'

'It proves familiarity, and familiarity implies the possession of mementoes, of relics. I can't tell you how that "Mr" touches me – how it bridges over the gulf of time and brings our hero near to me – nor what an edge it gives to my desire to see Juliana. You don't say "Mr" Shakespeare.'

'Would I, any more, if I had a box full of his letters?'

'Yes, if he had been your lover and some one wanted them!' And I added that John Cumnor was so convinced, and so all the more convinced by Miss Bordereau's tone, that he would have come himself to Venice on the business were it not that for him there was the obstacle that it would be difficult to disprove his identity with the person who had written to them, which the old ladies would be sure to suspect in spite of dissimulation and a change of name. If they were to ask him point-blank if he were not their correspondent it would be too awkward for him to lie; whereas I was fortunately not tied in that way. I was a fresh hand and could say no without lying.

'But you will have to change your name,' said Mrs Prest. 'Juliana lives out of the world as much as it is possible to live, but none the less she has probably heard of Mr Aspern's editors; she perhaps possesses what you have published.'

'I have thought of that,' I returned; and I drew out of my pocket-book a visiting-card, neatly engraved with a name that was not my own.

'You are very extravagant; you might have written it,' said my companion.

'This looks more genuine.'

'Certainly, you are prepared to go far! But it will be awkward about your letters; they won't come to you in that mask.'

'My banker will take them in and I will go every day to fetch them. It will give me a little walk.'

'Shall you only depend upon that?' asked Mrs Prest. 'Aren't you coming to see me?'

'Oh, you will have left Venice, for the hot months, long before there are any results. I am prepared to roast all summer – as well as hereafter, perhaps you'll say! Meanwhile, John Cumnor will bombard me with letters addressed, in my feigned name, to the care of the *padrona*.'[7]

'She will recognize his hand,' my companion suggested.

'On the envelope he can disguise it.'

'Well, you're a precious pair! Doesn't it occur to you that even if you are able to say you are not Mr Cumnor in person they may still suspect you of being his emissary?'

'Certainly, and I see only one way to parry that.'

'And what may that be?'

I hesitated a moment. 'To make love to the niece.'

'Ah,' cried Mrs Prest, 'wait till you see her!'

II

'I must work the garden – I must work the garden,' I said to myself, five minutes later, as I waited, upstairs, in the long, dusky sala, where the bare scagliola[8] floor gleamed vaguely in a chink of the closed shutters. The place was impressive but it looked cold and cautious. Mrs Prest had floated away, giving me a rendezvous at the end of half an hour by some neighbouring water-steps; and I had been let into the house, after pulling the rusty bell-wire, by a little red-headed, white-faced maid-servant, who was very young and not ugly and wore clicking pattens and a shawl in the fashion of a hood. She had not contented herself with opening the door from above by the usual arrangement of a creaking pulley, though she had looked down at me first from an upper window, dropping the inevitable challenge which in Italy precedes the hospitable act. As a general thing I was irritated by this survival of mediæval manners, though as I liked the old I suppose I ought to have liked it; but I was so determined to be genial that I took my false card out of my pocket and held it up to her, smiling as if it were a magic token. It had the effect of one indeed, for it brought her, as I say, all the way down. I begged her to hand it to her mistress, having first written on it in Italian the words, 'Could you very kindly see a gentleman, an American, for a moment?' The little maid was not hostile, and I reflected that even that was perhaps something gained. She coloured, she smiled and looked both frightened and pleased. I could see that my arrival was a great affair, that visits were rare in that house, and that she was a person who would have liked a sociable place. When she pushed forward the heavy door behind me I felt that I had a foot in the citadel. She pattered across the damp, stony lower hall and I followed her up the high staircase – stonier still, as it seemed – without an invitation. I think she had meant I should wait for her below, but such was not my idea, and I took up my station in the sala. She flitted, at the far end of it, into impenetrable regions, and I looked at the place with my heart beating as I had known it to do in the dentist's parlour. It was gloomy and stately, but it owed its character almost entirely to its noble shape and to the fine architectural doors – as high as the doors of houses – which, leading into the various rooms, repeated themselves on either side at intervals. They were surmounted with old faded painted escutcheons, and here and there, in the spaces between them, brown pictures, which I perceived to be bad, in battered frames, were suspended. With the exception of several straw-bottomed chairs with their backs to the wall, the grand obscure vista contained nothing else to minister to effect. It was evidently never used save as a passage, and little even as that. I may add that by the time the door opened again through which the maid-servant had escaped, my eyes had grown used to the want of light.

I had not meant by my private ejaculation that I must myself cultivate the soil of the tangled enclosure which lay beneath the windows, but the lady who came toward me from the distance over the hard, shining floor might have supposed as much from the way in which, as I went rapidly to meet her, I exclaimed, taking care to speak Italian: 'The garden, the garden – do me the pleasure to tell me if it's yours!'

She stopped short, looking at me with wonder; and then, 'Nothing here is mine,' she answered in English, coldly and sadly.

'Oh, you are English; how delightful!' I remarked, ingenuously. 'But surely the garden belongs to the house?'

'Yes, but the house doesn't belong to me.' She was a long, lean, pale person, habited apparently in a dull-coloured dressing-gown, and she spoke with a kind of mild literalness. She did not ask me to sit down, any more than years before (if she were the niece) she had asked Mrs Prest, and we stood face to face in the empty pompous hall.

'Well then, would you kindly tell me to whom I must address myself? I'm afraid you'll think me odiously intrusive, but you know I *must* have a garden – upon my honour I must!'

Her face was not young, but it was simple; it was not fresh, but it was mild. She had large eyes which were not bright, and a great deal of hair which was not 'dressed', and long fine hands which were – possibly – not clean. She clasped these members almost convulsively as, with a confused, alarmed look, she broke out, 'Oh, don't take it away from us; we like it ourselves!'

'You have the use of it then?'

'Oh yes. If it wasn't for that!' And she gave a shy, melancholy smile.

'Isn't it a luxury, precisely? That's why, intending to be in Venice some weeks, possibly all summer, and having some literary work, some reading and writing to do, so that I must be quiet, and yet if possible a great deal in the open air – that's why I have felt that a garden is really indispensable. I appeal to your own experience,' I went on, smiling. 'Now can't I look at yours?'

'I don't know, I don't understand,' the poor woman murmured, planted there and letting her embarrassed eyes wander all over my strangeness.

'I mean only from one of those windows – such grand ones as you have here – if you will let me open the shutters.' And I walked toward the back of the house. When I had advanced half-way I stopped and waited, as if I took it for granted she would accompany me. I had been of necessity very abrupt, but I strove at the same time to give her the impression of extreme courtesy. 'I have been looking at furnished rooms all over the place, and it seems impossible to find any with a garden attached. Naturally in a place like Venice gardens are rare. It's absurd if you like, for a man, but I can't live without flowers.'

'There are none to speak of down there.' She came nearer to me, as if, though she mistrusted me, I had drawn her by an invisible thread. I went on again, and she continued as she followed me: 'We have a few, but they are very common. It costs too much to cultivate them; one has to have a man.'

'Why shouldn't I be the man?' I asked. 'I'll work without

wages; or rather I'll put in a gardener. You shall have the sweetest flowers in Venice.'

She protested at this, with a queer little sigh which might also have been a gush of rapture at the picture I presented. Then she observed, 'We don't know you – we don't know you.'

'You know me as much as I know you; that is much more, because you know my name. And if you are English I am almost a countryman.'

'We are not English,' said my companion, watching me helplessly while I threw open the shutters of one of the divisions of the wide high window.

'You speak the language so beautifully: might I ask what you are?' Seen from above the garden was certainly shabby; but I perceived at a glance that it had great capabilities. She made no rejoinder, she was so lost in staring at me, and I exclaimed, 'You don't mean to say you are also by chance American?'

'I don't know; we used to be.'

'Used to be? Surely you haven't changed?'

'It's so many years ago – we are nothing.'

'So many years that you have been living here? Well, I don't wonder at that; it's a grand old house. I suppose you all use the garden,' I went on, 'but I assure you I shouldn't be in your way. I would be very quiet and stay in one corner.'

'We all use it?' she repeated after me, vaguely, not coming close to the window but looking at my shoes. She appeared to think me capable of throwing her out.

'I mean all your family, as many as you are.'

'There is only one other; she is very old – she never goes down.'

'Only one other, in all this great house!' I feigned to be not only amazed but almost scandalized. 'Dear lady, you must have space then to spare!'

'To spare?' she repeated, in the same dazed way.

'Why, you surely don't live (two quiet women – I see *you* are quiet, at any rate) in fifty rooms!' Then with a burst of hope and cheer I demanded: 'Couldn't you let me two or three? That would set me up!'

I had now struck the note that translated my purpose and I

need not reproduce the whole of the tune I played. I ended by making my interlocutress believe that I was an honourable person, though of course I did not even attempt to persuade her that I was not an eccentric one. I repeated that I had studies to pursue; that I wanted quiet; that I delighted in a garden and had vainly sought one up and down the city; that I would undertake that before another month was over the dear old house should be smothered in flowers. I think it was the flowers that won my suit, for I afterwards found that Miss Tita (for such the name of this high tremulous spinster proved somewhat incongruously to be) had an insatiable appetite for them. When I speak of my suit as won I mean that before I left her she had promised that she would refer the question to her aunt. I inquired who her aunt might be and she answered, 'Why, Miss Bordereau!' with an air of surprise, as if I might have been expected to know. There were contradictions like this in Tita Bordereau which, as I observed later, contributed to make her an odd and affecting person. It was the study of the two ladies to live so that the world should not touch them, and yet they had never altogether accepted the idea that it never heard of them. In Tita at any rate a grateful susceptibility to human contact had not died out, and contact of a limited order there would be if I should come to live in the house.

'We have never done anything of the sort; we have never had a lodger or any kind of inmate.' So much as this she made a point of saying to me. 'We are very poor, we live very badly. The rooms are very bare – that you might take; they have nothing in them. I don't know how you would sleep, how you would eat.'

'With your permission, I could easily put in a bed and a few tables and chairs. *C'est la moindre des choses*[9] and the affair of an hour or two. I know a little man from whom I can hire what I should want for a few months, for a trifle, and my gondolier can bring the things round in his boat. Of course in this great house you must have a second kitchen, and my servant, who is a wonderfully handy fellow' (this personage was an evocation of the moment), 'can easily cook me a chop there. My tastes and habits are of the simplest; I live on flowers!' And then I ventured to add that if they were very poor it was all the more reason they should let their rooms. They were bad economists – I had never heard of such a waste of material.

I saw in a moment that the good lady had never before been spoken to in that way, with a kind of humorous firmness which did not exclude sympathy but was on the contrary founded on it. She might easily have told me that my sympathy was impertinent, but this by good fortune did not occur to her. I left her with the understanding that she would consider the matter with her aunt and that I might come back the next day for their decision.

'The aunt will refuse; she will think the whole proceeding very *louche*!' Mrs Prest declared shortly after this, when I had resumed my place in her gondola. She had put the idea into my head and now (so little are women to be counted on) she appeared to take a despondent view of it. Her pessimism provoked me and I pretended to have the best hopes; I went so far as to say that I had a distinct presentiment that I should succeed. Upon this Mrs Prest broke out, 'Oh, I see what's in your head! You fancy you have made such an impression in a quarter of an hour that she is dying for you to come and can be depended upon to bring the old one round. If you do get in you'll count it as a triumph.'

I did count it as a triumph, but only for the editor (in the last analysis), not for the man, who had not the tradition of personal conquest. When I went back on the morrow the little maid-servant conducted me straight through the long sala (it opened there as before in perfect perspective and was lighter now, which I thought a good omen) into the apartment from which the recipient of my former visit had emerged on that occasion. It was a large shabby parlour, with a fine old painted ceiling and a strange figure sitting alone at one of the windows. They come back to me now almost with the palpitation they caused, the successive feelings that accompanied my consciousness that as the door of the room closed behind me I was really face to face with the Juliana of some of Aspern's most exquisite and most renowned lyrics. I grew used to her afterwards, though never completely; but as she sat there before me my heart beat as fast as if the miracle of resurrection had taken place for my benefit. Her presence seemed somehow to contain his, and I felt nearer to him at that first moment of seeing her than I ever had been before or ever have been since. Yes, I remember my emotions in their order, even including a curious little tremor that took me when I saw that the niece was not there. With her, the day before, I had become sufficiently familiar, but it almost exceeded my courage (much as I had longed for the event) to be left alone with such a terrible relic as the aunt. She was too strange, too literally resurgent. Then came a check, with the perception that we were not really face to face, inasmuch as she had over her eyes a horrible green shade which, for her, served almost as a mask. I believed for the instant that she had put it on expressly, so that from underneath it she might scrutinize me without being scrutinized herself. At the same time it increased the presumption that there was a ghastly death's-head lurking behind it. The divine Juliana as a grinning skull – the vision hung there until it passed. Then it came to me that she *was* tremendously old – so old that death might take her at any moment, before I had time to get what I wanted from her. The next thought was a correction to that; it lighted up the situation. She would die next week, she would die to-morrow – then I could seize her papers. Meanwhile she sat there neither moving nor speaking. She was very small and shrunken, bent forward, with her hands in her lap. She was dressed in black and her head was wrapped in a piece of old black lace which showed no hair.

My emotion keeping me silent she spoke first, and the remark she made was exactly the most unexpected.

III

'Our house is very far from the centre, but the little canal is very *comme il faut*.'

'It's the sweetest corner of Venice and I can imagine nothing more charming,' I hastened to reply. The old lady's voice was very thin and weak, but it had an agreeable, cultivated murmur and there was wonder in the thought that that individual note had been in Jeffrey Aspern's ear.

'Please to sit down there. I hear very well,' she said quietly, as if perhaps I had been shouting at her; and the chair she pointed to was at a certain distance. I took possession of it, telling her that I was perfectly aware that I had intruded, that I had not been properly introduced and could only throw myself upon her indulgence. Perhaps the other lady, the one I had had the honour of seeing the day before, would have explained to her about the garden. That was literally what had given me courage to take a step so unconventional. I had fallen in love at sight with the whole place (she herself probably was so used to it that she did not know the impression it was capable of making on a stranger), and I had felt it was really a case to risk something. Was her own kindness in receiving me a sign that I was not wholly out in my calculation? It would render me extremely happy to think so. I could give her my word of honour that I was a most respectable, inoffensive person and that as an inmate they would be barely conscious of my existence. I would conform to any regulations, any restrictions if they would only let me enjoy the garden. Moreover I should be delighted to give her references, guarantees; they would be of the very best, both in Venice and in England as well as in America.

She listened to me in perfect stillness and I felt that she was looking at me with great attention, though I could see only the lower part of her bleached and shrivelled face. Independently of the refining process of old age it had a delicacy which once must have been great. She had been very fair, she had had a wonderful complexion. She was silent a little after I had ceased speaking; then she inquired, 'If you are so fond of a garden why don't you go to *terra firma*, where there are so many far better than this?'

'Oh, it's the combination!' I answered, smiling; and then, with rather a flight of fancy, 'It's the idea of a garden in the middle of the sea.'

'It's not in the middle of the sea; you can't see the water.'

I stared a moment, wondering whether she wished to convict me of fraud. 'Can't see the water? Why, dear madam, I can come up to the very gate in my boat.'

She appeared inconsequent, for she said vaguely in reply to

this, 'Yes, if you have got a boat. I haven't any; it's many years since I have been in one of the gondolas.' She uttered these words as if the gondolas were a curious far-away craft which she knew only by hearsay.

'Let me assure you of the pleasure with which I would put mine at your service!' I exclaimed. I had scarcely said this however before I became aware that the speech was in questionable taste and might also do me the injury of making me appear too eager, too possessed of a hidden motive. But the old woman remained impenetrable and her attitude bothered me by suggesting that she had a fuller vision of me than I had of her. She gave me no thanks for my somewhat extravagant offer but remarked that the lady I had seen the day before was her niece; she would presently come in. She had asked her to stay away a little on purpose, because she herself wished to see me at first alone. She relapsed into silence and I asked myself why she had judged this necessary and what was coming yet; also whether I might venture on some judicious remark in praise of her companion. I went so far as to say that I should be delighted to see her again: she had been so very courteous to me, considering how odd she must have thought me – a declaration which drew from Miss Bordereau another of her whimsical speeches.

'She has very good manners; I bred her up myself!' I was on the point of saying that that accounted for the easy grace of the niece, but I arrested myself in time, and the next moment the old woman went on: 'I don't care who you may be – I don't want to know; it signifies very little to-day.' This had all the air of being a formula of dismissal, as if her next words would be that I might take myself off now that she had had the amusement of looking on the face of such a monster of indiscretion. Therefore I was all the more surprised when she added, with her soft, venerable quaver, 'You may have as many rooms as you like – if you will pay a good deal of money.'

I hesitated but for a single instant, long enough to ask myself what she meant in particular by this condition. First it struck me that she must have really a large sum in her mind; then I reasoned quickly that her idea of a large sum would probably not correspond to my own. My deliberation, I think, was not so visible as to diminish the promptitude with which I replied, 'I will pay with pleasure and of course in advance whatever you may think it proper to ask me.'

'Well then, a thousand francs a month,'[10] she rejoined instantly, while her baffling green shade continued to cover her attitude.

The figure, as they say, was startling and my logic had been at fault. The sum she had mentioned was, by the Venetian measure of such matters, exceedingly large; there was many an old palace in an out-of-the-way corner that I might on such terms have enjoyed by the year. But so far as my small means allowed I was prepared to spend money, and my decision was quickly taken. I would pay her with a smiling face what she asked, but in that case I would give myself the compensation of extracting the papers from her for nothing. Moreover if she had asked five times as much I should have risen to the occasion; so odious would it have appeared to me to stand chaffering with Aspern's Juliana. It was queer enough to have a question of money with her at all. I assured her that her views perfectly met my own and that on the morrow I should have the pleasure of putting three months' rent into her hand. She received this announcement with serenity and with no apparent sense that after all it would be becoming of her to say that I ought to see the rooms first. This did not occur to her and indeed her serenity was mainly what I wanted. Our little bargain was just concluded when the door opened and the younger lady appeared on the threshold. As soon as Miss Bordereau saw her niece she cried out almost gaily, 'He will give three thousand – three thousand to-morrow!'

Miss Tita stood still, with her patient eyes turning from one of us to the other; then she inquired, scarcely above her breath, 'Do you mean francs?'

'Did you mean francs or dollars?' the old woman asked of me at this.

'I think francs were what you said,' I answered, smiling.

'That is very good,' said Miss Tita, as if she had become conscious that her own question might have looked overreaching.

'What do *you* know? You are ignorant,' Miss Bordereau remarked; not with acerbity but with a strange, soft coldness.

'Yes, of money – certainly of money!' Miss Tita hastened to exclaim.

'I am sure you have your own branches of knowledge,' I took the liberty of saying, genially. There was something painful to me, somehow, in the turn the conversation had taken, in the discussion of the rent.

'She had a very good education when she was young. I looked into that myself,' said Miss Bordereau. Then she added, 'But she has learned nothing since.'

'I have always been with you,' Miss Tita rejoined very mildly, and evidently with no intention of making an epigram.

'Yes, but for that!' her aunt declared, with more satirical force. She evidently meant that but for this her niece would never have got on at all; the point of the observation however being lost on Miss Tita, though she blushed at hearing her history revealed to a stranger. Miss Bordereau went on, addressing herself to me: 'And what time will you come to-morrow with the money?'

'The sooner the better. If it suits you I will come at noon.'

'I am always here but I have my hours,' said the old woman, as if her convenience were not to be taken for granted.

'You mean the times when you receive?'

'I never receive. But I will see you at noon, when you come with the money.'

'Very good, I shall be punctual'; and I added, 'May I shake hands with you, on our contract?' I thought there ought to be some little form, it would make me really feel easier, for I foresaw that there would be no other. Besides, though Miss Bordereau could not to-day be called personally attractive and there was something even in her wasted antiquity that bade one stand at one's distance, I felt an irresistible desire to hold in my own for a moment the hand that Jeffrey Aspern had pressed.

For a minute she made no answer and I saw that my proposal failed to meet with her approbation. She indulged in no movement of withdrawal, which I half expected; she only said coldly, 'I belong to a time when that was not the custom.'

I felt rather snubbed but I exclaimed good-humouredly to Miss Tita, 'Oh, you will do as well!' I shook hands with her while she replied, with a small flutter, 'Yes, yes, to show it's all arranged!'

'Shall you bring the money in gold?' Miss Bordereau demanded, as I was turning to the door.

I looked at her a moment. 'Aren't you a little afraid, after all, of keeping such a sum as that in the house?' It was not that I was annoyed at her avidity but I was really struck with the disparity between such a treasure and such scanty means of guarding it.

'Whom should I be afraid of if I am not afraid of you?' she asked with her shrunken grimness.

'Ah well,' said I, laughing, 'I shall be in point of fact a protector and I will bring gold if you prefer.'

'Thank you,' the old woman returned with dignity and with an inclination of her head which evidently signified that I might depart. I passed out of the room, reflecting that it would not be easy to circumvent her. As I stood in the sala again I saw that Miss Tita had followed me and I supposed that as her aunt had neglected to suggest that I should take a look at my quarters it was her purpose to repair the omission. But she made no such suggestion; she only stood there with a dim, though not a languid smile, and with an effect of irresponsible, incompetent youth which was almost comically at variance with the faded facts of her person. She was not infirm, like her aunt, but she struck me as still more helpless, because her inefficiency was spiritual, which was not the case with Miss Bordereau's. I waited to see if she would offer to show me the rest of the house, but I did not precipitate the question, inasmuch as my plan was from this moment to spend as much of my time as possible in her society. I only observed at the end of a minute:

'I have had better fortune than I hoped. It was very kind of her to see me. Perhaps you said a good word for me.'

'It was the idea of the money,' said Miss Tita.

'And did you suggest that?'

'I told her that you would perhaps give a good deal.'

'What made you think that?'

'I told her I thought you were rich.'

'And what put that idea into your head?'

'I don't know; the way you talked.'

'Dear me, I must talk differently now,' I declared. 'I'm sorry to say it's not the case.'

'Well,' said Miss Tita, 'I think that in Venice the *forestieri*,[11] in general, often give a great deal for something that after all isn't much.' She appeared to make this remark with a comforting intention, to wish to remind me that if I had been extravagant I was not really foolishly singular. We walked together along the sala, and as I took its magnificent measure I said to her that I was afraid it would not form a part of my *quartiere*.[12] Were my rooms by chance to be among those that opened into it? 'Not if you go above, on the second floor,' she answered with a little startled air, as if she had rather taken for granted I would know my proper place.

'And I infer that that's where your aunt would like me to be.'

'She said your apartments ought to be very distinct.'

'That certainly would be best.' And I listened with respect while she told me that up above I was free to take whatever I liked; that there was another staircase, but only from the floor on which we stood, and that to pass from it to the garden-storey or to come up to my lodging I should have in effect to cross the great hall. This was an immense point gained; I foresaw that it would constitute my whole leverage in my relations with the two ladies. When I asked Miss Tita how I was to manage at present to find my way up she replied with an access of that sociable shyness which constantly marked her manner.

'Perhaps you can't. I don't see – unless I should go with you.' She evidently had not thought of this before.

We ascended to the upper floor and visited a long succession of empty rooms. The best of them looked over the garden; some of the others had a view of the blue lagoon, above the opposite rough-tiled housetops. They were all dusty and even a little disfigured with long neglect, but I saw that by spending a few hundred francs I should be able to convert three or four of them into a convenient habitation. My experiment was turning out costly, yet now that I had all but taken possession I ceased to allow this to trouble me. I mentioned to my companion a few of the things that I should put in, but she replied rather more precipitately than usual that I might do exactly what I liked; she seemed to wish to notify me that the Misses Bordereau would take no overt interest in my proceedings. I guessed that her aunt had instructed her to adopt this tone, and I may as well say now that I came afterwards to distinguish perfectly (as I believed) between the speeches she made on her own responsibility and those the old lady imposed upon her. She took no notice of the unswept condition of the rooms and indulged in no explanations nor apologies. I said to myself that this was a sign that Juliana and her niece (disenchanting idea!) were untidy persons, with a low Italian standard; but I afterwards recognized that a lodger who had forced an entrance had no *locus standi*[13] as a critic. We looked out of a good many windows, for there was nothing within the rooms to look at, and still I wanted to linger. I asked her what several different objects in the prospect might be, but in no case did she appear to know. She was evidently not familiar with the view – it was as if she had not looked at it for years – and I presently saw that she was too preoccupied with something else to pretend to care for it. Suddenly she said – the remark was not suggested:

'I don't know whether it will make any difference to you, but the money is for me.'

'The money?'

'The money you are going to bring.'

'Why, you'll make me wish to stay here two or three years.' I spoke as benevolently as possible, though it had begun to act on my nerves that with these women so associated with Aspern the pecuniary question should constantly come back.

'That would be very good for me,' she replied, smiling.

'You put me on my honour!'

She looked as if she failed to understand this, but went on: 'She wants me to have more. She thinks she is going to die.'

'Ah, not soon, I hope!' I exclaimed, with genuine feeling. I had perfectly considered the possibility that she would destroy her papers on the day she should feel her end really approach. I believed that she would cling to them till then and I think I had an idea that she read Aspern's letters over every night or at least pressed them to her withered lips. I would have given a good deal to have a glimpse of the latter spectacle. I asked Miss Tita if the old lady were seriously ill and she replied that she was only very tired – she had lived so very, very long. That was what she said herself – she wanted to die for a change. Besides, all her friends were dead long ago; either they ought to have remained or she ought to have gone. That was another thing her aunt often said – she was not at all content.

'But people don't die when they like, do they?' Miss Tita inquired. I took the liberty of asking why, if there was actually enough money to maintain both of them, there would not be more than enough in case of her being left alone. She considered this difficult problem a moment and then she said, 'Oh, well, you know, she takes care of me. She thinks that when I'm alone I shall be a great fool, I shall not know how to manage.'

'I should have supposed rather that you took care of her. I'm afraid she is very proud.'

'Why, have you discovered that already?' Miss Tita cried, with the glimmer of an illumination in her face.

'I was shut up with her there for a considerable time, and she struck me, she interested me extremely. It didn't take me long to make my discovery. She won't have much to say to me while I'm here.'

'No, I don't think she will,' my companion averred.

'Do you suppose she has some suspicion of me?'

Miss Tita's honest eyes gave me no sign that I had touched a mark. 'I shouldn't think so – letting you in after all so easily.'

'Oh, so easily! she has covered her risk. But where is it that one could take an advantage of her?'

'I oughtn't to tell you if I knew, ought I?' And Miss Tita added, before I had time to reply to this, smiling dolefully, 'Do you think we have any weak points?'

'That's exactly what I'm asking. You would only have to mention them for me to respect them religiously.'

She looked at me, at this, with that air of timid but candid and even gratified curiosity with which she had confronted me from the first; and then she said, 'There is nothing to tell. We are terribly quiet. I don't know how the days pass. We have no life.'

'I wish I might think that I should bring you a little.'

'Oh, we know what we want,' she went on. 'It's all right.'

There were various things I desired to ask her: how in the world they did live; whether they had any friends or visitors, any relations in America or in other countries. But I judged such an inquiry would be premature; I must leave it to a later chance. 'Well, don't *you* be proud,' I contented myself with saying. 'Don't hide from me altogether.'

'Oh, I must stay with my aunt,' she returned, without looking at me. And at the same moment, abruptly, without any ceremony of parting, she quitted me and disappeared, leaving me to make my own way downstairs. I remained a while longer, wandering about the bright desert (the sun was pouring in) of the old house, thinking the situation over on the spot. Not even the pattering little *serva* came to look after me and I reflected that after all this treatment showed confidence.

IV

Perhaps it did, but all the same, six weeks later, towards the middle of June, the moment when Mrs Prest undertook her annual migration, I had made no measureable advance. I was obliged to confess to her that I had no results to speak of. My first step had been unexpectedly rapid, but there was no appearance that it would be followed by a second. I was a thousand miles from taking tea with my hostesses – that privilege of which, as I reminded Mrs Prest, we both had had a vision. She reproached me with wanting boldness and I answered that even to be bold you must have an opportunity: you may push on through a breach but you can't batter down a dead wall. She answered that the breach I had already made was big enough to admit an army and accused me of wasting precious hours in whimpering in her salon when I ought to have been carrying on the struggle in the field. It is true that I went to see her very often, on the theory that it would console me (I freely expressed my discouragement) for my want of success on my own premises. But I began to perceive that it did not console me to be perpetually chaffed for my scruples, especially when I was really so vigilant; and I was rather glad when my derisive friend closed her house for the summer. She had expected to gather amusement from the drama of my intercourse with the Misses Bordereau and she was disappointed that the intercourse, and consequently the drama, had not come off. 'They'll lead you on to your ruin,' she said before she left Venice. 'They'll get all your money without showing you a scrap.' I think I settled down to my business with more concentration after she had gone away.

It was a fact that up to that time I had not, save on a single brief occasion, had even a moment's contact with my queer hostesses. The exception had occurred when I carried them according to my promise the terrible three thousand francs. Then I found Miss Tita waiting for me in the hall, and she took the money from my hand so that I did not see her aunt. The old lady had promised to receive me, but she apparently thought nothing of breaking that vow. The money was contained in a bag of chamois leather, of respectable dimensions, which my banker had given me, and Miss Tita had to make a big fist to receive it. This she did with extreme solemnity, though I tried to treat the affair a little as a joke. It was in no jocular strain, yet it was with simplicity, that she inquired, weighing the money in her two palms: 'Don't you think it's too much?' To which I replied that that would depend upon the amount of pleasure I should get for it. Hereupon she turned away from me quickly, as she had done the day before, murmuring in a tone different from any she had used hitherto: 'Oh, pleasure, pleasure – there's no pleasure in this house!'

After this, for a long time, I never saw her, and I wondered that the common chances of the day should not have helped us to meet. It could only be evident that she was immensely on her guard against them; and in addition to this the house was so big that for each other we were lost in it. I used to look out for her hopefully as I crossed the sala in my comings and goings, but I was not rewarded with a glimpse of the tail of her dress. It was as if she never peeped out of her aunt's apartment. I used to wonder what she did there week after week and year after year. I had never encountered such a violent *parti pris*[14] of seclusion; it was more than keeping quiet – it was like hunted creatures feigning death. The two ladies appeared to have no visitors whatever and no sort of contact with the world. I judged at least that people could not have come to the house and that Miss Tita could not have gone out without my having some observation of it. I did what I disliked myself for doing (reflecting that it was only once in a way): I questioned my servant about their habits and let him divine that I should be interested in any information he could pick up. But he picked up amazingly little for a knowing Venetian: it must be added that where there is a perpetual fast there are very few crumbs on the floor. His cleverness in other ways was sufficient, if it was not quite all that I had attributed to him on the occasion of my first interview with Miss Tita. He had helped my gondolier to bring me round a boat-load of furniture; and when these articles had been carried to the top of the palace and distributed according to our associated wisdom he organized my household with such promptitude as was consistent with the fact that it was composed exclusively of himself. He made me in short as comfortable as I could be with my indifferent prospects. I should have been glad if he had fallen in love with Miss Bordereau's maid or, failing this, had taken her in aversion; either event might have brought about some kind of catastrophe and a catastrophe might have led to some parley. It was my idea that she would have been sociable, and I myself on various occasions saw her flit to and fro on domestic errands, so that I was sure she was accessible. But I tasted of no gossip from that fountain, and I afterwards learned that Pasquale's affections were fixed upon an object that made him heedless of other women. This was a young lady with a powdered face, a yellow cotton gown and much leisure, who used often to come to see him. She practised, at her convenience, the art of a stringer of beads[15] (these ornaments are made in Venice, in profusion; she had her pocket full of them and I used to find them on the floor of my apartment), and kept an eye on the maiden in the house. It was not for me of course to make the domestics tattle, and I never said a word to Miss Bordereau's cook.

It seemed to me a proof of the old lady's determination to have nothing to do with me that she should never have sent me a receipt for my three months' rent. For some days I looked out for it and then, when I had given it up, I wasted a good deal of time in wondering what her reason had been for neglecting so indispensable and familiar a form. At first I was tempted to send her a reminder, after which I relinquished the idea (against my judgment as to what was right in the particular case), on the general ground of wishing to keep quiet. If Miss Bordereau suspected me of ulterior aims she would suspect me less if I should be businesslike, and yet I consented not to be so. It was possible she intended her omission as an impertinence, a visible irony, to show how she could overreach people who attempted to overreach her. On that hypothesis it was well to let her see that one did not notice her little tricks. The real reading of the matter, I afterwards perceived, was simply the poor old woman's desire to emphasize the fact that I was in the enjoyment of a favour as rigidly limited as it had been liberally bestowed. She had given me part of her house and now she would not give me even a morsel of paper with her name on it. Let me say that even at first this did not make me too miserable, for the whole episode was essentially delightful to me. I foresaw that I should have a summer after my own literary heart, and the sense of holding my opportunity was much greater than the sense of losing it. There could be no Venetian business without patience, and since I adored the place I was much more in the spirit of it for having laid in a large provision. That spirit kept me perpetual company and seemed to look out at me from the revived immortal face – in which all his genius shone – of the great poet who was my prompter. I had invoked him and he had come; he hovered before me half the time; it was as if his bright ghost had returned to earth to tell me that he regarded the affair as his own no less than mine and that we should see it fraternally, cheerfully to a conclusion. It was as if he had said, 'Poor dear, be easy with her; she has some natural prejudices; only give her time. Strange as it may appear to you she was very attractive in 1820. Meanwhile are we not in Venice together, and what better place is there for the meeting of dear friends? See how it glows with the advancing summer; how the sky and the sea and the rosy air and the marble of the palaces all shimmer and melt together.' My eccentric private errand became a part of the general romance and the general glory – I felt even a mystic companionship, a moral fraternity with all those who in the past had been in the service of art. They had worked for beauty, for a devotion; and what else was I doing? That element was in everything that Jeffrey Aspern had written and I was only bringing it to the light.

I lingered in the sala when I went to and fro; I used to watch – as long as I thought decent – the door that led to Miss Bordereau's part of the house. A person observing me might have supposed I was trying to cast a spell upon it or attempting some odd experiment in hypnotism. But I was only praying it would open or thinking what treasure probably lurked behind it. I hold it singular, as I look back, that I should never have doubted for a moment that the sacred relics were there; never have failed to feel a certain joy at being under the same roof with them. After all they were under my hand – they had not escaped me yet; and they made my life continuous, in a fashion, with the illustrious life they had touched at the other end. I lost myself in this satisfaction to the point of assuming – in my quiet extravagance – that poor Miss Tita also went back, went back, as I used to phrase it. She did indeed, the gentle spinster, but not quite so far as Jeffrey Aspern, who was simple hearsay to her, quite as he was to me. Only she had lived for years with Juliana, she had seen and handled the papers and (even though she was stupid) some esoteric knowledge had rubbed off on her. That was what the old woman represented – esoteric knowledge; and this was the idea with which my editorial heart used to thrill. It literally beat faster often, of an evening, when I had been out, as I stopped with my candle in the re-echoing hall on my way up to bed. It was as if at such a moment as that, in the stillness, after the long contradiction of the day, Miss Bordereau's secrets were in the air, the wonder of her survival more palpable. These were the acute impressions. I had them in another form, with more of a certain sort of reciprocity, during the hours that I sat in the garden looking up over the top of my book at the closed windows of my hostess. In these windows no sign of life ever appeared; it was as if, for fear of my

catching a glimpse of them, the two ladies passed their days in
the dark. But this only proved to me that they had something
to conceal; which was what I had wished to demonstrate. Their
motionless shutters became as expressive as eyes consciously
closed, and I took comfort in thinking that at all events though
invisible themselves they saw me between the lashes.

I made a point of spending as much time as possible in the
garden, to justify the picture I had originally given of my horti-
cultural passion. And I not only spent time, but (hang it! as I
said) I spent money. As soon as I had got my rooms arranged
and could give the proper thought to the matter I surveyed the
place with a clever expert and made terms for having it put in
order. I was sorry to do this, for personally I liked it better as it
was, with its weeds and its wild, rough tangle, its sweet, characteristic Venetian shabbiness. I had to be consistent, to keep
my promise that I would smother the house in flowers. Moreover I formed this graceful project that by flowers I would
make my way – I would succeed by big nosegays. I would batter the old women with lilies – I would bombard their citadel
with roses. Their door would have to yield to the pressure
when a mountain of carnations should be piled up against it.
The place in truth had been brutally neglected. The Venetian
capacity for dawdling is of the largest, and for a good many
days unlimited litter was all my gardener had to show for his
ministrations. There was a great digging of holes and carting
about of earth, and after a while I grew so impatient that I had
thoughts of sending for my bouquets to the nearest stand. But
I reflected that the ladies would see through the chinks of their
shutters that they must have been bought and might make up
their minds from this that I was a humbug. So I composed
myself and finally, though the delay was long, perceived some
appearances of bloom. This encouraged me and I waited
serenely enough till they multiplied. Meanwhile the real summer days arrived and began to pass, and as I look back upon
them they seem to me almost the happiest of my life. I took
more and more care to be in the garden whenever it was not
too hot. I had an arbour arranged and a low table and an armchair put into it; and I carried out books and portfolios (I had

always some business of writing in hand), and worked and waited and mused and hoped, while the golden hours elapsed and the plants drank in the light and the inscrutable old palace turned pale and then, as the day waned, began to flush in it and my papers rustled in the wandering breeze of the Adriatic.

Considering how little satisfaction I got from it at first it is remarkable that I should not have grown more tired of wondering what mystic rites of ennui the Misses Bordereau celebrated in their darkened rooms; whether this had always been the tenor of their life and how in previous years they had escaped elbowing their neighbours. It was clear that they must have had other habits and other circumstances; that they must once have been young or at least middle-aged. There was no end to the questions it was possible to ask about them and no end to the answers it was not possible to frame. I had known many of my country-people in Europe and was familiar with the strange ways they were liable to take up there; but the Misses Bordereau formed altogether a new type of the American absentee. Indeed it was plain that the American name had ceased to have any application to them – I had seen this in the ten minutes I spent in the old woman's room. You could never have said whence they came, from the appearance of either of them; wherever it was they had long ago dropped the local accent and fashion. There was nothing in them that one recognized, and putting the question of speech aside they might have been Norwegians or Spaniards. Miss Bordereau, after all, had been in Europe nearly threequarters of a century; it appeared by some verses addressed to her by Aspern on the occasion of his own second absence from America – verses of which Cumnor and I had after infinite conjecture established solidly enough the date – that she was even then, as a girl of twenty, on the foreign side of the sea. There was an implication in the poem (I hope not just for the phrase) that he had come back for her sake. We had no real light upon her circumstances at that moment, any more than we had upon her origin, which we believed to be of the sort usually spoken of as modest. Cumnor had a theory that she had been a governess in some family in which the poet visited and that, in consequence of her position, there was from the first something unavowed, or rather something positively clandestine, in their relations. I on the other hand had hatched a little romance according to which she was the daughter of an artist, a painter or a sculptor, who had left the western world when the century was fresh, to study in the ancient schools. It was essential to my hypothesis that this amiable man should have lost his wife, should have been poor and unsuccessful and should have had a second daughter, of a disposition quite different from Juliana's. It was also indispensable that he should have been accompanied to Europe by these young ladies and should have established himself there for the remainder of a struggling, saddened life. There was a further implication that Miss Bordereau had had in her youth a perverse and adventurous, albeit a generous and fascinating character, and that she had passed through some singular vicissitudes. By what passions had she been ravaged, by what sufferings had she been blanched, what store of memories had she laid away for the monotonous future?

I asked myself these things as I sat spinning theories about her in my arbour and the bees droned in the flowers. It was incontestable that, whether for right or for wrong, most readers of certain of Aspern's poems (poems not as ambiguous as the sonnets – scarcely more divine, I think – of Shakespeare) had taken for granted that Juliana had not always adhered to the steep footway of renunciation. There hovered about her name a perfume of reckless passion, an intimation that she had not been exactly as the respectable young person in general. Was this a sign that her singer had betrayed her, had given her away, as we say nowadays, to posterity? Certain it is that it would have been difficult to put one's finger on the passage in which her fair fame suffered an imputation. Moreover was not any fame fair enough that was so sure of duration and was associated with works immortal through their beauty? It was a part of my idea that the young lady had had a foreign lover (and an unedifying tragical rupture) before her meeting with Jeffrey Aspern. She had lived with her father and sister in a queer old-fashioned, expatriated, artistic Bohemia, in the days when the æsthetic was only the academic and the painters who

knew the best models for a *contadina* and *pifferaro*[16] wore
peaked hats and long hair. It was a society less furnished than
the coteries of to-day (in its ignorance of the wonderful chances,
the opportunities of the early bird, with which its path was
strewn), with tatters of old stuff and fragments of old crockery;
so that Miss Bordereau appeared not to have picked up or have
inherited many objects of importance. There was no enviable
bric-à-brac, with its provoking legend of cheapness, in the
room in which I had seen her. Such a fact as that suggested
bareness, but none the less it worked happily into the sentimental interest I had always taken in the early movements of my
countrymen as visitors to Europe. When Americans went
abroad in 1820 there was something romantic, almost heroic
in it, as compared with the perpetual ferryings of the present
hour, when photography and other conveniences have annihilated surprise.[17] Miss Bordereau sailed with her family on a
tossing brig, in the days of long voyages and sharp differences;
she had her emotions on the top of yellow diligences, passed
the night at inns where she dreamed of travellers' tales, and
was struck, on reaching the eternal city, with the elegance of
Roman pearls and scarfs. There was something touching to me
in all that and my imagination frequently went back to the
period. If Miss Bordereau carried it there of course Jeffrey
Aspern at other times had done so a great deal more. It was a
much more important fact, if one were looking at his genius
critically, that he had lived in the days before the general trans-
fusion. It had happened to me to regret that he had known
Europe at all; I should have liked to see what he would have
written without that experience, by which he had incontestably
been enriched. But as his fate had ordered otherwise I went
with him – I tried to judge how the old world would have
struck him. It was not only there, however, that I watched him;
the relations he had entertained with the new had even a livelier
interest. His own country after all had had most of his life, and
his muse, as they said at that time, was essentially American.
That was originally what I had loved him for: that at a period
when our native land was nude and crude and provincial, when
the famous 'atmosphere' it is supposed to lack was not even

missed, when literature was lonely there and art and form almost impossible, he had found means to live and write like one of the first; to be free and general and not at all afraid; to feel, understand and express everything.

V

I was seldom at home in the evening, for when I attempted to occupy myself in my apartments the lamplight brought in a swarm of noxious insects, and it was too hot for closed windows. Accordingly I spent the late hours either on the water (the moonlight of Venice is famous), or in the splendid square which serves as a vast forecourt to the strange old basilica of Saint Mark. I sat in front of Florian's *café*, eating ices, listening to music, talking with acquaintances: the traveller will remember how the immense cluster of tables and little chairs stretches like a promontory into the smooth lake of the Piazza.[18] The whole place, of a summer's evening, under the stars and with all the lamps, all the voices and light footsteps on marble (the only sounds of the arcades that enclose it), is like an open-air saloon dedicated to cooling drinks and to a still finer degustation – that of the exquisite impressions received during the day. When I did not prefer to keep mine to myself there was always a stray tourist, disencumbered of his Bädeker,[19] to discuss them with, or some domesticated painter rejoicing in the return of the season of strong effects. The wonderful church, with its low domes and bristling embroideries, the mystery of its mosaic and sculpture, looked ghostly in the tempered gloom, and the sea-breeze passed between the twin columns of the Piazzetta, the lintels of a door no longer guarded, as gently as if a rich curtain were swaying there. I used sometimes on these occasions to think of the Misses Bordereau and of the pity of their being shut up in apartments which in the Venetian July even Venetian vastness did not prevent from being stuffy. Their life seemed miles away from the life of the Piazza, and no doubt it was really too late to make the austere Juliana change her habits. But poor Miss Tita would have enjoyed one of Florian's ices, I was sure; sometimes I even had thoughts of carrying one home to her. Fortunately my patience bore fruit and I was not obliged to do anything so ridiculous.

One evening about the middle of July I came in earlier than usual – I forget what chance had led to this – and instead of going up to my quarters made my way into the garden. The temperature was very high; it was such a night as one would gladly have spent in the open air and I was in no hurry to go to bed. I had floated home in my gondola, listening to the slow splash of the oar in the narrow dark canals, and now the only thought that solicited me was the vague reflection that it would be pleasant to recline at one's length in the fragrant darkness on a garden bench. The odour of the canal was doubtless at the bottom of that aspiration and the breath of the garden, as I entered it, gave consistency to my purpose. It was delicious – just such an air as must have trembled with Romeo's vows when he stood among the flowers and raised his arms to his mistress's balcony. I looked at the windows of the palace to see if by chance the example of Verona (Verona being not far off) had been followed; but everything was dim, as usual, and everything was still. Juliana, on summer nights in her youth, might have murmured down from open windows at Jeffrey Aspern, but Miss Tita was not a poet's mistress any more than I was a poet. This however did not prevent my gratification from being great as I became aware on reaching the end of the garden that Miss Tita was seated in my little bower. At first I only made out an indistinct figure, not in the least counting on such an overture from one of my hostesses; it even occurred to me that some sentimental maid-servant had stolen in to keep a tryst with her sweetheart. I was going to turn away, not to frighten her, when the figure rose to its height and I recognized Miss Bordereau's niece. I must do myself the justice to say that I did not wish to frighten her either, and much as I had longed for some such accident I should have been capable of retreating. It was as if I had laid a trap for her by coming home earlier than usual and adding to that eccentricity by creeping into the garden. As she rose she spoke to me, and then I reflected that perhaps, secure in my almost inveterate absence, it was her nightly practice to take a lonely airing. There was no trap, in truth, because I had had no suspicion. At first I took for granted that the words she uttered expressed discomfiture at my arrival; but as she repeated them – I had not caught them clearly – I had the surprise of hearing her say, 'Oh, dear, I'm so very glad you've come!' She and her aunt had in common the property of unexpected speeches. She came out of the arbour almost as if she were going to throw herself into my arms.

I hasten to add that she did nothing of the kind; she did not even shake hands with me. It was a gratification to her to see me and presently she told me why – because she was nervous when she was out-of-doors at night alone. The plants and bushes looked so strange in the dark, and there were all sorts of queer sounds – she could not tell what they were – like the noises of animals. She stood close to me, looking about her with an air of greater security but without any demonstration of interest in me as an individual. Then I guessed that nocturnal prowlings were not in the least her habit, and I was also reminded (I had been struck with the circumstance in talking with her before I took possession) that it was impossible to overestimate her simplicity.

'You speak as if you were lost in the backwoods,' I said, laughing. 'How you manage to keep out of this charming place when you have only three steps to take to get into it, is more than I have yet been able to discover. You hide away mighty well so long as I am on the premises, I know; but I had a hope that you peeped out a little at other times. You and your poor aunt are worse off than Carmelite nuns[20] in their cells. Should you mind telling me how you exist without air, without exercise, without any sort of human contact? I don't see how you carry on the common business of life.'

She looked at me as if I were talking some strange tongue and her answer was so little of an answer that I was considerably irritated. 'We go to bed very early – earlier than you would believe.' I was on the point of saying that this only deepened the mystery when she gave me some relief by adding, 'Before you came we were not so private. But I never have been out at night.'

'Never in these fragrant alleys, blooming here under your nose?'

'Ah,' said Miss Tita, 'they were never nice till now!' There was an unmistakable reference in this and a flattering comparison, so that it seemed to me I had gained a small advantage. As it would help me to follow it up to establish a sort of grievance I asked her why, since she thought my garden nice, she had never thanked me in any way for the flowers I had been sending up in such quantities for the previous three weeks. I had not been discouraged – there had been, as she would have observed, a daily armful; but I had been brought up in the common forms and a word of recognition now and then would have touched me in the right place.

'Why I didn't know they were for me!'

'They were for both of you. Why should I make a difference?'

Miss Tita reflected as if she might be thinking of a reason for that, but she failed to produce one. Instead of this she asked abruptly, 'Why in the world do you want to know us?'

'I ought after all to make a difference,' I replied. 'That question is your aunt's; it isn't yours. You wouldn't ask it if you hadn't been put up to it.'

'She didn't tell me to ask you,' Miss Tita replied, without confusion; she was the oddest mixture of the shrinking and the direct.

'Well, she has often wondered about it herself and expressed her wonder to you. She has insisted on it, so that she has put the idea into your head that I am unsufferably pushing. Upon my word I think I have been very discreet. And how completely your aunt must have lost every tradition of sociability, to see anything out of the way in the idea that respectable intelligent people, living as we do under the same roof, should occasionally exchange a remark! What could be more natural? We are of the same country and we have at least some of the same tastes, since, like you, I am intensely fond of Venice.'

My interlocutress appeared incapable of grasping more than one clause in any proposition, and she declared quickly, eagerly, as if she were answering my whole speech: 'I am not in the least fond of Venice. I should like to go far away!'

'Has she always kept you back so?' I went on, to show her that I could be as irrelevant as herself.

'She told me to come out to-night; she has told me very often,' said Miss Tita. 'It is I who wouldn't come. I don't like to leave her.'

'Is she too weak, is she failing?' I demanded, with more emotion, I think, than I intended to show. I judged this by the way her eyes rested upon me in the darkness. It embarrassed me a little, and to turn the matter off I continued genially: 'Do let us sit down together comfortably somewhere and you will tell me all about her.'

Miss Tita made no resistance to this. We found a bench less secluded, less confidential, as it were, than the one in the arbour; and we were still sitting there when I heard midnight ring out from those clear bells of Venice which vibrate with a solemnity of their own over the lagoon and hold the air so much more than the chimes of other places. We were together more than an hour and our interview gave, as it struck me, a great lift to my undertaking. Miss Tita accepted the situation without a protest; she had avoided me for three months, yet now she treated me almost as if these three months had made me an old friend. If I had chosen I might have inferred from this that though she had avoided me she had given a good deal of consideration to doing so. She paid no attention to the flight of time – never worried at my keeping her so long away from her aunt. She talked freely, answering questions and asking them and not even taking advantage of certain longish pauses with which they inevitably alternated to say she thought she had better go in. It was almost as if she were waiting for something – something I might say to her – and intended to give me my opportunity. I was the more struck by this as she told me that her aunt had been less well for a good many days and in a way that was rather new. She was weaker; at moments it seemed as if she had no strength at all; yet more than ever before she wished to be left alone. That was why she had told her to come out – not even to remain in her own room, which was alongside; she said her niece irritated her, made her nervous. She sat still for hours together, as if she were asleep; she had always done that, musing and dozing; but at such times formerly she gave at intervals some small sign of life, of interest, liking her companion to be near her with her work. Miss Tita confided to me that at present her aunt was so motionless that she sometimes feared she was dead; moreover she took hardly any food – one couldn't see what she lived on. The great thing was that she still on most days got up; the serious job was to dress her, to wheel her out of her bedroom. She clung to as many of her old habits as possible and she had always, little company as they had received for years, made a point of sitting in the parlour.

I scarcely knew what to think of all this – of Miss Tita's sudden conversion to sociability and of the strange circumstance that the more the old lady appeared to decline toward her end the less she should desire to be looked after. The story did not hang together, and I even asked myself whether it were not a trap laid for me, the result of a design to make me show my hand. I could not have told why my companions (as they could only by courtesy be called) should have this purpose – why they should try to trip up so lucrative a lodger. At any rate I kept on my guard, so that Miss Tita should not have occasion again to ask me if I had an *arrière-pensée*.[21] Poor woman, before we parted for the night my mind was at rest as to *her* capacity for entertaining one.

She told me more about their affairs than I had hoped; there was no need to be prying, for it evidently drew her out simply to feel that I listened, that I cared. She ceased wondering why I cared, and at last, as she spoke of the brilliant life they had led years before, she almost chattered. It was Miss Tita who judged it brilliant; she said that when they first came to live in Venice, years and years before (I saw that her mind was essentially vague about dates and the order in which events had occurred), there was scarcely a week that they had not some visitor or did not make some delightful *passeggio*[22] in the city. They had seen all the curiosities; they had even been to the Lido[23] in a boat (she spoke as if I might think there was a way on foot); they had had a collation there, brought in three baskets and spread out on the grass. I asked her what people they had known and

she said, Oh! very nice ones – the Cavaliere Bombicci and the
Contessa Altemura, with whom they had had a great friendship. Also English people – the Churtons and the Goldies and
Mrs Stock-Stock, whom they had loved dearly; she was dead
and gone, poor dear. That was the case with most of their
pleasant circle (this expression was Miss Tita's own), though a
few were left, which was a wonder considering how they had
neglected them. She mentioned the names of two or three Venetian old women; of a certain doctor, very clever, who was so
kind – he came as a friend, he had really given up practice; of
the *avvocato*[24] Pochintesta, who wrote beautiful poems and
had addressed one to her aunt. These people came to see them
without fail every year, usually at the *capo d'anno*,[25] and of old
her aunt used to make them some little present – her aunt and
she together: small things that she, Miss Tita, made herself, like
paper lamp-shades or mats for the decanters of wine at dinner
or those woollen things that in cold weather were worn on the
wrists. The last few years there had not been many presents;
she could not think what to make and her aunt had lost her
interest and never suggested. But the people came all the same;
if the Venetians liked you once they liked you for ever.

There was something affecting in the good faith of this
sketch of former social glories; the picnic at the Lido had
remained vivid through the ages and poor Miss Tita evidently
was of the impression that she had had a brilliant youth. She
had in fact had a glimpse of the Venetian world in its gossip-
ing, home-keeping, parsimonious, professional walks; for I
observed for the first time that she had acquired by contact
something of the trick of the familiar, soft-sounding, almost
infantile speech of the place. I judged that she had imbibed this
invertebrate dialect, from the natural way the names of things
and people – mostly purely local – rose to her lips. If she knew
little of what they represented she knew still less of anything
else. Her aunt had drawn in – her failing interest in the
table-mats and lamp-shades was a sign of that – and she had
not been able to mingle in society or to entertain it alone; so
that the matter of her reminiscences struck one as an old world
altogether. If she had not been so decent her references would

have seemed to carry one back to the queer rococo Venice of Casanova.[26] I found myself falling into the error of thinking of her too as one of Jeffrey Aspern's contemporaries; this came from her having so little in common with my own. It was possible, I said to myself, that she had not even heard of him; it might very well be that Juliana had not cared to lift even for her the veil that covered the temple of her youth. In this case she perhaps would not know of the existence of the papers, and I welcomed that presumption – it made me feel more safe with her – until I remembered that we had believed the letter of disavowal received by Cumnor to be in the handwriting of the niece. If it had been dictated to her she had of course to know what it was about; yet after all the effect of it was to repudiate the idea of any connection with the poet. I held it probable at all events that Miss Tita had not read a word of his poetry. Moreover if, with her companion, she had always escaped the interviewer there was little occasion for her having got it into her head that people were 'after' the letters. People had not been after them, inasmuch as they had not heard of them; and Cumnor's fruitless feeler would have been a solitary accident.

When midnight sounded Miss Tita got up; but she stopped at the door of the house only after she had wandered two or three times with me round the garden. 'When shall I see you again?' I asked, before she went in; to which she replied with promptness that she should like to come out the next night. She added however that she should not come – she was so far from doing everything she liked.

'You might do a few things that *I* like,' I said with a sigh.

'Oh, you – I don't believe you!' she murmured, at this, looking at me with her simple solemnity.

'Why don't you believe me?'

'Because I don't understand you.'

'That is just the sort of occasion to have faith.' I could not say more, though I should have liked to, as I saw that I only mystified her; for I had no wish to have it on my conscience that I might pass for having made love to her. Nothing less should I have seemed to do had I continued to beg a lady to 'believe in me' in an Italian garden on a mid-summer night.

There was some merit in my scruples, for Miss Tita lingered and lingered: I perceived that she felt that she should not really soon come down again and wished therefore to protract the present. She insisted too on making the talk between us personal to ourselves; and altogether her behaviour was such as would have been possible only to a completely innocent woman.

'I shall like the flowers better now that I know they are also meant for me.'

'How could you have doubted it? If you will tell me the kind you like best I will send a double lot of them.'

'Oh, I like them all best!' Then she went on, familiarly: 'Shall you study – shall you read and write – when you go up to your rooms?'

'I don't do that at night, at this season. The lamplight brings in the animals.'

'You might have known that when you came.'

'I did know it!'

'And in winter do you work at night?'

'I read a good deal, but I don't often write.' She listened as if these details had a rare interest, and suddenly a temptation quite at variance with the prudence I had been teaching myself associated itself with her plain, mild face. Ah yes, she was safe and I could make her safer! It seemed to me from one moment to another that I could not wait longer – that I really must take a sounding. So I went on: 'In general before I go to sleep – very often in bed (it's a bad habit, but I confess to it), I read some great poet. In nine cases out of ten it's a volume of Jeffrey Aspern.'

I watched her well as I pronounced that name but I saw nothing wonderful. Why should I indeed – was not Jeffrey Aspern the property of the human race?

'Oh, we read him – we *have* read him,' she quietly replied.

'He is my poet of poets – I know him almost by heart.'

For an instant Miss Tita hesitated; then her sociability was too much for her.

'Oh, by heart – that's nothing!' she murmured, smiling. 'My aunt used to know him – to know him' – she paused an instant and I wondered what she was going to say – 'to know him as a visitor.'

'As a visitor?' I repeated, staring.

'He used to call on her and take her out.'

I continued to stare. 'My dear lady, he died a hundred years ago!'

'Well,' she said, mirthfully, 'my aunt is a hundred and fifty.'

'Mercy on us!' I exclaimed; 'why didn't you tell me before? I should like so to ask her about him.'

'She wouldn't care for that – she wouldn't tell you,' Miss Tita replied.

'I don't care what she cares for! She *must* tell me – it's not a chance to be lost.'

'Oh, you should have come twenty years ago: then she still talked about him.'

'And what did she say?' I asked, eagerly.

'I don't know – that he liked her immensely.'

'And she – didn't she like him?'

'She said he was a god.' Miss Tita gave me this information flatly, without expression; her tone might have made it a piece of trivial gossip. But it stirred me deeply as she dropped the words into the summer night; it seemed such a direct testimony.

'Fancy, fancy!' I murmured. And then, 'Tell me this, please – has she got a portrait of him? They are distressingly rare.'

'A portrait? I don't know,' said Miss Tita; and now there was discomfiture in her face. 'Well, good-night!' she added; and she turned into the house.

I accompanied her into the wide, dusky, stone-paved passage which on the ground floor corresponded with our grand sala. It opened at one end into the garden, at the other upon the canal, and was lighted now only by the small lamp that was always left for me to take up as I went to bed. An extinguished candle which Miss Tita apparently had brought down with her stood on the same table with it. 'Good-night, good-night!' I replied, keeping beside her as she went to get her light. 'Surely you would know, shouldn't you, if she had one?'

'If she had what?' the poor lady asked, looking at me queerly over the flame of her candle.

'A portrait of the god. I don't know what I wouldn't give to see it.'

'I don't know what she has got. She keeps her things locked up.' And Miss Tita went away, toward the staircase, with the sense evidently that she had said too much.

I let her go – I wished not to frighten her – and I contented myself with remarking that Miss Bordereau would not have locked up such a glorious possession as that – a thing a person would be proud of and hang up in a prominent place on the parlour-wall. Therefore of course she had not any portrait. Miss Tita made no direct answer to this and candle in hand, with her back to me, ascended two or three stairs. Then she stopped short and turned round, looking at me across the dusky space.

'Do you write – do you write?' There was a shake in her voice – she could scarcely bring out what she wanted to ask.

'Do I write? Oh, don't speak of my writing on the same day with Aspern's!'

'Do you write about *him* – do you pry into his life?'

'Ah, that's your aunt's question; it can't be yours!' I said, in a tone of slightly wounded sensibility.

'All the more reason then that you should answer it. Do you, please?'

I thought I had allowed for the falsehoods I should have to tell; but I found that in fact when it came to the point I had not. Besides, now that I had an opening there was a kind of relief in being frank. Lastly (it was perhaps fanciful, even fatuous), I guessed that Miss Tita personally would not in the last resort be less my friend. So after a moment's hesitation I answered, 'Yes, I have written about him and I am looking for more material. In heaven's name have you got any?'

'*Santo Dio!*' she exclaimed, without heeding my question; and she hurried upstairs and out of sight. I might count upon her in the last resort, but for the present she was visibly alarmed. The proof of it was that she began to hide again, so that for a fortnight I never beheld her. I found my patience ebbing and after four or five days of this I told the gardener to stop the flowers.

VI

One afternoon, as I came down from my quarters to go out, I found Miss Tita in the sala: it was our first encounter on that ground since I had come to the house. She put on no air of being there by accident; there was an ignorance of such arts in her angular, diffident directness. That I might be quite sure she was waiting for me she informed me of the fact and told me that Miss Bordereau wished to see me: she would take me into the room at that moment if I had time. If I had been late for a love-tryst I would have stayed for this, and I quickly signified that I should be delighted to wait upon the old lady. 'She wants to talk with you – to know you,' Miss Tita said, smiling as if she herself appreciated that idea; and she led me to the door of her aunt's apartment. I stopped her a moment before she had opened it, looking at her with some curiosity. I told her that this was a great satisfaction to me and a great honour; but all the same I should like to ask what had made Miss Bordereau change so suddenly. It was only the other day that she wouldn't suffer me near her. Miss Tita was not embarrassed by my question; she had as many little unexpected serenities as if she told fibs, but the odd part of them was that they had on the contrary their source in her truthfulness. 'Oh, my aunt changes,' she answered; 'it's so terribly dull – I suppose she's tired.'

'But you told me that she wanted more and more to be alone.'

Poor Miss Tita coloured, as if she found me over-insistent. 'Well, if you don't believe she wants to see you – I haven't invented it! I think people often are capricious when they are very old.'

'That's perfectly true. I only wanted to be clear as to whether you have repeated to her what I told you the other night.'

'What you told me?'

'About Jeffrey Aspern – that I am looking for materials.'

'If I had told her do you think she would have sent for you?'

'That's exactly what I want to know. If she wants to keep him to herself she might have sent for me to tell me so.'

'She won't speak of him,' said Miss Tita. Then as she opened the door she added in a lower tone, 'I have told her nothing.'

The old woman was sitting in the same place in which I had seen her last, in the same position, with the same mystifying bandage over her eyes. Her welcome was to turn her almost invisible face to me and show me that while she sat silent she saw me clearly. I made no motion to shake hands with her; I felt too well on this occasion that that was out of place for ever. It had been sufficiently enjoined upon me that she was too sacred for that sort of reciprocity – too venerable to touch. There was something so grim in her aspect (it was partly the accident of her green shade), as I stood there to be measured, that I ceased on the spot to feel any doubt as to her knowing my secret, though I did not in the least suspect that Miss Tita had not just spoken the truth. She had not betrayed me, but the old woman's brooding instinct had served her; she had turned me over and over in the long, still hours and she had guessed. The worst of it was that she looked terribly like an old woman who at a pinch would burn her papers. Miss Tita pushed a chair forward, saying to me, 'This will be a good place for you to sit.' As I took possession of it I asked after Miss Bordereau's health; expressed the hope that in spite of the very hot weather it was satisfactory. She replied that it was good enough – good enough; that it was a great thing to be alive.

'Oh, as to that, it depends upon what you compare it with!' I exclaimed, laughing.

'I don't compare – I don't compare. If I did that I should have given everything up long ago.'

I liked to think that this was a subtle allusion to the rapture she had known in the society of Jeffrey Aspern – though it was true that such an allusion would have accorded ill with the wish I imputed to her to keep him buried in her soul. What it accorded with was my constant conviction that no human being had ever had a more delightful social gift than his, and what it seemed to convey was that nothing in the world was worth speaking of if one pretended to speak of that. But one did not! Miss Tita sat down beside her aunt, looking as if she had reason to believe some very remarkable conversation would come off between us.

'It's about the beautiful flowers,' said the old lady; 'you sent us so many – I ought to have thanked you for them before. But I don't write letters and I receive only at long intervals.'

She had not thanked me while the flowers continued to come, but she departed from her custom so far as to send for me as soon as she began to fear that they would not come any more. I noted this; I remembered what an acquisitive propensity she had shown when it was a question of extracting gold from me, and I privately rejoiced at the happy thought I had had in suspending my tribute. She had missed it and she was willing to make a concession to bring it back. At the first sign of this concession I could only go to meet her. 'I am afraid you have not had many, of late, but they shall begin again immediately – to-morrow, to-night.'

'Oh, do send us some to-night!' Miss Tita cried, as if it were an immense circumstance.

'What else should you do with them? It isn't a manly taste to make a bower of your room,' the old woman remarked.

'I don't make a bower of my room, but I am exceedingly fond of growing flowers, of watching their ways. There is nothing unmanly in that: it has been the amusement of philosophers, of statesmen in retirement; even I think of great captains.'

'I suppose you know you can sell them – those you don't use,' Miss Bordereau went on. 'I daresay they wouldn't give you much for them; still, you could make a bargain.'

'Oh, I have never made a bargain, as you ought to know. My gardener disposes of them and I ask no questions.'

'I would ask a few, I can promise you!' said Miss Bordereau; and it was the first time I had heard her laugh. I could not get used to the idea that this vision of pecuniary profit was what drew out the divine Juliana most.

'Come into the garden yourself and pick them; come as often as you like; come every day. They are all for you,' I pursued, addressing Miss Tita and carrying off this veracious statement by treating it as an innocent joke. 'I can't imagine why she doesn't come down,' I added, for Miss Bordereau's benefit.

'You must make her come; you must come up and fetch her,' said the old woman, to my stupefaction. 'That odd thing you have made in the corner would be a capital place for her to sit.'

The allusion to my arbour was irreverent; it confirmed the impression I had already received that there was a flicker of impertinence in Miss Bordereau's talk, a strange mocking lambency which must have been a part of her adventurous youth and which had outlived passions and faculties. None the less I asked, 'Wouldn't it be possible for you to come down there yourself? Wouldn't it do you good to sit there in the shade, in the sweet air?'

'Oh, sir, when I move out of this it won't be to sit in the air, and I'm afraid that any that may be stirring around me won't be particularly sweet! It will be a very dark shade indeed. But that won't be just yet,' Miss Bordereau continued, cannily, as if to correct any hopes that this courageous allusion to the last receptacle of her mortality might lead me to entertain. 'I have sat here many a day and I have had enough of arbours in my time. But I'm not afraid to wait till I'm called.'

Miss Tita had expected some interesting talk, but perhaps she found it less genial on her aunt's side (considering that I had been sent for with a civil intention) than she had hoped. As if to give the conversation a turn that would put our companion in a light more favourable she said to me, 'Didn't I tell you the other night that she had sent me out? You see that I can do what I like!'

'Do you pity her – do you teach her to pity herself?' Miss Bordereau demanded, before I had time to answer this appeal. 'She has a much easier life than I had when I was her age.'

'You must remember that it has been quite open to me to think you rather inhuman.'

'Inhuman? That's what the poets used to call the women a hundred years ago. Don't try that; you won't do as well as they!' Juliana declared. 'There is no more poetry in the world – that I know of at least. But I won't bandy words with you,' she pursued, and I well remember the old-fashioned, artificial sound she gave to the speech. 'You have made me talk, talk! It isn't good for me at all.' I got up at this and told her I would take no more of her time; but she detained me to ask, 'Do you remember, the day I saw you about the rooms, that you offered us the use of your gondola?' And when I assented, promptly, struck again with her disposition to make a 'good thing' of being there and wondering what she now had in her eye, she broke out, 'Why don't you take that girl out in it and show her the place?'

'Oh dear aunt, what do you want to do with me?' cried the 'girl', with a piteous quaver. 'I know all about the place!'

'Well then, go with him as a cicerone!'[27] said Miss Bordereau, with an effect of something like cruelty in her implacable power of retort – an incongruous suggestion that she was a sarcastic, profane, cynical old woman. 'Haven't we heard that there have been all sorts of changes[28] in all these years? You ought to see them and at your age (I don't mean because you're so young), you ought to take the chances that come. You're old enough, my dear, and this gentleman won't hurt you. He will show you the famous sunsets, if they still go on – *do* they go on? The sun set for me so long ago. But that's not a reason. Besides, I shall never miss you; you think you are too important. Take her to the Piazza; it used to be very pretty,' Miss Bordereau continued, addressing herself to me. 'What have they done with the funny old church? I hope it hasn't tumbled down. Let her look at the shops; she may take some money, she may buy what she likes.'

Poor Miss Tita had got up, discountenanced and helpless, and as we stood there before her aunt it would certainly have seemed to a spectator of the scene that the old woman was amusing herself at our expense. Miss Tita protested, in a confusion of exclamations and murmurs; but I lost no time in saying that if she would do me the honour to accept the hospitality of my boat I would engage that she should not be bored. Or if she did not want so much of my company the boat itself, with the gondolier, was at her service; he was a capital oar and she might have every confidence. Miss Tita, without definitely answering this speech, looked away from me, out of the window, as if she were going to cry; and I remarked that once we had Miss Bordereau's approval we could easily come to an understanding. We would take an hour, whichever she liked, one of the very next days. As I made my obeisance to the old lady I asked her if she would kindly permit me to see her again.

For a moment she said nothing; then she inquired, 'Is it very necessary to your happiness?'

'It diverts me more than I can say.'

'You are wonderfully civil. Don't you know it almost kills *me*?'

'How can I believe that when I see you more animated, more brilliant than when I came in?'

'That is very true, aunt,' said Miss Tita. 'I think it does you good.'

'Isn't it touching, the solicitude we each have that the other shall enjoy herself?' sneered Miss Bordereau. 'If you think me brilliant to-day you don't know what you are talking about; you have never seen an agreeable woman. Don't try to pay me a compliment; I have been spoiled,' she went on. 'My door is shut, but you may sometimes knock.'

With this she dismissed me and I left the room. The latch closed behind me, but Miss Tita, contrary to my hope, had remained within. I passed slowly across the hall and before taking my way downstairs I waited a little. My hope was answered; after a minute Miss Tita followed me. 'That's a delightful idea about the Piazza,' I said. 'When will you go – to-night, to-morrow?'

She had been disconcerted, as I have mentioned, but I had already perceived and I was to observe again that when Miss Tita was embarrassed she did not (as most women would have done) turn away from you and try to escape, but came closer, as it were, with a deprecating, clinging appeal to be spared, to be protected. Her attitude was perpetually a sort of prayer for assistance, for explanation; and yet no woman in the world could have been less of a comedian. From the moment you were kind to her she depended on you absolutely; her self-consciousness dropped from her and she took the greatest intimacy, the innocent intimacy which was the only thing she could conceive, for granted. She told me she did not know what had got into her aunt; she had changed so quickly, she had got some idea. I replied that she must find out what the idea was and then let me know; we would go and have an ice together at Florian's and she should tell me while we listened to the band.

'Oh, it will take me a long time to find out!' she said, rather ruefully; and she could promise me this satisfaction neither for that night nor for the next. I was patient now, however, for I felt that I had only to wait; and in fact at the end of the week, one lovely evening after dinner, she stepped into my gondola, to which in honour of the occasion I had attached a second oar.

We swept in the course of five minutes into the Grand Canal; whereupon she uttered a murmur of ecstasy as fresh as if she had been a tourist just arrived. She had forgotten how splendid the great water-way looked on a clear, hot summer evening, and how the sense of floating between marble palaces and reflected lights disposed the mind to sympathetic talk. We floated long and far, and though Miss Tita gave no high-pitched voice to her satisfaction I felt that she surrendered herself. She was more than pleased, she was transported; the whole thing was an immense liberation. The gondola moved with slow strokes, to give her time to enjoy it, and she listened to the plash of the oars, which grew louder and more musically liquid as we passed into narrow canals, as if it were a revelation of Venice. When I asked her how long it was since she had been in a boat she answered, 'Oh, I don't know; a long time – not since my aunt began to be ill.' This was not the only example she gave me of her extreme vagueness about the previous years and the line which marked off the period when Miss Bordereau flourished. I was not at liberty to keep her out too long, but we took a considerable *giro*[29] before going to the Piazza. I asked her no questions, keeping the conversation on purpose away from her domestic situation and the things I wanted to know; I poured treasures of information about Venice into her ears, described Florence and Rome, discoursed to her on the charms and advantages of travel. She reclined, receptive, on the deep leather cushions, turned her eyes conscientiously to everything I pointed out to her, and never mentioned to me till some time afterwards that she might be supposed to know Florence better than I, as she had lived there for years with Miss Bordereau. At last she asked, with the shy impatience of a child, 'Are we not really going to the Piazza? That's what I want to see!' I immediately gave the order that we should go straight; and then we sat silent with the expectation of arrival. As some time still passed, however, she said suddenly, of her own movement, 'I have found out what is the matter with my aunt: she is afraid you will go!'

'What has put that into her head?'

'She has had an idea you have not been happy. That is why she is different now.'

'You mean she wants to make me happier?'

'Well, she wants you not to go; she wants you to stay.'

'I suppose you mean on account of the rent,' I remarked candidly.

Miss Tita's candour showed itself a match for my own. 'Yes, you know; so that I shall have more.'

'How much does she want you to have?' I asked, laughing. 'She ought to fix the sum, so that I may stay till it's made up.'

'Oh, that wouldn't please me,' said Miss Tita. 'It would be unheard of, your taking that trouble.'

'But suppose I should have my own reasons for staying in Venice?'

'Then it would be better for you to stay in some other house.'

'And what would your aunt say to that?'

'She wouldn't like it at all. But I should think you would do well to give up your reasons and go away altogether.'

'Dear Miss Tita,' I said, 'it's not so easy to give them up!'

She made no immediate answer to this, but after a moment she broke out: 'I think I know what your reasons are!'

'I daresay, because the other night I almost told you how I wish you would help me to make them good.'

'I can't do that without being false to my aunt.'

'What do you mean, being false to her?'

'Why, she would never consent to what you want. She has been asked, she has been written to. It made her fearfully angry.'

'Then she *has* got papers of value?' I demanded, quickly.

'Oh, she has got everything!' sighed Miss Tita, with a curious weariness, a sudden lapse into gloom.

These words caused all my pulses to throb, for I regarded them as precious evidence. For some minutes I was too agitated to speak, and in the interval the gondola approached the Piazzetta. After we had disembarked I asked my companion whether she would rather walk round the square or go and sit at the door of the café; to which she replied that she would do whichever I liked best – I must only remember again how little time she had. I assured her there was plenty to do both, and we made the circuit of the long arcades. Her spirits revived at the sight of the bright shop-windows, and she lingered and stopped, admiring or disapproving of their contents, asking me what I thought of things, theorizing about prices. My attention wandered from her; her words of a while before, 'Oh, she has got everything!' echoed so in my consciousness. We sat down at last in the crowded circle at Florian's, finding an unoccupied table among those that were ranged in the square. It was a splendid night and all the world was out-of-doors; Miss Tita could not have wished the elements more auspicious for her return to society. I saw that she enjoyed it even more than she told; she was agitated with the multitude of her impressions. She had forgotten what an attractive thing the world is, and it was coming over her that somehow she had for the best years of her life been cheated of it. This did not make her angry; but as she looked all over the charming scene her face had, in spite of its smile of appreciation, the flush of a sort of wounded surprise. She became silent, as if she were thinking with a secret sadness of opportunities, for ever lost, which ought to have been easy; and this gave me a chance to say to her, 'Did you mean a while ago that your aunt has a plan of keeping me on by admitting me occasionally to her presence?'

'She thinks it will make a difference with you if you sometimes see her. She wants you so much to stay that she is willing to make that concession.'

'And what good does she consider that I think it will do me to see her?'

'I don't know; she thinks it's interesting,' said Miss Tita, simply. 'You told her you found it so.'

'So I did; but every one doesn't think so.'

'No, of course not, or more people would try.'

'Well, if she is capable of making that reflection she is capable also of making this further one,' I went on: 'that I must have a particular reason for not doing as others do, in spite of the interest she offers – for not leaving her alone.' Miss Tita looked as if she failed to grasp this rather complicated proposition; so I continued, 'If you have not told her what I said to you the other night may she not at least have guessed it?'

'I don't know; she is very suspicious.'

'But she has not been made so by indiscreet curiosity, by persecution?'

'No, no; it isn't that,' said Miss Tita, turning on me a somewhat troubled face. 'I don't know how to say it: it's on account of something – ages ago, before I was born – in her life.'

'Something? What sort of thing?' I asked, as if I myself could have no idea.

'Oh, she has never told me,' Miss Tita answered; and I was sure she was speaking the truth.

Her extreme limpidity was almost provoking, and I felt for the moment that she would have been more satisfactory if she had been less ingenuous. 'Do you suppose it's something to which Jeffrey Aspern's letters and papers – I mean the things in her possession – have reference?'

'I daresay it is!' my companion exclaimed, as if this were a very happy suggestion. 'I have never looked at any of those things.'

'None of them? Then how do you know what they are?'

'I don't,' said Miss Tita, placidly. 'I have never had them in my hands. But I have seen them when she has had them out.'

'Does she have them out often?'

'Not now, but she used to. She is very fond of them.'

'In spite of their being compromising?'

'Compromising?' Miss Tita repeated, as if she was ignorant of the meaning of the word. I felt almost as one who corrupts the innocence of youth.

'I mean their containing painful memories.'

'Oh, I don't think they are painful.'

'You mean you don't think they affect her reputation?'

At this a singular look came into the face of Miss Bordereau's niece – a kind of confession of helplessness, an appeal to me to deal fairly, generously with her. I had brought her to the Piazza, placed her among charming influences, paid her an attention she appreciated, and now I seemed to let her perceive that all this had been a bribe – a bribe to make her turn in some way against her aunt. She was of a yielding nature and capable of doing almost anything to please a person who was kind to her; but the greatest kindness of all would be not to presume too much on this. It was strange enough, as I afterwards thought, that she had not the least air of resenting my want of consideration for her aunt's character, which would have been in the worst possible taste if anything less vital (from my point of view) had been at stake. I don't think she really measured it. 'Do you mean that she did something bad?' she asked in a moment.

'Heaven forbid I should say so, and it's none of my business. Besides, if she did,' I added, laughing, 'it was in other ages, in another world. But why should she not destroy her papers?'

'Oh, she loves them too much.'

'Even now, when she may be near her end?'

'Perhaps when she's sure of that she will.'

'Well, Miss Tita,' I said, 'it's just what I should like you to prevent.'

'How can I prevent it?'

'Couldn't you get them away from her?'

'And give them to you?'

This put the case very crudely, though I am sure there was no irony in her intention. 'Oh, I mean that you might let me see them and look them over. It isn't for myself; there is no personal avidity in my desire. It is simply that they would be of such immense interest to the public, such immeasurable importance as a contribution to Jeffrey Aspern's history.'

She listened to me in her usual manner, as if my speech were full of reference to things she had never heard of, and I felt particularly like the reporter of a newspaper who forces his way into a house of mourning. This was especially the case when after a moment she said, 'There was a gentleman who some time ago wrote to her in very much those words. He also wanted her papers.'

'And did she answer him?' I asked, rather ashamed of myself for not having her rectitude.

'Only when he had written two or three times. He made her very angry.'

'And what did she say?'

'She said he was a devil,' Miss Tita replied, simply.

'She used that expression in her letter?'

'Oh no; she said it to me. She made me write to him.'

'And what did you say?'

'I told him there were no papers at all.'

'Ah, poor gentleman!' I exclaimed.

'I knew there were, but I wrote what she bade me.'

'Of course you had to do that. But I hope I shall not pass for a devil.'

'It will depend upon what you ask me to do for you,' said Miss Tita, smiling.

'Oh, if there is a chance of *your* thinking so my affair is in a bad way! I shan't ask you to steal for me, nor even to fib – for you can't fib, unless on paper. But the principal thing is this – to prevent her from destroying the papers.'

'Why, I have no control of her,' said Miss Tita. 'It's she who controls me.'

'But she doesn't control her own arms and legs, does she? The way she would naturally destroy her letters would be to burn them. Now she can't burn them without fire, and she can't get fire unless you give it to her.'

'I have always done everything she has asked,' my companion rejoined. 'Besides, there's Olimpia.'

I was on the point of saying that Olimpia was probably corruptible, but I thought it best not to sound that note. So I simply inquired if that faithful domestic could not be managed.

'Every one can be managed by my aunt,' said Miss Tita. And then she observed that her holiday was over; she must go home.

I laid my hand on her arm, across the table, to stay her a moment. 'What I want of you is a general promise to help me.'

'Oh, how can I – how can I?' she asked, wondering and troubled. She was half surprised, half frightened at my wishing to make her play an active part.

'This is the main thing: to watch her carefully and warn me in time, before she commits that horrible sacrilege.'

'I can't watch her when she makes me go out.'

'That's very true.'

'And when you do too.'

'Mercy on us; do you think she will have done anything to-night?'

'I don't know; she is very cunning.'

'Are you trying to frighten me?' I asked.

I felt this inquiry sufficiently answered when my companion murmured in a musing, almost envious way, 'Oh, but she loves them – she loves them!'

This reflection, repeated with such emphasis, gave me great comfort; but to obtain more of that balm I said, 'If she shouldn't intend to destroy the objects we speak of before her death she will probably have made some disposition by will.'

'By will?'

'Hasn't she made a will for your benefit?'

'Why, she has so little to leave. That's why she likes money,' said Miss Tita.

'Might I ask, since we are really talking things over, what you and she live on?'

'On some money that comes from America, from a lawyer. He sends it every quarter. It isn't much!'

'And won't she have disposed of that?'

My companion hesitated – I saw she was blushing. 'I believe it's mine,' she said; and the look and tone which accompanied these words betrayed so the absence of the habit of thinking of herself that I almost thought her charming. The next instant she added, 'But she had a lawyer once, ever so long ago. And some people came and signed something.'

'They were probably witnesses. And you were not asked to

sign? Well then,' I argued, rapidly and hopefully, 'it is because
you are the legatee; she has left all her documents to you!'

'If she has it's with very strict conditions,' Miss Tita
responded, rising quickly, while the movement gave the words
a little character of decision. They seemed to imply that the
bequest would be accompanied with a command that the articles
bequeathed should remain concealed from every inquisitive eye
and that I was very much mistaken if I thought she was the
person to depart from an injunction so solemn.

'Oh, of course you will have to abide by the terms,' I said;
and she uttered nothing to mitigate the severity of this conclusion. None the less, later, just before we disembarked at her
own door, on our return, which had taken place almost in
silence, she said to me abruptly, 'I will do what I can to help
you.' I was grateful for this – it was very well so far as it went;
but it did not keep me from remembering that night in a worried waking hour that I now had her word for it to reinforce
my own impression that the old woman was very cunning.

VII

The fear of what this side of her character might have led her to
do made me nervous for days afterwards. I waited for an intimation from Miss Tita; I almost figured to myself that it was her
duty to keep me informed, to let me know definitely whether or
no Miss Bordereau had sacrificed her treasures. But as she gave
no sign I lost patience and determined to judge so far as was
possible with my own senses. I sent late one afternoon to ask if
I might pay the ladies a visit, and my servant came back with
surprising news. Miss Bordereau could be approached without
the least difficulty; she had been moved out into the sala and
was sitting by the window that overlooked the garden. I
descended and found this picture correct; the old lady had been
wheeled forth into the world and had a certain air, which came
mainly perhaps from some brighter element in her dress, of
being prepared again to have converse with it. It had not yet,
however, begun to flock about her; she was perfectly alone and,

though the door leading to her own quarters stood open, I had at first no glimpse of Miss Tita. The window at which she sat had the afternoon shade and, one of the shutters having been pushed back, she could see the pleasant garden, where the summer sun had by this time dried up too many of the plants – she could see the yellow light and the long shadows.

'Have you come to tell me that you will take the rooms for six months more?' she asked, as I approached her, startling me by something coarse in her cupidity almost as much as if she had not already given me a specimen of it. Juliana's desire to make our acquaintance lucrative had been, as I have sufficiently indicated, a false note in my image of the woman who had inspired a great poet with immortal lines; but I may say here definitely that I recognized after all that it behoved me to make a large allowance for her. It was I who had kindled the unholy flame; it was I who had put into her head that she had the means of making money. She appeared never to have thought of that; she had been living wastefully for years, in a house five times too big for her, on a footing that I could explain only by the presumption that, excessive as it was, the space she enjoyed cost her next to nothing and that small as were her revenues they left her, for Venice, an appreciable margin. I had descended on her one day and taught her to calculate, and my almost extravagant comedy on the subject of the garden had presented me irresistibly in the light of a victim. Like all persons who achieve the miracle of changing their point of view when they are old she had been intensely converted; she had seized my hint with a desperate, tremulous clutch.

I invited myself to go and get one of the chairs that stood, at a distance, against the wall (she had given herself no concern as to whether I should sit or stand); and while I placed it near her I began, gaily, 'Oh, dear madam, what an imagination you have, what an intellectual sweep! I am a poor devil of a man of letters who lives from day to day. How can I take palaces by the year? My existence is precarious. I don't know whether six months hence I shall have bread to put in my mouth. I have treated myself for once; it has been an immense luxury. But when it comes to going on—!'

'Are your rooms too dear? if they are you can have more for the same money,' Juliana responded. 'We can arrange, we can *combinare*, as they say here.'

'Well yes, since you ask me, they are too dear,' I said. 'Evidently you suppose me richer than I am.'

She looked at me in her barricaded way. 'If you write books don't you sell them?'

'Do you mean don't people buy them? A little – not so much as I could wish. Writing books, unless one be a great genius – and even then! – is the last road to fortune. I think there is no more money to be made by literature.'

'Perhaps you don't choose good subjects. What do you write about?' Miss Bordereau inquired.

'About the books of other people. I'm a critic, an historian, in a small way.' I wondered what she was coming to.

'And what other people, now?'

'Oh, better ones than myself: the great writers mainly – the great philosophers and poets of the past; those who are dead and gone and can't speak for themselves.'

'And what do you say about them?'

'I say they sometimes attached themselves to very clever women!' I answered, laughing. I spoke with great deliberation, but as my words fell upon the air they struck me as imprudent. However, I risked them and I was not sorry, for perhaps after all the old woman would be willing to treat. It seemed to be tolerably obvious that she knew my secret: why therefore drag the matter out? But she did not take what I had said as a confession; she only asked:

'Do you think it's right to rake up the past?'

'I don't know that I know what you mean by raking it up; but how can we get at it unless we dig a little? The present has such a rough way of treading it down.'

'Oh, I like the past, but I don't like critics,' the old woman declared, with her fine tranquillity.

'Neither do I, but I like their discoveries.'

'Aren't they mostly lies?'

'The lies are what they sometimes discover,' I said, smiling at the quiet impertinence of this. 'They often lay bare the truth.'

'The truth is God's, it isn't man's; we had better leave it
alone. Who can judge of it – who can say?'

'We are terribly in the dark, I know,' I admitted; 'but if we
give up trying what becomes of all the fine things? What
becomes of the work I just mentioned, that of the great philosophers and poets? It is all vain words if there is nothing to
measure it by.'

'You talk as if you were a tailor,' said Miss Bordereau,
whimsically; and then she added quickly, in a different manner,
'This house is very fine; the proportions are magnificent. To-day
I wanted to look at this place again. I made them bring me out
here. When your man came, just now, to learn if I would see
you, I was on the point of sending for you, to ask if you didn't
mean to go on. I wanted to judge what I'm letting you have.
This sala is very grand,' she pursued, like an auctioneer, moving a little, as I guessed, her invisible eyes. 'I don't believe you
often have lived in such a house, eh?'

'I can't often afford to!' I said.

'Well then, how much will you give for six months?'

I was on the point of exclaiming – and the air of excruci-
ation in my face would have denoted a moral fact – 'Don't,
Juliana; for *his* sake, don't!' But I controlled myself and asked
less passionately: 'Why should I remain so long as that?'

'I thought you liked it,' said Miss Bordereau, with her shrivelled dignity.

'So I thought I should.'

For a moment she said nothing more, and I left my own
words to suggest to her what they might. I half expected her to
say, coldly enough, that if I had been disappointed we need not
continue the discussion, and this in spite of the fact that I
believed her now to have in her mind (however it had come
there), what would have told her that my disappointment was
natural. But to my extreme surprise she ended by observing: 'If
you don't think we have treated you well enough perhaps we
can discover some way of treating you better.' This speech was
somehow so incongruous that it made me laugh again, and I
excused myself by saying that she talked as if I were a sulky
boy, pouting in the corner, to be 'brought round'. I had not a

grain of complaint to make; and could anything have exceeded Miss Tita's graciousness in accompanying me a few nights before to the Piazza? At this the old woman went on: 'Well, you brought it on yourself!' And then in a different tone, 'She is a very nice girl.' I assented cordially to this proposition, and she expressed the hope that I did so not merely to be obliging, but that I really liked her. Meanwhile I wondered still more what Miss Bordereau was coming to. 'Except for me, to-day,' she said, 'she has not a relation in the world.' Did she by describing her niece as amiable and unencumbered wish to represent her as a *parti*?[30]

It was perfectly true that I could not afford to go on with my rooms at a fancy price and that I had already devoted to my undertaking almost all the hard cash I had set apart for it. My patience and my time were by no means exhausted, but I should be able to draw upon them only on a more usual Venetian basis. I was willing to pay the venerable woman with whom my pecuniary dealings were such a discord twice as much as any other *padrona di casa* would have asked, but I was not willing to pay her twenty times as much. I told her so plainly, and my plainness appeared to have some success, for she exclaimed, 'Very good; you have done what I asked – you have made an offer!'

'Yes, but not for half a year. Only by the month.'

'Oh, I must think of that then.' She seemed disappointed that I would not tie myself to a period, and I guessed that she wished both to secure me and to discourage me; to say, severely, 'Do you dream that you can get off with less than six months? Do you dream that even by the end of that time you will be appreciably nearer your victory?' What was more in my mind was that she had a fancy to play me the trick of making me engage myself when in fact she had annihilated the papers. There was a moment when my suspense on this point was so acute that I all but broke out with the question, and what kept it back was but a kind of instinctive recoil (lest it should be a mistake), from the last violence of self-exposure. She was such a subtle old witch that one could never tell where one stood with her. You may imagine whether it cleared up the puzzle when, just after she had said she would think of my proposal and without any formal transition, she drew out of her pocket with an embarrassed hand a small object wrapped in crumpled white paper. She held it there a moment and then she asked, 'Do you know much about curiosities?'

'About curiosities?'

'About antiquities, the old gimcracks that people pay so much for to-day. Do you know the kind of price they bring?'

I thought I saw what was coming, but I said ingenuously, 'Do you want to buy something?'

'No, I want to sell. What would an amateur give me for that?' She unfolded the white paper and made a motion for me to take from her a small oval portrait. I possessed myself of it with a hand of which I could only hope that she did not perceive the tremor, and she added, 'I would part with it only for a good price.'

At the first glance I recognized Jeffrey Aspern, and I was well aware that I flushed with the act. As she was watching me however I had the consistency to exclaim, 'What a striking face! Do tell me who it is.'

'It's an old friend of mine, a very distinguished man in his day. He gave it to me himself, but I'm afraid to mention his name, lest you never should have heard of him, critic and historian as you are. I know the world goes fast and one generation forgets another. He was all the fashion when I was young.'

She was perhaps amazed at my assurance, but I was surprised at hers; at her having the energy, in her state of health and at her time of life, to wish to sport with me that way simply for her private entertainment – the humour to test me and practise on me. This, at least, was the interpretation that I put upon her production of the portrait, for I could not believe that she really desired to sell it or cared for any information I might give her. What she wished was to dangle it before my eyes and put a prohibitive price on it. 'The face comes back to me, it torments me,' I said, turning the object this way and that and looking at it very critically. It was a careful but not a supreme work of art, larger than the ordinary miniature and representing a young man with a remarkably handsome face, in a high-collared green coat and a buff waistcoat. I judged the picture to have a valuable quality of resemblance and to have been painted when the model was about twenty-five years old. There are, as all the world knows, three other portraits of the poet in existence, but none of them is of so early a date as this elegant production. 'I have never seen the original but I have seen other likenesses,' I went on. 'You expressed doubt of this generation having heard of the gentleman, but he strikes me for all the world as a celebrity. Now who is he? I can't put my finger on him – I can't give him a label. Wasn't he a writer? Surely he's a poet.' I was determined that it should be she, not I, who should first pronounce Jeffrey Aspern's name.

My resolution was taken in ignorance of Miss Bordereau's extremely resolute character, and her lips never formed in my hearing the syllables that meant so much for her. She neglected to answer my question but raised her hand to take back the picture, with a gesture which though ineffectual was in a high degree peremptory. 'It's only a person who should know for himself that would give me my price,' she said with a certain dryness.

'Oh, then, you have a price?' I did not restore the precious thing; not from any vindictive purpose but because I instinctively clung to it. We looked at each other hard while I retained it.

'I know the least I would take. What it occurred to me to ask you about is the most I shall be able to get.'

She made a movement, drawing herself together as if, in a spasm of dread at having lost her treasure, she were going to attempt the immense effort of rising to snatch it from me. I instantly placed it in her hand again, saying as I did so, 'I should like to have it myself, but with your ideas I could never afford it.'

She turned the small oval plate over in her lap, with its face down, and I thought I saw her catch her breath a little, as if she had had a strain or an escape. This however did not prevent her saying in a moment, 'You would buy a likeness of a person you don't know, by an artist who has no reputation?'

'The artist may have no reputation, but that thing is wonderfully well painted,' I replied, to give myself a reason.

'It's lucky you thought of saying that, because the painter was my father.'

'That makes the picture indeed precious!' I exclaimed, laughing; and I may add that a part of my laughter came from my satisfaction in finding that I had been right in my theory of Miss Bordereau's origin. Aspern had of course met the young lady when he went to her father's studio as a sitter. I observed to Miss Bordereau that if she would entrust me with her property for twenty-four hours I should be happy to take advice upon it; but she made no answer to this save to slip it in silence into her pocket. This convinced me still more that she had no sincere intention of selling it during her lifetime, though she may have desired to satisfy herself as to the sum her niece, should she leave it to her, might expect eventually to obtain for it. 'Well, at any rate I hope you will not offer it without giving me notice,' I said as she remained irresponsive. 'Remember that I am a possible purchaser.'

'I should want your money first!' she returned, with unexpected rudeness; and then, as if she bethought herself that I had just cause to complain of such an insinuation and wished to turn the matter off, asked abruptly what I talked about with her niece when I went out with her that way in the evening.

'You speak as if we had set up the habit,' I replied. 'Certainly I should be very glad if it were to become a habit. But in that case I should feel a still greater scruple at betraying a lady's confidence.'

'Her confidence? Has she got confidence?'

'Here she is – she can tell you herself,' I said; for Miss Tita now appeared on the threshold of the old woman's parlour. 'Have you got confidence, Miss Tita? Your aunt wants very much to know.'

'Not in her, not in her!' the younger lady declared, shaking her head with a dolefulness that was neither jocular nor affected. 'I don't know what to do with her; she has fits of horrid imprudence. She is so easily tired – and yet she has begun to roam – to drag herself about the house.' And she stood looking down at her immemorial companion with a sort of helpless wonder, as if all their years of familiarity had not made her perversities, on occasion, any more easy to follow.

'I know what I'm about. I'm not losing my mind. I daresay you would like to think so,' said Miss Bordereau, with a cynical little sigh.

'I don't suppose you came out here yourself. Miss Tita must have had to lend you a hand,' I interposed, with a pacifying intention.

'Oh, she insisted that we should push her; and when she insists!' said Miss Tita, in the same tone of apprehension; as if there were no knowing what service that she disapproved of her aunt might force her next to render.

'I have always got most things done I wanted, thank God! The people I have lived with have humoured me,' the old woman continued, speaking out of the grey ashes of her vanity.

'I suppose you mean that they have obeyed you.'

'Well, whatever it is, when they like you.'

'It's just because I like you that I want to resist,' said Miss Tita, with a nervous laugh.

'Oh, I suspect you'll bring Miss Bordereau upstairs next, to pay me a visit,' I went on; to which the old lady replied:

'Oh no; I can keep an eye on you from here!'

'You are very tired; you will certainly be ill to-night!' cried Miss Tita.

'Nonsense, my dear; I feel better at this moment than I have done for a month. To-morrow I shall come out again. I want to be where I can see this clever gentleman.'

'Shouldn't you perhaps see me better in your sitting-room?' I inquired.

'Don't you mean shouldn't you have a better chance at me?' she returned, fixing me a moment with her green shade.

'Ah, I haven't that anywhere! I look at you but I don't see you.'

'You excite her dreadfully – and that is not good,' said Miss Tita, giving me a reproachful, appealing look.

'I want to watch you – I want to watch you!' the old lady went on.

'Well then, let us spend as much of our time together as possible – I don't care where – and that will give you every facility.'

'Oh, I've seen you enough for to-day. I'm satisfied. Now I'll go home.' Miss Tita laid her hands on the back of her aunt's chair and began to push, but I begged her to let me take her place. 'Oh yes, you may move me this way – you shan't in any other!' Miss Bordereau exclaimed, as she felt herself propelled firmly and easily over the smooth, hard floor. Before we reached the door of her own apartment she commanded me to stop, and she took a long, last look up and down the noble sala. 'Oh, it's a magnificent house!' she murmured; after which I pushed her forward. When we had entered the parlour Miss Tita told me that she should now be able to manage, and at the same moment the little red-haired *donna* came to meet her mistress. Miss Tita's idea was evidently to get her aunt immediately back to bed. I confess that in spite of this urgency I was guilty of the indiscretion of lingering; it held me there to think that I was nearer the documents I coveted – that they were probably put away somewhere in the faded, unsociable room. The place had indeed a bareness which did not suggest hidden treasures; there were no dusky nooks nor curtained corners, no massive cabinets nor chests with iron bands. Moreover it was possible, it was perhaps even probable that the old lady had consigned her relics to her bedroom, to some battered box that was shoved under the bed, to the drawer of some lame dressing-table, where they would be in the range of vision by the dim night-lamp. None the less I scrutinized every article of furniture, every conceivable cover for a hoard, and noticed that there were half a dozen things with drawers, and in particular a tall old secretary, with brass ornaments of the style of the Empire – a receptacle somewhat rickety but still capable of keeping a great many secrets. I don't know why this article fascinated me so, inasmuch as I certainly had no definite purpose of break-ing into it; but I stared at it so hard that Miss Tita noticed me and changed colour. Her doing this made me think I was right and that wherever they might have been before the Aspern papers at that moment languished behind the peevish little lock of the secretary. It was hard to remove my eyes from the dull mahogany front when I reflected that a simple panel div-ided me from the goal of my hopes; but I remembered my

delighted to bring some one; but hadn't we better send my man instead, so that I may stay with you?'

Miss Tita assented to this and I despatched my servant for the best doctor in the neighbourhood. I hurried downstairs with her, and on the way she told me that an hour after I quitted them in the afternoon Miss Bordereau had had an attack of 'oppression', a terrible difficulty in breathing. This had subsided but had left her so exhausted that she did not come up: she seemed all gone. I repeated that she was not gone, that she would not go yet; whereupon Miss Tita gave me a sharper sidelong glance than she had ever directed at me and said, 'Really, what do you mean? I suppose you don't accuse her of making-believe!' I forget what reply I made to this, but I grant that in my heart I thought the old woman capable of any weird manœuvre. Miss Tita wanted to know what I had done to her; her aunt had told her that I had made her so angry. I declared I had done nothing – I had been exceedingly careful; to which my companion rejoined that Miss Bordereau had assured her she had had a scene with me – a scene that had upset her. I answered with some resentment that it was a scene of her own making – that I couldn't think what she was angry with me for unless for not seeing my way to give a thousand pounds for the portrait of Jeffrey Aspern. 'And did she show you that? Oh gracious – oh deary me!' groaned Miss Tita, who appeared to feel that the situation was passing out of her control and that the elements of her fate were thickening around her. I said that I would give anything to possess it, yet that I had not a thousand pounds; but I stopped when we came to the door of Miss Bordereau's room. I had an immense curiosity to pass it, but I thought it my duty to represent to Miss Tita that if I made the invalid angry she ought perhaps to be spared the sight of me. 'The sight of you? Do you think she can *see*?' my companion demanded, almost with indignation. I did think so but forbore to say it, and I softly followed my conductress.

I remember that what I said to her as I stood for a moment beside the old woman's bed was, 'Does she never show you her eyes then? Have you never seen them?' Miss Bordereau had been divested of her green shade, but (it was not my fortune to behold Juliana in her nightcap) the upper half of her face was covered by the fall of a piece of dingy lacelike muslin, a sort of extemporized hood which, wound round her head, descended to the end of her nose, leaving nothing visible but her white withered cheeks and puckered mouth, closed tightly and, as it were, consciously. Miss Tita gave me a glance of surprise, evidently not seeing a reason for my impatience. 'You mean that she always wears something? She does it to preserve them.'

'Because they are so fine?'

'Oh, to-day, to-day!' And Miss Tita shook her head, speaking very low. 'But they used to be magnificent!'

'Yes indeed, we have Aspern's word for that.' And as I looked again at the old woman's wrappings I could imagine that she had not wished to allow people a reason to say that the great poet had overdone it. But I did not waste my time in considering Miss Bordereau, in whom the appearance of respiration was so slight as to suggest that no human attention could ever help her more. I turned my eyes all over the room, rummaging with them the closets, the chests of drawers, the tables. Miss Tita met them quickly and read, I think, what was in them; but she did not answer it, turning away restlessly, anxiously, so that I felt rebuked, with reason, for a preoccupation that was almost profane in the presence of our dying companion. All the same I took another look, endeavouring to pick out mentally the place to try first, for a person who should wish to put his hand on Miss Bordereau's papers directly after her death. The room was a dire confusion; it looked like the room of an old actress. There were clothes hanging over chairs, odd-looking, shabby bundles here and there, and various pasteboard boxes piled together, battered, bulging and discoloured, which might have been fifty years old. Miss Tita after a moment noticed the direction of my eyes again and, as if she guessed how I judged the air of the place (forgetting I had no business to judge it at all), said, perhaps to defend herself from the imputation of complicity in such untidiness:

'She likes it this way; we can't move things. There are old bandboxes she has had most of her life.' Then she added, half taking pity on my real thought, 'Those things were *there*.' And she pointed to a small, low trunk which stood under a sofa where there was just room for it. It appeared to be a queer, superannuated coffer, of painted wood, with elaborate handles and shrivelled straps and with the colour (it had last been endued with a coat of light green) much rubbed off. It evidently had travelled with Juliana in the olden time – in the days of her adventures, which it had shared. It would have made a strange figure arriving at a modern hotel.

'*Were* there – they aren't now?' I asked, startled by Miss Tita's implication.

She was going to answer, but at that moment the doctor came in – the doctor whom the little maid had been sent to fetch and whom she had at last overtaken. My servant, going on his own errand, had met her with her companion in tow, and in the sociable Venetian spirit, retracing his steps with them, had also come up to the threshold of Miss Bordereau's room, where I saw him peeping over the doctor's shoulder. I motioned him away the more instantly that the sight of his prying face reminded me that I myself had almost as little to do there – an admonition confirmed by the sharp way the little doctor looked at me, appearing to take me for a rival who had the field before him. He was a short, fat, brisk gentleman who wore the tall hat of his profession and seemed to look at everything but his patient. He looked particularly at me, as if it struck him that I should be better for a dose, so that I bowed to him and left him with the women, going down to smoke a cigar in the garden. I was nervous; I could not go further; I could not leave the place. I don't know exactly what I thought might happen, but it seemed to me important to be there. I wandered about in the alleys – the warm night had come on – smoking cigar after cigar and looking at the light in Miss Bordereau's windows. They were open now, I could see; the situation was different. Sometimes the light moved, but not quickly; it did not suggest the hurry of a crisis. Was the old woman dying or was she already dead? Had the doctor said that there was nothing to be done at her tremendous age but to let her quietly pass away; or had he simply announced with a look a little more conventional that the end of the end had come? Were the other two women moving about to perform the offices that follow in such a case? It made me uneasy not to be nearer, as if I thought the doctor himself might carry away the papers with him. I bit my cigar hard as it came over me again that perhaps there were now no papers to carry!

I wandered about for an hour – for an hour and a half. I looked out for Miss Tita at one of the windows, having a vague idea that she might come there to give me some sign. Would she not see the red tip of my cigar moving about in the dark and feel that I wanted eminently to know what the doctor had said? I am afraid it is a proof my anxieties had made me gross that I should have taken in some degree for granted that at such an hour, in the midst of the greatest change that could take place in her life, they were uppermost also in poor Miss Tita's mind. My servant came down and spoke to me; he knew nothing save that the doctor had gone after a visit of half an hour. If he had stayed half an hour then Miss Bordereau was still alive: it could not have taken so much time as that to enunciate the contrary. I sent the man out of the house; there were moments when the sense of his curiosity annoyed me and this was one of them. *He* had been watching my cigar-tip from an upper window, if Miss Tita had not; he could not know what I was after and I could not tell him, though I was conscious he had fantastic private theories about me which he thought fine and which I, had I known them, should have thought offensive.

I went upstairs at last but I ascended no higher than the sala. The door of Miss Bordereau's apartment was open, showing from the parlour the dimness of a poor candle. I went toward it with a light tread and at the same moment Miss Tita appeared and stood looking at me as I approached. 'She's better – she's better,' she said, even before I had asked. 'The doctor has given her something; she woke up, came back to life while he was there. He says there is no immediate danger.'

'No immediate danger? Surely he thinks her condition strange!'

'Yes, because she had been excited. That affects her dreadfully.'

'It will do so again then, because she excites herself. She did so this afternoon.'

'Yes; she mustn't come out any more,' said Miss Tita, with one of her lapses into a deeper placidity.

'What is the use of making such a remark as that if you begin to rattle her about again the first time she bids you?'

'I won't – I won't do it any more.'

'You must learn to resist her,' I went on.

'Oh yes, I shall; I shall do so better if you tell me it's right.'

'You mustn't do it for me; you must do it for yourself. It all comes back to you, if you are frightened.'

'Well, I am not frightened now,' said Miss Tita, cheerfully. 'She is very quiet.'

'Is she conscious again – does she speak?'

'No, she doesn't speak, but she takes my hand. She holds it fast.'

'Yes,' I rejoined, 'I can see what force she still has by the way she grabbed that picture this afternoon. But if she holds you fast how comes it that you are here?'

Miss Tita hesitated a moment; though her face was in deep shadow (she had her back to the light in the parlour and I had put down my own candle far off, near the door of the sala), I thought I saw her smile ingenuously. 'I came on purpose – I heard your step.'

'Why, I came on tiptoe, as inaudibly as possible.'

'Well, I heard you,' said Miss Tita.

'And is your aunt alone now?'

'Oh no; Olimpia is sitting there.'

On my side I hesitated. 'Shall we then step in there?' And I nodded at the parlour; I wanted more and more to be on the spot.

'We can't talk there – she will hear us.'

I was on the point of replying that in that case we would sit silent, but I was too conscious that this would not do, as there was something I desired immensely to ask her. So I proposed that we should walk a little in the sala, keeping more at the other end, where we should not disturb the old lady. Miss Tita assented unconditionally; the doctor was coming again, she said, and she would be there to meet him at the door. We strolled through the fine superfluous hall, where on the marble floor – particularly as at first we said nothing – our footsteps were more audible than I had expected. When we reached the other end – the wide window, inveterately closed, connecting with the balcony that overhung the canal – I suggested that we should remain there, as she would see the doctor arrive still better. I opened the window and we passed out on the balcony. The air of the canal seemed even heavier, hotter than that of the sala. The place was hushed and void; the quiet neighbourhood had gone to sleep. A lamp, here and there, over the narrow black water, glimmered in double; the voice of a man going homeward singing, with his jacket on his shoulder and his hat on his ear, came to us from a distance. This did not prevent the scene from being very *comme il faut*, as Miss Bordereau had called it the first time I saw her. Presently a gondola passed along the canal with its slow rhythmical plash, and as we listened we watched it in silence. It did not stop, it did not carry the doctor; and after it had gone on I said to Miss Tita:

'And where are they now – the things that were in the trunk?'

'In the trunk?'

'That green box you pointed out to me in her room. You said her papers had been there; you seemed to imply that she had transferred them.'

'Oh yes; they are not in the trunk,' said Miss Tita.

'May I ask if you have looked?'

'Yes, I have looked – for you.'

'How for me, dear Miss Tita? Do you mean you would have given them to me if you had found them?' I asked, almost trembling.

She delayed to reply and I waited. Suddenly she broke out, 'I don't know what I would do – what I wouldn't!'

'Would you look again – somewhere else?'

She had spoken with a strange, unexpected emotion, and she went on in the same tone: 'I can't – I can't – while she lies there. It isn't decent.'

'No, it isn't decent,' I replied, gravely. 'Let the poor lady rest in peace.' And the words, on my lips, were not hypocritical, for I felt reprimanded and shamed.

Miss Tita added in a moment, as if she had guessed this and were sorry for me, but at the same time wished to explain that I did drive her on or at least did insist too much: 'I can't deceive her that way. I can't deceive her – perhaps on her deathbed.'

'Heaven forbid I should ask you, though I have been guilty myself!'

'You have been guilty?'

'I have sailed under false colours.' I felt now as if I must tell her that I had given her an invented name, on account of my fear that her aunt would have heard of me and would refuse to take me in. I explained this and also that I had really been a party to the letter written to them by John Cumnor months before.

She listened with great attention, looking at me with parted lips, and when I had made my confession she said, 'Then your real name – what is it?' She repeated it over twice when I had told her, accompanying it with the exclamation 'Gracious, gracious!' Then she added, 'I like your own best.'

'So do I,' I said, laughing. 'Ouf! it's a relief to get rid of the other.'

'So it was a regular plot – a kind of conspiracy?'

'Oh, a conspiracy – we were only two,' I replied, leaving out Mrs Prest of course.

She hesitated; I thought she was perhaps going to say that we had been very base. But she remarked after a moment, in a candid, wondering way, 'How much you must want them!'

'Oh, I do, passionately!' I conceded, smiling. And this chance made me go on, forgetting my compunction of a moment before. 'How can she possibly have changed their place herself? How can she walk? How can she arrive at that sort of muscular exertion? How can she lift and carry things?'

'Oh, when one wants and when one has so much will!' said Miss Tita, as if she had thought over my question already herself and had simply had no choice but that answer – the idea that in the dead of night, or at some moment when the coast was clear, the old woman had been capable of a miraculous effort.

'Have you questioned Olimpia? Hasn't she helped her – hasn't she done it for her?' I asked; to which Miss Tita replied promptly and positively that their servant had had nothing to do with the matter, though without admitting definitely that she had spoken to her. It was as if she were a little shy, a little ashamed now of letting me see how much she had entered into my uneasiness and had me on her mind. Suddenly she said to me, without any immediate relevance:

'I feel as if you were a new person, now that you have got a new name.'

'It isn't a new one; it is a very good old one, thank heaven!'

She looked at me a moment. 'I do like it better.'

'Oh, if you didn't I would almost go on with the other!'

'Would you really?'

I laughed again, but for all answer to this inquiry I said, 'Of course if she can rummage about that way she can perfectly have burnt them.'

'You must wait – you must wait,' Miss Tita moralized mournfully; and her tone ministered little to my patience, for it seemed after all to accept that wretched possibility. I would teach myself to wait, I declared nevertheless; because in the first place I could not do otherwise and in the second I had her promise, given me the other night, that she would help me.

'Of course if the papers are gone that's no use,' she said; not as if she wished to recede, but only to be conscientious.

'Naturally. But if you could only find out!' I groaned, quivering again.

'I thought you said you would wait.'

'Oh, you mean wait even for that?'

'For what then?'

'Oh, nothing,' I replied, rather foolishly, being ashamed to tell her what had been implied in my submission to delay – the idea that she would do more than merely find out. I know not whether she guessed this; at all events she appeared to become aware of the necessity for being a little more rigid.

'I didn't promise to deceive, did I? I don't think I did.'

'It doesn't much matter whether you did or not, for you couldn't!'

I don't think Miss Tita would have contested this even had she not been diverted by our seeing the doctor's gondola shoot into the little canal and approach the house. I noted that he came as fast as if he believed that Miss Bordereau was still in danger. We looked down at him while he disembarked and then went back into the sala to meet him. When he came up however I naturally left Miss Tita to go off with him alone, only asking her leave to come back later for news.

I went out of the house and took a long walk, as far as the Piazza, where my restlessness declined to quit me. I was unable to sit down (it was very late now but there were people still at the little tables in front of the cafés); I could only walk round and round, and I did so half a dozen times. I was uncomfortable, but it gave me a certain pleasure to have told Miss Tita who I really was. At last I took my way home again, slowly getting all but inextricably lost, as I did whenever I went out in Venice: so that it was considerably past midnight when I reached my door. The sala, upstairs, was as dark as usual and my lamp as I crossed it found nothing satisfactory to show me. I was disappointed, for I had notified Miss Tita that I would come back for a report, and I thought she might have left a light there as a sign. The door of the ladies' apartment was closed; which seemed an intimation that my faltering friend had gone to bed, tired of waiting for me. I stood in the middle of the place, considering, hoping she would hear me and perhaps peep out, saying to myself too that she would never go to bed with her aunt in a state so critical; she would sit up and watch – she would be in a chair, in her dressing-gown. I went nearer the door; I stopped there and listened. I heard nothing at all and at last I tapped gently. No answer came and after another minute I turned the handle. There was no light in the room; this ought to have prevented me from going in, but it had no such effect. If I have candidly narrated the importunities, the indelicacies, of which my desire to possess myself of Jeffrey Aspern's papers had rendered me capable I need not shrink from confessing this last indiscretion. I think it was the worst thing I did; yet there were extenuating circumstances. I was deeply though doubtless not disinterestedly anxious for more news of the old lady, and Miss Tita had accepted from me, as it were, a rendezvous which it might have been a point of honour with me to keep. It may be said that her leaving the place dark was a positive sign that she released me, and to this I can only reply that I desired not to be released.

The door of Miss Bordereau's room was open and I could see beyond it the faintness of a taper. There was no sound – my footstep caused no one to stir. I came further into the room; I lingered there with my lamp in my hand. I wanted to give Miss Tita a chance to come to me if she were with her aunt, as she must be. I made no noise to call her; I only waited to see if she would not notice my light. She did not, and I explained this (I found afterwards I was right) by the idea that she had fallen asleep. If she had fallen asleep her aunt was not on her mind, and my explanation ought to have led me to go out as I had come. I must repeat again that it did not, for I found myself at the same moment thinking of something else. I had no definite purpose, no bad intention, but I felt myself held to the spot by an acute, though absurd, sense of opportunity. For what I could not have said, inasmuch as it was not in my mind that I might commit a theft. Even if it had been I was confronted with the evident fact that Miss Bordereau did not leave her secretary, her cupboard and the drawers of her tables gaping. I had no keys, no tools and no ambition to smash her furniture. None the less it came to me that I was now, perhaps alone, unmolested, at the hour of temptation and secrecy, nearer to the tormenting treasure than I had ever been. I held up my lamp, let the light play on the different objects as if it could tell me something. Still there came no movement from the other room. If Miss Tita was sleeping she was sleeping sound. Was she doing so – generous creature – on purpose to leave me the field? Did she know I was there and was she just keeping quiet to see what I would do – what I *could* do? But what could I do, when it came to that? She herself knew even better than I how little.

I stopped in front of the secretary, looking at it very idiotic-ally; for what had it to say to me after all? In the first place it was locked, and in the second it almost surely contained nothing in which I was interested. Ten to one the papers had been destroyed; and even if they had not been destroyed the old woman would not have put them in such a place as that after removing them from the green trunk – would not have transferred them, if she had the idea of their safety on her brain, from the better hiding-place to the worse. The secretary was more conspicuous, more accessible in a room in which she could no longer mount guard. It opened with a key, but there was a little brass handle, like a button, as well; I saw this as I played my lamp over it. I did something more than this at that moment: I caught a glimpse of the possibility that Miss Tita wished me really to understand. If she did not wish me to understand, if she wished me to keep away, why had she not locked the door of communication between the sitting-room and the sala? That would have been a definite sign that I was to leave them alone. If I did not leave them alone she meant me to come for a purpose – a purpose now indicated by the quick, fantastic idea that to oblige me she had unlocked the secretary. She had not left the key, but the lid would probably move if I touched the button. This theory fascinated me, and I bent over very close to judge. I did not propose to do anything, not even – not in the least – to let down the lid; I only wanted to test my theory, to see if the cover *would* move. I touched the button with my hand – a mere touch would tell me; and as I did so (it is embarrassing for me to relate it), I looked over my shoulder. It was a chance, an instinct, for I had not heard anything. I almost let my luminary drop and certainly I stepped back, straightening myself up at what I saw. Miss Bordereau stood there in her night-dress, in the doorway of her room, watching me; her hands were raised, she had lifted the everlasting curtain that covered half her face, and for the first, the last, the only time I beheld her extraordinary eyes. They glared at me, they made me horribly ashamed. I never shall forget her strange little bent white tottering figure, with its lifted head, her attitude, her expression; neither shall I forget the tone in which as I turned, looking at her, she hissed out passionately, furiously:

'Ah, you publishing scoundrel!'

I know not what I stammered, to excuse myself, to explain;

but I went towards her, to tell her I meant no harm. She waved me off with her old hands, retreating before me in horror; and the next thing I knew she had fallen back with a quick spasm, as if death had descended on her, into Miss Tita's arms.

IX

I left Venice the next morning, as soon as I learnt that the old lady had not succumbed, as I feared at the moment, to the shock I had given her – the shock I may also say she had given me. How in the world could I have supposed her capable of getting out of bed by herself? I failed to see Miss Tita before going; I only saw the *donna*, whom I entrusted with a note for her younger mistress. In this note I mentioned that I should be absent but for a few days. I went to Treviso, to Bassano, to Castelfranco;[31] I took walks and drives and looked at musty old churches with ill-lighted pictures and spent hours seated smoking at the doors of cafés, where there were flies and yellow curtains, on the shady side of sleepy little squares. In spite of these pastimes, which were mechanical and perfunctory, I scantily enjoyed my journey: there was too strong a taste of the disagreeable in my life. It had been devilish awkward, as the young men say, to be found by Miss Bordereau in the dead of night examining the attachment of her bureau; and it had not been less so to have to believe for a good many hours afterward that it was highly probable I had killed her. In writing to Miss Tita I attempted to minimize these irregularities; but as she gave me no word of answer I could not know what impression I made upon her. It rankled in my mind that I had been called a publishing scoundrel, for certainly I did publish and certainly I had not been very delicate. There was a moment when I stood convinced that the only way to make up for this latter fault was to take myself away altogether on the instant; to sacrifice my hopes and relieve the two poor women for ever of the oppression of my intercourse. Then I reflected that I had better try a short absence first, for I must already have had a sense (unexpressed and dim) that in disappearing completely it would not be merely my own hopes that I should condemn to extinction. It would perhaps be sufficient if I stayed away long enough to give the elder lady time to think she was rid of me. That she would wish to be rid of me after this (if I was not rid of her) was now not to be doubted: that nocturnal scene would have cured her of the disposition to put up with my company for the sake of my dollars. I said to myself that after all I could not abandon Miss Tita, and I continued to say this even while I observed that she quite failed to comply with my earnest request (I had given her two or three addresses, at little towns, *poste restante*)[32] that she would let me know how she was getting on. I would have made my servant write to me but that he was unable to manage a pen. It struck me there was a kind of scorn in Miss Tita's silence (little disdainful as she had ever been), so that I was uncomfortable and sore. I had scruples about going back and yet I had others about not doing so, for I wanted to put myself on a better footing. The end of it was that I did return to Venice on the twelfth day; and as my gondola gently bumped against Miss Bordereau's steps a certain palpitation of suspense told me that I had done myself a violence in holding off so long.

I had faced about so abruptly that I had not telegraphed to my servant. He was therefore not at the station to meet me, but he poked out his head from an upper window when I reached the house. 'They have put her into the earth, *la vecchia*,'[33] he said to me in the lower hall, while he shouldered my valise; and he grinned and almost winked, as if he knew I should be pleased at the news.

'She's dead!' I exclaimed, giving him a very different look.

'So it appears, since they have buried her.'

'It's all over? When was the funeral?'

'The other yesterday. But a funeral you could scarcely call it, signore; it was a dull little passeggio of two gondolas. Poveretta!'[34] the man continued, referring apparently to Miss Tita. His conception of funerals was apparently that they were mainly to amuse the living.

I wanted to know about Miss Tita – how she was and where she was – but I asked him no more questions till we had got

upstairs. Now that the fact had met me I took a bad view of it,
especially of the idea that poor Miss Tita had had to manage by
herself after the end. What did she know about arrangements,
about the steps to take in such a case? Poveretta indeed! I could
only hope that the doctor had given her assistance and that she
had not been neglected by the old friends of whom she had told
me, the little band of the faithful whose fidelity consisted in
coming to the house once a year. I elicited from my servant that
two old ladies and an old gentleman had in fact rallied round
Miss Tita and had supported her (they had come for her in a
gondola of their own) during the journey to the cemetery, the
little red-walled island of tombs which lies to the north of the
town, on the way to Murano.[35] It appeared from these circumstances that the Misses Bordereau were Catholics, a discovery I
had never made, as the old woman could not go to church and
her niece, so far as I perceived, either did not or went only to
early mass in the parish, before I was stirring. Certainly even
the priests respected their seclusion; I had never caught the
whisk of the curato's skirt. That evening, an hour later, I sent
my servant down with five words written on a card, to ask
Miss Tita if she would see me for a few moments. She was not
in the house, where he had sought her, he told me when he
came back, but in the garden walking about to refresh herself
and gathering flowers. He had found her there and she would
be very happy to see me.

I went down and passed half an hour with poor Miss Tita.
She had always had a look of musty mourning (as if she were
wearing out old robes of sorrow that would not come to an
end), and in this respect there was no appreciable change in her
appearance. But she evidently had been crying, crying a great
deal – simply, satisfyingly, refreshingly, with a sort of primi-
tive, retarded sense of loneliness and violence. But she had
none of the formalism or the self-consciousness of grief, and I
was almost surprised to see her standing there in the first dusk
with her hands full of flowers, smiling at me with her reddened
eyes. Her white face, in the frame of her mantilla, looked
longer, leaner than usual. I had had an idea that she would be
a good deal disgusted with me – would consider that I ought to

have been on the spot to advise her, to help her; and, though I was sure there was no rancour in her composition and no great conviction of the importance of her affairs, I had prepared myself for a difference in her manner, for some little injured look, half familiar, half estranged, which should say to my conscience, 'Well, you are a nice person to have professed things!' But historic truth compels me to declare that Tita Bordereau's countenance expressed unqualified pleasure in seeing her late aunt's lodger. That touched him extremely and he thought it simplified his situation until he found it did not. I was as kind to her that evening as I knew how to be, and I walked about the garden with her for half an hour. There was no explanation of any sort between us; I did not ask her why she had not answered my letter. Still less did I repeat what I had said to her in that communication; if she chose to let me suppose that she had forgotten the position in which Miss Bordereau surprised me that night and the effect of the discovery on the old woman I was quite willing to take it that way: I was grateful to her for not treating me as if I had killed her aunt.

We strolled and strolled and really not much passed between us save the recognition of her bereavement, conveyed in my manner and in a visible air that she had of depending on me now, since I let her see that I took an interest in her. Miss Tita had none of the pride that makes a person wish to preserve the look of independence; she did not in the least pretend that she knew at present what would become of her. I forbore to touch particularly on that however, for I certainly was not prepared to say that I would take charge of her. I was cautious; not ignobly, I think, for I felt that her knowledge of life was so small that in her unsophisticated vision there would be no reason why – since I seemed to pity her – I should not look after her. She told me how her aunt had died, very peacefully at the last, and how everything had been done afterwards by the care of her good friends (fortunately, thanks to me, she said, smiling, there was money in the house; and she repeated that when once the Italians like you they are your friends for life); and when we had gone into this she asked me about my *giro*, my impressions, the places I had seen. I told her what I could, making it up partly, I am afraid, as in my depression I had not seen much; and after she had heard me she exclaimed, quite as if she had forgotten her aunt and her sorrow, 'Dear, dear, how much I should like to do such things – to take a little journey!' It came over me for the moment that I ought to propose some tour, say I would take her anywhere she liked; and I remarked at any rate that some excursion – to give her a change – might be managed: we would think of it, talk it over. I said never a word to her about the Aspern documents; asked no questions as to what she had ascertained or what had otherwise happened with regard to them before Miss Bordereau's death. It was not that I was not on pins and needles to know, but that I thought it more decent not to betray my anxiety so soon after the catastrophe. I hoped she herself would say something, but she never glanced that way, and I thought this natural at the time. Later however, that night, it occurred to me that her silence was somewhat strange; for if she had talked of my movements, of anything so detached as the Giorgione at Castelfranco,[36] she might have alluded to what she could easily remember was in my mind. It was not to be supposed that the emotion produced by her aunt's death had blotted out the recollection that I was interested in that lady's relics, and I fidgeted afterwards as it came to me that her reticence might very possibly mean simply that nothing had been found. We separated in the garden (it was she who said she must go in); now that she was alone in the rooms I felt that (judged, at any rate, by Venetian ideas) I was on rather a different footing in regard to visiting her there. As I shook hands with her for good-night I asked her if she had any general plan – had thought over what she had better do. 'Oh yes, oh yes, but I haven't settled anything yet,' she replied, quite cheerfully. Was her cheerfulness explained by the impression that I would settle for her?

I was glad the next morning that we had neglected practical questions, for this gave me a pretext for seeing her again immediately. There was a very practical question to be touched upon. I owed it to her to let her know formally that of course I did not expect her to keep me on as a lodger, and also to show some interest in her own tenure, what she might have on her hands in the way of a lease. But I was not destined, as it happened, to converse with her for more than an instant on either of these points. I sent her no message; I simply went down to the sala and walked to and fro there. I knew she would come out; she would very soon discover I was there. Somehow I preferred not to be shut up with her; gardens and big halls seemed better places to talk. It was a splendid morning, with something in the air that told of the waning of the long Venetian summer; a freshness from the sea which stirred the flowers in the garden and made a pleasant draught in the house, less shuttered and darkened now than when the old woman was alive. It was the beginning of autumn, of the end of the golden months. With this it was the end of my experiment – or would be in the course of half an hour, when I should really have learned that the papers had been reduced to ashes. After that there would be nothing left for me but to go to the station; for seriously (and as it struck me in the morning light) I could not linger there to act as guardian to a piece of middle-aged female helplessness. If she had not saved the papers wherein should I be indebted to her? I think I winced a little as I asked myself how much, if she *had* saved them, I should have to recognize and, as it were, to reward such a courtesy. Might not that circumstance after all saddle me with a guardianship? If this idea did not make me more uncomfortable as I walked up and down it was because I was convinced I had nothing to look to. If the old woman had not destroyed everything before she pounced upon me in the parlour she had done so afterwards.

It took Miss Tita rather longer than I had expected to guess that I was there; but when at last she came out she looked at me without surprise. I said to her that I had been waiting for her and she asked why I had not let her know. I was glad the next day that I had checked myself before remarking that I had wished to see if a friendly intuition would not tell her: it became a satisfaction to me that I had not indulged in that rather tender joke. What I did say was virtually the truth – that I was too nervous, since I expected her now to settle my fate.

'Your fate?' said Miss Tita, giving me a queer look; and as she spoke I noticed a rare change in her. She was different from what she had been the evening before – less natural, less quiet. She had been crying the day before and she was not crying now, and yet she struck me as less confident. It was as if something had happened to her during the night, or at least as if she had thought of something that troubled her – something in particular that affected her relations with me, made them more embarrassing and complicated. Had she simply perceived that her aunt's not being there now altered my position?

'I mean about our papers. *Are* there any? You must know now.'

'Yes, there are a great many; more than I supposed.' I was struck with the way her voice trembled as she told me this.

'Do you mean that you have got them in there – and that I may see them?'

'I don't think you can see them,' said Miss Tita, with an extraordinary expression of entreaty in her eyes, as if the dearest hope she had in the world now was that I would not take them from her. But how could she expect me to make such a sacrifice as that after all that had passed between us? What had I come back to Venice for but to see them, to take them? My delight at learning they were still in existence was such that if the poor woman had gone down on her knees to beseech me never to mention them again I would have treated the proceeding as a bad joke. 'I have got them but I can't show them,' she added.

'Not even to me? Ah, Miss Tita!' I groaned, with a voice of infinite remonstrance and reproach.

She coloured and the tears came back to her eyes; I saw that it cost her a kind of anguish to take such a stand but that a dreadful sense of duty had descended upon her. It made me quite sick to find myself confronted with that particular obstacle; all the more that it appeared to me I had been extremely encouraged to leave it out of account. I almost considered that Miss Tita had assured me that if she had no greater hindrance than that—! 'You don't mean to say you made her a deathbed promise? It was precisely against your doing anything of that sort that I thought I was safe. Oh, I would rather she had burned the papers outright than that!'

'No, it isn't a promise,' said Miss Tita.

'Pray what is it then?'

She hesitated and then she said, 'She tried to burn them, but I prevented it. She had hid them in her bed.'

'In her bed?'

'Between the mattresses. That's where she put them when she took them out of the trunk. I can't understand how she did it, because Olimpia didn't help her. She tells me so and I believe her. My aunt only told her afterwards, so that she shouldn't touch the bed – anything but the sheets. So it was badly made,' added Miss Tita, simply.

'I should think so! And how did she try to burn them?'

'She didn't try much; she was too weak, those last days. But she told me – she charged me. Oh, it was terrible! She couldn't speak after that night; she could only make signs.'

'And what did you do?'

'I took them away. I locked them up.'

'In the secretary?'

'Yes, in the secretary,' said Miss Tita, reddening again.

'Did you tell her you would burn them?'

'No, I didn't – on purpose.'

'On purpose to gratify me?'

'Yes, only for that.'

'And what good will you have done me if after all you won't show them?'

'Oh, none; I know that – I know that.'

'And did she believe you had destroyed them?'

'I don't know what she believed at the last. I couldn't tell – she was too far gone.'

'Then if there was no promise and no assurance I can't see what ties you.'

'Oh, she hated it so – she hated it so! She was so jealous. But here's the portrait – you may have that,' Miss Tita announced, taking the little picture, wrapped up in the same manner in which her aunt had wrapped it, out of her pocket.

'I may have it – do you mean you give it to me?' I questioned, staring, as it passed into my hand.

'Oh yes.'

'But it's worth money – a large sum.'

'Well!' said Miss Tita, still with her strange look.

I did not know what to make of it, for it could scarcely mean that she wanted to bargain like her aunt. She spoke as if she wished to make me a present. 'I can't take it from you as a gift,' I said, 'and yet I can't afford to pay you for it according to the ideas Miss Bordereau had of its value. She rated it at a thousand pounds.'

'Couldn't we sell it?' asked Miss Tita.

'God forbid! I prefer the picture to the money.'

'Well then keep it.'

'You are very generous.'

'So are you.'

'I don't know why you should think so,' I replied, and this was a truthful speech, for the singular creature appeared to have some very fine reference in her mind, which I did not in the least seize.

'Well, you have made a great difference for me,' said Miss Tita.

I looked at Jeffrey Aspern's face in the little picture, partly in order not to look at that of my interlocutress, which had begun to trouble me, even to frighten me a little – it was so self-conscious, so unnatural. I made no answer to this last declaration; I only privately consulted Jeffrey Aspern's delightful eyes with my own (they were so young and brilliant, and yet so wise, so full of vision); I asked him what on earth was the matter with Miss Tita. He seemed to smile at me with friendly mockery, as if he were amused at my case. I had got into a pickle for him – as if he needed it! He was unsatisfactory, for the only moment since I had known him. Nevertheless, now that I held the little picture in my hand I felt that it would be a precious possession. 'Is this a bribe to make me give up the papers?' I demanded in a moment, perversely. 'Much as I value it, if I were to be obliged to choose, the papers are what I should prefer. Ah, but ever so much!'

'How can you choose – how can you choose?' Miss Tita asked, slowly, lamentably.

'I see! Of course there is nothing to be said, if you regard the interdiction that rests upon you as quite insurmountable. In this case it must seem to you that to part with them would be an impiety of the worst kind, a simple sacrilege!'

Miss Tita shook her head, full of her dolefulness. 'You would understand if you had known her. I'm afraid,' she quavered suddenly – 'I'm afraid! She was terrible when she was angry.'

'Yes, I saw something of that, that night. She was terrible. Then I saw her eyes. Lord, they were fine!'

'I see them – they stare at me in the dark!' said Miss Tita.

'You are nervous, with all you have been through.'

'Oh yes, very – very!'

'You mustn't mind; that will pass away,' I said, kindly. Then I added, resignedly, for it really seemed to me that I must accept the situation, 'Well, so it is, and it can't be helped. I must renounce.' Miss Tita, at this, looking at me, gave a low, soft moan, and I went on: 'I only wish to heaven she had destroyed them; then there would be nothing more to say. And I can't understand why, with her ideas, she didn't.'

'Oh, she lived on them!' said Miss Tita.

'You can imagine whether that makes me want less to see them,' I answered, smiling. 'But don't let me stand here as if I had it in my soul to tempt you to do anything base. Naturally you will understand I give up my rooms. I leave Venice immediately.' And I took up my hat, which I had placed on a chair. We were still there rather awkwardly, on our feet, in the middle of the sala. She had left the door of the apartments open behind her but she had not led me that way.

A kind of spasm came into her face as she saw me take my hat. 'Immediately – do you mean to-day?' The tone of the words was tragical – they were a cry of desolation.

'Oh no; not so long as I can be of the least service to you.'

'Well, just a day or two more – just two or three days,' she panted. Then controlling herself she added in another manner, 'She wanted to say something to me – the last day – something very particular, but she couldn't.'

'Something very particular?'

'Something more about the papers.'

'And did you guess – have you any idea?'

'No, I have thought – but I don't know. I have thought all kinds of things.'

'And for instance?'

'Well, that if you were a relation it would be different.'

'If I were a relation?'

'If you were not a stranger. Then it would be the same for you as for me. Anything that is mine – would be yours, and you could do what you like. I couldn't prevent you – and you would have no responsibility.'

She brought out this droll explanation with a little nervous rush, as if she were speaking words she had got by heart. They gave me an impression of subtlety and at first I failed to follow. But after a moment her face helped me to see further, and then a light came into my mind. It was embarrassing, and I bent my head over Jeffrey Aspern's portrait. What an odd expression was in his face! 'Get out of it as you can, my dear fellow!' I put the picture into the pocket of my coat and said to Miss Tita, 'Yes, I'll sell it for you. I shan't get a thousand pounds by any means, but I shall get something good.'

She looked at me with tears in her eyes, but she seemed to try to smile as she remarked, 'We can divide the money.'

'No, no, it shall be all yours.' Then I went on, 'I think I know what your poor aunt wanted to say. She wanted to give directions that her papers should be buried with her.'

Miss Tita appeared to consider this suggestion for a moment; after which she declared, with striking decision, 'Oh no, she wouldn't have thought that safe!'

'It seems to me nothing could be safer.'

'She had an idea that when people want to publish they are capable—' And she paused, blushing.

'Of violating a tomb?[37] Mercy on us, what must she have thought of me!'

'She was not just, she was not generous!' Miss Tita cried with sudden passion.

The light that had come into my mind a moment before increased. 'Ah, don't say that, for we *are* a dreadful race.' Then I pursued, 'If she left a will, that may give you some idea.'

'I have found nothing of the sort – she destroyed it. She was very fond of me,' Miss Tita added, incongruously. 'She wanted me to be happy. And if any person should be kind to me – she wanted to speak of that.'

I was almost awestricken at the astuteness with which the good lady found herself inspired, transparent astuteness as it was and sewn, as the phrase is, with white thread. 'Depend upon it she didn't want to make any provision that would be agreeable to me.'

'No, not to you but to me. She knew I should like it if you could carry out your idea. Not because she cared for you but because she did think of me,' Miss Tita went on, with her unexpected, persuasive volubility. 'You could see them – you could use them.' She stopped, seeing that I perceived the sense of that conditional – stopped long enough for me to give some sign which I did not give. She must have been conscious however that though my face showed the greatest embarrassment that was ever painted on a human countenance it was not set as a stone, it was also full of compassion. It was a comfort to me a long time afterwards to consider that she could not have seen in me the smallest symptom of disrespect. 'I don't know what to do; I'm too tormented, I'm too ashamed!' she continued, with vehemence. Then turning away from me and burying her face in her hands she burst into a flood of tears. If she did not know what to do it may be imagined whether I did any better. I stood there dumb, watching her while her sobs resounded in the great empty hall. In a moment she was facing me again, with her streaming eyes. 'I would give you everything – and she would understand, where she is – she would forgive me!'

'Ah, Miss Tita – ah, Miss Tita,' I stammered, for all reply. I did not know what to do, as I say, but at a venture I made a wild, vague movement, in consequence of which I found myself at the door. I remember standing there and saying, 'It wouldn't do – it wouldn't do!' pensively, awkwardly, grotesquely, while I looked away to the opposite end of the sala as if there were a beautiful view there. The next thing I remember is that I was downstairs and out of the house. My gondola was there and my gondolier, reclining on the cushions, sprang up as soon as

he saw me. I jumped in and to his usual '*Dove commanda?*'[38] I
replied, in a tone that made him stare, 'Anywhere, anywhere;
out into the lagoon!'

He rowed me away and I sat there prostrate, groaning softly
to myself, with my hat pulled over my face. What in the name
of the preposterous did she mean if she did not mean to offer
me her hand? That was the price – that was the price! And did
she think I wanted it, poor deluded, infatuated, extravagant
lady? My gondolier, behind me, must have seen my ears red as
I wondered, sitting there under the fluttering *tenda*,[39] with my
hidden face, noticing nothing as we passed – wondered whether
her delusion, her infatuation had been my own reckless work.
Did she think I had made love to her, even to get the papers? I
had not, I had not; I repeated that over to myself for an hour,
for two hours, till I was wearied if not convinced. I don't know
where my gondolier took me; we floated aimlessly about on the
lagoon, with slow, rare strokes. At last I became conscious that
we were near the Lido, far up, on the right hand, as you turn
your back to Venice, and I made him put me ashore. I wanted
to walk, to move, to shed some of my bewilderment. I crossed
the narrow strip and got to the sea-beach – I took my way
toward Malamocco.[40] But presently I flung myself down again
on the warm sand, in the breeze, on the coarse dry grass. It
took it out of me to think I had been so much at fault, that I
had unwittingly but none the less deplorably trifled. But I had
not given her cause – distinctly I had not. I had said to Mrs Prest
that I would make love to her; but it had been a joke without
consequences and I had never said it to Tita Bordereau. I had
been as kind as possible, because I really liked her; but since
when had that become a crime where a woman of such an age
and such an appearance was concerned? I am far from remembering clearly the succession of events and feelings during this
long day of confusion, which I spent entirely in wandering
about, without going home, until late at night; it only comes
back to me that there were moments when I pacified my conscience and others when I lashed it into pain. I did not laugh all
day – that I do recollect; the case, however it might have struck
others, seemed to me so little amusing. It would have been

better perhaps for me to feel the comic side of it. At any rate, whether I had given cause or not it went without saying that I could not pay the price. I could not accept. I could not, for a bundle of tattered papers, marry a ridiculous, pathetic, provincial old woman. It was a proof that she did not think the idea would come to me, her having determined to suggest it herself in that practical, argumentative, heroic way, in which the timidity however had been so much more striking than the boldness that her reasons appeared to come first and her feelings afterward.

As the day went on I grew to wish that I had never heard of Aspern's relics, and I cursed the extravagant curiosity that had put John Cumnor on the scent of them. We had more than enough material without them and my predicament was the just punishment of that most fatal of human follies, our not having known when to stop. It was very well to say it was no predicament, that the way out was simple, that I had only to leave Venice by the first train in the morning, after writing a note to Miss Tita, to be placed in her hand as soon as I got clear of the house; for it was a strong sign that I was embarrassed that when I tried to make up the note in my mind in advance (I would put it on paper as soon as I got home, before going to bed), I could not think of anything but 'How can I thank you for the rare confidence you have placed in me?' That would never do; it sounded exactly as if an acceptance were to follow. Of course I might go away without writing a word, but that would be brutal and my idea was still to exclude brutal solutions. As my confusion cooled I was lost in wonder at the importance I had attached to Miss Bordereau's crumpled scraps; the thought of them became odious to me and I was as vexed with the old witch for the superstition that had prevented her from destroying them as I was with myself for having already spent more money than I could afford in attempting to control their fate. I forget what I did, where I went after leaving the Lido and at what hour or with what recovery of composure I made my way back to my boat. I only know that in the afternoon, when the air was aglow with the sunset, I was standing before the church of Saints John and Paul and looking up at the

small square-jawed face of Bartolommeo Colleoni,[41] the terrible *condottiere* who sits so sturdily astride of his huge bronze
horse, on the high pedestal on which Venetian gratitude main-
tains him. The statue is incomparable, the finest of all mounted
figures, unless that of Marcus Aurelius, who rides benignant
before the Roman Capitol, be finer: but I was not thinking of
that; I only found myself staring at the triumphant captain as if
he had an oracle on his lips. The western light shines into all his
grimness at that hour and makes it wonderfully personal. But
he continued to look far over my head, at the red immersion of
another day – he had seen so many go down into the lagoon
through the centuries – and if he were thinking of battles and
stratagems they were of a different quality from any I had to
tell him of. He could not direct me what to do, gaze up at him
as I might. Was it before this or after that I wandered about for
an hour in the small canals, to the continued stupefaction of
my gondolier, who had never seen me so restless and yet so
void of a purpose and could extract from me no order but 'Go
anywhere – everywhere – all over the place'? He reminded me
that I had not lunched and expressed therefore respectfully the
hope that I would dine earlier. He had had long periods of leisure during the day, when I had left the boat and rambled, so
that I was not obliged to consider him, and I told him that that
day, for a change, I would touch no meat. It was an effect of
poor Miss Tita's proposal, not altogether auspicious, that I had
quite lost my appetite. I don't know why it happened that on
this occasion I was more than ever struck with that queer air of
sociability, of cousinship and family life, which makes up half
the expression of Venice. Without streets and vehicles, the
uproar of wheels, the brutality of horses, and with its little
winding ways where people crowd together, where voices
sound as in the corridors of a house, where the human step
circulates as if it skirted the angles of furniture and shoes never
wear out, the place has the character of an immense collective
apartment, in which Piazza San Marco is the most ornamented
corner and palaces and churches, for the rest, play the part of
great divans of repose, tables of entertainment, expanses of
decoration. And somehow the splendid common domicile,

familiar, domestic and resonant, also resembles a theatre, with actors clicking over bridges and, in straggling processions, tripping along fondamentas.[42] As you sit in your gondola the footways that in certain parts edge the canals assume to the eye the importance of a stage, meeting it at the same angle, and the Venetian figures, moving to and fro against the battered scenery of their little houses of comedy, strike you as members of an endless dramatic troupe.

I went to bed that night very tired, without being able to compose a letter to Miss Tita. Was this failure the reason why I became conscious the next morning as soon as I awoke of a determination to see the poor lady again the first moment she would receive me? That had something to do with it, but what had still more was the fact that during my sleep a very odd revulsion had taken place in my spirit. I found myself aware of this almost as soon as I opened my eyes; it made me jump out of my bed with the movement of a man who remembers that he has left the house-door ajar or a candle burning under a shelf. Was I still in time to save my goods? That question was in my heart; for what had now come to pass was that in the unconscious cerebration of sleep I had swung back to a passionate appreciation of Miss Bordereau's papers. They were now more precious than ever and a kind of ferocity had come into my desire to possess them. The condition Miss Tita had attached to the possession of them no longer appeared an obstacle worth thinking of, and for an hour, that morning, my repentant imagination brushed it aside. It was absurd that I should be able to invent nothing; absurd to renounce so easily and turn away helpless from the idea that the only way to get hold of the papers was to unite myself to her for life. I would not unite myself and yet I would have them. I must add that by the time I sent down to ask if she would see me I had invented no alternative, though to do so I had had all the time that I was dressing. This failure was humiliating, yet what could the alternative be? Miss Tita sent back word that I might come; and as I descended the stairs and crossed the sala to her door – this time she received me in her aunt's forlorn parlour – I hoped she would not think my errand was to tell her I accepted her hand. She

certainly would have made the day before the reflection that I
declined it.

As soon as I came into the room I saw that she had drawn
this inference, but I also saw something which had not been in
my forecast. Poor Miss Tita's sense of her failure had produced
an extraordinary alteration in her, but I had been too full of my
literary concupiscence to think of that. Now I perceived it; I
can scarcely tell how it startled me. She stood in the middle of
the room with a face of mildness bent upon me, and her look
of forgiveness, of absolution made her angelic. It beautified
her; she was younger; she was not a ridiculous old woman.
This optical trick gave her a sort of phantasmagoric brightness,
and while I was still the victim of it I heard a whisper somewhere in the depths of my conscience: 'Why not, after all – why
not?' It seemed to me I was ready to pay the price. Still more
distinctly however than the whisper I heard Miss Tita's own
voice. I was so struck with the different effect she made upon
me that at first I was not clearly aware of what she was saying;
then I perceived she had bade me good-bye – she said something about hoping I should be very happy.

'Good-bye – good-bye?' I repeated, with an inflection inter-
rogative and probably foolish.

I saw she did not feel the interrogation, she only heard the
words; she had strung herself up to accepting our separation and
they fell upon her ear as a proof. 'Are you going to-day?' she
asked. 'But it doesn't matter, for whenever you go I shall not see
you again. I don't want to.' And she smiled strangely, with an
infinite gentleness. She had never doubted that I had left her the
day before in horror. How could she, since I had not come back
before night to contradict, even as a simple form, such an idea?
And now she had the force of soul – Miss Tita with force of soul
was a new conception – to smile at me in her humiliation.

'What shall you do – where shall you go?' I asked.

'Oh, I don't know. I have done the great thing. I have
destroyed the papers.'

'Destroyed them?' I faltered.

'Yes; what was I to keep them for? I burnt them last night,
one by one, in the kitchen.'

'One by one?' I repeated, mechanically.

'It took a long time – there were so many.' The room seemed to go round me as she said this and a real darkness for a moment descended upon my eyes. When it passed Miss Tita was there still, but the transfiguration was over and she had changed back to a plain, dingy, elderly person. It was in this character she spoke as she said, 'I can't stay with you longer, I can't'; and it was in this character that she turned her back upon me, as I had turned mine upon her twenty-four hours before, and moved to the door of her room. Here she did what I had not done when I quitted her – she paused long enough to give me one look. I have never forgotten it and I sometimes still suffer from it, though it was not resentful. No, there was no resentment, nothing hard or vindictive in poor Miss Tita; for when, later, I sent her in exchange for the portrait of Jeffrey Aspern a larger sum of money than I had hoped to be able to gather for her, writing to her that I had sold the picture, she kept it with thanks; she never sent it back. I wrote to her that I had sold the picture, but I admitted to Mrs Prest, at the time (I met her in London, in the autumn), that it hangs above my writing-table. When I look at it my chagrin at the loss of the letters becomes almost intolerable.[43]

THE LESSON OF
THE MASTER

He had been informed that the ladies were at church, but that
was corrected by what he saw from the top of the steps (they
descended from a great height in two arms, with a circular
sweep of the most charming effect) at the threshold of the door
which, from the long, bright gallery, overlooked the immense
lawn. Three gentlemen, on the grass, at a distance, sat under
the great trees; but the fourth figure was not a gentleman, the
one in the crimson dress which made so vivid a spot, told so as
a 'bit of colour' amid the fresh, rich green. The servant had
come so far with Paul Overt to show him the way and had
asked him if he wished first to go to his room. The young man
declined this privilege, having no disorder to repair after so
short and easy a journey and liking to take a general perceptive
possession of the new scene immediately, as he always did. He
stood there a little with his eyes on the group and on the admirable picture – the wide grounds of an old country-house near
London (that only made it better), on a splendid Sunday in
June. 'But that lady, who is she?' he said to the servant before
the man went away.

'I think it's Mrs St George, sir.'

'Mrs St George, the wife of the distinguished—' Then Paul
Overt checked himself, doubting whether the footman would
know.

'Yes, sir – probably, sir,' said the servant, who appeared to
wish to intimate that a person staying at Summersoft would
naturally be, if only by alliance, distinguished. His manner,
however, made poor Overt feel for the moment as if he himself
were but little so.

'And the gentlemen?' he inquired.

'Well, sir, one of them is General Fancourt.'

'Ah yes, I know; thank you.' General Fancourt was distinguished, there was no doubt of that, for something he had done, or perhaps even had not done (the young man could not remember which) some years before in India. The servant went away, leaving the glass doors open into the gallery, and Paul Overt remained at the head of the wide double staircase, saying to himself that the place was sweet and promised a pleasant visit, while he leaned on the balustrade of fine old ironwork which, like all the other details, was of the same period as the house. It all went together and spoke in one voice – a rich English voice of the early part of the eighteenth century. It might have been church-time on a summer's day in the reign of Queen Anne; the stillness was too perfect to be modern, the nearness counted so as distance and there was something so fresh and sound in the originality of the large smooth house, the expanse of whose beautiful brickwork, which had been kept clear of messy creepers (as a woman with a rare complexion disdains a veil), was pink rather than red. When Paul Overt perceived that the people under the trees were noticing him he turned back through the open doors into the great gallery which was the pride of the place. It traversed the mansion from end to end and seemed – with its bright colours, its high panelled windows, its faded, flowered chintzes, its quickly-recognized portraits and pictures, the blue and white china of its cabinets and the attenuated festoons and rosettes of its ceiling – a cheerful upholstered avenue into the other century.

The young man was slightly nervous; that belonged in general to his disposition as a student of fine prose, with his dose of the artist's restlessness; and there was a particular excitement in the idea that Henry St George might be a member of the party. For the younger writer he had remained a high literary figure, in spite of the lower range of production to which he had fallen after his three first great successes, the comparative absence of quality in his later work. There had been moments when Paul Overt almost shed tears upon this; but now that he was near him (he had never met him), he was conscious only of the fine original source and of his own immense debt. After he had taken a turn or two up and down the gallery he came out again and descended the steps. He was but slenderly supplied with a certain social boldness (it was really a weakness in him), so that, conscious of a want of acquaintance with the four persons in the distance, he indulged in a movement as to which he had a certain safety in feeling that it did not necessarily appear to commit him to an attempt to join them. There was a fine English awkwardness in it – he felt this too as he sauntered vaguely and obliquely across the lawn, as if to take an independent line. Fortunately there was an equally fine English directness in the way one of the gentlemen presently rose and made as if to approach him, with an air of conciliation and reassurance. To this demonstration Paul Overt instantly responded, though he knew the gentleman was not his host. He was tall, straight and elderly, and had a pink, smiling face and a white moustache. Our young man met him half way while he laughed and said: 'A – Lady Watermouth told us you were coming; she asked me just to look after you.' Paul Overt thanked him (he liked him without delay), and turned round with him, walking toward the others. 'They've all gone to church – all except us,' the stranger continued as they went; 'we're just sitting here – it's so jolly.' Overt rejoined that it was jolly indeed – it was such a lovely place; he mentioned that he had not seen it before – it was a charming impression.

'Ah, you've not been here before?' said his companion. 'It's a nice little place – not much to *do*, you know.' Overt wondered what he wanted to 'do' – he felt as if he himself were doing a good deal. By the time they came to where the others sat he had guessed his initiator was a military man, and (such was the turn of Overt's imagination), this made him still more sympathetic. He would naturally have a passion for activity – for deeds at variance with the pacific, pastoral scene. He was evidently so good-natured, however, that he accepted the inglorious hour for what it was worth. Paul Overt shared it with him and with his companions for the next twenty minutes; the latter looked at him and he looked at them without knowing much who they were, while the talk went on without enlightening him much as to what it was about. It was indeed about nothing in particular, and wandered, with casual, pointless pauses and short terrestrial flights, amid the names of persons and places – names which, for him, had no great power of evocation. It was all sociable and slow, as was right and natural on a warm Sunday morning.

Overt's first attention was given to the question, privately considered, of whether one of the two younger men would be Henry St George. He knew many of his distinguished contemporaries by their photographs, but he had never, as it happened, seen a portrait of the great misguided novelist. One of the gentlemen was out of the question – he was too young; and the other scarcely looked clever enough, with such mild, undiscriminating eyes. If those eyes were St George's the problem presented by the ill-matched parts of his genius was still more difficult of solution. Besides, the deportment of the personage possessing them was not, as regards the lady in the red dress, such as could be natural, towards his wife, even to a writer accused by several critics of sacrificing too much to manner. Lastly, Paul Overt had an indefinite feeling that if the gentleman with the sightless eyes bore the name that had set his heart beating faster (he also had contradictory, conventional whiskers – the young admirer of the celebrity had never in a mental vision seen *his* face in so vulgar a frame), he would have given him a sign of recognition or of friendliness – would have heard of him a little, would know something about *Ginistrella*,[1] would have gathered at least that that recent work of fiction had made an impression on the discerning. Paul Overt had a dread of being grossly proud, but it seemed to him that his self-consciousness took no undue licence in thinking that the authorship of *Ginistrella* constituted a degree of identity. His soldierly friend became clear enough; he was 'Fancourt', but he was also the General; and he mentioned to our young man in the course of a few moments that he had but lately returned from twenty years' service abroad.

'And do you mean to remain in England?' Overt asked.

'Oh yes, I have bought a little house in London.'

'And I hope you like it,' said Overt, looking at Mrs St George.

'Well, a little house in Manchester Square[2] – there's a limit to the enthusiasm that that inspires.'

'Oh, I meant being at home again – being in London.'

'My daughter likes it – that's the main thing. She's very fond of art and music and literature and all that kind of thing. She missed it in India and she finds it in London, or she hopes she will find it. Mr St George has promised to help her – he has been awfully kind to her. She has gone to church – she's fond of that too – but they'll all be back in a quarter of an hour. You must let me introduce you to her – she will be so glad to know you. I daresay she has read every word you have written.'

'I shall be delighted – I haven't written very many,' said Overt, who felt without resentment that the General at least was very vague about that. But he wondered a little why, since he expressed this friendly disposition, it did not occur to him to pronounce the word which would put him in relation with Mrs St George. If it was a question of introductions Miss Fancourt (apparently she was unmarried), was far away and the wife of his illustrious *confrère*[3] was almost between them. This lady struck Paul Overt as a very pretty woman, with a surprising air of youth and a high smartness of aspect which seemed to him (he could scarcely have said why), a sort of mystification. St George certainly had every right to a charming wife, but he himself would never have taken the important little woman in the aggressively Parisian dress for the domestic partner of a man of letters. That partner in general, he knew, was far from presenting herself in a single type: his observation had instructed him that she was not inveterately, not necessarily dreary. But he had never before seen her look so much as if her prosperity had deeper foundations than an ink-spotted study-table littered with proof-sheets. Mrs St George might have been the wife of a gentleman who 'kept' books rather than wrote them, who carried on great affairs in the City and made better bargains than those that poets make with publishers. With this she hinted at a success more personal, as if she had been the most characteristic product of an age in which society, the world of conversation, is a great drawing-room with the City for its antechamber. Overt judged her at first to be about thirty years of age; then, after a while, he perceived that she was much nearer fifty. But she juggled away the twenty years somehow – you only saw them in a rare glimpse, like the rabbit in the conjurer's sleeve. She was extraordinarily white, and everything about her was pretty – her eyes, her ears, her hair, her voice, her hands, her feet (to which her relaxed attitude in her wicker chair gave a great publicity), and the numerous ribbons and trinkets with which she was bedecked. She looked as if she had put on her best clothes to go to church and then had decided that they were too good for that and had stayed at home. She told a story of some length about the shabby way Lady Jane had treated the Duchess, as well as an anecdote in relation to a purchase she had made in Paris (on her way back from Cannes), for Lady Egbert, who had never refunded the money. Paul Overt suspected her of a tendency to figure great people as larger than life, until he noticed the manner in which she handled Lady Egbert, which was so subversive that it reassured him. He felt that he should have understood her better if he might have met her eye; but she scarcely looked at him. 'Ah, here they come – all the good ones!' she said at last; and Paul Overt saw in the distance the return of the churchgoers – several persons, in couples and threes, advancing in a flicker of sun and shade at the end of a large green vista formed by the level grass and the overarching boughs.

'If you mean to imply that we are bad, I protest,' said one of the gentlemen – 'after making oneself agreeable all the morning!'

'Ah, if they've found you agreeable!' Mrs St George exclaimed, smiling. 'But if we are good the others are better.'

'They must be angels then,' observed the General.

'Your husband was an angel, the way he went off at your bidding,' the gentleman who had first spoken said to Mrs St George.

'At my bidding?'

'Didn't you make him go to church?'

'I never made him do anything in my life but once, when I made him burn up a bad book. That's all!' At her 'That's all!'

Paul broke into an irrepressible laugh; it lasted only a second, but it drew her eyes to him. His own met them, but not long enough to help him to understand her; unless it were a step towards this that he felt sure on the instant that the burnt book (the way she alluded to it!) was one of her husband's finest things.

'A bad book?' her interlocutor repeated.

'I didn't like it. He went to church because your daughter went,' she continued, to General Fancourt. 'I think it my duty to call your attention to his demeanour to your daughter.'

'Well, if you don't mind it, I don't,' the General laughed.

'*Il s'attache à ses pas.*[4] But I don't wonder – she's so charming.'

'I hope she won't make him burn any books!' Paul Overt ventured to exclaim.

'If she would make him write a few it would be more to the purpose,' said Mrs St George. 'He has been of an indolence this year!'

Our young man stared – he was so struck with the lady's phraseology. Her 'Write a few' seemed to him almost as good as her 'That's all.' Didn't she, as the wife of a rare artist, know what it was to produce *one* perfect work of art? How in the world did she think they were turned off? His private conviction was that admirably as Henry St George wrote, he had written for the last ten years, and especially for the last five, only too much, and there was an instant during which he felt the temptation to make this public. But before he had spoken a diversion was effected by the return of the absent guests. They strolled up dispersedly – there were eight or ten of them – and the circle under the trees rearranged itself as they took their place in it. They made it much larger; so that Paul Overt could feel (he was always feeling that sort of thing, as he said to himself), that if the company had already been interesting to watch it would now become a great deal more so. He shook hands with his hostess, who welcomed him without many words, in the manner of a woman able to trust him to understand – conscious that, in every way, so pleasant an occasion would speak for itself. She offered him no particular

facility for sitting by her, and when they had all subsided again
he found himself still next General Fancourt, with an unknown
lady on his other flank.

'That's my daughter – that one opposite,' the General said to
him without loss of time. Overt saw a tall girl, with magnificent
red hair, in a dress of a pretty grey-green tint and of a limp
silken texture, in which every modern effect had been avoided.
It had therefore somehow the stamp of the latest thing, so that
Overt quickly perceived she was eminently a contemporary
young lady.

'She's very handsome – very handsome,' he repeated, looking at her. There was something noble in her head, and she
appeared fresh and strong.

Her father surveyed her with complacency; then he said:
'She looks too hot – that's her walk. But she'll be all right presently. Then I'll make her come over and speak to you.'

'I should be sorry to give you that trouble; if you were to
take me over there—' the young man murmured.

'My dear sir, do you suppose I put myself out that way? I
don't mean for you, but for Marian,' the General added.

'*I* would put myself out for her, soon enough,' Overt replied;
after which he went on: 'Will you be so good as to tell me
which of those gentlemen is Henry St George?'

'The fellow talking to my girl. By Jove, he *is* making up to
her – they're going off for another walk.'

'Ah, is that he, really?' The young man felt a certain surprise,
for the personage before him contradicted a preconception
which had been vague only till it was confronted with the reality. As soon as this happened the mental image, retiring with a
sigh, became substantial enough to suffer a slight wrong. Overt,
who had spent a considerable part of his short life in foreign
lands, made now, but not for the first time, the reflection that
whereas in those countries he had almost always recognized
the artist and the man of letters by his personal 'type', the
mould of his face, the character of his head, the expression of
his figure and even the indications of his dress, in England
this identification was as little as possible a matter of course,
thanks to the greater conformity, the habit of sinking the

profession instead of advertising it, the general diffusion of the air of the gentleman – the gentleman committed to no particular set of ideas. More than once, on returning to his own country, he had said to himself in regard to the people whom he met in society: 'One sees them about and one even talks with them; but to find out what they *do* one would really have to be a detective.' In respect to several individuals whose work he was unable to like (perhaps he was wrong) he found himself adding, 'No wonder they conceal it – it's so bad!' He observed that oftener than in France and in Germany his artist looked like a gentleman (that is, like an English one), while he perceived that outside of a few exceptions his gentleman didn't look like an artist. St George was not one of the exceptions; that circumstance he definitely apprehended before the great man had turned his back to walk off with Miss Fancourt. He certainly looked better behind than any foreign man of letters, and beautifully correct in his tall black hat and his superior frock coat. Somehow, all the same, these very garments (he wouldn't have minded them so much on a weekday), were disconcerting to Paul Overt, who forgot for the moment that the head of the profession was not a bit better dressed than himself. He had caught a glimpse of a regular face, with a fresh colour, a brown moustache and a pair of eyes surely never visited by a fine frenzy,[5] and he promised himself to study it on the first occasion. His temporary opinion was that St George looked like a lucky stockbroker – a gentleman driving eastward every morning from a sanitary suburb in a smart dog-cart. That carried out the impression already derived from his wife. Paul Overt's glance, after a moment, travelled back to this lady, and he saw that her own had followed her husband as he moved off with Miss Fancourt. Overt permitted himself to wonder a little whether she were jealous when another woman took him away. Then he seemed to perceive that Mrs St George was not glaring at the indifferent maiden – her eyes rested only on her husband, and with unmistakable serenity. That was the way she wanted him to be – she liked his conventional uniform. Overt had a great desire to hear more about the book she had induced him to destroy.

II

As they all came out from luncheon General Fancourt took hold of Paul Overt and exclaimed, 'I say, I want you to know my girl!' as if the idea had just occurred to him and he had not spoken of it before. With the other hand he possessed himself of the young lady and said: 'You know all about him. I've seen you with his books. She reads everything – everything!' he added to the young man. The girl smiled at him and then laughed at her father. The General turned away and his daughter said:

'Isn't papa delightful?'

'He is indeed, Miss Fancourt.'

'As if I read you because I read "everything"!'

'Oh, I don't mean for saying that,' said Paul Overt. 'I liked him from the moment he spoke to me. Then he promised me this privilege.'

'It isn't for you he means it, it's for me. If you flatter yourself that he thinks of anything in life but me you'll find you are mistaken. He introduces every one to me. He thinks me insatiable.'

'You speak like him,' said Paul Overt, laughing.

'Ah, but sometimes I want to,' the girl replied, colouring. 'I don't read everything – I read very little. But I *have* read you.'

'Suppose we go into the gallery,' said Paul Overt. She pleased him greatly, not so much because of this last remark (though that of course was not disagreeable to him), as because, seated opposite to him at luncheon, she had given him for half an hour the impression of her beautiful face. Something else had come with it – a sense of generosity, of an enthusiasm which, unlike many enthusiasms, was not all manner. That was not spoiled for him by the circumstance that the repast had placed her again in familiar contact with Henry St George. Sitting next to her he was also opposite to our young man, who had been able to observe that he multiplied the attentions which his wife had brought to the General's notice. Paul Overt had been able to observe further that this lady was not in the least discomposed by these demonstrations and that she gave every sign of an unclouded spirit. She had Lord Masham on one side of her and on the other the accomplished Mr Mulliner, editor of the new high-class, lively evening paper which was expected to meet a want felt in circles increasingly conscious that Conservatism must be made amusing, and unconvinced when assured by those of another political colour that it was already amusing enough. At the end of an hour spent in her company Paul Overt thought her still prettier than she had appeared to him at first, and if her profane allusions to her husband's work had not still rung in his ears he should have liked her – so far as it could be a question of that in connection with a woman to whom he had not yet spoken and to whom probably he should never speak if it were left to her. Pretty women evidently were necessary to Henry St George, and for the moment it was Miss Fancourt who was most indispensable. If Overt had promised himself to take a better look at him the opportunity now was of the best, and it brought consequences which the young man felt to be important. He saw more in his face, and he liked it the better for its not telling its whole story in the first three minutes. That story came out as one read, in little instalments (it was excusable that Overt's mental comparisons should be somewhat professional), and the text was a style considerably involved – a language not easy to translate at sight. There were shades of meaning in it and a vague perspective of history which receded as you advanced. Of two facts Paul Overt had taken especial notice. The first of these was that he liked the countenance of the illustrious novelist much better when it was in repose than when it smiled; the smile displeased him (as much as anything from that source could), whereas the quiet face had a charm which increased in proportion as it became completely quiet. The change to the expression of gaiety excited on Overt's part a private protest which resembled that of a person sitting in the twilight and enjoying it, when the lamp is brought in too soon. His second reflection was that, though generally he disliked the sight of a man of that age using arts to make himself agreeable to a pretty girl, he was not struck in this case by the ugliness of the thing, which seemed to prove that St George had a light hand or the air of being younger than he was, or else that Miss Fancourt showed that *she* was not conscious of an anomaly.

Overt walked with her into the gallery, and they strolled to the end of it, looking at the pictures, the cabinets, the charming vista, which harmonized with the prospect of the summer afternoon, resembling it in its long brightness, with great divans and old chairs like hours of rest. Such a place as that had the added merit of giving persons who came into it plenty to talk about. Miss Fancourt sat down with Paul Overt on a flowered sofa, the cushions of which, very numerous, were tight, ancient cubes, of many sizes, and presently she said: 'I'm so glad to have a chance to thank you.'

'To thank me?'

'I liked your book so much. I think it's splendid.'

She sat there smiling at him, and he never asked himself which book she meant; for after all he had written three or four. That seemed a vulgar detail, and he was not even gratified by the idea of the pleasure she told him – her bright, handsome face told him – he had given her. The feeling she appealed to, or at any rate the feeling she excited, was something larger – something that had little to do with any quickened pulsation of his own vanity. It was responsive admiration of the life she embodied, the young purity and richness of which appeared to imply that real success was to resemble *that*, to live, to bloom, to present the perfection of a fine type, not to have hammered out headachy fancies with a bent back at an ink-stained table. While her grey eyes rested on him (there was a wideish space between them, and the division of her rich-coloured hair, which was so thick that it ventured to be smooth, made a free arch above them), he was almost ashamed of that exercise of the pen which it was her present inclination to eulogize. He was conscious that he should have liked better to please her in some other way. The lines of her face were those of a woman grown, but there was something childish in her complexion and the sweetness of her mouth. Above all she was natural – that was indubitable now – more natural than he had supposed at first, perhaps on account of her æsthetic drapery, which was conventionally unconventional, suggesting a tortuous spontaneity.

He had feared that sort of thing in other cases, and his fears had been justified; though he was an artist to the essence, the modern reactionary nymph, with the brambles of the woodland caught in her folds and a look as if the satyrs had toyed with her hair,[6] was apt to make him uncomfortable. Miss Fancourt was really more candid than her costume, and the best proof of it was her supposing that such garments suited her liberal character. She was robed like a pessimist, but Overt was sure she liked the taste of life. He thanked her for her appreciation – aware at the same time that he didn't appear to thank her enough and that she might think him ungracious. He was afraid she would ask him to explain something that he had written, and he always shrank from that (perhaps too timidly), for to his own ear the explanation of a work of art sounded fatuous. But he liked her so much as to feel a confidence that in the long run he should be able to show her that he was not rudely evasive. Moreover it was very certain that she was not quick to take offence; she was not irritable, she could be trusted to wait. So when he said to her, 'Ah! don't talk of anything I have done, *here*; there is another man in the house who is the actuality!' when he uttered this short, sincere protest, it was with the sense that she would see in the words neither mock humility nor the ungraciousness of a successful man bored with praise.

'You mean Mr St George – isn't he delightful?'

Paul Overt looked at her a moment; there was a species of morning-light in her eyes.

'Alas, I don't know him. I only admire him at a distance.'

'Oh, you must know him – he wants so to talk to you,' rejoined Miss Fancourt, who evidently had the habit of saying the things that, by her quick calculation, would give people pleasure. Overt divined that she would always calculate on everything's being simple between others.

'I shouldn't have supposed he knew anything about me,' Paul said, smiling.

'He does then – everything. And if he didn't, I should be able to tell him.'

'To tell him everything?'

'You talk just like the people in your book!' the girl exclaimed.

'Then they must all talk alike.'

'Well, it must be so difficult. Mr St George tells me it is, terribly. I've tried too and I find it so. I've tried to write a novel.'

'Mr St George oughtn't to discourage you,' said Paul Overt.

'You do much more – when you wear that expression.'

'Well, after all, why try to be an artist?' the young man went on. 'It's so poor – so poor!'

'I don't know what you mean,' said Marian Fancourt, looking grave.

'I mean as compared with being a person of action – as living your works.'

'But what is art but a life – if it be real?' asked the girl. 'I think it's the only one – everything else is so clumsy!' Paul Overt laughed, and she continued: 'It's so interesting, meeting so many celebrated people.'

'So I should think; but surely it isn't new to you.'

'Why, I have never seen any one – any one: living always in Asia.'

'But doesn't Asia swarm with personages? Haven't you administered provinces in India and had captive rajahs and tributary princes chained to your car?'

'I was with my father, after I left school to go out there. It was delightful being with him – we are alone together in the world, he and I – but there was none of the society I like best. One never heard of a picture – never of a book, except bad ones.'

'Never of a picture? Why, wasn't all life a picture?'

Miss Fancourt looked over the delightful place where they sat. 'Nothing to compare with this. I adore England!' she exclaimed.

'Ah, of course I don't deny that we must do something with it yet.'

'It hasn't been touched, really,' said the girl.

'Did Henry St George say that?'

There was a small and, as he felt it, venial intention of irony in his question; which, however, the girl took very simply, not noticing the insinuation. 'Yes, he says it has not been touched – not touched comparatively,' she answered, eagerly. 'He's so interesting about it. To listen to him makes one want so to do something.'

'It would make me want to,' said Paul Overt, feeling strongly, on the instant, the suggestion of what she said and of the emotion with which she said it, and what an incentive, on St George's lips, such a speech might be.

'Oh, you – as if you hadn't! I should like so to hear you talk together,' the girl added, ardently.

'That's very genial of you; but he would have it all his own way. I'm prostrate before him.'

Marian Fancourt looked earnest for a moment. 'Do you think then he's so perfect?'

'Far from it. Some of his later books seem to me awfully queer.'

'Yes, yes – he knows that.'

Paul Overt stared. 'That they seem to me awfully queer?'

'Well yes, or at any rate that they are not what they should be. He told me he didn't esteem them. He has told me such wonderful things – he's so interesting.'

There was a certain shock for Paul Overt in the knowledge that the fine genius they were talking of had been reduced to so explicit a confession and had made it, in his misery, to the first comer; for though Miss Fancourt was charming, what was she after all but an immature girl encountered at a country-house? Yet precisely this was a part of the sentiment that he himself had just expressed; he would make way completely for the poor peccable great man, not because he didn't read him clear, but altogether because he did. His consideration was half composed of tenderness for superficialities which he was sure St George judged privately with supreme sternness and which denoted some tragic intellectual secret. He would have his reasons for his psychology *à fleur de peau*,[7] and these reasons could only be cruel ones, such as would make him dearer to those who already were fond of him. 'You excite my envy. I judge him, I discriminate – but I love him,' Overt said in a moment.

'And seeing him for the first time this way is a great event for me.'

'How momentous – how magnificent!' cried the girl. 'How delicious to bring you together!'

'*Your* doing it – that makes it perfect,' Overt responded.

'He's as eager as you', Miss Fancourt went on. 'But it's so odd you shouldn't have met.'

'It's not so odd as it seems. I've been out of England so much – repeated absences during all these last years.'

'And yet you write of it as well as if you were always here.'

'It's just the being away perhaps. At any rate the best bits, I suspect, are those that were done in dreary places abroad.'

'And why were they dreary?'

'Because they were health-resorts – where my poor mother was dying.'

'Your poor mother?' the girl murmured, kindly.

'We went from place to place to help her to get better. But she never did. To the deadly Riviera (I hate it!) to the high Alps, to Algiers, and far away – a hideous journey – to Colorado.'

'And she isn't better?' Miss Fancourt went on.

'She died a year ago.'

'Really? – like mine! Only that is far away. Some day you must tell me about your mother,' she added.

Overt looked at her a moment. 'What right things you say! If you say them to St George I don't wonder he's in bondage.'

'I don't know what you mean. He doesn't make speeches and professions at all – he isn't ridiculous.'

'I'm afraid you consider that I am.'

'No, I don't,' the girl replied, rather shortly. 'He understands everything.'

Overt was on the point of saying jocosely: 'And I don't – is that it?' But these words, before he had spoken, changed themselves into others slightly less trivial: 'Do you suppose he understands his wife?'

Miss Fancourt made no direct answer to his question; but after a moment's hesitation she exclaimed: 'Isn't she charming?'

'Not in the least!'

'Here he comes. Now you must know him,' the girl went on. A small group of visitors had gathered at the other end of the gallery and they had been joined for a moment by Henry St George, who strolled in from a neighbouring room. He stood near them a moment, not, apparently, falling into the conversation, but taking up an old miniature from a table and vaguely examining it. At the end of a minute he seemed to perceive Miss Fancourt and her companion in the distance; whereupon, laying down his miniature, he approached them with the same procrastinating air, with his hands in his pockets, looking to right and left at the pictures. The gallery was so long that this transit took some little time, especially as there was a moment when he stopped to admire the fine Gainsborough. 'He says she has been the making of him,' Miss Fancourt continued, in a voice slightly lowered.

'Ah, he's often obscure!' laughed Paul Overt.

'Obscure?' she repeated, interrogatively. Her eyes rested upon her other friend, and it was not lost upon Paul that they appeared to send out great shafts of softness. 'He is going to speak to us!' she exclaimed, almost breathlessly. There was a sort of rapture in her voice; Paul Overt was startled. 'Bless my soul, is she so fond of him as that – is she in love with him?' he mentally inquired. 'Didn't I tell you he was eager?' she added, to her companion.

'It's eagerness dissimulated,' the young man rejoined, as the subject of their observation lingered before his Gainsborough. 'He edges toward us shyly. Does he mean that she saved him by burning that book?'

'That book? what book did she burn?' The girl turned her face quickly upon him.

'Hasn't he told you, then?'

'Not a word.'

'Then he doesn't tell you everything!' Paul Overt had guessed that Miss Fancourt pretty much supposed he did. The great man had now resumed his course and come nearer; nevertheless Overt risked the profane observation: 'St George and the dragon, the anecdote suggests!'

Miss Fancourt, however, did not hear it; she was smiling at her approaching friend. 'He *is* eager – he is!' she repeated.

'Eager for you – yes.'

The girl called out frankly, joyously: 'I know you want to know Mr Overt. You'll be great friends, and it will always be delightful to me to think that I was here when you first met and that I had something to do with it.'

There was a freshness of intention in this speech which carried it off; nevertheless our young man was sorry for Henry St George, as he was sorry at any time for any one who was publicly invited to be responsive and delightful. He would have been so contented to believe that a man he deeply admired attached an importance to him that he was determined not to play with such a presumption if it possibly were vain. In a single glance of the eye of the pardonable master he discovered (having the sort of divination that belonged to his talent), that this personage was full of general good-will, but had not read a word he had written. There was even a relief, a simplification, in that: liking him so much already for what he had done, how could he like him more for having been struck with a certain promise? He got up, trying to show his compassion, but at the same instant he found himself encompassed by St George's happy personal art – a manner of which it was the essence to conjure away false positions. It all took place in a moment. He was conscious that he knew him now, conscious of his handshake and of the very quality of his hand; of his face, seen nearer and consequently seen better, of a general fraternizing assurance, and in particular of the circumstance that St George didn't dislike him (as yet at least), for being imposed by a charming but too gushing girl, valuable enough without such danglers. At any rate no irritation was reflected in the voice with which he questioned Miss Fancourt in respect to some project of a walk – a general walk of the company round the park. He had said something to Overt about a talk – 'We must have a tremendous lot of talk; there are so many things, aren't there?' – but Paul perceived that this idea would not in the present case take very immediate effect. All the same he was extremely happy, even after the matter of the walk had been settled (the three presently passed back to the other part of the gallery, where it was discussed with several members of the party), even when, after they had all gone out together, he found himself for half an hour in contact with Mrs St George. Her husband had taken the advance with Miss Fancourt, and this pair were quite out of sight. It was the prettiest of rambles for a summer afternoon – a grassy circuit, of immense extent, skirting the limit of the park within. The park was completely surrounded by its old mottled but perfect red wall, which, all the way on their left, made a picturesque accompaniment. Mrs St George mentioned to him the surprising number of acres that were thus enclosed, together with numerous other facts relating to the property and the family, and its other properties: she could not too strongly urge upon him the importance of seeing their other houses. She ran over the names of these and rang the changes on them with the facility of practice, making them appear an almost endless list. She had received Paul Overt very amiably when he broke ground with her by telling her that he had just had the joy of making her husband's acquaintance, and struck him as so alert and so accommodating a little woman that he was rather ashamed of his *mot*[8] about her to Miss Fancourt; though he reflected that a hundred other people, on a hundred occasions, would have been sure to make it. He got on with Mrs St George, in short, better than he expected; but this did not prevent her from suddenly becoming aware that she was faint with fatigue and must take her way back to the house by the shortest cut. She hadn't the strength of a kitten, she said – she was awfully seedy; a state of things that Overt had been too preoccupied to perceive – preoccupied with a private effort to ascertain in what sense she could be held to have been the making of her husband. He had arrived at a glimmering of the answer when she announced that she must leave him, though this perception was of course provisional. While he was in the very act of placing himself at her disposal for the return the situation underwent a change; Lord Masham suddenly turned up, coming back to them, overtaking them, emerging from the shrubbery – Overt could scarcely have said how he appeared, and Mrs St George had protested that she wanted to be left alone and not to break up the party. A moment later she was walking off with Lord Masham. Paul Overt fell back and joined Lady Watermouth, to whom he presently mentioned that Mrs St George had been obliged to renounce the attempt to go further.

'She oughtn't to have come out at all,' her ladyship remarked, rather grumpily.

'Is she so very much of an invalid?'

'Very bad indeed.' And his hostess added, with still greater austerity: 'She oughtn't to come to stay with one!' He wondered what was implied by this, and presently gathered that it was not a reflection on the lady's conduct or her moral nature: it only represented that her strength was not equal to her aspirations.

III

The smoking-room at Summersoft was on the scale of the rest of the place; that is it was high and light and commodious, and decorated with such refined old carvings and mouldings that it seemed rather a bower for ladies who should sit at work at fading crewels than a parliament of gentlemen smoking strong cigars. The gentlemen mustered there in considerable force on the Sunday evening, collecting mainly at one end, in front of one of the cool fair fireplaces of white marble, the entablature of which was adorned with a delicate little Italian 'subject'. There was another in the wall that faced it, and, thanks to the mild summer night, there was no fire in either; but a nucleus for aggregation was furnished on one side by a table in the chimney-corner laden with bottles, decanters and tall tumblers. Paul Overt was an insincere smoker; he puffed cigarettes occasionally for reasons with which tobacco had nothing to do. This was particularly the case on the occasion of which I speak; his motive was the vision of a little direct talk with Henry St George. The 'tremendous' communion of which the great man had held out hopes to him earlier in the day had not yet come off, and this saddened him considerably, for the party was to go its several ways immediately after breakfast on

the morrow. He had, however, the disappointment of finding
that apparently the author of *Shadowmere* was not disposed to
prolong his vigil. He was not among the gentlemen assembled
in the smoking-room when Overt entered it, nor was he one of
those who turned up, in bright habiliments, during the next ten
minutes. The young man waited a little, wondering whether he
had only gone to put on something extraordinary; this would
account for his delay as well as contribute further to Overt's
observation of his tendency to do the approved superficial
thing. But he didn't arrive – he must have been putting on
something more extraordinary than was probable. Paul gave
him up, feeling a little injured, a little wounded at his not having managed to say twenty words to him. He was not angry,
but he puffed his cigarette sighingly, with the sense of having
lost a precious chance. He wandered away with his regret,
moved slowly round the room, looking at the old prints on the
walls. In this attitude he presently felt a hand laid on his shoulder and a friendly voice in his ear. 'This is good. I hoped I
should find you. I came down on purpose.' St George was
there, without a change of dress and with a kind face – his
graver one – to which Overt eagerly responded. He explained
that it was only for the Master[9] – the idea of a little talk – that
he had sat up and that, not finding him, he had been on the
point of going to bed.

'Well, you know, I don't smoke – my wife doesn't let me,'
said St George, looking for a place to sit down. 'It's very good
for me – very good for me. Let us take that sofa.'

'Do you mean smoking is good for you?'

'No, no, her not letting me. It's a great thing to have a wife
who proves to one all the things one can do without. One might
never find them out for oneself. She doesn't allow me to touch
a cigarette.'

They took possession of the sofa, which was at a distance
from the group of smokers, and St George went on: 'Have you
got one yourself?'

'Do you mean a cigarette?'

'Dear no! a wife.'

'No; and yet I would give up my cigarette for one.'

'You would give up a good deal more than that,' said St George. 'However, you would get a great deal in return. There is a great deal to be said for wives,' he added, folding his arms and crossing his outstretched legs. He declined tobacco altogether and sat there without returning fire. Paul Overt stopped smoking, touched by his courtesy; and after all they were out of the fumes, their sofa was in a far-away corner. It would have been a mistake, St George went on, a great mistake for them to have separated without a little chat; 'for I know all about you,' he said, 'I know you're very remarkable. You've written a very distinguished book.'

'And how do you know it?' Overt asked.

'Why, my dear fellow, it's in the air, it's in the papers, it's everywhere,' St George replied, with the immediate familiarity of a *confrère* – a tone that seemed to his companion the very rustle of the laurel. 'You're on all men's lips and, what's better, you're on all women's. And I've just been reading your book.'

'Just? You hadn't read it this afternoon,' said Overt.

'How do you know that?'

'You know how I know it,' the young man answered, laughing.

'I suppose Miss Fancourt told you.'

'No, indeed; she led me rather to suppose that you had.'

'Yes; that's much more what she would do. Doesn't she shed a rosy glow over life? But you didn't believe her?' asked St George.

'No, not when you came to us there.'

'Did I pretend? did I pretend badly?' But without waiting for an answer to this St George went on: 'You ought always to believe such a girl as that – always, always. Some women are meant to be taken with allowances and reserves; but you must take *her* just as she is.'

'I like her very much,' said Paul Overt.

Something in his tone appeared to excite on his companion's part a momentary sense of the absurd; perhaps it was the air of deliberation attending this judgment. St George broke into a laugh and returned: 'It's the best thing you can do with her.

She's a rare young lady! In point of fact, however, I confess I hadn't read you this afternoon.'

'Then you see how right I was in this particular case not to believe Miss Fancourt.'

'How right? how can I agree to that, when I lost credit by it?'

'Do you wish to pass for exactly what she represents you? Certainly you needn't be afraid,' Paul said.

'Ah, my dear young man, don't talk about passing – for the likes of me! I'm passing away – nothing else than that. She has a better use for her young imagination (isn't it fine?) than in "representing" in any way such a weary, wasted, used-up animal!' St George spoke with a sudden sadness which produced a protest on Paul's part; but before the protest could be uttered he went on, reverting to the latter's successful novel: 'I had no idea you were so good – one hears of so many things. But you're surprisingly good.'

'I'm going to be surprisingly better,' said Overt.

'I see that and it's what fetches me. I don't see so much else – as one looks about – that's going to be surprisingly better. They're going to be consistently worse – most of the things. It's so much easier to be worse – heaven knows I've found it so. I'm not in a great glow, you know, about what's being attempted, what's being done. But you *must* be better – you must keep it up. I haven't, of course. It's very difficult – that's the devil of the whole thing; but I see you can. It will be a great disgrace if you don't.'

'It's very interesting to hear you speak of yourself; but I don't know what you mean by your allusions to your having fallen off,' Paul Overt remarked, with pardonable hypocrisy. He liked his companion so much now that it had ceased for the moment to be vivid to him that there had been any decline.

'Don't say that – don't say that,' St George replied gravely, with his head resting on the top of the back of the sofa and his eyes on the ceiling. 'You know perfectly what I mean. I haven't read twenty pages of your book without seeing that you can't help it.'

'You make me very miserable,' Paul murmured.

'I'm glad of that, for it may serve as a kind of warning.

Shocking enough it must be, especially to a young, fresh mind,
full of faith, – the spectacle of a man meant for better things
sunk at my age in such dishonour.' St George, in the same con-
templative attitude, spoke softly but deliberately, and without
perceptible emotion. His tone indeed suggested an impersonal
lucidity which was cruel – cruel to himself – and which made
Paul lay an argumentative hand on his arm. But he went on,
while his eyes seemed to follow the ingenuities of the beautiful
Adam ceiling:[10] 'Look at me well and take my lesson to heart,
for it *is* a lesson. Let that good come of it at least that you shud-
der with your pitiful impression and that this may help to keep
you straight in the future. Don't become in your old age what I
am in mine – the depressing, the deplorable illustration of the
worship of false gods!'

'What do you mean by your old age?' Paul Overt asked.

'It has made me old. But I like your youth.'

Overt answered nothing – they sat for a minute in silence.
They heard the others talking about the governmental major-
ity. Then, 'What do you mean by false gods?' Paul inquired.

'The idols of the market – money and luxury and "the world",
placing one's children and dressing one's wife – everything that
drives one to the short and easy way. Ah, the vile things they
make one do!'

'But surely one is right to want to place one's children.'

'One has no business to have any children,' St George
declared, placidly. 'I mean of course if one wants to do something good.'

'But aren't they an inspiration – an incentive?'

'An incentive to damnation, artistically speaking.'

'You touch on very deep things – things I should like to discuss with you,' Paul Overt said. 'I should like you to tell me
volumes about yourself. This is a festival for *me*!'

'Of course it is, cruel youth. But to show you that I'm still
not incapable, degraded as I am, of an act of faith, I'll tie my
vanity to the stake for you and burn it to ashes. You must come
and see me – you must come and see us. Mrs St George is
charming; I don't know whether you have had any opportunity
to talk with her. She will be delighted to see you; she likes great

celebrities, whether incipient or predominant. You must come and dine – my wife will write to you. Where are you to be found?'

'This is my little address' – and Overt drew out his pocket-book and extracted a visiting-card. On second thoughts, however, he kept it back, remarking that he would not trouble his friend to take charge of it but would come and see him straightway in London and leave it at his door if he should fail to obtain admittance.

'Ah! you probably will fail; my wife's always out, or when she isn't out she's knocked up from having been out. You must come and dine – though that won't do much good either, for my wife insists on big dinners. You must come down and see us in the country, that's the best way; we have plenty of room, and it isn't bad.'

'You have a house in the country?' Paul asked, enviously.

'Ah, not like this! But we have a sort of place we go to – an hour from Euston.[11] That's one of the reasons.'

'One of the reasons?'

'Why my books are so bad.'

'You must tell me all the others!' Paul exclaimed, laughing.

St George made no direct rejoinder to this; he only inquired rather abruptly: 'Why have I never seen you before?'

The tone of the question was singularly flattering to his new comrade; it seemed to imply that he perceived now that for years he had missed something. 'Partly, I suppose, because there has been no particular reason why you should see me. I haven't lived in the world – in your world. I have spent many years out of England, in different places abroad.'

'Well, please don't do it any more. You must do England – there's such a lot of it.'

'Do you mean I must write about it?' Paul asked, in a voice which had the note of the listening candour of a child.

'Of course you must. And tremendously well, do you mind? That takes off a little of my esteem for this thing of yours – that it goes on abroad. Hang abroad! Stay at home and do things here – do subjects we can measure.'

'I'll do whatever you tell me,' said Paul Overt, deeply

attentive. 'But excuse me if I say I don't understand how you have been reading my book,' he subjoined. 'I've had you before me all the afternoon, first in that long walk, then at tea on the lawn, till we went to dress for dinner, and all the evening at dinner and in this place.'

St George turned his face round with a smile. 'I only read for a quarter of an hour.'

'A quarter of an hour is liberal, but I don't understand where you put it in. In the drawing-room, after dinner, you were not reading, you were talking to Miss Fancourt.'

'It comes to the same thing, because we talked about *Ginistrella*. She described it to me – she lent it to me.'

'Lent it to you?'

'She travels with it.'

'It's incredible,' Paul Overt murmured, blushing.

'It's glorious for you; but it also turned out very well for me. When the ladies went off to bed she kindly offered to send the book down to me. Her maid brought it to me in the hall and I went to my room with it. I hadn't thought of coming here, I do that so little. But I don't sleep early, I always have to read for an hour or two. I sat down to your novel on the spot, without undressing, without taking off anything but my coat. I think that's a sign that my curiosity had been strongly roused about it. I read a quarter of an hour, as I tell you, and even in a quarter of an hour I was greatly struck.'

'Ah, the beginning isn't very good – it's the whole thing!' said Overt, who had listened to this recital with extreme interest. 'And you laid down the book and came after me?' he asked.

'That's the way it moved me. I said to myself, "I see it's off his own bat, and he's there, by the way, and the day's over and I haven't said twenty words to him." It occurred to me that you would probably be in the smoking-room and that it wouldn't be too late to repair my omission. I wanted to do something civil to you, so I put on my coat and came down. I shall read your book again when I go up.'

Paul Overt turned round in his place – he was exceedingly touched by the picture of such a demonstration in his favour.

'You're really the kindest of men. *Cela s'est passé comme ça?*[12] and I have been sitting here with you all this time and never apprehended it and never thanked you!'

'Thank Miss Fancourt – it was she who wound me up. She has made me feel as if I had read your novel.'

'She's an angel from heaven!' Paul Overt exclaimed.

'She is indeed. I have never seen anyone like her. Her interest in literature is touching – something quite peculiar to herself; she takes it all so seriously. She feels the arts and she wants to feel them more. To those who practise them it's almost humiliating – her curiosity, her sympathy, her good faith. How can anything be as fine as she supposes it?'

'She's a rare organization,' Paul Overt sighed.

'The richest I have ever seen – an artistic intelligence really of the first order. And lodged in such a form!' St George exclaimed.

'One would like to paint such a girl as that,' Overt continued.

'Ah, there it is – there's nothing like life! When you're finished, squeezed dry and used up and you think the sack's empty, you're still spoken to, you still get touches and thrills, the idea springs up – out of the lap of the actual – and shows you there's always something to be done. But I shan't do it – she's not for me!'

'How do you mean, not for you?'

'Oh, it's all over – she's for you, if you like.'

'Ah, much less!' said Paul Overt. 'She's not for a dingy little man of letters; she's for the world, the bright rich world of bribes and rewards. And the world will take hold of her – it will carry her away.'

'It will try; but it's just a case in which there may be a fight. It would be worth fighting, for a man who had it in him, with youth and talent on his side.'

These words rang not a little in Paul Overt's consciousness – they held him silent a moment. 'It's a wonder she has remained as she is – giving herself away so, with so much to give away.'

'Do you mean so ingenuous – so natural? Oh, she doesn't care a straw – she gives away because she overflows. She has her own feelings, her own standards; she doesn't keep remembering that she must be proud. And then she hasn't been here long enough to be spoiled; she has picked up a fashion or two, but only the amusing ones. She's a provincial – a provincial of genius; her very blunders are charming, her mistakes are interesting. She has come back from Asia with all sorts of excited curiosities and unappeased appetites. She's first-rate herself and she expends herself on the second-rate. She's life herself and she takes a rare interest in imitations. She mixes all things up, but there are none in regard to which she hasn't perceptions. She sees things in a perspective – as if from the top of the Himalayas – and she enlarges everything she touches. Above all she exaggerates – to herself, I mean. She exaggerates you and me!'

There was nothing in this description to allay the excitement produced in the mind of our younger friend by such a sketch of a fine subject. It seemed to him to show the art of St George's admired hand, and he lost himself in it, gazing at the vision (it hovered there before him), of a woman's figure which should be part of the perfection of a novel. At the end of a moment he became aware that it had turned into smoke, and out of the smoke – the last puff of a big cigar – proceeded the voice of General Fancourt, who had left the others and come and planted himself before the gentlemen on the sofa. 'I suppose that when you fellows get talking you sit up half the night.'

'Half the night? – *jamais de la vie!*[13] I follow a hygiene,' St George replied, rising to his feet.

'I see, you're hothouse plants,' laughed the General. 'That's the way you produce your flowers.'

'I produce mine between ten and one[14] every morning; I bloom with a regularity!' St George went on.

'And with a splendour!' added the polite General, while Paul Overt noted how little the author of *Shadowmere* minded, as he phrased it to himself, when he was addressed as a celebrated story-teller. The young man had an idea that *he* should never get used to that – it would always make him uncomfortable (from the suspicion that people would think they had to), and he would want to prevent it. Evidently his more illustrious congener had toughened and hardened – had made himself a surface. The group of men had finished their cigars and taken up their bedroom candlesticks; but before they all passed out Lord Watermouth invited St George and Paul Overt to drink something. It happened that they both declined, upon which General Fancourt said: 'Is that the hygiene? You don't sprinkle the flowers?'

'Oh, I should drown them!' St George replied; but leaving the room beside Overt he added whimsically, for the latter's benefit, in a lower tone: 'My wife doesn't let me.'

'Well, I'm glad I'm not one of you fellows!' the General exclaimed.

The nearness of Summersoft to London had this consequence, chilling to a person who had had a vision of sociability in a railway-carriage, that most of the company, after breakfast, drove back to town, entering their own vehicles, which had come out to fetch them, while their servants returned by train with their luggage. Three or four young men, among whom was Paul Overt, also availed themselves of the common convenience; but they stood in the portico of the house and saw the others roll away. Miss Fancourt got into a victoria with her father, after she had shaken hands with Paul Overt and said, smiling in the frankest way in the world – 'I *must* see you more. Mrs St George is so nice: she has promised to ask us both to dinner together.' This lady and her husband took their places in a perfectly-appointed brougham[15] (she required a closed carriage), and as our young man waved his hat to them in response to their nods and flourishes he reflected that, taken together, they were an honourable image of success, of the material rewards and the social credit of literature. Such things were not the full measure, but all the same he felt a little proud for literature.

IV

Before a week had elapsed Paul Overt met Miss Fancourt in Bond Street, at a private view of the works of a young artist in 'black and white' who had been so good as to invite him to the stuffy scene. The drawings were admirable, but the crowd in the one little room was so dense that he felt as if he were up to his neck in a big sack of wool. A fringe of people at the outer edge endeavoured by curving forward their backs and presenting, below them, a still more convex surface of resistance to the pressure of the mass, to preserve an interval between their noses and the glazed mounts of the pictures; while the central body, in the comparative gloom projected by a wide horizontal screen, hung under the skylight and allowing only a margin for the day, remained upright, dense and vague, lost in the contemplation of its own ingredients. This contemplation sat especially in the sad eyes of certain female heads, surmounted with hats of strange convolution and plumage, which rose on long necks above the others. One of the heads, Paul Overt perceived, was much the most beautiful of the collection, and his next discovery was that it belonged to Miss Fancourt. Its beauty was enhanced by the glad smile that she sent him across surrounding obstructions, a smile which drew him to her as fast as he could make his way. He had divined at Summersoft that the last thing her nature contained was an affectation of indifference; yet even with this circumspection he had a freshness of pleasure in seeing that she did not pretend to await his arrival with composure. She smiled as radiantly as if she wished to make him hurry, and as soon as he came within earshot she said to him, in her voice of joy: 'He's here – he's here – he's coming back in a moment!'

'Ah, your father?' Paul responded, as she offered him her hand.

'Oh dear no, this isn't in my poor father's line. I mean Mr St George. He has just left me to speak to some one – he's coming back. It's he who brought me – wasn't it charming?'

'Ah, that gives him a pull over me – I couldn't have "brought" you, could I?'

'If you had been so kind as to propose it – why not you as well as he?' the girl asked, with a face which expressed no cheap coquetry, but simply affirmed a happy fact.

'Why, he's a *père de famille*.[16] They have privileges,' Paul

Overt explained. And then, quickly: 'Will you go to see places with *me*?' he broke out.

'Anything you like!' she smiled. 'I know what you mean, that girls have to have a lot of people—' She interrupted herself to say: 'I don't know; I'm free. I have always been like that,' she went on; 'I can go anywhere with any one. I'm so glad to meet you,' she added, with a sweet distinctness that made the people near her turn round.

'Let me at least repay that speech by taking you out of this squash,' said Paul Overt. 'Surely people are not happy here!'

'No, they are *mornes*,[17] aren't they? But I am very happy indeed, and I promised Mr St George to remain in this spot till he comes back. He's going to take me away. They send him invitations for things of this sort – more than he wants. It was so kind of him to think of me.'

'They also send me invitations of this kind – more than I want. And if thinking of *you* will do it—!' Paul went on.

'Oh, I delight in them – everything that's life – everything that's London!'

'They don't have private views in Asia, I suppose. But what a pity that for this year, in this fertile city, they are pretty well over.'

'Well, next year will do, for I hope you believe we are going to be friends always. Here he comes!' Miss Fancourt continued, before Paul had time to respond.

He made out St George in the gaps of the crowd, and this perhaps led to his hurrying a little to say: 'I hope that doesn't mean that I'm to wait till next year to see you.'

'No, no; are we not to meet at dinner on the 25th?' she answered, with an eagerness greater even than his own.

'That's almost next year. Is there no means of seeing you before?'

She stared, with all her brightness. 'Do you mean that you would *come*?'

'Like a shot, if you'll be so good as to ask me!'

'On Sunday, then – this next Sunday?'

'What have I done that you should doubt it?' the young man demanded, smiling.

Miss Fancourt turned instantly to St George, who had now

joined them, and announced triumphantly: 'He's coming on Sunday – this next Sunday!'

'Ah, my day – my day too!' said the famous novelist, laughing at Paul Overt.

'Yes, but not yours only. You shall meet in Manchester Square; you shall talk – you shall be wonderful!'

'We don't meet often enough,' St George remarked, shaking hands with his disciple. 'Too many things – ah, too many things! But we must make it up in the country in September. You won't forget that you've promised me that?'

'Why, he's coming on the 25th; you'll see him then,' said Marian Fancourt.

'On the 25th?' St George asked, vaguely.

'We dine with you; I hope you haven't forgotten. He's dining out,' she added gaily to Paul Overt.

'Oh, bless me, yes; that's charming! And you're coming? My wife didn't tell me,' St George said to Paul. 'Too many things – too many things!' he repeated.

'Too many people – too many people!' Paul exclaimed, giving ground before the penetration of an elbow.

'You oughtn't to say that; they all read you.'

'Me? I should like to see them! Only two or three at most,' the young man rejoined.

'Did you ever hear anything like that? he knows how good he is!' St George exclaimed, laughing, to Miss Fancourt. 'They read *me*, but that doesn't make me like them any better. Come away from them, come away!' And he led the way out of the exhibition.

'He's going to take me to the Park,' the girl said, with elation, to Paul Overt, as they passed along the corridor which led to the street.

'Ah, does he go there?' Paul asked, wondering at the idea as a somewhat unexpected illustration of St George's *moeurs*.[18]

'It's a beautiful day; there will be a great crowd. We're going to look at the people, to look at types,' the girl went on. 'We shall sit under the trees; we shall walk by the Row.'[19]

'I go once a year, on business,' said St George, who had overheard Paul's question.

'Or with a country cousin, didn't you tell me? I'm the coun-try cousin!' she went on, over her shoulder, to Paul, as her companion drew her toward a hansom[20] to which he had sig-nalled. The young man watched them get in; he returned, as he stood there, the friendly wave of the hand with which, ensconced in the vehicle beside Miss Fancourt, St George took leave of him. He even lingered to see the vehicle start away and lose itself in the confusion of Bond Street. He followed it with his eyes; it was embarrassingly suggestive. 'She's not for me!' the great novelist had said emphatically at Summersoft; but his manner of conducting himself toward her appeared not exactly in harmony with such a conviction. How could he have behaved differently if she *had* been for him? An indefinite envy rose in Paul Overt's heart as he took his way on foot alone, and the singular part of it was that it was directed to each of the occu-pants of the hansom. How much he should like to rattle about London with such a girl! How much he should like to go and look at 'types' with St George!

The next Sunday, at four o'clock, he called in Manchester Square, where his secret wish was gratified by his finding Miss Fancourt alone. She was in a large, bright, friendly, occupied room, which was painted red all over, draped with the quaint, cheap, florid stuffs that are represented as coming from south-ern and eastern countries, where they are fabled to serve as the counterpanes of the peasantry, and bedecked with pot-tery of vivid hues, ranged on casual shelves, and with many water-colour drawings from the hand (as the visitor learned), of the young lady, commemorating, with courage and skill, the sunsets, the mountains, the temples and palaces of India. Overt sat there an hour – more than an hour, two hours – and all the while no one came in. Miss Fancourt was so good as to remark, with her liberal humanity, that it was delightful they were not interrupted; it was so rare in London, especially at that season, that people got a good talk. But fortunately now, of a fine Sunday, half the world went out of town, and that made it better for those who didn't go, when they were in sympathy. It was the defect of London (one of two or three, the very short list of those she recognized in the teeming world-city that she adored), that there were too few good chances for talk; one never had time to carry anything far.

'Too many things – too many things!' Paul Overt said, quoting St George's exclamation of a few days before.

'Ah yes, for him there are too many; his life is too complicated.'

'Have you seen it *near*? That's what I should like to do; it might explain some mysteries,' Paul Overt went on. The girl asked him what mysteries he meant, and he said: 'Oh, peculiarities of his work, inequalities, superficialities. For one who looks at it from the artistic point of view it contains a bottomless ambiguity.'

'Oh, do describe that more – it's so interesting. There are no such suggestive questions. I'm so fond of them. He thinks he's a failure – fancy!' Miss Fancourt added.

'That depends upon what his ideal may have been. Ah, with his gifts it ought to have been high. But till one knows what he really proposed to himself – Do *you* know, by chance?' the young man asked, breaking off.

'Oh, he doesn't talk to me about himself. I can't make him. It's too provoking.'

Paul Overt was on the point of asking what then he did talk about; but discretion checked this inquiry, and he said instead: 'Do you think he's unhappy at home?'

'At home?'

'I mean in his relations with his wife. He has a mystifying little way of alluding to her.'

'Not to me,' said Marian Fancourt, with her clear eyes. 'That wouldn't be right, would it?' she asked, seriously.

'Not particularly; so I am glad he doesn't mention her to you. To praise her might bore you, and he has no business to do anything else. Yet he knows you better than me.'

'Ah, but he respects *you*!' the girl exclaimed, enviously.

Her visitor stared a moment; then he broke into a laugh. 'Doesn't he respect you?'

'Of course, but not in the same way. He respects what you've done – he told me so, the other day.'

'When you went to look at types?'

'Ah, we found so many – he has such an observation of them! He talked a great deal about your book. He says it's really important.'

'Important! Ah! the grand creature,' Paul murmured, hilarious.

'He was wonderfully amusing, he was inexpressibly droll, while we walked about. He sees everything; he has so many comparisons, and they are always exactly right. *C'est d'un trouvé!*[21] as they say.'

'Yes, with his gifts, such things as he ought to have done!' Paul Overt remarked.

'And don't you think he *has* done them?'

He hesitated a moment. 'A part of them – and of course even that part is immense. But he might have been one of the greatest! However, let us not make this an hour of qualifications. Even as they stand, his writings are a mine of gold.'

To this proposition Marian Fancourt ardently responded, and for half an hour the pair talked over the master's principal productions. She knew them well – she knew them even better than her visitor, who was struck with her critical intelligence and with something large and bold in the movement in her mind. She said things that startled him and that evidently had come to her directly; they were not picked-up phrases, she placed them too well. St George had been right about her being first-rate, about her not being afraid to gush, not remembering that she must be proud. Suddenly something reminded her, and she said: 'I recollect that he did speak of Mrs St George to me once. He said, *à propos* of something or other, that she didn't care for perfection.'

'That's a great crime, for an artist's wife,' said Paul Overt.

'Yes, poor thing!' and the young lady sighed, with a suggestion of many reflections, some of them mitigating. But she added in a moment, 'Ah, perfection, perfection – how one ought to go in for it! I wish I could.'

'Every one can, in his way,' said Paul Overt.

'In *his* way, yes; but not in hers. Women are so hampered – so condemned! But it's a kind of dishonour if you don't, when you want to *do* something, isn't it?' Miss Fancourt pursued,

dropping one train in her quickness to take up another, an accident that was common with her. So these two young persons
sat discussing high themes in their eclectic drawing-room, in
their London season – discussing, with extreme seriousness, the
high theme of perfection. And it must be said, in extenuation of
this eccentricity, that they were interested in the business; their
tone was genuine, their emotion real; they were not posturing
for each other or for some one else.

The subject was so wide that they found it necessary to contract it; the perfection to which for the moment they agreed to
confine their speculations was that of which the valid work of
art is susceptible. Miss Fancourt's imagination, it appeared,
had wandered far in that direction, and her visitor had the rare
delight of feeling that their conversation was a full interchange.
This episode will have lived for years in his memory and even
in his wonder; it had the quality that fortune distils in a single
drop at a time – the quality that lubricates ensuing weeks and
months. He has still a vision of the room, whenever he likes –
the bright, red, sociable, talkative room, with the curtains that,
by a stroke of successful audacity, had the note of vivid blue.
He remembers where certain things stood, the book that was
open on the table and the particular odour of the flowers that
were placed on the left, somewhere behind him. These facts
were the fringe, as it were, of a particular consciousness which
had its birth in those two hours and of which perhaps the most
general description would be to mention that it led him to say
over and over again to himself: 'I had no idea there was any
one like this – I had no idea there was any one like this!' Her
freedom amazed him and charmed him – it seemed so to
simplify the practical question. She was on the footing of an
independent personage – a motherless girl who had passed out
of her teens and had a position, responsibilities, and was not
held down to the limitations of a little miss. She came and went
without the clumsiness of a chaperon; she received people alone
and, though she was totally without hardness, the question of
protection or patronage had no relevancy in regard to her. She
gave such an impression of purity combined with naturalness
that, in spite of her eminently modern situation, she suggested

no sort of sisterhood with the 'fast' girl. Modern she was, indeed, and made Paul Overt, who loved old colour, the golden glaze of time, think with some alarm of the muddled palette of the future. He couldn't get used to her interest in the arts he cared for; it seemed too good to be real – it was so unlikely an adventure to tumble into such a well of sympathy. One might stray into the desert easily – that was on the cards and that was the law of life; but it was too rare an accident to stumble on a crystal well. Yet if her aspirations seemed at one moment too extravagant to be real, they struck him at the next as too intelligent to be false. They were both noble and crude, and whims for whims, he liked them better than any he had met. It was probable enough she would leave them behind – exchange them for politics, or 'smartness', or mere prolific maternity, as was the custom of scribbling, daubing, educated, flattered girls, in an age of luxury and a society of leisure. He noted that the water-colours on the walls of the room she sat in had mainly the quality of being *naïves*, and reflected that *naïveté* in art is like a cipher in a number: its importance depends upon the figure it is united with. But meanwhile he had fallen in love with her.

Before he went away he said to Miss Fancourt: 'I thought St George was coming to see you to-day – but he doesn't turn up.'

For a moment he supposed she was going to reply, '*Comment donc?*[22] Did you come here only to meet him?' But the next he became aware of how little such a speech would have fallen in with any flirtatious element he had as yet perceived in her. She only replied: 'Ah yes, but I don't think he'll come. He recommended me not to expect him.' Then she added, laughing: 'He said it wasn't fair to you. But I think I could manage two.'

'So could I,' Paul Overt rejoined, stretching the point a little to be humorous. In reality his appreciation of the occasion was so completely an appreciation of the woman before him that another figure in the scene, even so esteemed a one as St George, might for the hour have appealed to him vainly. As he went away he wondered what the great man had meant by its not being fair to him; and, still more than that, whether he had actually stayed away out of the delicacy of such an idea. As he took his course, swinging his stick, through the Sunday solitude of Manchester Square, with a good deal of emotion fermenting in his soul, it appeared to him that he was living in a world really magnanimous. Miss Fancourt had told him that there was an uncertainty about her being, and her father's being, in town on the following Sunday, but that she had the hope of a visit from him if they should not go away. She promised to let him know if they stayed at home, then he could act accordingly. After he had passed into one of the streets that lead out of the square, he stopped, without definite intentions, looking sceptically for a cab. In a moment he saw a hansom roll through the square from the other side and come a part of the way toward him. He was on the point of hailing the driver when he perceived that he carried a fare; then he waited, seeing him prepare to deposit his passenger by pulling up at one of the houses. The house was apparently the one he himself had just quitted; at least he drew that inference as he saw that the person who stepped out of the hansom was Henry St George. Paul Overt turned away quickly, as if he had been caught in the act of spying. He gave up his cab – he preferred to walk; he would go nowhere else. He was glad St George had not given up his visit altogether – that would have been too absurd. Yes, the world was magnanimous, and Overt felt so too as, on looking at his watch, he found it was only six o'clock, so that he could mentally congratulate his successor on having an hour still to sit in Miss Fancourt's drawing-room. He himself might use that hour for another visit, but by the time he reached the Marble Arch the idea of another visit had become incongruous to him. He passed beneath that architectural effort and walked into the Park till he got upon the grass. Here he continued to walk; he took his way across the elastic turf and came out by the Serpentine. He watched with a friendly eye the diversions of the London people, and bent a glance almost encouraging upon the young ladies paddling their sweethearts on the lake, and the guardsmen tickling tenderly with their bearskins the artificial flowers in the Sunday hats of their partners. He prolonged his meditative walk; he went into Kensington Gardens[23] – he sat upon the penny chairs – he looked at the little sail-boats launched upon the round pond – he was glad he had no engagement to dine. He repaired for this purpose, very late, to his club, where he found himself unable to order a repast and told the waiter to bring whatever he would. He did not even observe what he was served with, and he spent the evening in the library of the establishment, pretending to read an article in an American magazine. He failed to discover what it was about; it appeared in a dim way to be about Marian Fancourt.

Quite late in the week she wrote to him that she was not to go into the country – it had only just been settled. Her father, she added, would never settle anything – he put it all on her. She felt her responsibility – she had to – and since she was forced that was the way she had decided. She mentioned no reasons, which gave Paul Overt all the clearer field for bold conjecture about them. In Manchester Square, on this second Sunday, he esteemed his fortune less good, for she had three or four other visitors. But there were three or four compensations; the greatest, perhaps, of which was that, learning from her that her father had, after all, at the last hour, gone out of town alone, the bold conjecture I just now spoke of found itself becoming a shade more bold. And then her presence was her presence, and the personal red room was there and was full of it, whatever phantoms passed and vanished, emitting incomprehensible sounds. Lastly, he had the resource of staying till every one had come and gone and of supposing that this pleased her, though she gave no particular sign. When they were alone together he said to her: 'But St George did come – last Sunday. I saw him as I looked back.'

'Yes; but it was the last time.'

'The last time?'

'He said he would never come again.'

Paul Overt stared. 'Does he mean that he wishes to cease to see you?'

'I don't know what he means,' the girl replied, smiling. 'He won't, at any rate, see me here.'

'And, pray, why not?'

'I don't know,' said Marian Fancourt; and her visitor thought he had not yet seen her more beautiful than in uttering these unsatisfactory words.

V

'Oh, I say, I want you to remain,' Henry St George said to him at eleven o'clock, the night he dined with the head of the profession. The company had been numerous and they were taking their leave; our young man, after bidding good-night to his hostess, had put out his hand in farewell to the master of the house. Besides eliciting from St George the protest I have quoted this movement provoked a further observation about such a chance to have a talk, their going into his room, his having still everything to say. Paul Overt was delighted to be asked to stay; nevertheless he mentioned jocularly the literal fact that he had promised to go to another place, at a distance.

'Well then, you'll break your promise, that's all. You humbug!' St George exclaimed, in a tone that added to Overt's contentment.

'Certainly, I'll break it; but it was a real promise.'

'Do you mean to Miss Fancourt? You're following her?' St George asked.

Paul Overt answered by a question. 'Oh, is *she* going?'

'Base impostor!' his ironic host went on; 'I've treated you handsomely on the article of that young lady: I won't make another concession. Wait three minutes – I'll be with you.' He gave himself to his departing guests, went with the long-trained ladies to the door. It was a hot night, the windows were open, the sound of the quick carriages and of the linkmen's[24] call came into the house. The company had been brilliant; a sense of festal things was in the heavy air: not only the influence of that particular entertainment, but the suggestion of the wide hurry of pleasure which, in London, on summer nights, fills so many of the happier quarters of the complicated town. Gradually Mrs St George's drawing-room emptied itself; Paul Overt

was left alone with his hostess, to whom he explained the
motive of his waiting. 'Ah yes, some intellectual, some *professional*, talk,' she smiled; 'at this season doesn't one miss it?
Poor dear Henry, I'm so glad!' The young man looked out of
the window a moment, at the called hansoms that lurched up,
at the smooth broughams that rolled away. When he turned
round Mrs St George had disappeared; her husband's voice
came up to him from below – he was laughing and talking, in
the portico, with some lady who awaited her carriage. Paul had
solitary possession, for some minutes, of the warm, deserted
rooms, where the covered, tinted lamplight was soft, the seats
had been pushed about and the odour of flowers lingered. They
were large, they were pretty, they contained objects of value;
everything in the picture told of a 'good house'. At the end
of five minutes a servant came in with a request from Mr
St George that he would join him downstairs; upon which,
descending, he followed his conductor through a long passage
to an apartment thrown out, in the rear of the habitation, for
the special requirements, as he guessed, of a busy man of letters.

St George was in his shirt-sleeves in the middle of a large,
high room – a room without windows, but with a wide skylight
at the top, like a place of exhibition. It was furnished as a
library, and the serried bookshelves rose to the ceiling, a surface of incomparable tone, produced by dimly-gilt 'backs',
which was interrupted here and there by the suspension of
old prints and drawings. At the end furthest from the door
of admission was a tall desk, of great extent, at which the
person using it could only write standing, like a clerk in a
counting-house; and stretching from the door to this structure
was a large plain band of crimson cloth, as straight as a
garden-path and almost as long, where, in his mind's eye, Paul
Overt immediately saw his host pace to and fro during his
hours of composition. The servant gave him a coat, an old
jacket with an air of experience, from a cupboard in the wall,
retiring afterwards with the garment he had taken off. Paul
Overt welcomed the coat; it was a coat for talk and promised
confidences – it must have received so many – and had pathetic literary elbows. 'Ah, we're practical – we're practical!'

St George said, as he saw his visitor looking the place over. 'Isn't it a good big cage, to go round and round? My wife invented it and she locks me up here every morning.'

'You don't miss a window – a place to look out?'

'I did at first, awfully; but her calculation was just. It saves time, it has saved me many months in these ten years. Here I stand, under the eye of day – in London of course, very often, it's rather a bleared old eye – walled in to my trade. I can't get away, and the room is a fine lesson in concentration. I've learned the lesson, I think; look at that big bundle of proof and admit that I have.' He pointed to a fat roll of papers, on one of the tables, which had not been undone.

'Are you bringing out another—?' Paul Overt asked, in a tone of whose deficiencies he was not conscious till his companion burst out laughing, and indeed not even then.

'You humbug – you humbug! Don't I know what you think of them?' St George inquired, standing before him with his hands in his pockets and with a new kind of smile. It was as if he were going to let his young votary know him well now.

'Upon my word, in that case you know more than I do!' Paul ventured to respond, revealing a part of the torment of being able neither clearly to esteem him nor distinctly to renounce him.

'My dear fellow,' said his companion, 'don't imagine I talk about my books, specifically; it isn't a decent subject – *il ne manquerait plus que ça*[25] – I'm not so bad as you may apprehend! About myself, a little, if you like; though it wasn't for that I brought you down here. I want to ask you something – very much indeed – I value this chance. Therefore sit down. We are practical, but there *is* a sofa, you see, for she does humour me a little, after all. Like all really great administrators she knows when to.' Paul Overt sank into the corner of a deep leathern couch, but his interlocutor remained standing and said: 'If you don't mind, in this room this is my habit. From the door to the desk and from the desk to the door. That shakes up my imagination, gently; and don't you see what a good thing it is that there's no window for her to fly out of? The eternal standing as I write (I stop at that bureau and put it down, when anything comes, and so we go on), was rather wearisome at first, but we adopted it with an eye to the long run; you're in better order (if your legs don't break down!) and you can keep it up for more years. Oh, we're practical – we're practical!' St George repeated, going to the table and taking up, mechanically, the bundle of proofs. He pulled off the wrapper, he turned the papers over with a sudden change of attention which only made him more interesting to Paul Overt. He lost himself a moment, examining the sheets of his new book, while the younger man's eyes wandered over the room again.

'Lord, what good things I should do if I had such a charming place as this to do them in!' Paul reflected. The outer world, the world of accident and ugliness was so successfully excluded, and within the rich, protecting square, beneath the patronizing sky, the figures projected for an artistic purpose could hold their particular revel. It was a prevision of Paul Overt's rather than an observation on actual data, for which the occasions had been too few, that his new friend would have the quality, the charming quality, of surprising him by flashing out in personal intercourse, at moments of suspended, or perhaps even of diminished expectation. A happy relation with him would be a thing proceeding by jumps, not by traceable stages.

'Do you read them – really?' he asked, laying down the proofs on Paul's inquiring of him how soon the work would be published. And when the young man answered, 'Oh yes, always,' he was moved to mirth again by something he caught in his manner of saying that. 'You go to see your grandmother on her birthday – and very proper it is, especially as she won't last for ever. She has lost every faculty and every sense; she neither sees, nor hears, nor speaks; but all customary pieties and kindly habits are respectable. But you're strong if you *do* read 'em! *I* couldn't, my dear fellow. You *are* strong, I know; and that's just a part of what I wanted to say to you. You're very strong indeed. I've been going into your other things – they've interested me exceedingly. Some one ought to have told me about them before – some one I could believe. But whom can one believe? You're wonderfully in the good direction – it's 'extremely curious work. Now do you mean to keep it up? – that's what I want to ask you.'

'Do I mean to do others?' Paul Overt asked, looking up from his sofa at his erect inquisitor and feeling partly like a happy little boy when the schoolmaster is gay and partly like some pilgrim of old who might have consulted the oracle. St George's own performance had been infirm, but as an adviser he would be infallible.

'Others – others? Ah, the number won't matter; one other would do, if it were really a further step – a throb of the same effort. What I mean is, have you it in your mind to go in for some sort of little perfection?'

'Ah, perfection!' Overt sighed, 'I talked of that the other Sunday with Miss Fancourt.'

'Oh yes, they'll talk of it, as much as you like! But they do mighty little to help one to it. There's no obligation, of course; only you strike me as capable,' St George went on. 'You must have thought it all over. I can't believe you're without a plan. That's the sensation you give me, and it's so rare that it really stirs up one; it makes you remarkable. If you haven't a plan and you don't mean to keep it up, of course it's all right, it's no one's business, no one can force you, and not more than two or three people will notice that you don't go straight. The others – *all* the rest, every blessed soul in England, will think you do – will think you *are* keeping it up: upon my honour they will! I shall be one of the two or three who know better. Now the question is whether you can do it for two or three. Is that the stuff you're made of?'

'I could do it for one, if you were the one.'

'Don't say that – I don't deserve it; it scorches me,' St George exclaimed, with eyes suddenly grave and glowing. 'The "one" is of course oneself – one's conscience, one's idea, the single-ness of one's aim. I think of that pure spirit as a man thinks of a woman whom, in some detested hour of his youth, he has loved and forsaken. She haunts him with reproachful eyes, she lives for ever before him. As an artist, you know, I've married for money.' Paul stared and even blushed a little, confounded by this avowal; whereupon his host, observing the expression of his face, dropped a quick laugh and went on: 'You don't follow my figure. I'm not speaking of my dear wife, who had a small fortune, which, however, was not my bribe. I fell in love with her, as many other people have done. I refer to the mercenary muse whom I led to the altar of literature. Don't do that, my boy. She'll lead you a life!'

'Haven't you been happy!'

'Happy? It's a kind of hell.'

'There are things I should like to ask you,' Paul Overt said, hesitating.

'Ask me anything in all the world. I'd turn myself inside out to save you.'

'To save me?' Paul repeated.

'To make you stick to it – to make you see it through. As I said to you the other night at Summersoft, let my example be vivid to you.'

'Why, your books are not so bad as that,' said Paul, laughing and feeling that he breathed the air of art.

'So bad as what?'

'Your talent is so great that it is in everything you do, in what's less good as well as in what's best. You've some forty volumes to show for it – forty volumes of life, of observation, of magnificent ability.'

'I'm very clever, of course I know that,' St George replied, quietly. 'Lord, what rot they'd all be if I hadn't been! I'm a successful charlatan – I've been able to pass off my system. But do you know what it is? It's *carton-pierre*.'

'*Carton-pierre?*'

'Lincrusta-Walton!'

'Ah, don't say such things – you make me bleed!' the younger man protested. 'I see you in a beautiful, fortunate home, living in comfort and honour.'

'Do you call it honour?' St George interrupted, with an intonation that often comes back to his companion. 'That's what I want *you* to go in for. I mean the real thing. This is brummagaem.'[26]

'Brummagaem?' Paul ejaculated, while his eyes wandered,

by a movement natural at the moment, over the luxurious room.

'Ah, they make it so well to-day; it's wonderfully deceptive!'

'Is it deceptive that I find you living with every appearance of domestic felicity – blessed with a devoted, accomplished wife, with children whose acquaintance I haven't yet had the pleasure of making, but who *must* be delightful young people, from what I know of their parents?'

'It's all excellent, my dear fellow – heaven forbid I should deny it. I've made a great deal of money; my wife has known how to take care of it, to use it without wasting it, to put a good bit of it by, to make it fructify. I've got a loaf on the shelf; I've got everything, in fact, but the great thing—'

'The great thing?'

'The sense of having done the best – the sense, which is the real life of the artist and the absence of which is his death, of having drawn from his intellectual instrument the finest music that nature had hidden in it, of having played it as it should be played. He either does that or he doesn't – and if he doesn't he isn't worth speaking of. And precisely those who really know don't speak of him. He may still hear a great chatter, but what he hears most is the incorruptible silence of Fame. I have squared her, you may say, for my little hour – but what is my little hour? Don't imagine for a moment I'm such a cad as to have brought you down here to abuse or to complain of my wife to you. She is a woman of very distinguished qualities, to whom my obligations are immense; so that, if you please, we will say nothing about her. My boys – my children are all boys – are straight and strong, thank God! and have no poverty of growth about them, no penury of needs. I receive, periodically, the most satisfactory attestation from Harrow, from Oxford, from Sandhurst (oh, we have done the best for them!) of their being living, thriving, consuming organisms.'

'It must be delightful to feel that the son of one's loins is at Sandhurst,' Paul remarked enthusiastically.

'It is – it's charming. Oh, I'm a patriot!'

'Then what did you mean – the other night at Summersoft – by saying that children are a curse?'

'My dear fellow, on what basis are we talking?' St George asked, dropping upon the sofa, at a short distance from his visitor. Sitting a little sideways he leaned back against the opposite arm with his hands raised and interlocked behind his head. 'On the supposition that a certain perfection is possible and even desirable – isn't it so? Well, all I say is that one's children interfere with perfection. One's wife interferes. Marriage interferes.'

'You think then the artist shouldn't marry?'

'He does so at his peril – he does so at his cost.'

'Not even when his wife is in sympathy with his work?'

'She never is – she can't be! Women don't know what work is.'

'Surely, they work themselves,' Paul Overt objected.

'Yes, very badly. Oh, of course, often, they think they understand, they think they sympathize. Then it is that they are most dangerous. Their idea is that you shall do a great lot and get a great lot of money. Their great nobleness and virtue, their exemplary conscientiousness as British females, is in keeping you up to that. My wife makes all my bargains with my publishers for me, and she has done so for twenty years. She does it consummately well; that's why I'm really pretty well off. Are you not the father of their innocent babes, and will you withhold from them their natural sustenance? You asked me the other night if they were not an immense incentive. Of course they are – there's no doubt of that!'

'For myself, I have an idea I need incentives,' Paul Overt dropped.

'Ah well, then, *n'en parlons plus*!'[27] said his companion, smiling.

'You are an incentive, I maintain,' the young man went on. 'You don't affect me in the way you apparently would like to. Your great success is what I see – the pomp of Ennismore Gardens!'[28]

'Success? – do you call it success to be spoken of as you would speak of me if you were sitting here with another artist – a young man intelligent and sincere like yourself? Do you call it success to make you blush – as you would blush – if some foreign critic (some fellow, of course, I mean, who should know what he was talking about and should have shown you he did, as foreign critics like to show it!) were to say to you: "He's the one, in this country, whom they consider the most perfect, isn't he?" Is it success to be the occasion of a young Englishman's having to stammer as you would have to stammer at such a moment for old England? No, no; success is to have made people tremble after another fashion. Do try it!'

'Try it?'

'Try to do some really good work.'

'Oh, I want to, heaven knows!'

'Well, you can't do it without sacrifices; don't believe that for a moment,' said Henry St George. 'I've made none. I've had everything. In other words, I've missed everything.'

'You've had the full, rich, masculine, human, general life, with all the responsibilities and duties and burdens and sorrows and joys – all the domestic and social initiations and complications. They must be immensely suggestive, immensely amusing.'

'Amusing?'

'For a strong man – yes.'

'They've given me subjects without number, if that's what you mean; but they've taken away at the same time the power to use them. I've touched a thousand things, but which one of them have I turned into gold? The artist has to do only with that – he knows nothing of any baser metal. I've led the life of the world, with my wife and my progeny; the clumsy, expensive, materialized, brutalized, Philistine, snobbish life of London. We've got everything handsome, even a carriage – we are prosperous, hospitable, eminent people. But, my dear fellow, don't try to stultify yourself and pretend you don't know what we *haven't* got. It's bigger than all the rest. Between artists – come! You know as well as you sit there that you would put a pistol-ball into your brain if you had written my books!'

It appeared to Paul Overt that the tremendous talk promised by the master at Summersoft had indeed come off, and with a promptitude, a fullness, with which his young imagination had scarcely reckoned. His companion made an immense impression on him and he throbbed with the excitement of such deep soundings and such strange confidences. He throbbed indeed with the conflict of his feelings – bewilderment and recognition and alarm, enjoyment and protest and assent, all commingled with tenderness (and a kind of shame in the participation), for the sores and bruises exhibited by so fine a creature, and with a sense of the tragic secret that he nursed under his trappings. The idea of *his* being made the occasion of such an act of humility made him flush and pant, at the same time that his perception, in certain directions, had been too much awakened to conceal from him anything that St George really meant. It had been his odd fortune to blow upon the deep waters, to make them surge and break in waves of strange eloquence. He launched himself into a passionate contradiction of his host's last declaration; tried to enumerate to him the parts of his work he loved, the splendid things he had found in it, beyond the compass of any other writer of the day. St George listened awhile, courteously; then he said, laying his hand on Paul Overt's:

'That's all very well; and if your idea is to do nothing better there is no reason why you shouldn't have as many good things as I – as many human and material appendages, as many sons or daughters, a wife with as many gowns, a house with as many servants, a stable with as many horses, a heart with as many aches.' He got up when he had spoken thus, and then stood a moment near the sofa, looking down on his agitated pupil. 'Are you possessed of any money?' it occurred to him to ask.

'None to speak of.'

'Oh, well, there's no reason why you shouldn't make a goodish income – if you set about it the right way. Study *me* for that – study me well. You may really have a carriage.'

Paul Overt sat there for some moments without speaking. He looked straight before him – he turned over many things. His friend had wandered away from him, taking up a parcel of letters that were on the table where the roll of proofs had lain. 'What was the book Mrs St George made you burn – the one she didn't like?' he abruptly inquired.

'The book she made me burn – how did you know that?' St George looked up from his letters.

'I heard her speak of it at Summersoft.'

'Ah, yes; she's proud of it. I don't know – it was rather good.'

'What was it about?'

'Let me see.' And St George appeared to make an effort to remember. 'Oh, yes, it was about myself.' Paul Overt gave an irrepressible groan for the disappearance of such a production, and the elder man went on: 'Oh, but *you* should write it – *you* should do me. There's a subject, my boy: no end of stuff in it!'

Again Paul was silent, but after a little he spoke. 'Are there no women that really understand – that can take part in a sacrifice?'

'How can they take part? They themselves are the sacrifice. They're the idol and the altar and the flame.'

'Isn't there even *one* who sees further?' Paul continued.

For a moment St George made no answer to this; then, having torn up his letters, he stood before his disciple again, ironic. 'Of course I know the one you mean. But not even Miss Fancourt.'

'I thought you admired her so much.'

'It's impossible to admire her more. Are you in love with her?' St George asked.

'Yes,' said Paul Overt.

'Well, then, give it up.'

Paul stared. 'Give up my love?'

'Bless me, no; your idea.'

'My idea?'

'The one you talked with her about. The idea of perfection.'

'She would help it – she would help it!' cried the young man.

'For about a year – the first year, yes. After that she would be as a millstone round its neck.'

'Why, she has a passion for completeness, for good work – for everything you and I care for most.'

' "You and I" is charming, my dear fellow! She has it indeed, but she would have a still greater passion for her children; and very proper too. She would insist upon everything's being made comfortable, advantageous, propitious for them. That isn't the artist's business.'

'The artist – the artist! Isn't he a man all the same?'

St George hesitated. 'Sometimes I really think not. You know as well as I what he has to do: the concentration, the finish, the independence that he must strive for, from the moment that he begins to respect his work. Ah, my young friend, his relation to women, especially in matrimony, is at the mercy of this damning fact – that whereas he can in the nature of things have but one standard, they have about fifty. That's what makes them so superior,' St George added, laughing. 'Fancy an artist with a plurality of standards,' he went on. 'To *do* it – to do it and make it divine is the only thing he has to think about. "Is it done or not?" is his only question. Not "Is it done as well as a proper solicitude for my dear little family will allow?" He has nothing to do with the relative, nothing to do with a dear little family!'

'Then you don't allow him the common passions and affections of men?'

'Hasn't he a passion, an affection, which includes all the rest? Besides, let him have all the passions he likes – if he only keeps his independence. He must afford to be poor.'

Paul Overt slowly got up. 'Why did you advise me to make up to her, then?'

St George laid his hand on his shoulder. 'Because she would make an adorable wife! And I hadn't read you then.'

'I wish you had left me alone!' murmured the young man.

'I didn't know that that wasn't good enough for you,' St George continued.

'What a false position, what a condemnation of the artist, that he's a mere disfranchised monk and can produce his effect only by giving up personal happiness. What an arraignment of art!' Paul Overt pursued, with a trembling voice.

'Ah, you don't imagine, by chance, that I'm defending art? Arraignment, I should think so! Happy the societies in which it hasn't made its appearance; for from the moment it comes they have a consuming ache, they have an incurable corruption in their bosom. Assuredly, the artist is in a false position. But I thought we were taking him for granted. Pardon me,' St George continued; '*Ginistrella* made me!'

Paul Overt stood looking at the floor – one o'clock struck, in the stillness, from a neighbouring church-tower. 'Do you think she would ever look at me?' he asked at last.

'Miss Fancourt – as a suitor? Why shouldn't I think it? That's why I've tried to favour you – I have had a little chance or two of bettering your opportunity.'

'Excuse my asking you, but do you mean by keeping away yourself?' Paul said, blushing.

'I'm an old idiot – my place isn't there,' St George replied, gravely.

'I'm nothing, yet; I've no fortune; and there must be so many others.'

'You're a gentleman and a man of genius. I think you might do something.'

'But if I must give that up – the genius?'

'Lots of people, you know, think I've kept mine.'

'You have a genius for torment!' Paul Overt exclaimed; but taking his companion's hand in farewell as a mitigation of this judgment.

'Poor child, I do bother you. Try, try, then! I think your chances are good, and you'll win a great prize.'

Paul held the other's hand a minute; he looked into his face. 'No, I *am* an artist – I can't help it!'

'Ah, show it then!' St George broke out – 'let me see before I die the thing I most want, the thing I yearn for – a life in which the passion is really intense. If you can be rare, don't fail of it! Think what it is – how it counts – how it lives!' They had moved to the door and St George had closed both his own hands over that of his companion. Here they paused again and Paul Overt ejaculated – 'I want to live!'

'In what sense?'

'In the greatest sense.'

'Well then, stick to it – see it through.'

'With your sympathy – your help?'

'Count on that – you'll be a great figure to me. Count on my highest appreciation, my devotion. You'll give me satisfaction! – if that has any weight with you.' And as Paul appeared still to waver, St George added: 'Do you remember what you said to me at Summersoft?'

'Something infatuated, no doubt!'

' "I'll do anything in the world you tell me." You said that.'

'And you hold me to it?'

'Ah, what am I?' sighed the master, shaking his head.

'Lord, what things I shall have to do!' Paul almost moaned as he turned away.

VI

'It goes on too much abroad – hang abroad!' These, or something like them, had been St George's remarkable words in relation to the action of *Ginistrella*; and yet, though they had made a sharp impression on Paul Overt, like almost all the master's spoken words, the young man, a week after the conversation I have narrated, left England for a long absence and full of projects of work. It is not a perversion of the truth to say that that conversation was the direct cause of his departure. If the oral utterance of the eminent writer had the privilege of moving him deeply it was especially on his turning it over at leisure, hours and days afterward, that it appeared to yield its full meaning and exhibit its extreme importance. He spent the summer in Switzerland, and having, in September, begun a new task, he determined not to cross the Alps till he should have made a good start. To this end he returned to a quiet corner that he knew well, on the edge of the Lake of Geneva, within sight of the towers of Chillon:[29] a region and a view for which he had an affection springing from old associations, capable of mysterious little revivals and refreshments. Here he lingered late, till the snow was on the nearer hills, almost down to the limit to which he could climb when his stint was done, on the shortening afternoons. The autumn was fine, the lake was blue, and his book took form and direction. These circumstances, for the time, embroidered his life, and he suffered it to cover him with its mantle. At the end of six weeks he appeared to himself to have learned St George's lesson by heart – to have tested and proved its doctrine. Nevertheless he did a very inconsistent thing: before crossing the Alps he wrote to Marian

Fancourt. He was aware of the perversity of this act, and it was only as a luxury, an amusement, the reward of a strenuous autumn, that he justified it. She had not asked any such favour of him when he went to see her three days before he left London – three days after their dinner in Ennismore Gardens. It is true that she had no reason to, for he had not mentioned that he was on the eve of such an excursion. He hadn't mentioned it because he didn't know it; it was that particular visit that made the matter clear. He had paid the visit to see how much he really cared for her, and quick departure, without so much as a farewell, was the sequel to this inquiry, the answer to which had been a distinct superlative. When he wrote to her from Clarens[30] he noted that he owed her an explanation (more than three months after!) for the omission of such a form.

She answered him briefly but very promptly, and gave him a striking piece of news: the death, a week before, of Mrs St George. This exemplary woman had succumbed, in the country, to a violent attack of inflammation of the lungs – he would remember that for a long time she had been delicate. Miss Fancourt added that she heard her husband was overwhelmed with the blow; he would miss her unspeakably – she had been everything to him. Paul Overt immediately wrote to St George. He had wished to remain in communication with him, but had hitherto lacked the right excuse for troubling so busy a man. Their long nocturnal talk came back to him in every detail, but this did not prevent his expressing a cordial sympathy with the head of the profession, for had not that very talk made it clear that the accomplished lady was the influence that ruled his life? What catastrophe could be more cruel than the extinction of such an influence? This was exactly the tone that St George took in answering his young friend, upwards of a month later. He made no allusion, of course, to their important discussion. He spoke of his wife as frankly and generously as if he had quite forgotten that occasion, and the feeling of deep bereavement was visible in his words. 'She took every thing off my hands – off my mind. She carried on our life with the greatest art, the rarest devotion, and I was free, as few men can have been, to drive my pen, to shut myself up with my trade. This was a rare service – the highest she could have rendered me. Would I could have acknowledged it more fitly!'

A certain bewilderment, for Paul Overt, disengaged itself from these remarks: they struck him as a contradiction, a retraction. He had certainly not expected his correspondent to rejoice in the death of his wife, and it was perfectly in order that the rupture of a tie of more than twenty years should have left him sore. But if she was such a benefactress as that, what in the name of consistency had St George meant by turning *him* upside down that night – by dosing him to that degree, at the most sensitive hour of his life, with the doctrine of renunciation? If Mrs St George was an irreparable loss, then her husband's inspired advice had been a bad joke and renunciation was a mistake. Overt was on the point of rushing back to London to show that, for his part, he was perfectly willing to consider it so, and he went so far as to take the manuscript of the first chapters of his new book out of his table-drawer, to insert it into a pocket of his portmanteau. This led to his catching a glimpse of some pages he had not looked at for months, and that accident, in turn, to his being struck with the high promise they contained – a rare result of such retrospections, which it was his habit to avoid as much as possible. They usually made him feel that the glow of composition might be a purely subjective and a very barren emotion. On this occasion a certain belief in himself disengaged itself whimsically from the serried erasures of his first draft, making him think it best after all to carry out his present experiment to the end. If he could write as well as that under the influence of renunciation, it would be a pity to change the conditions before the termination of the work. He would go back to London of course, but he would go back only when he should have finished his book. This was the vow he privately made, restoring his manuscript to the table-drawer. It may be added that it took him a long time to finish his book, for the subject was as difficult as it was fine and he was literally embarrassed by the fullness of his notes. Something within him told him that he must make it supremely good – otherwise he should lack, as regards his private behaviour, a handsome excuse. He had a horror of this deficiency and found himself as firm as need be on the question of the lamp and the file. He crossed the Alps at last and spent the winter, the spring, the ensuing summer, in Italy, where still, at the end of a twelve-month, his task was unachieved. 'Stick to it – see it through': this general injunction of St George's was good also for the particular case. He applied it to the utmost, with the result that when in its slow order, the summer had come round again he felt that he had given all that was in him. This time he put his papers into his portmanteau, with the address of his publisher attached, and took his way northward.

He had been absent from London for two years – two years which were a long period and had made such a difference in his own life (through the production of a novel far stronger, he believed, than *Ginistrella*) that he turned out into Piccadilly, the morning after his arrival, with an indefinite expectation of changes, of finding that things had happened. But there were few transformations in Piccadilly (only three or four big red houses where there had been low black ones), and the brightness of the end of June peeped through the rusty railings of the Green Park and glittered in the varnish of the rolling carriages as he had seen it in other, more cursory Junes. It was a greeting that he appreciated; it seemed friendly and pointed, added to the exhilaration of his finished book, of his having his own country and the huge, oppressive, amusing city that suggested everything, that contained everything, under his hand again. 'Stay at home and do things here – do subjects we can measure,' St George had said; and now it appeared to him that he should ask nothing better than to stay at home for ever. Late in the afternoon he took his way to Manchester Square, looking out for a number he had not forgotten. Miss Fancourt, however, was not within, so that he turned, rather dejectedly, from the door. This movement brought him face to face with a gentleman who was approaching it and whom he promptly perceived to be Miss Fancourt's father. Paul saluted this personage, and the General returned his greeting with his customary good

manner – a manner so good, however, that you could never tell
whether it meant that he placed you. Paul Overt felt the impulse
to speak to him; then, hesitating, became conscious both that
he had nothing particular to say and that though the old soldier
remembered him he remembered him wrong. He therefore
passed on, without calculating on the irresistible effect that his
own evident recognition would have upon the General, who
never neglected a chance to gossip. Our young man's face was
expressive, and observation seldom let it pass. He had not
taken ten steps before he heard himself called after with a
friendly, semi-articulate 'A – I beg your pardon!' He turned
round and the General, smiling at him from the steps, said:
'Won't you come in? I won't leave you the advantage of me!'
Paul declined to come in, and then was sorry he had done so,
for Miss Fancourt, so late in the afternoon, might return at any
moment. But her father gave him no second chance; he appeared
mainly to wish not to have struck him as inhospitable. A further look at the visitor told him more about him, enough at
least to enable him to say – 'You've come back, you've come
back?' Paul was on the point of replying that he had come back
the night before, but he bethought himself to suppress this
strong light on the immediacy of his visit, and, giving merely
a general assent, remarked that he was extremely sorry not
to have found Miss Fancourt. He had come late, in the hope
that she would be in. 'I'll tell her – I'll tell her,' said the old man;
and then he added quickly, gallantly, 'You'll be giving us something new? It's a long time, isn't it?' Now he remembered him
right.

'Rather long. I'm very slow,' said Paul. 'I met you at Summersoft a long time ago.'

'Oh, yes, with Henry St George. I remember very well.
Before his poor wife—' General Fancourt paused a moment,
smiling a little less. 'I daresay you know.'

'About Mrs St George's death? Oh yes, I heard at the time.'

'Oh no; I mean – I mean he's to be married.'

'Ah! I've not heard that.' Just as Paul was about to add, 'To
whom?' the General crossed his intention with a question.

'When did you come back? I know you've been away – from

my daughter. She was very sorry. You ought to give her something new.'

'I came back last night,' said our young man, to whom something had occurred which made his speech, for the moment, a little thick.

'Ah, most kind of you to come so soon. Couldn't you turn up at dinner?'

'At dinner?' Paul Overt repeated, not liking to ask whom St George was going to marry, but thinking only of that.

'There are several people, I believe. Certainly St George. Or afterwards, if you like better. I believe my daughter expects—.' He appeared to notice something in Overt's upward face (on his steps he stood higher) which led him to interrupt himself, and the interruption gave him a momentary sense of awkwardness, from which he sought a quick issue. 'Perhaps then you haven't heard she's to be married.'

'To be married?' Paul stared.

'To Mr St George – it has just been settled. Odd marriage, isn't it?' Paul uttered no opinion on this point: he only continued to stare. 'But I daresay it will do – she's so awfully literary!' said the General.

Paul had turned very red. 'Oh, it's a surprise – very interesting, very charming! I'm afraid I can't dine – so many thanks!'

'Well, you must come to the wedding!' cried the General. 'Oh, I remember that day at Summersoft. He's a very good fellow.'

'Charming – charming!' Paul stammered, retreating. He shook hands with the General and got off. His face was red and he had the sense of its growing more and more crimson. All the evening at home – he went straight to his rooms and remained there dinnerless – his cheek burned at intervals as if it had been smitten. He didn't understand what had happened to him, what trick had been played him, what treachery practised. 'None, none,' he said to himself. 'I've nothing to do with it. I'm out of it – it's none of my business.' But that bewildered murmur was followed again and again by the incongruous ejaculation – 'Was it a plan – was it a plan?' Sometimes he cried to himself, breathless, 'Am I a dupe – am I a dupe?' If he was, he was an absurd, and abject one. It seemed to him he had never lost her till now. He had renounced her, yes; but that was another affair – that was a closed but not a locked door. Now he felt as if the door had been slammed in his face. Did he expect her to wait – was she to give him his time like that: two years at a stretch? He didn't know what he had expected – he only knew what he hadn't. It wasn't this – it wasn't this. Mystification, bitterness and wrath rose and boiled in him when he thought of the deference, the devotion, the credulity with which he had listened to St George. The evening wore on and the light was long; but even when it had darkened he remained without a lamp. He had flung himself on the sofa, and he lay there through the hours with his eyes either closed or gazing into the gloom, in the attitude of a man teaching himself to bear something, to bear having been made a fool of. He had made it too easy – that idea passed over him like a hot wave. Suddenly, as he heard eleven o'clock strike, he jumped up, remembering what General Fancourt had said about his coming after dinner. He would go – he would see her at least; perhaps he should see what it meant. He felt as if some of the elements of a hard sum had been given him and the others were wanting: he couldn't do his sum till he was in possession of them all.

He dressed quickly, so that by half-past eleven he was at Manchester Square. There were a good many carriages at the door – a party was going on; a circumstance which at the last gave him a slight relief, for now he would rather see her in a crowd. People passed him on the staircase; they were going away, going 'on', with the hunted, herdlike movement of London society at night. But sundry groups remained in the drawing-room, and it was some minutes, as she didn't hear him announced, before he discovered her and spoke to her. In this short interval he had perceived that St George was there, talking to a lady before the fireplace; but he looked away from him, for the moment, and therefore failed to see whether the author of *Shadowmere* noticed him. At all events he didn't come to him. Miss Fancourt did, as soon as she saw him; she almost rushed at him, smiling, rustling, radiant, beautiful. He had forgotten what her head, what her face offered to the sight; she was in white, there were gold figures on her dress, and her hair was like a casque of gold. In a single moment he saw she was happy, happy with a kind of aggressiveness, of splendour. But she would not speak to him of that, she would speak only of himself.

'I'm so delighted; my father told me. How kind of you to come!' She struck him as so fresh and brave, while his eyes moved over her, that he said to himself, irresistibly: 'Why to *him*, why not to youth, to strength, to ambition, to a future? Why, in her rich young capacity, to failure, to abdication, to superannuation?' In his thought, at that sharp moment, he blasphemed even against all that had been left of his faith in the peccable master. 'I'm so sorry I missed you,' she went on. 'My father told me. How charming of you to have come so soon!'

'Does that surprise you?' Paul Overt asked.

'The first day? No, from you – nothing that's nice.' She was interrupted by a lady who bade her good-night, and he seemed to read that it cost her nothing to speak to one in that tone; it was her old bounteous, demonstrative way, with a certain added amplitude that time had brought; and if it began to oper-ate on the spot, at such a juncture in her history, perhaps in the other days too it had meant just as little or as much – a sort of mechanical charity, with the difference now that she was satisfied, ready to give but asking nothing. Oh, she was satisfied – and why shouldn't she be? Why shouldn't she have been surprised at his coming the first day – for all the good she had ever got from him? As the lady continued to hold her atten-tion Paul Overt turned from her with a strange irritation in his complicated artistic soul and a kind of disinterested disap-pointment. She was so happy that it was almost stupid – it seemed to deny the extraordinary intelligence he had formerly found in her. Didn't she know how bad St George could be, hadn't she perceived the deplorable thinness—? If she didn't she was nothing, and if she did why such an insolence of seren-ity? This question expired as our young man's eyes settled at last upon the genius who had advised him in a great crisis.

St George was still before the chimney-piece, but now he was alone (fixed, waiting, as if he meant to remain after every one), and he met the clouded gaze of the young friend who was tormented with uncertainty as to whether he had the right (which his resentment would have enjoyed), to regard himself as his victim. Somehow, the fantastic inquiry I have just noted was answered by St George's aspect. It was as fine in its way as Marian Fancourt's – it denoted the happy human being; but somehow it represented to Paul Overt that the author of *Shadowmere* had now definitively ceased to count – ceased to count as a writer. As he smiled a welcome across the room he was almost *banal*, he was almost smug. Paul had the impression that for a moment he hesitated to make a movement forward, as if he had a bad conscience; but the next they had met in the middle of the room and had shaken hands, expressively, cordially on St George's part. Then they had passed together to where the elder man had been standing, while St George said: 'I hope you are never going away again. I have been dining here; the General told me.' He was handsome, he was young, he looked as if he had still a great fund of life. He bent the friendliest, most unconfessing eyes upon Paul Overt; asked him about everything, his health, his plans, his late occupations, the new book. 'When will it be out – soon, soon, I hope? Splendid, eh? That's right; you're a comfort! I've read you all over again, the last six months.' Paul waited to see if he would tell him what the General had told him in the afternoon, and what Miss Fancourt, verbally at least, of course had not. But as it didn't come out he asked at last: 'Is it true, the great news I hear, that you're to be married?'

'Ah, you *have* heard it then?'

'Didn't the General tell you?' Paul Overt went on.

'Tell me what?'

'That he mentioned it to me this afternoon?'

'My dear fellow, I don't remember. We've been in the midst of people. I'm sorry, in that case, that I lose the pleasure, myself, of announcing to you a fact that touches me so nearly. It *is* a fact, strange as it may appear. It has only just become one. Isn't it ridiculous?' St George made this speech without confusion, but on the other hand, so far as Paul could see, without latent impudence. It appeared to his interlocutor that, to talk so comfortably and coolly, he must simply have forgotten what had passed between them. His next words, however, showed that he had not, and they had, as an appeal to Paul's own memory, an effect which would have been ludicrous if it had not been cruel. 'Do you recollect the talk we had at my house that night, into which Miss Fancourt's name entered? I've often thought of it since.'

'Yes – no wonder you said what you did,' said Paul, looking at him.

'In the light of the present occasion? Ah! but there was no light then. How could I have foreseen this hour?'

'Didn't you think it probable?'

'Upon my honour, no,' said Henry St George. 'Certainly, I owe you that assurance. Think how my situation has changed.'

'I see – I see,' Paul murmured.

His companion went on, as if, now that the subject had been broached, he was, as a man of imagination and tact, perfectly ready to give every satisfaction – being able to enter fully into everything another might feel. 'But it's not only that – for honestly, at my age, I never dreamed – a widower, with big boys and with so little else! It has turned out differently from any possible calculation, and I am fortunate beyond all measure. She has been so free, and yet she consents. Better than any one else perhaps – for I remember how you liked her, before you went away, and how she liked you – you can intelligently congratulate me.'

'She has been so free!' Those words made a great impression on Paul Overt, and he almost writhed under that irony in them as to which it little mattered whether it was intentional or casual. Of course she had been free and, appreciably perhaps, by his own act; for was not St George's allusion to her having liked him a part of the irony too? 'I thought that by your theory you disapproved of a writer's marrying.'

'Surely – surely. But you don't call me a writer?'

'You ought to be ashamed,' said Paul.

'Ashamed of marrying again?'

'I won't say that – but ashamed of your reasons.'

'You must let me judge of them, my friend.'

'Yes; why not? For you judged wonderfully of mine.'

The tone of these words appeared suddenly, for Henry St George, to suggest the unsuspected. He stared as if he read a bitterness in them. 'Don't you think I have acted fair?'

'You might have told me at the time, perhaps.'

'My dear fellow, when I say I couldn't pierce futurity!'

'I mean afterwards.'

St George hesitated. 'After my wife's death?'

'When this idea came to you.'

'Ah, never, never! I wanted to save you, rare and precious as you are.'

'Are you marrying Miss Fancourt to save me?'

'Not absolutely, but it adds to the pleasure. I shall be the making of you,' said St George, smiling. 'I was greatly struck, after our talk, with the resolute way you quitted the country and still more, perhaps, with your force of character in remaining abroad. You're very strong – you're wonderfully strong.'

Paul Overt tried to sound his pleasant eyes; the strange thing was that he appeared sincere – not a mocking fiend. He turned away, and as he did so he heard St George say something about his giving them the proof, being the joy of his old age. He faced him again, taking another look. 'Do you mean to say you've stopped writing?'

'My dear fellow, of course I have. It's too late. Didn't I tell you?'

'I can't believe it!'

'Of course you can't – with your own talent! No, no; for the rest of my life I shall only read you.'

'Does she know that – Miss Fancourt?'

'She will – she will.' Our young man wondered whether St George meant this as a covert intimation that the assistance he should derive from that young lady's fortune, moderate as it was, would make the difference of putting it in his power to cease to work, ungratefully, an exhausted vein. Somehow, standing there in the ripeness of his successful manhood, he did not suggest that any of his veins were exhausted. 'Don't you remember the moral I offered myself to you – that night – as pointing?' St George continued. 'Consider, at any rate, the warning I am at present.'

This was too much – he *was* the mocking fiend. Paul separated from him with a mere nod for good-night; the sense that he might come back to him some time in the far future but could not fraternize with him now. It was necessary to his sore spirit to believe for the hour that he had a grievance – all the more cruel for not being a legal one. It was doubtless in the attitude of hugging this wrong that he descended the stairs without taking leave of Miss Fancourt, who had not been in view at the moment he quitted the room. He was glad to get out into the honest, dusky, unsophisticating night, to move fast, to take his way home on foot. He walked a long time, missing his way, not thinking of it. He was thinking of too many other things. His steps recovered their direction, however, and at the end of an hour he found himself before his door, in the small, inexpensive, empty street. He lingered, questioning himself still, before going in, with nothing around and above him but moonless blackness, a bad lamp or two and a few faraway dim stars. To these last faint features he raised his eyes; he had been saying to himself that there would have been mockery indeed if now, on his new foundation, at the end of a year, St George should put forth something with his early quality – something of the type of *Shadowmere* and finer than his finest. Greatly as he admired his talent Paul literally hoped such an incident would not occur; it seemed to him just then that he scarcely should be able to endure it. St George's words were still in his ears, 'You're very strong – wonderfully strong.' Was he really? Certainly, he would have to be; and it would be a sort of revenge. *Is* he? the reader may ask in turn, if his interest has followed the perplexed young man so far. The best answer to that perhaps is that he is doing his best but that it is too soon to say. When the new book came out in the autumn Mr and Mrs St George found it really magnificent. The former

THE REAL THING

When the porter's wife (she used to answer the house-bell), announced 'A gentleman – with a lady, sir,' I had, as I often had in those days, for the wish was father to the thought, an immediate vision of sitters. Sitters my visitors in this case proved to be; but not in the sense I should have preferred. However, there was nothing at first to indicate that they might not have come for a portrait. The gentleman, a man of fifty, very high and very straight, with a moustache slightly grizzled and a dark grey walking-coat admirably fitted, both of which I noted professionally – I don't mean as a barber or yet as a tailor – would have struck me as a celebrity if celebrities often were striking. It was a truth of which I had for some time been conscious that a figure with a good deal of front-age was, as one might say, almost never a public institution. A glance at the lady helped to remind me of this paradoxical law: she also looked too distinguished to be a 'personality'. Moreover one would scarcely come across two variations together.

Neither of the pair spoke immediately – they only prolonged the preliminary gaze which suggested that each wished to give the other a chance. They were visibly shy; they stood there letting me take them in – which, as I afterwards perceived, was the most practical thing they could have done. In this way their embarrassment served their cause. I had seen people painfully reluctant to mention that they desired anything so gross as to be represented on canvas; but the scruples of my new friends appeared almost insurmountable. Yet the gentleman might have said 'I should like a portrait of my wife,' and the lady might have said 'I should like a portrait of my husband.' Perhaps they were not husband and wife – this naturally would make the matter more delicate. Perhaps they wished to be done together – in which case they ought to have brought a third person to break the news.

'We come from Mr Rivet,' the lady said at last, with a dim smile which had the effect of a moist sponge passed over a 'sunk' piece of painting,[1] as well as of a vague allusion to vanished beauty. She was as tall and straight, in her degree, as her companion, and with ten years less to carry. She looked as sad as a woman could look whose face was not charged with expression; that is her tinted oval mask showed friction as an exposed surface shows it. The hand of time had played over her freely, but only to simplify. She was slim and stiff, and so well-dressed, in dark blue cloth, with lappets[2] and pockets and buttons, that it was clear she employed the same tailor as her husband. The couple had an indefinable air of prosperous thrift – they evidently got a good deal of luxury for their money. If I was to be one of their luxuries it would behove me to consider my terms.

'Ah, Claude Rivet recommended me?' I inquired; and I added that it was very kind of him, though I could reflect that, as he only painted landscape, this was not a sacrifice.

The lady looked very hard at the gentleman, and the gentleman looked round the room. Then staring at the floor a moment and stroking his moustache, he rested his pleasant eyes on me with the remark: 'He said you were the right one.'

'I try to be, when people want to sit.'

'Yes, we should like to,' said the lady anxiously.

'Do you mean together?'

My visitors exchanged a glance. 'If you could do anything with *me*, I suppose it would be double,' the gentleman stammered.

'Oh yes, there's naturally a higher charge for two figures than for one.'

'We should like to make it pay,' the husband confessed.

'That's very good of you,' I returned, appreciating so unwonted a sympathy – for I supposed he meant pay the artist.

A sense of strangeness seemed to dawn on the lady. 'We mean for the illustrations – Mr Rivet said you might put one in.'

'Put one in – an illustration?' I was equally confused.

'Sketch her off, you know,' said the gentleman, colouring.

It was only then that I understood the service Claude Rivet had rendered me; he had told them that I worked in black and white, for magazines, for story-books, for sketches of contemporary life, and consequently had frequent employment for models. These things were true, but it was not less true (I may confess it now – whether because the aspiration was to lead to everything or to nothing I leave the reader to guess), that I couldn't get the honours, to say nothing of the emoluments, of a great painter of portraits out of my head. My 'illustrations' were my pot-boilers; I looked to a different branch of art (far and away the most interesting it had always seemed to me), to perpetuate my fame. There was no shame in looking to it also to make my fortune; but that fortune was by so much further from being made from the moment my visitors wished to be 'done' for nothing. I was disappointed; for in the pictorial sense I had immediately *seen* them. I had seized their type – I had already settled what I would do with it. Something that wouldn't absolutely have pleased them, I afterwards reflected.

'Ah, you're – you're – a—?' I began, as soon as I had mastered my surprise. I couldn't bring out the dingy word 'models'; it seemed to fit the case so little.

'We haven't had much practice,' said the lady.

'We've got to *do* something, and we've thought that an artist in your line might perhaps make something of us,' her husband threw off. He further mentioned that they didn't know many artists and that they had gone first, on the off-chance (he painted views of course, but sometimes put in figures – perhaps I remembered), to Mr Rivet, whom they had met a few years before at a place in Norfolk where he was sketching.

'We used to sketch a little ourselves,' the lady hinted.

'It's very awkward, but we absolutely *must* do something,' her husband went on.

'Of course, we're not so *very* young,' she admitted, with a wan smile.

With the remark that I might as well know something more about them, the husband had handed me a card extracted from a neat new pocket-book (their appurtenances were all of the freshest) and inscribed with the words 'Major Monarch'. Impressive as these words were they didn't carry my knowledge much further; but my visitor presently added: 'I've left the army, and we've had the misfortune to lose our money. In fact our means are dreadfully small.'

'It's an awful bore,' said Mrs Monarch.

They evidently wished to be discreet – to take care not to swagger because they were gentlefolks. I perceived they would have been willing to recognize this as something of a drawback, at the same time that I guessed at an underlying sense – their consolation in adversity – that they *had* their points. They certainly had; but these advantages struck me as preponderantly social; such for instance as would help to make a drawing-room look well. However, a drawing-room was always, or ought to be, a picture.

In consequence of his wife's allusion to their age Major Monarch observed: 'Naturally, it's more for the figure that we thought of going in. We can still hold ourselves up.' On the instant I saw that the figure was indeed their strong point. His 'naturally' didn't sound vain, but it lighted up the question. '*She* has got the best,' he continued, nodding at his wife, with a pleasant after-dinner absence of circumlocution. I could only reply, as if we were in fact sitting over our wine, that this didn't prevent his own from being very good; which led him in turn to rejoin: 'We thought that if you ever have to do people like us, we might be something like it. *She*, particularly – for a lady in a book, you know.'

I was so amused by them that, to get more of it, I did my best to take their point of view; and though it was an embarrassment to find myself appraising physically, as if they were animals on hire or useful blacks, a pair whom I should have expected to meet only in one of the relations in which criticism is tacit, I looked at Mrs Monarch judicially enough to be able to exclaim, after a moment, with conviction: 'Oh yes, a lady in a book!' She was singularly like a bad illustration.

'We'll stand up, if you like,' said the Major; and he raised himself before me with a really grand air.

I could take his measure at a glance – he was six feet two and a perfect gentleman. It would have paid any club in process of formation and in want of a stamp to engage him at a salary to stand in the principal window. What struck me immediately was that in coming to me they had rather missed their vocation; they could surely have been turned to better account for advertising purposes. I couldn't of course see the thing in detail, but I could see them make someone's fortune – I don't mean their own. There was something in them for a waistcoat-maker, an hotel-keeper or a soap-vendor. I could imagine 'We always use it' pinned on their bosoms with the greatest effect; I had a vision of the promptitude with which they would launch a table d'hôte.

Mrs Monarch sat still, not from pride but from shyness, and presently her husband said to her: 'Get up my dear and show how smart you are.' She obeyed, but she had no need to get up to show it. She walked to the end of the studio, and then she came back blushing, with her fluttered eyes on her husband. I was reminded of an incident I had accidentally had a glimpse of in Paris – being with a friend there, a dramatist about to produce a play – when an actress came to him to ask to be entrusted with a part. She went through her paces before him, walked up and down as Mrs Monarch was doing. Mrs Monarch did it quite as well, but I abstained from applauding. It was very odd to see such people apply for such poor pay. She looked as if she had ten thousand a year. Her husband had used the word that described her: she was, in the London current jargon, essentially and typically 'smart'. Her figure was, in the same order of ideas, conspicuously and irreproachably 'good'. For a woman of her age her waist was surprisingly small; her elbow moreover had the orthodox crook. She held her head at the conventional angle; but why did she come to *me*? She ought to have tried on jackets at a big shop. I feared my visitors were not only destitute, but 'artistic' – which would be a great complication. When she sat down again I thanked her, observing that what a draughtsman most valued in his model was the faculty of keeping quiet.

'Oh, *she* can keep quiet,' said Major Monarch. Then he added, jocosely: 'I've always kept her quiet.'

'I'm not a nasty fidget, am I?' Mrs Monarch appealed to her husband.

He addressed his answer to me. 'Perhaps it isn't out of place to mention – because we ought to be quite business-like, oughtn't we? – that when I married her she was known as the Beautiful Statue.'

'Oh dear!' said Mrs Monarch, ruefully.

'Of course I should want a certain amount of expression,' I rejoined.

'Of *course*!' they both exclaimed.

'And then I suppose you know that you'll get awfully tired.'

'Oh, we *never* get tired!' they eagerly cried.

'Have you had any kind of practice?'

They hesitated – they looked at each other. 'We've been photographed, *immensely*,' said Mrs Monarch.

'She means the fellows have asked us,' added the Major.

'I see – because you're so good-looking.'

'I don't know what they thought, but they were always after us.'

'We always got our photographs for nothing,' smiled Mrs Monarch.

'We might have brought some, my dear,' her husband remarked.

'I'm not sure we have any left. We've given quantities away,' she explained to me.

'With our autographs and that sort of thing,' said the Major.

'Are they to be got in the shops?' I inquired, as a harmless pleasantry.

'Oh, yes; *hers* – they used to be.'

'Not now,' said Mrs Monarch, with her eyes on the floor.

II

I could fancy the 'sort of thing' they put on the presentation-copies of their photographs, and I was sure they wrote a beautiful hand. It was odd how quickly I was sure of everything that concerned them. If they were now so poor as to have to earn shillings and pence, they never had had much of a margin. Their good looks had been their capital, and they had good-humouredly made the most of the career that this resource marked out for them. It was in their faces, the blankness, the deep intellectual repose of the twenty years of country-house visiting which had given them pleasant intonations. I could see the sunny drawing-rooms, sprinkled with periodicals she didn't read, in which Mrs Monarch had continuously sat; I could see the wet shrubberies in which she had walked, equipped to admiration for either exercise. I could see the rich covers the Major had helped to shoot and the wonderful garments in which, late at night, he repaired to the smoking-room to talk about them. I could imagine their leggings and waterproofs, their knowing tweeds and rugs, their rolls of sticks and cases of tackle and neat umbrellas; and I could evoke the exact appearance of their servants and the compact variety of their luggage on the platforms of country stations.

They gave small tips, but they were liked; they didn't do anything themselves, but they were welcome. They looked so well everywhere; they gratified the general relish for stature, complexion and 'form'. They knew it without fatuity or vulgarity, and they respected themselves in consequence. They were not superficial; they were thorough and kept themselves up – it had been their line. People with such a taste for activity had to have some line. I could feel how, even in a dull house, they could have been counted upon for cheerfulness. At present something had happened – it didn't matter what, their little income had grown less, it had grown least – and they had to do something for pocket-money. Their friends liked them, but didn't like to support them. There was something about them that represented credit – their clothes, their manners, their type;

but if credit is a large empty pocket in which an occasional chink reverberates, the chink at least must be audible. What they wanted of me was to help to make it so. Fortunately they had no children – I soon divined that. They would also perhaps wish our relations to be kept secret: this was why it was 'for the figure' – the reproduction of the face would betray them.

I liked them – they were so simple; and I had no objection to them if they would suit. But, somehow, with all their perfections I didn't easily believe in them. After all they were amateurs, and the ruling passion of my life was the detestation of the amateur. Combined with this was another perversity – an innate preference for the represented subject over the real one: the defect of the real one was so apt to be a lack of representation. I liked things that appeared; then one was sure. Whether they *were* or not was a subordinate and almost always a profitless question. There were other considerations, the first of which was that I already had two or three people in use, notably a young person with big feet, in alpaca, from Kilburn,[3] who for a couple of years had come to me regularly for my illustrations and with whom I was still – perhaps ignobly – satisfied. I frankly explained to my visitors how the case stood; but they had taken more precautions than I supposed. They had reasoned out their opportunity, for Claude Rivet had told them of the projected *édition de luxe* of one of the writers of our day – the rarest of the novelists – who, long neglected by the multitudinous vulgar and dearly prized by the attentive (need I mention Philip Vincent?)[4] had had the happy fortune of seeing, late in life, the dawn and then the full light of a higher criticism – an estimate in which, on the part of the public, there was something really of expiation. The edition in question, planned by a publisher of taste, was practically an act of high reparation; the wood-cuts with which it was to be enriched were the homage of English art to one of the most independent representatives of English letters. Major and Mrs Monarch confessed to me that they had hoped I might be able to work *them* into my share of the enterprise. They knew I was to do the first of the books, 'Rutland Ramsay', but I had to make clear to them that my participation in the rest of the affair – this first book was to be a test – was to depend on the satisfaction I should give. If this should be limited my employers would drop me without a scruple. It was therefore a crisis for me, and naturally I was making special preparations, looking about for new people, if they should be necessary, and securing the best types. I admitted however that I should like to settle down to two or three good models who would do for everything.

'Should we have often to – a – put on special clothes?' Mrs Monarch timidly demanded.

'Dear, yes – that's half the business.'

'And should we be expected to supply our own costumes?'

'Oh, no; I've got a lot of things. A painter's models put on – or put off – anything he likes.'

'And do you mean – a – the same?'

'The same?'

Mrs Monarch looked at her husband again.

'Oh, she was just wondering,' he explained, 'if the costumes are in *general* use.' I had to confess that they were, and I mentioned further that some of them (I had a lot of genuine, greasy last-century things), had served their time, a hundred years ago, on living, world-stained men and women. 'We'll put on anything that *fits*,' said the Major.

'Oh, I arrange that – they fit in the pictures.'

'I'm afraid I should do better for the modern books. I would come as you like,' said Mrs Monarch.

'She has got a lot of clothes at home: they might do for contemporary life,' her husband continued.

'Oh, I can fancy scenes in which you'd be quite natural.' And indeed I could see the slipshod rearrangements of stale properties – the stories I tried to produce pictures for without the exasperation of reading them – whose sandy tracts the good lady might help to people. But I had to return to the fact that for this sort of work – the daily mechanical grind – I was already equipped; the people I was working with were fully adequate.

'We only thought we might be more like *some* characters,' said Mrs Monarch mildly, getting up.

Her husband also rose; he stood looking at me with a dim wistfulness that was touching in so fine a man. 'Wouldn't it be rather a pull sometimes to have – a – to have—?' He hung fire; he wanted me to help him by phrasing what he meant. But I couldn't – I didn't know. So he brought it out, awkwardly: 'The *real* thing; a gentleman, you know, or a lady.' I was quite ready to give a general assent – I admitted that there was a great deal in that. This encouraged Major Monarch to say, following up his appeal with an unacted gulp: 'It's awfully hard – we've tried everything.' The gulp was communicative; it proved too much for his wife. Before I knew it Mrs Monarch had dropped again upon a divan and burst into tears. Her husband sat down beside her, holding one of her hands; whereupon she quickly dried her eyes with the other, while I felt embarrassed as she looked up at me. 'There isn't a confounded job I haven't applied for – waited for – prayed for. You can fancy we'd be pretty bad first. Secretaryships and that sort of thing? You might as well ask for a peerage. I'd be *anything* – I'm strong; a messenger or a coalheaver. I'd put on a gold-laced cap and open carriage-doors in front of the haberdasher's; I'd hang about a station, to carry portmanteaus; I'd be a postman. But they won't *look* at you; there are thousands, as good as yourself, already on the ground. *Gentlemen*, poor beggars, who have drunk their wine, who have kept their hunters!'

I was as reassuring as I knew how to be, and my visitors were presently on their feet again while, for the experiment, we agreed on an hour. We were discussing it when the door opened and Miss Churm came in with a wet umbrella. Miss Churm had to take the omnibus to Maida Vale[5] and then walk half-a-mile. She looked a trifle blowsy and slightly splashed. I scarcely ever saw her come in without thinking afresh how odd it was that, being so little in herself, she should yet be so much in others. She was a meagre little Miss Churm, but she was an ample heroine of romance. She was only a freckled cockney, but she could represent everything, from a fine lady to a shepherdess; she had the faculty, as she might have had a fine voice or long hair. She couldn't spell, and she loved beer, but she had two or three 'points', and practice, and a knack, and mother-wit, and a kind of whimsical sensibility, and a love of the theatre, and seven sisters, and not an ounce of respect, especially for the *h*.[6] The first thing my visitors saw was that her umbrella was wet, and in their spotless perfection they visibly winced at it. The rain had come on since their arrival.

'I'm all in a soak; there *was* a mess of people in the 'bus. I wish you lived near a stytion,' said Miss Churm. I requested her to get ready as quickly as possible, and she passed into the room in which she always changed her dress. But before going out she asked me what she was to get into this time.

'It's the Russian princess, don't you know?' I answered; 'the one with the "golden eyes", in black velvet, for the long thing in the *Cheapside*.'[7]

'Golden eyes? I *say*!' cried Miss Churm, while my companions watched her with intensity as she withdrew. She always arranged herself, when she was late, before I could turn round; and I kept my visitors a little, on purpose, so that they might get an idea, from seeing her, what would be expected of themselves. I mentioned that she was quite my notion of an excellent model – she was really very clever.

'Do you think she looks like a Russian princess?' Major Monarch asked, with lurking alarm.

'When I make her, yes.'

'Oh, if you have to *make* her—!' he reasoned, acutely.

'That's the most you can ask. There are so many that are not makeable.'

'Well now, *here's* a lady' – and with a persuasive smile he passed his arm into his wife's – 'who's already made!'

'Oh, I'm not a Russian princess,' Mrs Monarch protested, a little coldly. I could see that she had known some and didn't like them. There, immediately, was a complication of a kind that I never had to fear with Miss Churm.

This young lady came back in black velvet – the gown was rather rusty and very low on her lean shoulders – and with a Japanese fan in her red hands. I reminded her that in the scene I was doing she had to look over someone's head. 'I forget whose it is; but it doesn't matter. Just look over a head.'

'I'd rather look over a stove,' said Miss Churm; and she took her station near the fire. She fell into position, settled herself into a tall attitude, gave a certain backward inclination to her head and a certain forward droop to her fan, and looked, at least to my prejudiced sense, distinguished and charming, foreign and dangerous. We left her looking so, while I went downstairs with Major and Mrs Monarch.

'I think I could come about as near it as that,' said Mrs Monarch.

'Oh, you think she's shabby, but you must allow for the alchemy of art.'

However, they went off with an evident increase of comfort, founded on their demonstrable advantage in being the real thing. I could fancy them shuddering over Miss Churm. She was very droll about them when I went back, for I told her what they wanted.

'Well, if *she* can sit I'll tyke to bookkeeping,' said my model.

'She's very lady-like,' I replied, as an innocent form of aggravation.

'So much the worse for *you*. That means she can't turn round.'

'She'll do for the fashionable novels.'

'Oh yes, she'll *do* for them!' my model humorously declared. 'Ain't they bad enough without her?' I had often sociably denounced them to Miss Churm.

III

It was for the elucidation of a mystery in one of these works that I first tried Mrs Monarch. Her husband came with her, to be useful if necessary – it was sufficiently clear that as a general thing he would prefer to come with her. At first I wondered if this were for 'propriety's' sake – if he were going to be jealous and meddling. The idea was too tiresome, and if it had been confirmed it would speedily have brought our acquaintance to a close. But I soon saw there was nothing in it and that if he accompanied Mrs Monarch it was (in addition to the chance of being wanted), simply because he had nothing else to do. When she was away from him his occupation was gone – she never *had* been away from him. I judged, rightly, that in their awkward situation their close union was their main comfort and that this union had no weak spot. It was a real marriage, an encouragement to the hesitating, a nut for pessimists to crack. Their address was humble (I remember afterwards thinking it had been the only thing about them that was really professional), and I could fancy the lamentable lodgings in which the Major would have been left alone. He could bear them with his wife – he couldn't bear them without her.

He had too much tact to try and make himself agreeable when he couldn't be useful; so he simply sat and waited, when I was too absorbed in my work to talk. But I liked to make him talk – it made my work, when it didn't interrupt it, less sordid, less special. To listen to him was to combine the excitement of going out with the economy of staying at home. There was only one hindrance: that I seemed not to know any of the people he and his wife had known. I think he wondered extremely, during the term of our intercourse, whom the deuce I *did* know. He hadn't a stray sixpence of an idea to fumble for; so we didn't spin it very fine – we confined ourselves to questions of leather and even of liquor (saddlers and breeches-makers and how to get good claret cheap), and matters like 'good trains' and the habits of small game. His lore on these last subjects was astonishing, he managed to interweave the station-master with the ornithologist. When he couldn't talk about greater things he could talk cheerfully about smaller, and since I couldn't accompany him into reminiscences of the fashionable world he could lower the conversation without a visible effort to my level.

So earnest a desire to please was touching in a man who could so easily have knocked one down. He looked after the fire and had an opinion on the draught of the stove, without my asking him, and I could see that he thought many of my arrangements not half clever enough. I remember telling him that if I were only rich I would offer him a salary to come and teach me how to live. Sometimes he gave a random sigh, of which the essence was: 'Give me even such a bare old barrack as *this*, and I'd do something with it!' When I wanted to use

him he came alone; which was an illustration of the superior
courage of women. His wife could bear her solitary second
floor, and she was in general more discreet; showing by various
small reserves that she was alive to the propriety of keeping our
relations markedly professional – not letting them slide into
sociability. She wished it to remain clear that she and the Major
were employed, not cultivated, and if she approved of me as a
superior, who could be kept in his place, she never thought me
quite good enough for an equal.

She sat with great intensity, giving the whole of her mind to
it, and was capable of remaining for an hour almost as motionless as if she were before a photographer's lens. I could see she
had been photographed often, but somehow the very habit that
made her good for that purpose unfitted her for mine. At first I
was extremely pleased with her lady-like air, and it was a satisfaction, on coming to follow her lines, to see how good they
were and how far they could lead the pencil. But after a few
times I began to find her too insurmountably stiff; do what I
would with it my drawing looked like a photograph or a copy
of a photograph. Her figure had no variety of expression – she
herself had no sense of variety. You may say that this was my
business, was only a question of placing her. I placed her in
every conceivable position, but she managed to obliterate their
differences. She was always a lady certainly, and into the bargain was always the same lady. She was the real thing, but
always the same thing. There were moments when I was
oppressed by the serenity of her confidence that she *was* the
real thing. All her dealings with me and all her husband's were
an implication that this was lucky for *me*. Meanwhile I found
myself trying to invent types that approached her own, instead
of making her own transform itself – in the clever way that was
not impossible, for instance, to poor Miss Churm. Arrange as I
would and take the precautions I would, she always, in my
pictures, came out too tall – landing me in the dilemma of having represented a fascinating woman as seven feet high, which,
out of respect perhaps to my own very much scantier inches,
was far from my idea of such a personage.

The case was worse with the Major – nothing I could do

would keep *him* down, so that he became useful only for the representation of brawny giants. I adored variety and range, I cherished human accidents, the illustrative note; I wanted to characterize closely, and the thing in the world I most hated was the danger of being ridden by a type. I had quarrelled with some of my friends about it – I had parted company with them for maintaining that one *had* to be, and that if the type was beautiful (witness Raphael and Leonardo), the servitude was only a gain. I was neither Leonardo nor Raphael; I might only be a presumptuous young modern searcher, but I held that everything was to be sacrificed sooner than character. When they averred that the haunting type in question could easily *be* character, I retorted, perhaps superficially: 'Whose?' It couldn't be everybody's – it might end in being nobody's.

After I had drawn Mrs Monarch a dozen times I perceived more clearly than before that the value of such a model as Miss Churm resided precisely in the fact that she had no positive stamp, combined of course with the other fact that what she did have was a curious and inexplicable talent for imitation. Her usual appearance was like a curtain which she could draw up at request for a capital performance. This performance was simply suggestive; but it was a word to the wise – it was vivid and pretty. Sometimes, even, I thought it, though she was plain herself, too insipidly pretty; I made it a reproach to her that the figures drawn from her were monotonously (*bêtement*,[8] as we used to say) graceful. Nothing made her more angry: it was so much her pride to feel that she could sit for characters that had nothing in common with each other. She would accuse me at such moments of taking away her 'reputytion'.

It suffered a certain shrinkage, this queer quantity, from the repeated visits of my new friends. Miss Churm was greatly in demand, never in want of employment, so I had no scruple in putting her off occasionally, to try them more at my ease. It was certainly amusing at first to do the real thing – it was amusing to do Major Monarch's trousers. They *were* the real thing, even if he did come out colossal. It was amusing to do his wife's back hair (it was so mathematically neat), and the particular 'smart' tension of her tight stays. She lent herself especially to positions in which the face was somewhat averted or blurred; she abounded in lady-like back views and *profils perdus*.[9] When she stood erect she took naturally one of the attitudes in which court-painters represent queens and princesses; so that I found myself wondering whether, to draw out this accomplishment, I couldn't get the editor of the *Cheapside* to publish a really royal romance, 'A Tale of Buckingham Palace'. Sometimes, however, the real thing and the make-believe came into contact; by which I mean that Miss Churm, keeping an appointment or coming to make one on days when I had much work in hand, encountered her invidious rivals. The encounter was not on their part, for they noticed her no more than if she had been the housemaid; not from intentional loftiness, but simply because, as yet, professionally, they didn't know how to fraternize, as I could guess that they would have liked – or at least that the Major would. They couldn't talk about the omnibus – they always walked; and they didn't know what else to try – she wasn't interested in good trains or cheap claret. Besides, they must have felt – in the air – that she was amused at them, secretly derisive of their ever knowing how. She was not a person to conceal her scepticism if she had had a chance to show it. On the other hand Mrs Monarch didn't think her tidy; for why else did she take pains to say to me (it was going out of the way, for Mrs Monarch), that she didn't like dirty women?

One day when my young lady happened to be present with my other sitters (she even dropped in, when it was convenient, for a chat), I asked her to be so good as to lend a hand in getting tea – a service with which she was familiar and which was one of a class that, living as I did in a small way, with slender domestic resources, I often appealed to my models to render. They liked to lay hands on my property, to break the sitting, and sometimes the china – I made them feel Bohemian. The next time I saw Miss Churm after this incident she surprised me greatly by making a scene about it – she accused me of having wished to humiliate her. She had not resented the outrage at the time, but had seemed obliging and amused, enjoying the comedy of asking Mrs Monarch, who sat vague and silent, whether she would have cream and sugar, and putting an exaggerated simper into the question. She had tried intonations – as if she too wished to pass for the real thing; till I was afraid my other visitors would take offence.

Oh, *they* were determined not to do this; and their touching patience was the measure of their great need. They would sit by the hour, uncomplaining, till I was ready to use them; they would come back on the chance of being wanted and would walk away cheerfully if they were not. I used to go to the door with them to see in what magnificent order they retreated. I tried to find other employment for them – I introduced them to several artists. But they didn't 'take', for reasons I could appreciate, and I became conscious, rather anxiously, that after such disappointments they fell back upon me with a heavier weight. They did me the honour to think that it was I who was most *their* form. They were not picturesque enough for the painters, and in those days there were not so many serious workers in black and white. Besides, they had an eye to the great job I had mentioned to them – they had secretly set their hearts on supplying the right essence for my pictorial vindication of our fine novelist. They knew that for this undertaking I should want no costume-effects, none of the frippery of past ages – that it was a case in which everything would be contemporary and satirical and, presumably, genteel. If I could work them into it their future would be assured, for the labour would of course be long and the occupation steady.

One day Mrs Monarch came without her husband – she explained his absence by his having had to go to the City. While she sat there in her usual anxious stiffness there came, at the door, a knock which I immediately recognized as the subdued appeal of a model out of work. It was followed by the entrance of a young man whom I easily perceived to be a foreigner and who proved in fact an Italian acquainted with no English word but my name, which he uttered in a way that made it seem to include all others. I had not then visited his country, nor was I proficient in his tongue; but as he was not so meanly constituted – what Italian is? – as to depend only on that member for expression he conveyed to me, in familiar but graceful mimicry, that he was in search of exactly the employment in which the lady before me was engaged. I was not struck with him at first, and while I continued to draw I emitted rough sounds of discouragement and dismissal. He stood his ground, however, not importunately, but with a dumb, dog-like fidelity in his eyes which amounted to innocent impudence – the manner of a devoted servant (he might have been in the house for years), unjustly suspected. Suddenly I saw that this very attitude and expression made a picture, whereupon I told him to sit down and wait till I should be free. There was another picture in the way he obeyed me, and I observed as I worked that there were others still in the way he looked wonderingly, with his head thrown back, about the high studio. He might have been crossing himself in St Peter's. Before I finished I said to myself: 'The fellow's a bankrupt orange-monger, but he's a treasure.'

When Mrs Monarch withdrew he passed across the room like a flash to open the door for her, standing there with the rapt, pure gaze of the young Dante spellbound by the young Beatrice. As I never insisted, in such situations, on the blankness of the British domestic, I reflected that he had the making of a servant (and I needed one, but couldn't pay him to be only that), as well as of a model; in short I made up my mind to adopt my bright adventurer if he would agree to officiate in the double capacity. He jumped at my offer, and in the event my rashness (for I had known nothing about him), was not brought home to me. He proved a sympathetic though a desultory ministrant, and had in a wonderful degree the *sentiment de la pose*. It was uncultivated, instinctive; a part of the happy instinct which had guided him to my door and helped him to spell out my name on the card nailed to it. He had had no other introduction to me than a guess, from the shape of my high north window, seen outside, that my place was a studio and that as a studio it would contain an artist. He had wandered to England in search of fortune, like other itinerants, and had embarked, with a partner and a small green handcart, on the sale of penny ices. The ices had melted away and the partner had dissolved in their train. My young man wore tight yellow trousers with reddish stripes and his name was Oronte. He was sallow but fair, and when I put him into some old clothes of my own he looked like an Englishman. He was as good as Miss Churm, who could look, when required, like an Italian.

IV

I thought Mrs Monarch's face slightly convulsed when, on her coming back with her husband, she found Oronte installed. It was strange to have to recognize in a scrap of a *lazzarone*[10] a competitor to her magnificent Major. It was she who scented danger first, for the Major was anecdotically unconscious. But Oronte gave us tea, with a hundred eager confusions (he had never seen such a queer process), and I think she thought better of me for having at last an 'establishment'. They saw a couple of drawings that I had made of the establishment, and Mrs Monarch hinted that it never would have struck her that he had sat for them. 'Now the drawings you make from *us*, they look exactly like us,' she reminded me, smiling in triumph; and I recognized that this was indeed just their defect. When I drew the Monarchs I couldn't, somehow, get away from them – get into the character I wanted to represent; and I had not the least desire my model should be discoverable in my picture. Miss Churm never was, and Mrs Monarch thought I hid her, very properly, because she was vulgar; whereas if she was lost it was only as the dead who go to heaven are lost – in the gain of an angel the more.

By this time I had got a certain start with 'Rutland Ramsay', the first novel in the great projected series; that is I had produced a dozen drawings, several with the help of the Major and his wife, and I had sent them in for approval. My understanding with the publishers, as I have already hinted, had been that I was to be left to do my work, in this particular case, as I liked, with the whole book committed to me; but my connection with the rest of the series was only contingent. There were moments when, frankly, it *was* a comfort to have the real thing under one's hand; for there were characters in 'Rutland Ramsay' that were very much like it. There were people presumably as

straight as the Major and women of as good a fashion as
Mrs Monarch. There was a great deal of country-house life –
treated, it is true, in a fine, fanciful, ironical, generalized
way – and there was a considerable implication of knicker-
bockers and kilts. There were certain things I had to settle at
the outset; such things for instance as the exact appearance of
the hero, the particular bloom of the heroine. The author of
course gave me a lead, but there was a margin for interpretation. I took the Monarchs into my confidence, I told them
frankly what I was about, I mentioned my embarrassments and
alternatives. 'Oh, take *him*!' Mrs Monarch murmured sweetly,
looking at her husband; and 'What could you want better than
my wife?' the Major inquired, with the comfortable candour
that now prevailed between us.

I was not obliged to answer these remarks – I was only
obliged to place my sitters. I was not easy in mind, and I post-
poned, a little timidly perhaps, the solution of the question.
The book was a large canvas, the other figures were numerous,
and I worked off at first some of the episodes in which the hero
and the heroine were not concerned. When once I had set *them*
up I should have to stick to them – I couldn't make my young
man seven feet high in one place and five feet nine in another. I
inclined on the whole to the latter measurement, though the
Major more than once reminded me that *he* looked about as
young as anyone. It was indeed quite possible to arrange him,
for the figure, so that it would have been difficult to detect his
age. After the spontaneous Oronte had been with me a month,
and after I had given him to understand several different times
that his native exuberance would presently constitute an insurmountable barrier to our further intercourse, I waked to a
sense of his heroic capacity. He was only five feet seven, but the
remaining inches were latent. I tried him almost secretly at first,
for I was really rather afraid of the judgment my other models
would pass on such a choice. If they regarded Miss Churm as
little better than a snare, what would they think of the representation by a person so little the real thing as an Italian
street-vendor of a protagonist formed by a public school?

If I went a little in fear of them it was not because they

bullied me, because they had got an oppressive foothold, but because in their really pathetic decorum and mysteriously permanent newness they counted on me so intensely. I was therefore very glad when Jack Hawley came home: he was always of such good counsel. He painted badly himself, but there was no one like him for putting his finger on the place. He had been absent from England for a year; he had been somewhere – I don't remember where – to get a fresh eye. I was in a good deal of dread of any such organ, but we were old friends; he had been away for months and a sense of emptiness was creeping into my life. I hadn't dodged a missile for a year.

He came back with a fresh eye, but with the same old black velvet blouse, and the first evening he spent in my studio we smoked cigarettes till the small hours. He had done no work himself, he had only got the eye; so the field was clear for the production of my little things. He wanted to see what I had done for the *Cheapside*, but he was disappointed in the exhib-ition. That at least seemed the meaning of two or three comprehensive groans which, as he lounged on my big divan, on a folded leg, looking at my latest drawings, issued from his lips with the smoke of the cigarette.

'What's the matter with you?' I asked.

'What's the matter with *you*?'

'Nothing save that I'm mystified.'

'You are indeed. You're quite off the hinge. What's the meaning of this new fad?' And he tossed me, with visible irrev-erence, a drawing in which I happened to have depicted both my majestic models. I asked if he didn't think it good, and he replied that it struck him as execrable, given the sort of thing I had always represented myself to him as wishing to arrive at; but I let that pass, I was so anxious to see exactly what he meant. The two figures in the picture looked colossal, but I supposed this was *not* what he meant, inasmuch as, for aught he knew to the contrary, I might have been trying for that. I maintained that I was working exactly in the same way as when he last had done me the honour to commend me. 'Well, there's a big hole somewhere,' he answered; 'wait a bit and I'll discover it.' I depended upon him to do so: where else was the fresh eye? But he produced at last nothing more luminous than 'I don't know – I don't like your types.' This was lame, for a critic who had never consented to discuss with me anything but the question of execution, the direction of strokes and the mystery of values.

'In the drawings you've been looking at I think my types are very handsome.'

'Oh, they won't do!'

'I've had a couple of new models.'

'I see you have. *They* won't do.'

'Are you very sure of that?'

'Absolutely – they're stupid.'

'You mean *I* am – for I ought to get round that.'

'You *can't* – with such people. Who are they?'

I told him, as far as was necessary, and he declared, heartlessly: '*Ce sont des gens qu'il faut mettre à la porte.*'[11]

'You've never seen them; they're awfully good,' I compassionately objected.

'Not seen them? Why, all this recent work of yours drops to pieces with them. It's all I want to see of them.'

'No one else has said anything against it – the *Cheapside* people are pleased.'

'Everyone else is an ass, and the *Cheapside* people the biggest asses of all. Come, don't pretend, at this time of day, to have pretty illusions about the public, especially about publishers and editors. It's not for *such* animals you work – it's for those who know, *coloro che sanno*;[12] so keep straight for *me* if you can't keep straight for yourself. There's a certain sort of thing you tried for from the first – and a very good thing it is. But this twaddle isn't *in* it.' When I talked with Hawley later about 'Rutland Ramsay' and its possible successors he declared that I must get back into my boat again or I would go to the bottom. His voice in short was the voice of warning.

I noted the warning, but I didn't turn my friends out of doors. They bored me a good deal; but the very fact that they bored me admonished me not to sacrifice them – if there was anything to be done with them – simply to irritation. As I look back at this phase they seem to me to have pervaded my life not a little.

I have a vision of them as most of the time in my studio, seated, against the wall, on an old velvet bench to be out of the way, and looking like a pair of patient courtiers in a royal ante-chamber. I am convinced that during the coldest weeks of the winter they held their ground because it saved them fire. Their newness was losing its gloss, and it was impossible not to feel that they were objects of charity. Whenever Miss Churm arrived they went away, and after I was fairly launched in 'Rutland Ramsay' Miss Churm arrived pretty often. They managed to express to me tacitly that they supposed I wanted her for the low life of the book, and I let them suppose it, since they had attempted to study the work – it was lying about the studio – without discovering that it dealt only with the highest circles. They had dipped into the most brilliant of our novelists without deciphering many passages. I still took an hour from them, now and again, in spite of Jack Hawley's warning: it would be time enough to dismiss them, if dismissal should be necessary, when the rigour of the season was over. Hawley had made their acquaintance – he had met them at my fireside – and thought them a ridiculous pair. Learning that he was a painter they tried to approach him, to show him too that they were the real thing; but he looked at them, across the big room, as if they were miles away: they were a compendium of everything that he most objected to in the social system of his country. Such people as that, all convention and patent-leather, with ejaculations that stopped conversation, had no business in a studio. A studio was a place to learn to see, and how could you see through a pair of feather beds?

The main inconvenience I suffered at their hands was that, at first, I was shy of letting them discover how my artful little servant had begun to sit to me for 'Rutland Ramsay'. They knew that I had been odd enough (they were prepared by this time to allow oddity to artists), to pick a foreign vagabond out of the streets, when I might have had a person with whiskers and credentials; but it was some time before they learned how high I rated his accomplishments. They found him in an attitude more than once, but they never doubted I was doing him as an organ-grinder. There were several things they never guessed, and one of them was that for a striking scene in the novel, in which a footman briefly figured, it occurred to me to make use of Major Monarch as the menial. I kept putting this off, I didn't like to ask him to don the livery – besides the difficulty of finding a livery to fit him. At last, one day late in the winter, when I was at work on the despised Oronte (he caught one's idea in an instant), and was in the glow of feeling that I was going very straight, they came in, the Major and his wife, with their society laugh about nothing (there was less and less to laugh at), like country-callers – they always reminded me of that – who have walked across the park after church and are presently persuaded to stay to luncheon. Luncheon was over, but they could stay to tea – I knew they wanted it. The fit was on me, however, and I couldn't let my ardour cool and my work wait, with the fading daylight, while my model prepared it. So I asked Mrs Monarch if she would mind laying it out – a request which, for an instant, brought all the blood to her face. Her eyes were on her husband's for a second, and some mute telegraphy passed between them. Their folly was over the next instant; his cheerful shrewdness put an end to it. So far from pitying their wounded pride, I must add, I was moved to give it as complete a lesson as I could. They bustled about together and got out the cups and saucers and made the kettle boil. I know they felt as if they were waiting on my servant, and when the tea was prepared I said: 'He'll have a cup, please – he's tired.' Mrs Monarch brought him one where he stood, and he took it from her as if he had been a gentleman at a party, squeezing a crush-hat with an elbow.

Then it came over me that she had made a great effort for me – made it with a kind of nobleness – and that I owed her a compensation. Each time I saw her after this I wondered what the compensation could be. I couldn't go on doing the wrong thing to oblige them. Oh, it *was* the wrong thing, the stamp of the work for which they sat – Hawley was not the only person to say it now. I sent in a large number of the drawings I had made for 'Rutland Ramsay', and I received a warning that was more to the point than Hawley's. The artistic adviser of the house for which I was working was of opinion that many of my illustrations were not what had been looked for. Most of these

illustrations were the subjects in which the Monarchs had figured. Without going into the question of what *had* been looked
for, I saw at this rate I shouldn't get the other books to do. I
hurled myself in despair upon Miss Churm, I put her through
all her paces. I not only adopted Oronte publicly as my hero,
but one morning when the Major looked in to see if I didn't
require him to finish a figure for the *Cheapside*, for which he
had begun to sit the week before, I told him that I had changed
my mind – I would do the drawing from my man. At this my
visitor turned pale and stood looking at me. 'Is *he* your idea of
an English gentleman?' he asked.

I was disappointed, I was nervous, I wanted to get on with
my work; so I replied with irritation: 'Oh, my dear Major – I
can't be ruined for *you*!'

He stood another moment; then, without a word, he quitted
the studio. I drew a long breath when he was gone, for I said to
myself that I shouldn't see him again. I had not told him definitely that I was in danger of having my work rejected, but I was
vexed at his not having felt the catastrophe in the air, read with
me the moral of our fruitless collaboration, the lesson that, in
the deceptive atmosphere of art, even the highest respectability
may fail of being plastic.

I didn't owe my friends money, but I did see them again.
They re-appeared together, three days later, and under the circumstances there was something tragic in the fact. It was a
proof to me that they could find nothing else in life to do. They
had threshed the matter out in a dismal conference – they had
digested the bad news that they were not in for the series. If
they were not useful to me even for the *Cheapside* their function seemed difficult to determine, and I could only judge at
first that they had come, forgivingly, decorously, to take a last
leave. This made me rejoice in secret that I had little leisure for
a scene; for I had placed both my other models in position
together and I was pegging away at a drawing from which I
hoped to derive glory. It had been suggested by the passage in
which Rutland Ramsay, drawing up a chair to Artemisia's
piano-stool, says extraordinary things to her while she osten-
sibly fingers out a difficult piece of music. I had done Miss Churm

at the piano before – it was an attitude in which she knew how to take on an absolutely poetic grace. I wished the two figures to 'compose' together, intensely, and my little Italian had entered perfectly into my conception. The pair were vividly before me, the piano had been pulled out; it was a charming picture of blended youth and murmured love, which I had only to catch and keep. My visitors stood and looked at it, and I was friendly to them over my shoulder.

They made no response, but I was used to silent company and went on with my work, only a little disconcerted (even though exhilarated by the sense that *this* was at least the ideal thing), at not having got rid of them after all. Presently I heard Mrs Monarch's sweet voice beside, or rather above me: 'I wish her hair was a little better done.' I looked up and she was staring with a strange fixedness at Miss Churm, whose back was turned to her. 'Do you mind my just touching it?' she went on – a question which made me spring up for an instant, as with the instinctive fear that she might do the young lady a harm. But she quieted me with a glance I shall never forget – I confess I should like to have been able to paint *that* – and went for a moment to my model. She spoke to her softly, laying a hand upon her shoulder and bending over her; and as the girl, understanding, gratefully assented, she disposed her rough curls, with a few quick passes, in such a way as to make Miss Churm's head twice as charming. It was one of the most heroic personal services I have ever seen rendered. Then Mrs Monarch turned away with a low sigh and, looking about her as if for something to do, stooped to the floor with a noble humility and picked up a dirty rag that had dropped out of my paint-box.

The Major meanwhile had also been looking for something to do and, wandering to the other end of the studio, saw before him my breakfast things, neglected, unremoved. 'I say, can't I be useful *here*?' he called out to me with an irrepressible quaver. I assented with a laugh that I fear was awkward and for the next ten minutes, while I worked, I heard the light clatter of china and the tinkle of spoons and glass. Mrs Monarch assisted her husband – they washed up my crockery, they put it away. They wandered off into my little scullery, and I afterwards found that they had cleaned my knives and that my slender stock of plate had an unprecedented surface. When it came over me, the latent eloquence of what they were doing, I confess that my drawing was blurred for a moment – the picture swam. They had accepted their failure, but they couldn't accept their fate. They had bowed their heads in bewilderment to the perverse and cruel law in virtue of which the real thing could be so much less precious than the unreal; but they didn't want to starve. If my servants were my models, my models might be my servants. They would reverse the parts – the others would sit for the ladies and gentlemen, and *they* would do the work. They would still be in the studio – it was an intense dumb appeal to me not to turn them out. 'Take us on,' they wanted to say – 'we'll do *anything*.'

When all this hung before me the *afflatus*[13] vanished – my pencil dropped from my hand. My sitting was spoiled and I got rid of my sitters, who were also evidently rather mystified and awestruck. Then, alone with the Major and his wife, I had a most uncomfortable moment. He put their prayer into a single sentence: 'I say, you know – just let *us* do for you, can't you?' I couldn't – it was dreadful to see them emptying my slops; but I pretended I could, to oblige them, for about a week. Then I gave them a sum of money to go away; and I never saw them again. I obtained the remaining books, but my friend Hawley repeats that Major and Mrs Monarch did me a permanent harm, got me into a second-rate trick. If it be true I am content to have paid the price – for the memory.

GREVILLE FANE

Coming in to dress for dinner, I found a telegram: 'Mrs Stormer dying; can you give us half a column for to-morrow evening? Let her off easy, but not too easy.' I was late; I was in a hurry; I had very little time to think, but at a venture I despatched a reply: 'Will do what I can.' It was not till I had dressed and was rolling away to dinner that, in the hansom, I bethought myself of the difficulty of the condition attached. The difficulty was not of course in letting her off easy but in qualifying that indulgence. 'I simply won't qualify it,' I said to myself. I didn't admire her, but I liked her, and I had known her so long that I almost felt heartless in sitting down at such an hour to a feast of indifference. I must have seemed abstracted, for the early years of my acquaintance with her came back to me. I spoke of her to the lady I had taken down, but the lady I had taken down had never heard of Greville Fane. I tried my other neighbour, who pronounced her books 'too vile'. I had never thought them very good, but I should let her off easier than that.

I came away early, for the express purpose of driving to ask about her. The journey took time, for she lived in the north-west district, in the neighbourhood of Primrose Hill.[1] My apprehension that I should be too late was justified in a fuller sense than I had attached to it – I had only feared that the house would be shut up. There were lights in the windows, and the temperate tinkle of my bell brought a servant immediately to the door, but poor Mrs Stormer had passed into a state in which the resonance of no earthly knocker was to be feared. A lady, in the hall, hovering behind the servant, came forward when she heard my voice. I recognized Lady Luard, but she had mistaken me for the doctor.

'Excuse my appearing at such an hour,' I said; 'it was the first possible moment after I heard.'

'It's all over,' Lady Luard replied. 'Dearest mamma!'

She stood there under the lamp with her eyes on me; she was very tall, very stiff, very cold, and always looked as if these things, and some others beside, in her dress, her manner and even her name, were an implication that she was very admirable. I had never been able to follow the argument, but that is a detail. I expressed briefly and frankly what I felt, while the little mottled maid-servant flattened herself against the wall of the narrow passage and tried to look detached without looking indifferent. It was not a moment to make a visit, and I was on the point of retreating when Lady Luard arrested me with a queer, casual, drawling 'Would you – a – would you, perhaps, be *writing* something?' I felt for the instant like an interviewer, which I was not. But I pleaded guilty to this intention, on which she rejoined: 'I'm so very glad – but I think my brother would like to see you.' I detested her brother, but it wasn't an occasion to act this out; so I suffered myself to be inducted, to my surprise, into a small back room which I immediately recognized as the scene, during the later years, of Mrs Stormer's imperturbable industry. Her table was there, the battered and blotted accessory to innumerable literary lapses, with its contracted space for the arms (she wrote only from the elbow down) and the confusion of scrappy, scribbled sheets which had already become literary remains. Leolin was also there, smoking a cigarette before the fire and looking impudent even in his grief, sincere as it well might have been.

To meet him, to greet him, I had to make a sharp effort; for the air that he wore to me as he stood before me was quite that of his mother's murderer. She lay silent for ever upstairs – as dead as an unsuccessful book, and his swaggering erectness was a kind of symbol of his having killed her. I wondered if he had already, with his sister, been calculating what they could get for the poor papers on the table; but I had not long to wait to learn, for in reply to the scanty words of sympathy I addressed him he puffed out: 'It's miserable, miserable, yes; but she has left three books complete.' His words had the oddest effect; they converted the cramped little room into a seat of trade and made the 'book' wonderfully feasible. He would certainly get all that could be got for the three. Lady Luard explained to me that her husband had been with them but had had to go down to the House. To her brother she explained that I was going to write something, and to me again she made it clear that she hoped I would 'do mamma justice'. She added that she didn't think this had ever been done. She said to her brother: 'Don't you think there are some things he ought thoroughly to understand?' and on his instantly exclaiming 'Oh, thoroughly – thoroughly!' she went on, rather austerely: 'I mean about mamma's birth.'

'Yes, and her connections,' Leolin added.

I professed every willingness, and for five minutes I listened, but it would be too much to say that I understood. I don't even now, but it is not important. My vision was of other matters than those they put before me, and while they desired there should be no mistake about their ancestors I became more and more lucid about themselves. I got away as soon as possible, and walked home through the great dusky, empty London – the best of all conditions for thought. By the time I reached my door my little article was practically composed – ready to be transferred on the morrow from the polished plate of fancy. I believe it attracted some notice, was thought 'graceful' and was said to be by some one else.[2] I had to be pointed without being lively, and it took some tact. But what I said was much less interesting than what I thought – especially during the half-hour I spent in my armchair by the fire, smoking the cigar I always light before going to bed. I went to sleep there, I believe; but I continued to moralize about Greville Fane. I am reluctant to lose that retrospect altogether, and this is a dim little memory of it, a document not to 'serve'. The dear woman had written a hundred stories, but none so curious as her own.

When first I knew her she had published half-a-dozen fictions, and I believe I had also perpetrated a novel. She was more than a dozen years older than I, but she was a person who always acknowledged her relativity. It was not so very long ago, but in London, amid the big waves of the present, even a near horizon gets hidden. I met her at some dinner and took her down, rather flattered at offering my arm to a celebrity. She didn't look like one, with her matronly, mild, inanimate face, but I supposed her greatness would come out in her conversation. I gave it all the opportunities I could, but I was not disappointed when I found her only a dull, kind woman. This was why I liked her – she rested me so from literature. To myself literature was an irritation, a torment; but Greville Fane slumbered in the intellectual part of it like a Creole in a hammock. She was not a woman of genius, but her faculty was so special, so much a gift out of hand, that I have often wondered why she fell below that distinction. This was doubtless because the transaction, in her case, had remained incomplete; genius always pays for the gift, feels the debt, and she was placidly unconscious of obligation. She could invent stories by the yard, but she couldn't write a page of English. She went down to her grave without suspecting that though she had contributed volumes to the diversion of her contemporaries she had not contributed a sentence to the language. This had not prevented bushels of criticism from being heaped upon her head; she was worth a couple of columns any day to the weekly papers, in which it was shown that her pictures of life were dreadful but her style really charming. She asked me to come and see her, and I went. She lived then in Montpelier Square;[3] which helped me to see how dissociated her imagination was from her character.

An industrious widow, devoted to her daily stint, to meeting the butcher and baker and making a home for her son and daughter, from the moment she took her pen in her hand she became a creature of passion. She thought the English novel deplorably wanting in that element, and the task she had cut out for herself was to supply the deficiency. Passion in high life was the general formula of this work, for her imagination was at home only in the most exalted circles. She adored, in truth, the aristocracy, and they constituted for her the romance of the world or, what is more to the point, the prime material of fiction. Their beauty and luxury, their loves and revenges, their temptations and surrenders, their immoralities and diamonds were as familiar to her as the blots on her writing-table. She was not a belated producer of the old fashionable novel, she had a cleverness and a modernness of her own, she had freshened up the fly-blown tinsel. She turned off plots by the hundred and – so far as her flying quill could convey her – was perpetually going abroad. Her types, her illustrations, her tone were nothing if not cosmopolitan. She recognized nothing less provincial than European society, and her fine folk knew each other and made love to each other from Doncaster to Bucharest.[4] She had an idea that she resembled Balzac, and her favourite historical characters were Lucien de Rubempré and the Vidame de Pamiers.[5] I must add that when I once asked her who the latter personage was she was unable to tell me. She was very brave and healthy and cheerful, very abundant and innocent and wicked. She was clever and vulgar and snobbish, and never so intensely British as when she was particularly foreign.

This combination of qualities had brought her early success, and I remember having heard with wonder and envy of what she 'got', in those days, for a novel. The revelation gave me a pang: it was such a proof that, practising a totally different style, I should never make my fortune. And yet when, as I knew her better she told me her real tariff and I saw how rumour had quadrupled it, I liked her enough to be sorry. After a while I discovered too that if she got less it was not that *I* was to get any more. My failure never had what Mrs Stormer would have called the banality of being relative – it was always admirably absolute. She lived at ease however in those days – ease is exactly the word, though she produced three novels a year. She scorned me when I spoke of difficulty – it was the only thing that made her angry. If I hinted that a work of art required a tremendous licking into shape she thought it a pretension and a *pose*. She never recognized the 'torment of form'; the furthest she went was to introduce into one of her books (in satire her hand was heavy) a young poet who was always talking about it. I couldn't quite understand her irritation on this score, for she had nothing at stake in the matter. She had a shrewd perception that form, in prose at least, never recommended any one to the public we were condemned to address, and therefore she lost nothing (putting her private humiliation aside) by not having any. She made no pretence of producing works of art, but had comfortable tea-drinking hours in which she freely confessed herself a common pastrycook, dealing in such tarts and puddings as would bring customers to the shop. She put in plenty of sugar and of cochineal, or whatever it is that gives these articles a rich and attractive colour. She had a serene superiority to observation and opportunity which constituted an inexpugnable strength and would enable her to go on indefinitely. It is only real success that wanes, it is only solid things that melt. Greville Fane's ignorance of life was a resource still more unfailing than the most approved receipt. On her saying once that the day would come when she should have written herself out I answered: 'Ah, you look into fairyland, and the fairies love you, and *they* never change. Fairyland is always there; it always was from the beginning of time, and it always will be to the end. They've given you the key and you can always open the door. With me it's different; I try, in my clumsy way, to be in some direct relation to life.' 'Oh, bother your direct relation to life!' she used to reply, for she was always annoyed by the phrase – which would not in the least prevent her from using it when she wished to try for style. With no more prejudices than an old sausage-mill, she would give forth again with patient punctuality any poor verbal scrap that had been dropped into her. I cheered her with saying that the dark day, at the end, would be for the like of *me*; inasmuch as, going in our small way by experience and observation, we depended not on a revelation, but on a little tiresome process. Observation depended on opportunity, and where should we be when opportunity failed?

One day she told me that as the novelist's life was so delightful and during the good years at least such a comfortable support (she had these staggering optimisms) she meant to train up her boy to follow it. She took the ingenious view that it was a profession like another and that therefore everything was to be gained by beginning young and serving an apprenticeship. Moreover the education would be less expensive than any other special course, inasmuch as she could administer it herself. She didn't profess to keep a school, but she could at least teach her own child. It was not that she was so very clever, but (she confessed to me as if she were afraid I would laugh at her) that *he* was. I didn't laugh at her for that, for I thought the boy sharp – I had seen him at sundry times. He was well grown and good-looking and unabashed, and both he and his sister made me wonder about their defunct papa, concerning whom the little I knew was that he had been a clergyman. I explained them to myself by suppositions and imputations possibly unjust to the departed; so little were they – superficially at least – the children of their mother. There used to be, on an easel in her drawing-room, an enlarged photograph of her husband, done by some horrible posthumous 'process' and draped, as to its florid frame, with a silken scarf, which testified to the candour of Greville Fane's bad taste. It made him look like an unsuccessful tragedian; but it was not a thing to trust. He may have been a successful comedian. Of the two children the girl was the elder, and struck me in all her younger years as singularly colourless. She was only very long, like an undecipherable letter. It was not till Mrs Stormer came back from a protracted residence abroad that Ethel (which was this young lady's name) began to produce the effect, which was afterwards remarkable in her, of a certain kind of high resolution. She made one apprehend that she meant to do something for herself. She was long-necked and near-sighted and striking, and I thought I had never seen sweet seventeen in a form so hard and high and dry. She was cold and affected and ambitious, and she carried an eyeglass with a long handle, which she put up whenever she wanted not to see. She had come out, as the phrase is, immensely; and yet I felt as if she were surrounded with a spiked iron railing. What she meant to do for herself was to marry, and it was the only thing, I think, that she meant to do for any one else; yet who would be inspired to clamber over that bristling barrier? What flower of tenderness or of intimacy would such an adventurer conceive as his reward?

This was for Sir Baldwin Luard to say; but he naturally never confided to me the secret. He was a joyless, jokeless young man, with the air of having other secrets as well, and a determination to get on politically that was indicated by his never having been known to commit himself – as regards any proposition whatever – beyond an exclamatory 'Oh!' His wife and he must have conversed mainly in prim ejaculations, but they understood sufficiently that they were kindred spirits. I remember being angry with Greville Fane when she announced these nuptials to me as magnificent; I remember asking her what splendour there was in the union of the daughter of a woman of genius with an irredeemable mediocrity. 'Oh! he's awfully clever,' she said; but she blushed for the maternal fib. What she meant was that though Sir Baldwin's estates were not vast (he had a dreary house in South Kensington and a still drearier 'Hall' somewhere in Essex, which was let), the connection was a 'smarter' one than a child of hers could have aspired to form. In spite of the social bravery of her novels she took a very humble and dingy view of herself, so that of all her productions 'my daughter Lady Luard' was quite the one she was proudest of. That personage thought her mother very vulgar and was distressed and perplexed by the occasional licence of her pen, but had a complicated attitude in regard to this indirect connection with literature. So far as it was lucrative her ladyship approved of it, and could compound with the inferiority of the pursuit by doing practical justice to some of its advantages. I had reason to know (my reason was simply that poor Mrs Stormer told me) that she suffered the inky fingers to press an occasional bank-note into her palm. On the other hand she deplored the 'peculiar style' to which Greville Fane had devoted herself, and wondered where an author who had the convenience of so lady-like a daughter could have picked up such views about the best society. 'She might know better, with Leolin and me,' Lady Luard had been known to remark; but it appeared that some of Greville Fane's superstitions were incurable. She didn't live in Lady Luard's society, and the best was not good enough for her – she must make it still better.

I could see that this necessity grew upon her during the years

she spent abroad, when I had glimpses of her in the shifting
sojourns that lay in the path of my annual ramble. She betook
herself from Germany to Switzerland and from Switzerland to
Italy; she favoured cheap places and set up her desk in the
smaller capitals. I took a look at her whenever I could, and I
always asked how Leolin was getting on. She gave me beautiful
accounts of him, and whenever it was possible the boy was
produced for my edification. I had entered from the first into
the joke of his career – I pretended to regard him as a conse-
crated child. It had been a joke for Mrs Stormer at first, but the
boy himself had been shrewd enough to make the matter serious. If his mother accepted the principle that the intending
novelist cannot begin too early to see life, Leolin was not interested in hanging back from the application of it. He was eager
to qualify himself, and took to cigarettes at ten, on the highest
literary grounds. His poor mother gazed at him with extravagant envy and, like Desdemona,[6] wished heaven had made *her*
such a man. She explained to me more than once that in her
profession she had found her sex a dreadful drawback. She
loved the story of Madame George Sand's[7] early rebellion
against this hindrance, and believed that if she had worn trousers she could have written as well as that lady. Leolin had for
the career at least the qualification of trousers, and as he grew
older he recognized its importance by laying in an immense
assortment. He grew up in gorgeous apparel, which was his
way of interpreting his mother's system. Whenever I met her I
found her still under the impression that she was carrying this
system out and that Leolin's training was bearing fruit. She was
giving him experience, she was giving him impressions, she was
putting a *gagne-pain*[8] into his hand. It was another name for
spoiling him with the best conscience in the world. The queerest pictures come back to me of this period of the good lady's
life and of the extraordinarily virtuous, muddled, bewildering
tenor of it. She had an idea that she was seeing foreign manners
as well as her petticoats would allow; but, in reality she was
not seeing anything, least of all fortunately how much she was
laughed at. She drove her whimsical pen at Dresden and at
Florence, and produced in all places and at all times the same

romantic and ridiculous fictions. She carried about her box of properties and fished out promptly the familiar, tarnished old puppets. She believed in them when others couldn't, and as they were like nothing that was to be seen under the sun it was impossible to prove by comparison that they were wrong. You can't compare birds and fishes; you could only feel that, as Greville Fane's characters had the fine plumage of the former species, human beings must be of the latter.

It would have been droll if it had not been so exemplary to see her tracing the loves of the duchesses beside the innocent cribs of her children. The immoral and the maternal lived together in her diligent days on the most comfortable terms, and she stopped curling the moustaches of her Guardsmen to pat the head of her babes. She was haunted by solemn spinsters who came to tea from continental *pensions*, and by unsophisticated Americans who told her she was just loved in *their* country. 'I had rather be just paid there,'[9] she usually replied; for this tribute of transatlantic opinion was the only thing that galled her. The Americans went away thinking her coarse; though as the author of so many beautiful love-stories she was disappointing to most of these pilgrims, who had not expected to find a shy, stout, ruddy lady in a cap like a crumbled pyramid. She wrote about the affections and the impossibility of controlling them, but she talked of the price of *pension* and the convenience of an English chemist. She devoted much thought and many thousands of francs to the education of her daughter, who spent three years at a very superior school at Dresden, receiving wonderful instruction in sciences, arts and tongues, and who, taking a different line from Leolin, was to be brought up wholly as a *femme du monde*.[10] The girl was musical and philological; she made a specialty of languages and learned enough about them to be inspired with a great contempt for her mother's artless accents. Greville Fane's French and Italian were droll; the imitative faculty had been denied her, and she had an unequalled gift, especially pen in hand, of squeezing big mistakes into small opportunities. She knew it, but she didn't care; correctness was the virtue in the world that, like her heroes and heroines, she valued least. Ethel, who had perceived in her pages some remarkable lapses, undertook at one time to revise her proofs; but I remember her telling me a year after the girl had left school that this function had been very briefly exercised. 'She can't read me,' said Mrs Stormer; 'I offend her taste. She tells me that at Dresden – at school – I was never allowed.' The good lady seemed surprised at this, having the best conscience in the world about her lucubrations. She had never meant to fly in the face of anything, and considered that she grovelled before the Rhadamanthus[11] of the English literary tribunal, the celebrated and awful Young Person.[12] I assured her, as a joke, that she was frightfully indecent (she hadn't in fact that reality any more than any other) my purpose being solely to prevent her from guessing that her daughter had dropped her not because she was immoral but because she was vulgar. I used to figure her children closeted together and asking each other while they exchanged a gaze of dismay: 'Why should she *be* so – and so *fearfully* so – when she has the advantage of our society? Shouldn't *we* have taught her better?' Then I imagined their recognizing with a blush and a shrug that she was unteachable, irreformable. Indeed she was, poor lady; but it is never fair to read by the light of taste things that were not written by it. Greville Fane had, in the topsy-turvy, a serene good faith that ought to have been safe from allusion, like a stutter or a *faux pas*.

She didn't make her son ashamed of the profession to which he was destined, however; she only made him ashamed of the way she herself exercised it. But he bore his humiliation much better than his sister, for he was ready to take for granted that he should one day restore the balance. He was a canny and far-seeing youth, with appetites and aspirations, and he had not a scruple in his composition. His mother's theory of the happy knack he could pick up deprived him of the wholesome discipline required to prevent young idlers from becoming cads. He had, abroad, a casual tutor and a snatch or two of a Swiss school, but no consecutive study, no prospect of a university or a degree. It may be imagined with what zeal, as the years went on, he entered into the pleasantry of there being no manual so important to him as the massive book of life. It was an expensive volume to peruse, but Mrs Stormer was willing to lay out a sum in what she would have called her *premiers frais*.[13] Ethel disapproved – she thought this education far too unconventional for an English gentleman. Her voice was for Eton and Oxford, or for any public school (she would have resigned herself) with the army to follow. But Leolin never was afraid of his sister, and they visibly disliked, though they some-times agreed to assist, each other. They could combine to work the oracle – to keep their mother at her desk.

When she came back to England, telling me she had got all the continent could give her, Leolin was a broad-shouldered, red-faced young man, with an immense wardrobe and an extra-ordinary assurance of manner. She was fondly obstinate about her having taken the right course with him, and proud of all that he knew and had seen. He was now quite ready to begin, and a little while later she told me he *had* begun. He had writ-ten something tremendously clever, and it was coming out in the *Cheapside*.[14] I believe it came out; I had no time to look for it; I never heard anything about it. I took for granted that if this contribution had passed through his mother's hands it had practically become a specimen of her own genius, and it was interesting to consider Mrs Stormer's future in the light of her having to write her son's novels as well as her own. This was not the way she looked at it herself; she took the charming ground that he would help her to write hers. She used to tell me that he supplied passages of the greatest value to her own work – all sorts of technical things, about hunting and yachting and wine – that she couldn't be expected to get very straight. It was all so much practice for him and so much alleviation for her. I was unable to identify these pages, for I had long since ceased to 'keep up' with Greville Fane; but I was quite able to believe that the wine-question had been put, by Leolin's good offices, on a better footing, for the dear lady used to mix her drinks (she was perpetually serving the most splendid suppers) in the queerest fashion. I could see that he was willing enough to accept a commission to look after that department. It occurred to me indeed, when Mrs Stormer settled in England again, that by making a shrewd use of both her children she might be able to rejuvenate her style. Ethel had come back to gratify her young ambition, and if she couldn't take her mother into society she would at least go into it herself. Silently, stiffly, almost grimly, this young lady held up her head, clenched her long teeth, squared her lean elbows and made her way up the staircases she had elected. The only communication she ever made to me, the only effusion of confidence with which she ever honoured me, was when she said: 'I don't want to know the people mamma knows; I mean to know others.' I took due note of the remark, for I was not one of the 'others'. I couldn't trace therefore the steps of her process; I could only admire it at a distance and congratulate her mother on the results. The results were that Ethel went to 'big' parties and got people to take her. Some of them were people she had met abroad, and others were people whom the people she had met abroad had met. They ministered alike to Miss Ethel's convenience, and I wondered how she extracted so many favours without the expenditure of a smile. Her smile was the dimmest thing in the world, diluted lemonade, without sugar, and she had arrived precociously at social wisdom, recognizing that if she was neither pretty enough nor rich enough nor clever enough, she could at least in her muscular youth be rude enough. Therefore if she was able to tell her mother what really took place in the mansions of the great, give her notes to work from, the quill could be driven at home to better purpose and precisely at a moment when it would have to be more active than ever. But if she did tell, it would appear that poor Mrs Stormer didn't believe. As regards many points this was not a wonder; at any rate I heard nothing of Greville Fane's having developed a new manner. She had only one manner from start to finish, as Leolin would have said.

She was tired at last, but she mentioned to me that she couldn't afford to pause. She continued to speak of Leolin's work as the great hope of their future (she had saved no money) though the young man wore to my sense an aspect more and more professional if you like, but less and less literary. At the end of a couple of years there was something monstrous in the impudence with which he played his part in the comedy. When

I wondered how she could play *her* part I had to perceive that her good faith was complete and that what kept it so was simply her extravagant fondness. She loved the young impostor with a simple, blind, benighted love, and of all the heroes of romance who had passed before her eyes he was by far the most brilliant. He was at any rate the most real – she could touch him, pay for him, suffer for him, worship him. He made her think of her princes and dukes, and when she wished to fix these figures in her mind's eye she thought of her boy. She had often told me she was carried away by her own creations, and she was certainly carried away by Leolin. He vivified, by potentialities at least, the whole question of youth and passion. She held, not unjustly, that the sincere novelist should feel the whole flood of life; she acknowledged with regret that she had not had time to feel it herself, and it was a joy to her that the deficiency might be supplied by the sight of the way it was rushing through this magnificent young man. She exhorted him, I suppose, to let it rush; she wrung her own flaccid little sponge into the torrent. I knew not what passed between them in her hours of tuition, but I gathered that she mainly impressed on him that the great thing was to live,[15] because that gave you material. He asked nothing better; he collected material, and the formula served as a universal pretext. You had only to look at him to see that, with his rings and breastpins, his cross-barred jackets, his early *embonpoint*,[16] his eyes that looked like imitation jewels, his various indications of a dense, full-blown temperament, his idea of life was singularly vulgar; but he was not so far wrong as that his response to his mother's expectations was not in a high degree practical. If she had imposed a profession on him from his tenderest years it was exactly a profession that he followed. The two were not quite the same, inasmuch as *his* was simply to live at her expense; but at least she couldn't say that he hadn't taken a line. If she insisted on believing in him he offered himself to the sacrifice. My impression is that her secret dream was that he should have a *liaison* with a countess, and he persuaded her without difficulty that he had one. I don't know what countesses are capable of, but I have a clear notion of what Leolin was.

He didn't persuade his sister, who despised him – she wished to work her mother in her own way, and I asked myself why the girl's judgment of him didn't make me like her better. It was because it didn't save her after all from a mute agreement with him to go halves. There were moments when I couldn't help looking hard into his atrocious young eyes, challenging him to confess his fantastic fraud and give it up. Not a little tacit conversation passed between us in this way, but he had always the best of it. If I said: 'Oh, come now, with *me* you needn't keep it up; plead guilty, and I'll let you off,' he wore the most ingenuous, the most candid expression, in the depths of which I could read: 'Oh, yes, I know it exasperates you – that's just why I do it.' He took the line of earnest inquiry, talked about Balzac and Flaubert, asked me if I thought Dickens *did* exaggerate and Thackeray *ought* to be called a pessimist. Once he came to see me, at his mother's suggestion he declared, on purpose to ask me how far, in my opinion, in the English novel, one really might venture to 'go'. He was not resigned to the usual pruderies – he suffered under them already. He struck out the brilliant idea that nobody knew how far we might go, for nobody had ever tried. Did I think *he* might safely try – would it injure his mother if he did? He would rather disgrace himself by his timidities than injure his mother, but certainly some one ought to try. Wouldn't *I* try – couldn't I be prevailed upon to look at it as a duty? Surely the ultimate point ought to be fixed – he was worried, haunted by the question. He patronized me unblushingly, made me feel like a foolish amateur, a helpless novice, inquired into my habits of work and conveyed to me that I was utterly *vieux jeu*[17] and had not had the advantage of an early training. I had not been brought up from the germ, I knew nothing of life – didn't go at it on *his* system. He had dipped into French feuilletons[18] and picked up plenty of phrases, and he made a much better show in talk than his poor mother, who never had time to read anything and could only be vivid with her pen. If I didn't kick him downstairs it was because he would have alighted on her at the bottom.

When she went to live at Primrose Hill I called upon her and found her weary and wasted. It had waned a good deal, the elation caused the year before by Ethel's marriage; the foam on the cup had subsided and there was a bitterness in the draught. She had had to take a cheaper house and she had to work still harder to pay even for that. Sir Baldwin was obliged to be close; his charges were fearful, and the dream of her living with her daughter (a vision she had never mentioned to me) must be renounced. 'I would have helped with things, and I could have lived perfectly in one room,' she said; 'I would have paid for everything, and – after all – I'm some one, ain't I? But I don't fit in, and Ethel tells me there are tiresome people she *must* receive. I can help them from here, no doubt, better than from there. She told me once, you know, what she thinks of my picture of life. "Mamma, your picture of life is preposterous!" No doubt it is, but she's vexed with me for letting my prices go down; and I had to write three novels to pay for all her marriage cost me. I did it very well – I mean the outfit and the wedding; but that's why I'm here. At any rate she doesn't want a dingy old woman in her house. I should give it an atmosphere of literary glory, but literary glory is only the eminence of nobodies. Besides, she doubts my glory – she knows I'm glorious only at Peckham and Hackney.[19] She doesn't want her friends to ask if I've never known nice people. She can't tell them I've never been in society. She tried to teach me better once, but I couldn't learn. It would seem too as if Peckham and Hackney had had enough of me; for (don't tell any one!) I've had to take less for my last than I ever took for anything.' I asked her how little this had been, not from curiosity, but in order to upbraid her, more disinterestedly than Lady Luard had done, for such concessions. She answered 'I'm ashamed to tell you,' and then she began to cry.

I had never seen her break down, and I was proportionately moved; she sobbed, like a frightened child, over the extinction of her vogue and the exhaustion of her vein. Her little work-room seemed indeed a barren place to grow flowers, and I wondered, in the after years (for she continued to produce and publish) by what desperate and heroic process she dragged them out of the soil. I remember asking her on that occasion what had become of Leolin, and how much longer she intended to allow him to amuse himself at her cost. She rejoined with spirit, wiping her eyes, that he was down at Brighton[20] hard at work – he was in the midst of a novel – and that he *felt* life so, in all its misery and mystery, that it was cruel to speak of such experiences as a pleasure. 'He goes beneath the surface,' she said, 'and he *forces* himself to look at things from which he would rather turn away. Do you call that amusing yourself? You should see his face sometimes! And he does it for me as much as for himself. He tells me everything – he comes home to me with his *trouvailles*.[21] We are artists together, and to the artist all things are pure. I've often heard you say so yourself.' The novel that Leolin was engaged in at Brighton was never published, but a friend of mine and of Mrs Stormer's who was staying there happened to mention to me later that he had seen the young apprentice to fiction driving, in a dog-cart, a young lady with a very pink face. When I suggested that she was perhaps a woman of title with whom he was conscientiously flirting my informant replied: 'She is indeed, but do you know what her title is?' He pronounced it – it was familiar and descriptive – but I won't reproduce it here. I don't know whether Leolin mentioned it to his mother: she would have needed all the purity of the artist to forgive him. I hated so to come across him that in the very last years I went rarely to see her, though I knew that she had come pretty well to the end of her rope. I didn't want her to tell me that she had fairly to give her books away – I didn't want to see her cry. She kept it up amazingly, and every few months, at my club, I saw three new volumes, in green, in crimson, in blue, on the book-table that groaned with light literature. Once I met her at the Academy[22] soirée, where you meet people you thought were dead, and she vouchsafed the information, as if she owed it to me in candour, that Leolin had been obliged to recognize insuperable difficulties in the question of *form*, he was so fastidious; so that she had now arrived at a definite understanding with him (it was such a comfort) that *she* would do the form if he would bring home the substance. That was now his position – he foraged for her in the great world at a salary. 'He's my "devil", don't you see? as if I were a great lawyer: he gets up the case and I argue it.' She mentioned further that in addition to his salary he was paid by the piece: he got so much for a striking character, so much for a pretty name, so much for a plot, so much for an incident, and had so much promised him if he would invent a new crime.

'He *has* invented one,' I said, 'and he's paid every day of his life.'

'What is it?' she asked, looking hard at the picture of the year, 'Baby's Tub', near which we happened to be standing.

I hesitated a moment. 'I myself will write a little story about it, and then you'll see.'

But she never saw; she had never seen anything, and she passed away with her fine blindness unimpaired. Her son published every scrap of scribbled paper that could be extracted from her table-drawers, and his sister quarrelled with him mortally about the proceeds, which showed that she only wanted a pretext, for they cannot have been great. I don't know what Leolin lives upon, unless it be on a queer lady many years older than himself, whom he lately married. The last time I met him he said to me with his infuriating smile: 'Don't you think we can go a little further still – just a little?' *He* really goes too far.

THE MIDDLE YEARS

The April day was soft and bright, and poor Dencombe, happy in the conceit of reasserted strength, stood in the garden of the hotel, comparing, with a deliberation in which, however, there was still something of languor, the attractions of easy strolls. He liked the feeling of the south, so far as you could have it in the north, he liked the sandy cliffs and the clustered pines, he liked even the colourless sea. 'Bournemouth as a health-resort' had sounded like a mere advertisement, but now he was reconciled to the prosaic. The sociable country postman, passing through the garden, had just given him a small parcel, which he took out with him, leaving the hotel to the right and creeping to a convenient bench that he knew of, a safe recess in the cliff. It looked to the south, to the tinted walls of the Island,[1] and was protected behind by the sloping shoulder of the down. He was tired enough when he reached it, and for a moment he was disappointed; he was better, of course, but better, after all, than what? He should never again, as at one or two great moments of the past, be better than himself. The infinite of life had gone, and what was left of the dose was a small glass engraved like a thermometer by the apothecary. He sat and stared at the sea, which appeared all surface and twinkle, far shallower than the spirit of man. It was the abyss of human illusion that was the real, the tideless deep. He held his packet, which had come by book-post, unopened on his knee, liking, in the lapse of so many joys (his illness had made him feel his age), to know that it was there, but taking for granted there could be no complete renewal of the pleasure, dear to young experience, of seeing one's self 'just out'. Dencombe, who had a reputation, had come out too often and knew too well in advance how he should look.

His postponement associated itself vaguely, after a little, with a group of three persons, two ladies and a young man, whom, beneath him, straggling and seemingly silent, he could see move slowly together along the sands. The gentleman had his head bent over a book and was occasionally brought to a stop by the charm of this volume, which, as Dencombe could perceive even at a distance, had a cover alluringly red. Then his companions, going a little further, waited for him to come up, poking their parasols into the beach, looking around them at the sea and sky and clearly sensible of the beauty of the day. To these things the young man with the book was still more clearly indifferent; lingering, credulous, absorbed, he was an object of envy to an observer from whose connection with literature all such artlessness had faded. One of the ladies was large and mature; the other had the spareness of comparative youth and of a social situation possibly inferior. The large lady carried back Dencombe's imagination to the age of crinoline; she wore a hat of the shape of a mushroom, decorated with a blue veil, and had the air, in her aggressive amplitude, of clinging to a vanished fashion or even a lost cause. Presently her companion produced from under the folds of a mantle a limp, portable chair which she stiffened out and of which the large lady took possession. This act, and something in the movement of either party, instantly characterized the performers – they performed for Dencombe's recreation – as opulent matron and humble dependant. What, moreover, was the use of being an approved novelist if one couldn't establish a relation between such figures; the clever theory, for instance, that the young man was the son of the opulent matron, and that the humble dependant, the daughter of a clergyman or an officer, nourished a secret passion for him? Was that not visible from the way she stole behind her protectress to look back at him? – back to where he had let himself come to a full stop when his mother sat down to rest. His book was a novel; it had the catchpenny[2] cover, and while the romance of life stood neglected at his side he lost himself in that of the circulating library.[3] He moved mechanically to where the sand was softer, and ended by plumping down in it to finish his chapter at his ease. The humble dependant, discouraged by his remoteness, wandered, with a martyred droop of the head, in another direction, and the exorbitant lady, watching the waves, offered a confused resemblance to a flying-machine that had broken down.

When his drama began to fail Dencombe remembered that he had, after all, another pastime. Though such promptitude on the part of the publisher was rare, he was already able to draw from its wrapper his 'latest', perhaps his last. The cover of 'The Middle Years'[4] was duly meretricious, the smell of the fresh pages the very odour of sanctity; but for the moment he went no further – he had become conscious of a strange alienation. He had forgotten what his book was about. Had the assault of his old ailment, which he had so fallaciously come to Bournemouth to ward off, interposed utter blankness as to what had preceded it? He had finished the revision of proof before quitting London, but his subsequent fortnight in bed had passed the sponge over colour.[5] He couldn't have chanted to himself a single sentence, couldn't have turned with curiosity or confidence to any particular page. His subject had already gone from him, leaving scarcely a superstition behind. He uttered a low moan as he breathed the chill of this dark void, so desperately it seemed to represent the completion of a sinister process. The tears filled his mild eyes; something precious had passed away. This was the pang that had been sharpest during the last few years – the sense of ebbing time, of shrinking opportunity; and now he felt not so much that his last chance was going as that it was gone indeed. He had done all that he should ever do, and yet he had not done what he wanted. This was the laceration – that practically his career was over: it was as violent as a rough hand at his throat. He rose from his seat nervously, like a creature hunted by a dread; then he fell back in his weakness and nervously opened his book. It was a single volume; he preferred single volumes and aimed at a rare compression. He began to read, and little by little, in this occupation, he was pacified and reassured. Everything came back to him, but came back with a wonder, came back, above all, with a high and magnificent beauty. He read his own prose, he turned his own leaves, and had, as he sat there with the spring sunshine on the page, an emotion peculiar and intense. His career was over, no doubt, but it was over, after all, with *that*.

He had forgotten during his illness the work of the previous year; but what he had chiefly forgotten was that it was extraordinarily good. He lived once more into his story and was drawn down, as by a siren's hand, to where, in the dim underworld of fiction, the great glazed tank of art, strange silent subjects float. He recognized his motive and surrendered to his talent. Never, probably, had that talent, such as it was, been so fine. His difficulties were still there, but what was also there, to his perception, though probably, alas! to nobody's else, was the art that in most cases had surmounted them. In his surprised enjoyment of this ability he had a glimpse of a possible reprieve. Surely its force was not spent – there was life and service in it yet. It had not come to him easily, it had been backward and roundabout. It was the child of time, the nursling of delay; he had struggled and suffered for it, making sacrifices not to be counted, and now that it was really mature was it to cease to yield, to confess itself brutally beaten? There was an infinite charm for Dencombe in feeling as he had never felt before that diligence *vincit omnia*.[6] The result produced in his little book was somehow a result beyond his conscious intention: it was as if he had planted his genius, had trusted his method, and they had grown up and flowered with this sweetness. If the achievement had been real, however, the process had been manful enough. What he saw so intensely to-day, what he felt as a nail driven in, was that only now, at the very last, had he come into possession. His development had been abnormally slow, almost grotesquely gradual. He had been hindered and retarded by experience, and for long periods had only groped his way. It had taken too much of his life to produce too little of his art. The art had come, but it had come after everything else. At such a rate a first existence was too short – long enough only to collect material; so that to fructify, to use the material, one must have a second age, an extension. This extension was what poor Dencombe sighed for. As he turned the last leaves of his volume he murmured: 'Ah for another go! – ah for a better chance!'

The three persons he had observed on the sands had vanished and then reappeared; they had now wandered up a path, an artificial and easy ascent, which led to the top of the cliff. Dencombe's bench was half-way down, on a sheltered ledge, and the large lady, a massive, heterogeneous person, with bold black eyes and kind red cheeks, now took a few moments to rest. She wore dirty gauntlets and immense diamond ear-rings; at first she looked vulgar, but she contradicted this announcement in an agreeable off-hand tone. While her companions stood waiting for her she spread her skirts on the end of Dencombe's seat. The young man had gold spectacles, through which, with his finger still in his red-covered book, he glanced at the volume, bound in the same shade of the same colour, lying on the lap of the original occupant of the bench. After an instant Dencombe understood that he was struck with a resemblance, had recognized the gilt stamp on the crimson cloth, was reading 'The Middle Years', and now perceived that somebody else had kept pace with him. The stranger was startled, possibly even a little ruffled, to find that he was not the only person who had been favoured with an early copy. The eyes of the two proprietors met for a moment, and Dencombe borrowed amusement from the expression of those of his competitor, those, it might even be inferred, of his admirer. They confessed to some resentment – they seemed to say: 'Hang it, has he got it *already*? – Of course he's a brute of a reviewer!' Dencombe shuffled his copy out of sight while the opulent matron, rising from her repose, broke out: 'I feel already the good of this air!'

'I can't say I do,' said the angular lady. 'I find myself quite let down.'

'I find myself horribly hungry. At what time did you order lunch?' her protectress pursued.

The young person put the question by. 'Doctor Hugh always orders it.'

'I ordered nothing to-day – I'm going to make you diet,' said their comrade.

'Then I shall go home and sleep. *Qui dort dine!*'[7]

'Can I trust you to Miss Vernham?' asked Doctor Hugh of his elder companion.

'Don't I trust *you*?' she archly inquired.

'Not too much!' Miss Vernham, with her eyes on the ground, permitted herself to declare. 'You must come with us at least to the house,' she went on, while the personage on whom they appeared to be in attendance began to mount higher. She had got a little out of ear-shot; nevertheless Miss Vernham became, so far as Dencombe was concerned, less distinctly audible to murmur to the young man: 'I don't think you realize all you owe the Countess!'

Absently, a moment, Doctor Hugh caused his gold-rimmed spectacles to shine at her.

'Is that the way I strike you? I see – I see!'

'She's awfully good to us,' continued Miss Vernham, compelled by her interlocutor's immovability to stand there in spite of his discussion of private matters. Of what use would it have been that Dencombe should be sensitive to shades had he not detected in that immovability a strange influence from the quiet old convalescent in the great tweed cape? Miss Vernham appeared suddenly to become aware of some such connection, for she added in a moment: 'If you want to sun yourself here you can come back after you've seen us home.'

Doctor Hugh, at this, hesitated, and Dencombe, in spite of a desire to pass for unconscious, risked a covert glance at him. What his eyes met this time, as it happened, was on the part of the young lady a queer stare, naturally vitreous, which made her aspect remind him of some figure (he couldn't name it) in a play or a novel, some sinister governess or tragic old maid. She seemed to scrutinize him, to challenge him, to say, from general spite: 'What have you got to do with us?' At the same instant the rich humour of the Countess reached them from above: 'Come, come, my little lambs, you should follow your old *bergère*!'[8] Miss Vernham turned away at this, pursuing the ascent, and Doctor Hugh, after another mute appeal to Dencombe and a moment's evident demur, deposited his book on the bench, as if to keep his place or even as a sign that he would return, and bounded without difficulty up the rougher part of the cliff.

Equally innocent and infinite are the pleasures of observation and the resources engendered by the habit of analysing life. It amused poor Dencombe, as he dawdled in his tepid air-bath, to think that he was waiting for a revelation of something at the back of a fine young mind. He looked hard at the book on the end of the bench, but he wouldn't have touched it for the world. It served his purpose to have a theory which should not be exposed to refutation. He already felt better of his melancholy; he had, according to his old formula, put his head at the window. A passing Countess could draw off the fancy when, like the elder of the ladies who had just retreated, she was as obvious as the giantess of a caravan. It was indeed general views that were terrible; short ones, contrary to an opinion sometimes expressed, were the refuge, were the remedy. Doctor Hugh couldn't possibly be anything but a reviewer who had understandings for early copies with publishers or with newspapers. He reappeared in a quarter of an hour, with visible relief at finding Dencombe on the spot, and the gleam of white teeth in an embarrassed but generous smile. He was perceptibly disappointed at the eclipse of the other copy of the book; it was a pretext the less for speaking to the stranger. But he spoke notwithstanding; he held up his own copy and broke out pleadingly:

'Do say, if you have occasion to speak of it, that it's the best thing he has done yet!'

Dencombe responded with a laugh: 'Done yet' was so amusing to him, made such a grand avenue of the future. Better still, the young man took *him* for a reviewer. He pulled out 'The Middle Years' from under his cape, but instinctively concealed any tell-tale look of fatherhood. This was partly because a person was always a fool for calling attention to his work. 'Is that what you're going to say yourself?' he inquired of his visitor.

'I'm not quite sure I shall write anything. I don't, as a regular thing – I enjoy in peace. But it's awfully fine.'

Dencombe debated a moment. If his interlocutor had begun to abuse him he would have confessed on the spot to his identity, but there was no harm in drawing him on a little to praise. He drew him on with such success that in a few moments his new acquaintance, seated by his side, was confessing candidly that Dencombe's novels were the only ones he could read a second time. He had come the day before from London, where a friend of his, a journalist, had lent him his copy of the last – the copy sent to the office of the journal and already the subject of a 'notice' which, as was pretended there (but one had to allow for 'swagger') it had taken a full quarter of an hour to prepare. He intimated that he was ashamed for his friend, and in the case of a work demanding and repaying study, of such inferior manners; and, with his fresh appreciation and inexplicable wish to express it, he speedily became for poor Dencombe a remarkable, a delightful apparition. Chance had brought the weary man of letters face to face with the greatest admirer in the new generation whom it was supposable he possessed. The admirer, in truth, was mystifying, so rare a case was it to find a bristling young doctor – he looked like a German physiologist – enamoured of literary form. It was an accident, but happier than most accidents, so that Dencombe, exhilarated as well as confounded, spent half an hour in making his visitor talk while he kept himself quiet. He explained his premature possession of 'The Middle Years' by an allusion to the friendship of the publisher, who, knowing he was at Bournemouth for his health, had paid him this graceful attention. He admitted that he had been ill, for Doctor Hugh would infallibly have guessed it; he even went so far as to wonder whether he mightn't look for some hygenic 'tip' from a personage combining so bright an enthusiasm with a presumable knowledge of the remedies now in vogue. It would shake his faith a little perhaps to have to take a doctor seriously who could take *him* so seriously, but he enjoyed this gushing modern youth and he felt with an acute pang that there would still be work to do in a world in which such odd combinations were presented. It was not true, what he had tried for renunciation's sake to believe, that all the combinations were exhausted. They were not, they were not – they were infinite: the exhaustion was in the miserable artist.

Doctor Hugh was an ardent physiologist, saturated with the spirit of the age – in other words he had just taken his degree; but he was independent and various, he talked like a man who would have preferred to love literature best. He would fain have made fine phrases, but nature had denied him the trick. Some of the finest in 'The Middle Years' had struck him inordinately, and he took the liberty of reading them to Dencombe in support of his plea. He grew vivid, in the balmy air, to his companion, for whose deep refreshment he seemed to have been sent; and was particularly ingenuous in describing how recently he had become acquainted, and how instantly infatuated, with the only man who had put flesh between the ribs of an art that was starving on superstitions. He had not yet written to him – he was deterred by a sentiment of respect. Dencombe at this moment felicitated himself more than ever on having never answered the photographers. His visitor's attitude promised him a luxury of intercourse, but he surmised that a certain security in it, for Doctor Hugh, would depend not a little on the Countess. He learned without delay with what variety of Countess they were concerned, as well as the nature of the tie that united the curious trio. The large lady, an Englishwoman by birth and the daughter of a celebrated baritone, whose taste, without his talent, she had inherited, was the widow of a French nobleman and mistress of all that remained of the handsome fortune, the fruit of her father's earnings, that had constituted her dower. Miss Vernham, an odd creature but an accomplished pianist, was attached to her person at a salary. The Countess was generous, independent, eccentric; she travelled with her minstrel and her medical man. Ignorant and passionate, she had nevertheless moments in which she was almost irresistible. Dencombe saw her sit for her portrait in Doctor Hugh's free sketch, and felt the picture of his young friend's relation to her frame itself in his mind. This young friend, for a representative of the new psychology, was himself easily hypnotized, and if he became abnormally communicative it was only a sign of his real subjection. Dencombe did accordingly what he wanted with him, even without being known as Dencombe.

Taken ill on a journey in Switzerland the Countess had picked him up at an hotel, and the accident of his happening to please her had made her offer him, with her imperious liberality, terms that couldn't fail to dazzle a practitioner without patients and whose resources had been drained dry by his studies. It was not the way he would have elected to spend his time, but it was time that would pass quickly, and meanwhile she was wonderfully kind. She exacted perpetual attention, but it was impossible not to like her. He gave details about his queer patient, a 'type' if there ever was one, who had in connection with her flushed obesity and in addition to the morbid strain of a violent and aimless will a grave organic disorder; but he came back to his loved novelist, whom he was so good as to pronounce more essentially a poet than many of those who went in for verse, with a zeal excited, as all his indiscretion had been excited, by the happy chance of Dencombe's sympathy and the coincidence of their occupation. Dencombe had confessed to a slight personal acquaintance with the author of 'The Middle Years', but had not felt himself as ready as he could have wished when his companion, who had never yet encountered a being so privileged, began to be eager for particulars. He even thought that Doctor Hugh's eye at that moment emitted a glimmer of suspicion. But the young man was too inflamed to be shrewd and repeatedly caught up the book to exclaim: 'Did you notice this?' or 'Weren't you immensely struck with that?' 'There's a beautiful passage toward the end,' he broke out; and again he laid his hand upon the volume. As he turned the pages he came upon something else, while Dencombe saw him suddenly change colour. He had taken up, as it lay on the bench, Dencombe's copy instead of his own, and his neighbour immediately guessed the reason of his start. Doctor Hugh looked grave an instant; then he said: 'I see you've been altering the text!' Dencombe was a passionate corrector, a fingerer of style; the last thing he ever arrived at was a form final for himself. His ideal would have been to publish secretly, and then, on the published text, treat himself to the terrified revise, sacrificing always a first edition and beginning for posterity and even for the collectors, poor dears, with a second. This morning, in 'The

Middle Years', his pencil had pricked a dozen lights. He was amused at the effect of the young man's reproach; for an instant it made him change colour. He stammered, at any rate, ambiguously; then, through a blur of ebbing consciousness, saw Doctor Hugh's mystified eyes. He only had time to feel he was about to be ill again – that emotion, excitement, fatigue, the heat of the sun, the solicitation of the air, had combined to play him a trick, before, stretching out a hand to his visitor with a plaintive cry, he lost his senses altogether.

Later he knew that he had fainted and that Doctor Hugh had got him home in a bath-chair,[9] the conductor of which, prowling within hail for custom, had happened to remember seeing him in the garden of the hotel. He had recovered his perception in the transit, and had, in bed, that afternoon, a vague recollection of Doctor Hugh's young face, as they went together, bent over him in a comforting laugh and expressive of something more than a suspicion of his identity. That identity was ineffaceable now, and all the more that he was disappointed, disgusted. He had been rash, been stupid, had gone out too soon, stayed out too long. He oughtn't to have exposed himself to strangers, he ought to have taken his servant. He felt as if he had fallen into a hole too deep to descry any little patch of heaven. He was confused about the time that had elapsed – he pieced the fragments together. He had seen his doctor, the real one, the one who had treated him from the first and who had again been very kind. His servant was in and out on tiptoe, looking very wise after the fact. He said more than once something about the sharp young gentleman. The rest was vagueness, in so far as it wasn't despair. The vagueness, however, justified itself by dreams, dozing anxieties from which he finally emerged to the consciousness of a dark room and a shaded candle.

'You'll be all right again – I know all about you now,' said a voice near him that he knew to be young. Then his meeting with Doctor Hugh came back. He was too discouraged to joke about it yet, but he was able to perceive, after a little, that the interest of it was intense for his visitor. 'Of course I can't attend you professionally – you've got your own man, with whom I've talked and who's excellent,' Doctor Hugh went on. 'But you must let me come to see you as a good friend. I've just looked in before going to bed. You're doing beautifully, but it's a good job I was with you on the cliff. I shall come in early to-morrow. I want to do something for you. I want to do everything. You've done a tremendous lot for me.' The young man held his hand, hanging over him, and poor Dencombe, weakly aware of this living pressure, simply lay there and accepted his devotion. He couldn't do anything less – he needed help too much.

The idea of the help he needed was very present to him that night, which he spent in a lucid stillness, an intensity of thought that constituted a reaction from his hours of stupor. He was lost, he was lost – he was lost if he couldn't be saved. He was not afraid of suffering, of death; he was not even in love with life; but he had had a deep demonstration of desire. It came over him in the long, quiet hours that only with 'The Middle Years' had he taken his flight; only on that day, visited by soundless processions, had he recognized his kingdom. He had had a revelation of his range. What he dreaded was the idea that his reputation should stand on the unfinished. It was not with his past but with his future that it should properly be concerned. Illness and age rose before him like spectres with pitiless eyes: how was he to bribe such fates to give him the second chance? He had had the one chance that all men have – he had had the chance of life. He went to sleep again very late, and when he awoke Doctor Hugh was sitting by his head. There was already, by this time, something beautifully familiar in him.

'Don't think I've turned out your physician,' he said; 'I'm acting with his consent. He has been here and seen you. Somehow he seems to trust me. I told him how we happened to come together yesterday, and he recognizes that I've a peculiar right.'

Dencombe looked at him with a calculating earnestness. 'How have you squared the Countess?'

The young man blushed a little, but he laughed. 'Oh, never mind the Countess!'

'You told me she was very exacting.'

Doctor Hugh was silent a moment. 'So she is.'

'And Miss Vernham's an *intrigante*.'

'How do you know that?'

'I know everything. One *has* to, to write decently!'

'I think she's mad,' said limpid Doctor Hugh.

'Well, don't quarrel with the Countess – she's a present help to you.'

'I don't quarrel,' Doctor Hugh replied. 'But I don't get on with silly women.' Presently he added: 'You seem very much alone.'

'That often happens at my age. I've outlived, I've lost by the way.'

Doctor Hugh hesitated; then surmounting a soft scruple: 'Whom have you lost?'

'Every one.'

'Ah, no,' the young man murmured, laying a hand on his arm.

'I once had a wife – I once had a son. My wife died when my child was born, and my boy, at school, was carried off by typhoid.'

'I wish I'd been there!' said Doctor Hugh simply.

'Well – if you're here!' Dencombe answered, with a smile that, in spite of dimness, showed how much he liked to be sure of his companion's whereabouts.

'You talk strangely of your age. You're not old.'

'Hypocrite – so early!'

'I speak physiologically.'

'That's the way I've been speaking for the last five years, and it's exactly what I've been saying to myself. It isn't till we *are* old that we begin to tell ourselves we're not!'

'Yet I know I myself am young,' Doctor Hugh declared.

'Not so well as I!' laughed his patient, whose visitor indeed would have established the truth in question by the honesty with which he changed the point of view, remarking that it must be one of the charms of age – at any rate in the case of high distinction – to feel that one has laboured and achieved. Doctor Hugh employed the common phrase about earning one's rest, and it made poor Dencombe, for an instant, almost angry. He recovered himself, however, to explain, lucidly enough, that if he, ungraciously, knew nothing of such a balm, it was doubtless because he had wasted inestimable years. He had followed literature from the first, but he had taken a lifetime to get alongside of her. Only to-day, at last, had he begun to *see*, so that what he had hitherto done was a movement without a direction. He had ripened too late and was so clumsily constituted that he had had to teach himself by mistakes.

'I prefer your flowers, then, to other people's fruit, and your mistakes to other people's successes,' said gallant Doctor Hugh. 'It's for your mistakes I admire you.'

'You're happy – you don't know,' Dencombe answered.

Looking at his watch the young man had got up; he named the hour of the afternoon at which he would return. Dencombe warned him against committing himself too deeply, and expressed again all his dread of making him neglect the Countess – perhaps incur her displeasure.

'I want to be like you – I want to learn by mistakes!' Doctor Hugh laughed.

'Take care you don't make too grave a one! But do come back,' Dencombe added, with the glimmer of a new idea.

'You should have had more vanity!' Doctor Hugh spoke as if he knew the exact amount required to make a man of letters normal.

'No, no – I only should have had more time. I want another go.'

'Another go?'

'I want an extension.'

'An extension?' Again Doctor Hugh repeated Dencombe's words, with which he seemed to have been struck.

'Don't you know? – I want to what they call "live".'

The young man, for good-bye, had taken his hand, which closed with a certain force. They looked at each other hard a moment. 'You *will* live,' said Doctor Hugh.

'Don't be superficial. It's too serious!'

'You *shall* live!' Dencombe's visitor declared, turning pale.

'Ah, that's better!' And as he retired the invalid, with a troubled laugh, sank gratefully back.

All that day and all the following night he wondered if it mightn't be arranged. His doctor came again, his servant was attentive, but it was to his confident young friend that he found himself mentally appealing. His collapse on the cliff was plausibly explained, and his liberation, on a better basis, promised for the morrow; meanwhile, however, the intensity of his meditations kept him tranquil and made him indifferent. The idea that occupied him was none the less absorbing because it was a morbid fancy. Here was a clever son of the age, ingenious and ardent, who happened to have set him up for connoisseurs to worship. This servant of his altar had all the new learning in science and all the old reverence in faith; wouldn't he therefore put his knowledge at the disposal of his sympathy, his craft at the disposal of his love? Couldn't he be trusted to invent a remedy for a poor artist to whose art he had paid a tribute? If he couldn't, the alternative was hard: Dencombe would have to surrender to silence, unvindicated and undivined. The rest of the day and all the next he toyed in secret with this sweet futility. Who would work the miracle for him but the young man who could combine such lucidity with such passion? He thought of the fairy-tales of science and charmed himself into forgetting that he looked for a magic that was not of this world. Doctor Hugh was an apparition, and that placed him above the law. He came and went while his patient, who sat up, followed him with supplicating eyes. The interest of knowing the great author had made the young man begin 'The Middle Years' afresh, and would help him to find a deeper meaning in its pages. Dencombe had told him what he 'tried for'; with all his intelligence, on a first perusal, Doctor Hugh had failed to guess it. The baffled celebrity wondered then who in the world *would* guess it: he was amused once more at the fine, full way with which an intention could be missed. Yet he wouldn't rail at the general mind to-day – consoling as that ever had been: the revelation of his own slowness had seemed to make all stupidity sacred.

Doctor Hugh, after a little, was visibly worried, confessing, on inquiry, to a source of embarrassment at home. 'Stick to the Countess – don't mind me,' Dencombe said, repeatedly; for his companion was frank enough about the large lady's attitude. She was so jealous that she had fallen ill – she resented such a breach of allegiance. She paid so much for his fidelity that she must have it all: she refused him the right to other sympathies, charged him with scheming to make her die alone, for it was needless to point out how little Miss Vernham was a resource in trouble. When Doctor Hugh mentioned that the Countess would already have left Bournemouth if he hadn't kept her in bed, poor Dencombe held his arm tighter and said with decision: 'Take her straight away.' They had gone out together, walking back to the sheltered nook in which, the other day, they had met. The young man, who had given his companion a personal support, declared with emphasis that his conscience was clear – he could ride two horses at once. Didn't he dream, for his future, of a time when he should have to ride five hundred? Longing equally for virtue, Dencombe replied that in that golden age no patient would pretend to have contracted with him for his whole attention. On the part of the Countess was not such an avidity lawful? Doctor Hugh denied it, said there was no contract but only a free understanding, and that a sordid servitude was impossible to a generous spirit; he liked moreover to talk about art, and that was the subject on which, this time, as they sat together on the sunny bench, he tried most to engage the author of 'The Middle Years'. Dencombe, soaring again a little on the weak wings of convalescence and still haunted by that happy notion of an organized rescue, found another strain of eloquence to plead the cause of a certain splendid 'last manner', the very citadel, as it would prove, of his reputation, the stronghold into which his real treasure would be gathered. While his listener gave up the morning and the great still sea appeared to wait, he had a wonderful explanatory hour. Even for himself he was inspired as he told of what his treasure would consist – the precious metals he would dig from the mine, the jewels rare, strings of pearls, he would hang between the columns of his temple. He was wonderful for himself, so thick his convictions crowded; but he was still more wonderful for Doctor Hugh, who assured him, none the less, that the very pages he had just published were already encrusted with gems. The young man, however, panted for the combinations to come, and, before the face of the beautiful day, renewed to Dencombe his guarantee that his profession would hold itself responsible for such a life. Then he suddenly clapped his hand upon his watch-pocket and asked leave to absent himself for half an hour. Dencombe waited there for his return, but was at last recalled to the actual by the fall of a shadow across the ground. The shadow darkened into that of Miss Vernham, the young lady in attendance on the Countess; whom Dencombe, recognizing her, perceived so clearly to have come to speak to him that he rose from his bench to acknowledge the civility. Miss Vernham indeed proved not particularly civil; she looked strangely agitated, and her type was now unmistakable.

'Excuse me if I inquire,' she said, 'whether it's too much to hope that you may be induced to leave Doctor Hugh alone.' Then, before Dencombe, greatly disconcerted, could protest: 'You ought to be informed that you stand in his light; that you may do him a terrible injury.'

'Do you mean by causing the Countess to dispense with his services?'

'By causing her to disinherit him.' Dencombe stared at this, and Miss Vernham pursued, in the gratification of seeing she could produce an impression: 'It has depended on himself to come into something very handsome. He has had a magnificent prospect, but I think you've succeeded in spoiling it.'

'Not intentionally, I assure you. Is there no hope the accident may be repaired?' Dencombe asked.

'She was ready to do anything for him. She takes great fancies, she lets herself go – it's her way. She has no relations, she's free to dispose of her money, and she's very ill.'

'I'm very sorry to hear it,' Dencombe stammered.

'Wouldn't it be possible for you to leave Bournemouth? That's what I've come to ask you.'

Poor Dencombe sank down on his bench. 'I'm very ill myself, but I'll try!'

Miss Vernham still stood there with her colourless eyes and the brutality of her good conscience. 'Before it's too late, please!' she said; and with this she turned her back, in order, quickly, as if it had been a business to which she could spare but a precious moment, to pass out of his sight.

Oh, yes, after this Dencombe was certainly very ill. Miss

Vernham had upset him with her rough, fierce news; it was the sharpest shock to him to discover what was at stake for a penniless young man of fine parts. He sat trembling on his bench, staring at the waste of waters, feeling sick with the directness of the blow. He was indeed too weak, too unsteady, too alarmed; but he would make the effort to get away, for he couldn't accept the guilt of interference, and his honour was really involved. He would hobble home, at any rate, and then he would think what was to be done. He made his way back to the hotel and, as he went, had a characteristic vision of Miss Vernham's great motive. The Countess hated women, of course; Dencombe was lucid about that; so the hungry pianist had no personal hopes and could only console herself with the bold conception of helping Doctor Hugh in order either to marry him after he should get his money or to induce him to recognize her title to compensation and buy her off. If she had befriended him at a fruitful crisis he would really, as a man of delicacy, and she knew what to think of that point, have to reckon with her.

At the hotel Dencombe's servant insisted on his going back to bed. The invalid had talked about catching a train and had begun with orders to pack; after which his humming nerves had yielded to a sense of sickness. He consented to see his physician, who immediately was sent for, but he wished it to be understood that his door was irrevocably closed to Doctor Hugh. He had his plan, which was so fine that he rejoiced in it after getting back to bed. Doctor Hugh, suddenly finding himself snubbed without mercy, would, in natural disgust and to the joy of Miss Vernham, renew his allegiance to the Countess. When his physician arrived Dencombe learned that he was feverish and that this was very wrong: he was to cultivate calmness and try, if possible, not to think. For the rest of the day he wooed stupidity; but there was an ache that kept him sentient, the probable sacrifice of his 'extension', the limit of his course. His medical adviser was anything but pleased; his successive relapses were ominous. He charged this personage to put out a strong hand and take Doctor Hugh off his mind – it would contribute so much to his being quiet. The agitating name, in his room, was not mentioned again, but his security was a smothered fear, and it was not confirmed by the receipt, at ten o'clock that evening, of a telegram which his servant opened and read for him and to which, with an address in London, the signature of Miss Vernham was attached. 'Beseech you to use all influence to make our friend join us here in the morning. Countess much the worse for dreadful journey, but everything may still be saved.' The two ladies had gathered themselves up and had been capable in the afternoon of a spiteful revolution. They had started for the capital, and if the elder one, as Miss Vernham had announced, was very ill, she had wished to make it clear that she was proportionately reckless. Poor Dencombe, who was not reckless and who only desired that everything should indeed be 'saved', sent this missive straight off to the young man's lodging and had on the morrow the pleasure of knowing that he had quitted Bournemouth by an early train.

Two days later he pressed in with a copy of a literary journal in his hand. He had returned because he was anxious and for the pleasure of flourishing the great review of 'The Middle Years'. Here at least was something adequate – it rose to the occasion; it was an acclamation, a reparation, a critical attempt to place the author in the niche he had fairly won. Dencombe accepted and submitted; he made neither objection nor inquiry, for old complications had returned and he had had two atrocious days. He was convinced not only that he should never again leave his bed, so that his young friend might pardonably remain, but that the demand he should make on the patience of beholders would be very moderate indeed. Doctor Hugh had been to town, and he tried to find in his eyes some confession that the Countess was pacified and his legacy clinched; but all he could see there was the light of his juvenile joy in two or three of the phrases of the newspaper. Dencombe couldn't read them, but when his visitor had insisted on repeating them more than once he was able to shake an unintoxicated head. 'Ah, no; but they would have been true of what I *could* have done!'

'What people "could have done" is mainly what they've in fact done,' Doctor Hugh contended.

'Mainly, yes; but I've been an idiot!' said Dencombe.

Doctor Hugh did remain; the end was coming fast. Two days later Dencombe observed to him, by way of the feeblest of jokes, that there would now be no question whatever of a second chance. At this the young man stared; then he exclaimed: 'Why, it has come to pass – it has come to pass! The second chance has been the public's – the chance to find the point of view, to pick up the pearl!'

'Oh, the pearl!' poor Dencombe uneasily sighed. A smile as cold as a winter sunset flickered on his drawn lips as he added: 'The pearl is the unwritten – the pearl is the unalloyed, the *rest*, the lost!'

From that moment he was less and less present, heedless to all appearance of what went on around him. His disease was definitely mortal, of an action as relentless, after the short arrest that had enabled him to fall in with Doctor Hugh, as a leak in a great ship. Sinking steadily, though this visitor, a man of rare resources, now cordially approved by his physician, showed endless art in guarding him from pain, poor Dencombe kept no reckoning of favour or neglect, betrayed no symptom of regret or speculation. Yet toward the last he gave a sign of having noticed that for two days Doctor Hugh had not been in his room, a sign that consisted of his suddenly opening his eyes to ask of him if had spent the interval with the Countess.

'The Countess is dead,' said Doctor Hugh. 'I knew that in a particular contingency she wouldn't resist. I went to her grave.'

Dencombe's eyes opened wider. 'She left you "something handsome"?'

The young man gave a laugh almost too light for a chamber of woe. 'Never a penny. She roundly cursed me.'

'Cursed you?' Dencombe murmured.

'For giving her up. I gave her up for *you*. I had to choose,' his companion explained.

'You chose to let a fortune go?'

'I chose to accept, whatever they might be, the consequences of my infatuation,' smiled Doctor Hugh. Then, as a larger pleasantry: 'A fortune be hanged! It's your own fault if I can't get your things out of my head.'

The immediate tribute to his humour was a long, bewildered

moan; after which, for many hours, many days, Dencombe lay motionless and absent. A response so absolute, such a glimpse of a definite result and such a sense of credit worked together in his mind and, producing a strange commotion, slowly altered and transfigured his despair. The sense of cold submersion left him – he seemed to float without an effort. The incident was extraordinary as evidence, and it shed an intenser light. At the last he signed to Doctor Hugh to listen, and, when he was down on his knees by the pillow, brought him very near.

'You've made me think it all a delusion.'

'Not your glory, my friend,' stammered the young man.

'Not my glory – what there is of it! It *is* glory – to have been tested, to have had our little quality and cast our little spell. The thing is to have made somebody care. You happen to be crazy, of course, but that doesn't affect the law.'

'You're a great success!' said Doctor Hugh, putting into his young voice the ring of a marriage-bell.

Dencombe lay taking this in; then he gathered strength to speak once more. 'A second chance – *that's* the delusion. There never was to be but one. We work in the dark – we do what we can – we give what we have. Our doubt is our passion and our passion is our task. The rest is the madness of art.'

'If you've doubted, if you've despaired, you've always "done" it,' his visitor subtly argued.

'We've done something or other,' Dencombe conceded.

'Something or other is everything. It's the feasible. It's *you*!'

'Comforter!' poor Dencombe ironically sighed.

'But it's true,' insisted his friend.

'It's true. It's frustration that doesn't count.'

'Frustration's only life,' said Doctor Hugh.

'Yes, it's what passes.' Poor Dencombe was barely audible, but he had marked with the words the virtual end of his first and only chance.

THE FIGURE IN
THE CARPET

I had done a few things and earned a few pence – I had perhaps even had time to begin to think I was finer than was perceived by the patronizing; but when I take the little measure of my course (a fidgety habit, for it's none of the longest yet) I count my real start from the evening George Corvick, breathless and worried, came in to ask me a service. He had done more things than I, and earned more pence, though there were chances for cleverness I thought he sometimes missed. I could only however that evening declare to him that he never missed one for kindness. There was almost rapture in hearing it proposed to me to prepare for *The Middle*,[1] the organ of our lucubrations, so called from the position in the week of its day of appearance, an article for which he had made himself responsible and of which, tied up with a stout string, he laid on my table the subject. I pounced upon my opportunity – that is on the first volume of it – and paid scant attention to my friend's explanation of his appeal. What explanation could be more to the point than my obvious fitness for the task? I had written on Hugh Vereker, but never a word in *The Middle*, where my dealings were mainly with the ladies and the minor poets. This was his new novel, an advance copy, and whatever much or little it should do for his reputation I was clear on the spot as to what it should do for mine. Moreover if I always read him as soon as I could get hold of him I had a particular reason for wishing to read him now: I had accepted an invitation to Bridges for the following Sunday, and it had been mentioned in Lady Jane's note that Mr Vereker was to be there. I was young enough to have an emotion about meeting a man of his renown and innocent enough to believe the occasion would demand the display of an acquaintance with his 'last'.

Corvick, who had promised a review of it, had not even had time to read it; he had gone to pieces in consequence of news requiring – as on precipitate reflection he judged – that he should catch the night-mail to Paris. He had had a telegram from Gwendolen Erme in answer to his letter offering to fly to her aid. I knew already about Gwendolen Erme; I had never seen her, but I had my ideas, which were mainly to the effect that Corvick would marry her if her mother would only die. That lady seemed now in a fair way to oblige him; after some dreadful mistake about some climate or some waters she had suddenly collapsed on the return from abroad. Her daughter, unsupported and alarmed, desiring to make a rush for home but hesitating at the risk, had accepted our friend's assistance, and it was my secret belief that at the sight of him Mrs Erme would pull round. His own belief was scarcely to be called secret; it discernibly at any rate differed from mine. He had showed me Gwendolen's photograph with the remark that she wasn't pretty but was awfully interesting; she had published at the age of nineteen a novel in three volumes, 'Deep Down', about which, in *The Middle*, he had been really splendid. He appreciated my present eagerness and undertook that the periodical in question should do no less; then at the last, with his hand on the door, he said to me: 'Of course you'll be all right, you know.' Seeing I was a trifle vague he added: 'I mean you won't be silly.'

'Silly – about Vereker! Why, what do I ever find him but awfully clever?'

'Well, what's that but silly? What on earth does "awfully clever" mean? For God's sake try to get *at* him. Don't let him suffer by our arrangement. Speak of him, you know, if you can, as *I* should have spoken of him.'

I wondered an instant. 'You mean as far and away the biggest of the lot – that sort of thing?'

Corvick almost groaned. 'Oh, you know, I don't put them back to back that way; it's the infancy of art! But he gives me a pleasure so rare; the sense of' – he mused a little – 'something or other.'

I wondered again. 'The sense, pray, of what?'

'My dear man, that's just what I want *you* to say!'

Even before Corvick had banged the door I had begun, book in hand, to prepare myself to say it. I sat up with Vereker half the night; Corvick couldn't have done more than that. He was awfully clever – I stuck to that, but he wasn't a bit the biggest of the lot. I didn't allude to the lot, however; I flattered myself that I emerged on this occasion from the infancy of art. 'It's all right,' they declared vividly at the office; and when the number appeared I felt there was a basis on which I could meet the great man. It gave me confidence for a day or two, and then that confidence dropped. I had fancied him reading it with relish, but if Corvick was not satisfied how could Vereker himself be? I reflected indeed that the heat of the admirer was sometimes grosser even than the appetite of the scribe. Corvick at all events wrote me from Paris a little ill-humouredly. Mrs Erme was pulling round, and I hadn't at all said what Vereker gave him the sense of.

II

The effect of my visit to Bridges was to turn me out for more profundity. Hugh Vereker, as I saw him there, was of a contact so void of angles that I blushed for the poverty of imagination involved in my small precautions. If he was in spirits it was not because he had read my review; in fact on the Sunday morning I felt sure he hadn't read it, though *The Middle* had been out three days and bloomed, I assured myself, in the stiff garden of periodicals which gave one of the ormolu tables the air of a stand at a station. The impression he made on me personally was such that I wished him to read it, and I corrected to this end with a surreptitious hand what might be wanting in the careless conspicuity of the sheet. I am afraid I even watched the result of my manœuvre, but up to luncheon I watched in vain.

When afterwards, in the course of our gregarious walk, I found myself for half an hour, not perhaps without another manœuvre, at the great man's side, the result of his affability was a still livelier desire that he should not remain in ignorance of the peculiar justice I had done him. It was not that he seemed to thirst for justice; on the contrary I had not yet caught in his talk the faintest grunt of a grudge – a note for which my young experience had already given me an ear. Of late he had had more recognition, and it was pleasant, as we used to say in *The Middle*, to see that it drew him out. He wasn't of course popular, but I judged one of the sources of his good humour to be precisely that his success was independent of that. He had none the less become in a manner the fashion; the critics at least had put on a spurt and caught up with him. We had found out at last how clever he was, and he had had to make the best of the loss of his mystery. I was strongly tempted, as I walked beside him, to let him know how much of that unveiling was my act; and there was a moment when I probably should have done so had not one of the ladies of our party, snatching a place at his other elbow, just then appealed to him in a spirit comparatively selfish. It was very discouraging: I almost felt the liberty had been taken with myself.

I had had on my tongue's end, for my own part, a phrase or two about the right word at the right time; but later on I was glad not to have spoken, for when on our return we clustered at tea I perceived Lady Jane, who had not been out with us, brandishing *The Middle* with her longest arm. She had taken it up at her leisure; she was delighted with what she had found, and I saw that, as a mistake in a man may often be a felicity in a woman, she would practically do for me what I hadn't been able to do for myself. 'Some sweet little truths that needed to be spoken,' I heard her declare, thrusting the paper at rather a bewildered couple by the fireplace. She grabbed it away from them again on the reappearance of Hugh Vereker, who after our walk had been upstairs to change something. 'I know you don't in general look at this kind of thing, but it's an occasion really for doing so. You *haven't* seen it? Then you must. The man has actually got *at* you, at what *I* always feel, you know.' Lady Jane threw into her eyes a look evidently intended to give an idea of what she always felt; but she added that she couldn't

have expressed it. The man in the paper expressed it in a striking manner. 'Just see there, and there, where I've dashed it, how
he brings it out.' She had literally marked for him the brightest
patches of my prose, and if I was a little amused Vereker himself may well have been. He showed how much he was when
before us all Lady Jane wanted to read something aloud. I liked
at any rate the way he defeated her purpose by jerking the
paper affectionately out of her clutch. He would take it upstairs
with him, would look at it on going to dress. He did this half
an hour later – I saw it in his hand when he repaired to his
room. That was the moment at which, thinking to give her
pleasure, I mentioned to Lady Jane that I was the author of the
review. I did give her pleasure, I judged, but perhaps not quite
so much as I had expected. If the author was 'only me' the
thing didn't seem quite so remarkable. Hadn't I had the effect
rather of diminishing the lustre of the article than of adding to
my own? Her ladyship was subject to the most extraordinary
drops. It didn't matter; the only effect I cared about was the
one it would have on Vereker up there by his bedroom fire.

At dinner I watched for the signs of this impression, tried to
fancy there was some happier light in his eyes; but to my disappointment Lady Jane gave me no chance to make sure. I had
hoped she would call triumphantly down the table, publicly
demand if she hadn't been right. The party was large – there
were people from outside as well, but I had never seen a table
long enough to deprive Lady Jane of a triumph. I was just
reflecting in truth that this interminable board would deprive
me of one when the guest next me, dear woman – she was Miss
Poyle, the vicar's sister, a robust, unmodulated person – had
the happy inspiration and the unusual courage to address herself across it to Vereker, who was opposite, but not directly, so
that when he replied they were both leaning forward. She
inquired, artless body, what he thought of Lady Jane's 'pan-
egyric', which she had read – not connecting it however with
her right-hand neighbour; and while I strained my ear for his
reply I heard him, to my stupefaction, call back gaily, with his
mouth full of bread: 'Oh, it's all right – it's the usual twaddle!'

I had caught Vereker's glance as he spoke, but Miss Poyle's

surprise was a fortunate cover for my own. 'You mean he doesn't do you justice?' said the excellent woman.

Vereker laughed out, and I was happy to be able to do the same. 'It's a charming article,' he tossed us.

Miss Poyle thrust her chin half across the cloth. 'Oh you're so deep!' she drove home.

'As deep as the ocean! All I pretend is, the author doesn't see—'

A dish was at this point passed over his shoulder, and we had to wait while he helped himself.

'Doesn't see what?' my neighbour continued.

'Doesn't see anything.'

'Dear me – how very stupid!'

'Not a bit,' Vereker laughed again. 'Nobody does.'

The lady on his further side appealed to him, and Miss Poyle sank back to me. 'Nobody sees anything!' she cheerfully announced; to which I replied that I had often thought so too, but had somehow taken the thought for a proof on my own part of a tremendous eye. I didn't tell her the article was mine; and I observed that Lady Jane, occupied at the end of the table, had not caught Vereker's words.

I rather avoided him after dinner, for I confess he struck me as cruelly conceited, and the revelation was a pain. 'The usual twaddle' – my acute little study! That one's admiration should have had a reserve or two could gall him to that point? I had thought him placid, and he was placid enough; such a surface was the hard, polished glass that encased the bauble of his vanity. I was really ruffled, and the only comfort was that if nobody saw anything George Corvick was quite as much out of it as I. This comfort however was not sufficient, after the ladies had dispersed, to carry me in the proper manner – I mean in a spotted jacket[2] and humming an air – into the smoking-room. I took my way in some dejection to bed; but in the passage I encountered Mr Vereker, who had been up once more to change, coming out of his room. *He* was humming an air and had on a spotted jacket, and as soon as he saw me his gaiety gave a start.

'My dear young man,' he exclaimed, 'I'm so glad to lay

hands on you! I'm afraid I most unwittingly wounded you by those words of mine at dinner to Miss Poyle. I learned but half an hour ago from Lady Jane that you wrote the little notice in *The Middle*.'

I protested that no bones were broken; but he moved with me to my own door, his hand, on my shoulder, kindly feeling for a fracture; and on hearing that I had come up to bed he asked leave to cross my threshold and just tell me in three words what his qualification of my remarks had represented. It was plain he really feared I was hurt, and the sense of his solicitude suddenly made all the difference to me. My cheap review fluttered off into space, and the best things I had said in it became flat enough beside the brilliancy of his being there. I can see him there still, on my rug, in the firelight and his spotted jacket, his fine, clear face all bright with the desire to be tender to my youth. I don't know what he had at first meant to say, but I think the sight of my relief touched him, excited him, brought up words to his lips from far within. It was so these words presently conveyed to me something that, as I afterwards knew, he had never uttered to any one. I have always done justice to the generous impulse that made him speak; it was simply compunction for a snub unconsciously administered to a man of letters in a position inferior to his own, a man of letters moreover in the very act of praising him. To make the thing right he talked to me exactly as an equal and on the ground of what we both loved best. The hour, the place, the unexpectedness deepened the impression: he couldn't have done anything more exquisitely successful.

III

'I don't quite know how to explain it to you,' he said, 'but it was the very fact that your notice of my book had a spice of intelligence, it was just your exceptional sharpness that produced the feeling – a very old story with me, I beg you to believe – under the momentary influence of which I used in speaking to that good lady the words you so naturally resent.

I don't read the things in the newspapers unless they're thrust upon me as that one was – it's always one's best friend that does it! But I used to read them sometimes – ten years ago. I daresay they were in general rather stupider then; at any rate it always seemed to me that they missed my little point with a perfection exactly as admirable when they patted me on the back as when they kicked me in the shins. Whenever since I've happened to have a glimpse of them they were still blazing away – still missing it, I mean, deliciously. *You* miss it, my dear fellow, with inimitable assurance; the fact of your being awfully clever and your article's being awfully nice doesn't make a hair's breadth of difference. It's quite with you rising young men,' Vereker laughed, 'that I feel most what a failure I am!'

I listened with intense interest; it grew intenser as he talked. '*You* a failure – heavens! What then may your "little point" happen to be?'

'Have I got to *tell* you, after all these years and labours?' There was something in the friendly reproach of this – jocosely exaggerated – that made me, as an ardent young seeker for truth, blush to the roots of my hair. I'm as much in the dark as ever, though I've grown used in a sense to my obtuseness; at that moment, however, Vereker's happy accent made me appear to myself, and probably to him, a rare donkey. I was on the point of exclaiming 'Ah, yes, don't tell me: for my honour, for that of the craft, don't!' when he went on in a manner that showed he had read my thought and had his own idea of the probability of our some day redeeming ourselves. 'By my little point I mean – what shall I call it? – the particular thing I've written my books most *for*. Isn't there for every writer a par-ticular thing of that sort, the thing that most makes him apply himself, the thing without the effort to achieve which he wouldn't write at all, the very passion of his passion, the part of the business in which, for him, the flame of art burns most intensely? Well, it's *that*!'

I considered a moment. I was fascinated – easily, you'll say; but I wasn't going after all to be put off my guard. 'Your description's certainly beautiful, but it doesn't make what you describe very distinct.'

'I promise you it would be distinct if it should dawn on you at all.' I saw that the charm of our topic overflowed for my companion into an emotion as lively as my own. 'At any rate,' he went on, 'I can speak for myself: there's an idea in my work without which I wouldn't have given a straw for the whole job. It's the finest, fullest intention of the lot, and the application of it has been, I think, a triumph of patience, of ingenuity. I ought to leave that to somebody else to say; but that nobody does say it is precisely what we're talking about. It stretches, this little trick of mine, from book to book, and everything else, comparatively, plays over the surface of it. The order, the form, the texture of my books will perhaps some day constitute for the initiated a complete representation of it. So it's naturally the thing for the critic to look for. It strikes me,' my visitor added, smiling, 'even as the thing for the critic to find.'

This seemed a responsibility indeed. 'You call it a little trick?'

'That's only my little modesty. It's really an exquisite scheme.'

'And you hold that you've carried the scheme out?'

'The way I've carried it out is the thing in life I think a bit well of myself for.'

I was silent a moment. 'Don't you think you ought – just a trifle – to assist the critic?'

'Assist him? What else have I done with every stroke of my pen? I've shouted my intention in his great blank face!' At this, laughing out again, Vereker laid his hand on my shoulder to show that the allusion was not to my personal appearance.

'But you talk about the initiated. There must therefore, you see, be initiation.'

'What else in heaven's name is criticism supposed to be?' I'm afraid I coloured at this too; but I took refuge in repeating that his account of his silver lining was poor in something or other that a plain man knows things by. 'That's only because you've never had a glimpse of it,' he replied. 'If you had had one the element in question would soon have become practically all you'd see. To me it's exactly as palpable as the marble of this chimney. Besides, the critic just *isn't* a plain man: if he were, pray, what would he be doing in his neighbour's garden? You're anything but a plain man yourself, and the very *raison d'être* of you all is that you're little demons of subtlety. If my great affair's a secret, that's only because it's a secret in spite of itself – the amazing event has made it one. I not only never took the smallest precaution to do so, but never dreamed of any such accident. If I had I shouldn't in advance have had the heart to go on. As it was I only became aware little by little, and meanwhile I had done my work.'

'And now you quite like it?' I risked.

'My work?'

'Your secret. It's the same thing.'

'Your guessing that,' Vereker replied, 'is a proof that you're as clever as I say!' I was encouraged by this to remark that he would clearly be pained to part with it, and he confessed that it was indeed with him now the great amusement of life. 'I live almost to see if it will ever be detected.' He looked at me for a jesting challenge; something at the back of his eyes seemed to peep out. 'But I needn't worry – it won't!'

'You fire me as I've never been fired,' I returned; 'you make me determined to do or die.' Then I asked: 'Is it a kind of esoteric message?'

His countenance fell at this – he put out his hand as if to bid me good-night. 'Ah, my dear fellow, it can't be described in cheap journalese!'

I knew of course he would be awfully fastidious, but our talk had made me feel how much his nerves were exposed. I was unsatisfied – I kept hold of his hand. 'I won't make use of the expression then,' I said, 'in the article in which I shall eventually announce my discovery, though I daresay I shall have hard work to do without it. But meanwhile, just to hasten that difficult birth, can't you give a fellow a clue?' I felt much more at my ease.

'My whole lucid effort gives him the clue – every page and line and letter. The thing's as concrete there as a bird in a cage, a bait on a hook, a piece of cheese in a mouse-trap. It's stuck into every volume as your foot is stuck into your shoe. It governs every line, it chooses every word, it dots every i, it places every comma.'

I scratched my head. 'Is it something in the style or something in the thought? An element of form or an element of feeling?'[3]

He indulgently shook my hand again, and I felt my questions to be crude and my distinctions pitiful. 'Good-night, my dear boy – don't bother about it. After all, you do like a fellow.'

'And a little intelligence might spoil it?' I still detained him.

He hesitated. 'Well, you've got a heart in your body. Is that an element of form or an element of feeling?[3] What I contend that nobody has ever mentioned in my work is the organ of life.'

'I see – it's some idea about life, some sort of philosophy. Unless it be,' I added with the eagerness of a thought perhaps still happier, 'some kind of game you're up to with your style, something you're after in the language. Perhaps it's a preference for the letter P!' I ventured profanely to break out. 'Papa, potatoes, prunes – that sort of thing?' He was suitably indulgent: he only said I hadn't got the right letter. But his amusement was over; I could see he was bored. There was nevertheless something else I had absolutely to learn. 'Should you be able, pen in hand, to state it clearly yourself – to name it, phrase it, formulate it?'

'Oh,' he almost passionately sighed, 'if I were only, pen in hand, one of *you* chaps!'

'That would be a great chance for you of course. But why should you despise us chaps for not doing what you can't do yourself?'

'Can't do?' He opened his eyes. 'Haven't I done it in twenty volumes? I do it in my way,' he continued. 'You don't do it in yours.'

'Ours is so devilish difficult,' I weakly observed.

'So is mine. We each choose our own. There's no compulsion. You won't come down and smoke?'

'No. I want to think this thing out.'

'You'll tell me then in the morning that you've laid me bare?'

'I'll see what I can do; I'll sleep on it. But just one word more,' I added. We had left the room – I walked again with him a few steps along the passage. 'This extraordinary "general intention", as you call it – for that's the most vivid description I can induce you to make of it – is then generally a sort of buried treasure?'

His face lighted. 'Yes, call it that, though it's perhaps not for me to do so.'

'Nonsense!' I laughed. 'You know you're hugely proud of it.'

'Well, I didn't propose to tell you so; but it *is* the joy of my soul!'

'You mean it's a beauty so rare, so great?'

He hesitated a moment. 'The loveliest thing in the world!' We had stopped, and on these words he left me; but at the end of the corridor, while I looked after him rather yearningly, he turned and caught sight of my puzzled face. It made him earnestly, indeed I thought quite anxiously, shake his head and wave his finger. 'Give it up – give it up!'

This wasn't a challenge – it was fatherly advice. If I had had one of his books at hand I would have repeated my recent act of faith – I would have spent half the night with him. At three o'clock in the morning, not sleeping, remembering moreover how indispensable he was to Lady Jane, I stole down to the library with a candle. There wasn't, so far as I could discover, a line of his writing in the house.

IV

Returning to town I feverishly collected them all; I picked out each in its order and held it up to the light. This gave me a maddening month, in the course of which several things took place. One of these, the last, I may as well immediately mention, was that I acted on Vereker's advice: I renounced my ridiculous attempt. I could really make nothing of the business; it proved a dead loss. After all, before, as he had himself observed, I liked him; and what now occurred was simply that my new intelligence and vain preoccupation damaged my liking. I not only failed to find his general intention – I found myself missing the subordinate intentions I had formerly found. His books didn't even remain the charming things they had been for me; the exasperation of my search put me out of conceit of them. Instead of being a pleasure the more they became a resource the less; for from the moment I was unable to follow up the author's hint I of course felt it a point of honour not to make use professionally of my knowledge of them. I *had* no knowledge – nobody had any. It was humiliating, but I could bear it – they only annoyed me now. At last they even bored me, and I accounted for my confusion – perversely, I confess – by the idea that Vereker had made a fool of me. The buried treasure was a bad joke, the general intention a monstrous *pose.*

The great incident of the time however was that I told George Corvick all about the matter and that my information had an immense effect upon him. He had at last come back, but so, unfortunately, had Mrs Erme, and there was as yet, I could see, no question of his nuptials. He was immensely stirred up by the anecdote I had brought from Bridges; it fell in so completely with the sense he had had from the first that there was more in Vereker than met the eye. When I remarked that the eye seemed what the printed page had been expressly invented to meet he immediately accused me of being spiteful because I had been foiled. Our commerce had always that pleasant latitude. The thing Vereker had mentioned to me was exactly the thing he, Corvick, had wanted me to speak of in my review. On my suggesting at last that with the assistance I had now given him he would doubtless be prepared to speak of it himself he admitted freely that before doing this there was more he must understand. What he would have said, had he reviewed the new book, was that there was evidently in the writer's inmost art something to *be* understood. I hadn't so much as hinted at that: no wonder the writer hadn't been flattered! I asked Corvick what he really considered he meant by his own supersubtlety, and, unmistakably kindled, he replied: 'It isn't for the vulgar – it isn't for the vulgar!' He had hold of the tail of something; he would pull hard, pull it right out. He pumped me dry on Vereker's strange confidence and, pronouncing me the luckiest of mortals, mentioned half a dozen questions he wished to goodness I had had the gumption to put. Yet on the other hand he didn't want to be told too much – it would spoil the fun of seeing what would come. The failure of my fun was at the moment of our meeting not complete, but I saw it ahead, and Corvick saw that I saw it. I, on my side, saw likewise that one of the first things he would do would be to rush off with my story to Gwendolen.

On the very day after my talk with him I was surprised by the receipt of a note from Hugh Vereker, to whom our encounter at Bridges had been recalled, as he mentioned, by his falling, in a magazine, on some article to which my signature was appended. 'I read it with great pleasure,' he wrote, 'and remembered under its influence our lively conversation by your bedroom fire. The consequence of this has been that I begin to measure the temerity of my having saddled you with a knowledge that you may find something of a burden. Now that the fit's over I can't imagine how I came to be moved so much beyond my wont. I had never before related, no matter in what expansion, the history of my little secret, and I shall never speak of the business again. I was accidentally so much more explicit with you than it had ever entered into my game to be, that I find this game – I mean the pleasure of playing it – suffers considerably. In short, if you can understand it, I've spoiled a part of my fun. I really don't want to give anybody what I believe you clever young men call the tip. That's of course a selfish solicitude, and I name it to you for what it may be worth to you. If you're disposed to humour me don't repeat my revelation. Think me demented – it's your right; but don't tell anybody why.'

The sequel to this communication was that as early on the morrow as I dared I drove straight to Mr Vereker's door. He occupied in those years one of the honest old houses in Kensington Square.[4] He received me immediately, and as soon as I came in I saw I had not lost my power to minister to his mirth. He laughed out at the sight of my face, which doubtless expressed my perturbation. I had been indiscreet – my compunction was great. 'I *have* told somebody,' I panted, 'and I'm sure that person will by this time have told somebody else! It's a woman, into the bargain.'

'The person you've told?'

'No, the other person. I'm quite sure he must have told her.'

'For all the good it will do her – or do *me*! A woman will never find out.'

'No, but she'll talk all over the place: she'll do just what you don't want.'

Vereker thought a moment, but he was not so disconcerted as I had feared: he felt that if the harm was done it only served him right. 'It doesn't matter – don't worry.'

'I'll do my best, I promise you, that your talk with me shall go no further.'

'Very good; do what you can.'

'In the meantime,' I pursued, 'George Corvick's possession of the tip may, on his part, really lead to something.'

'That will be a brave day.'

I told him about Corvick's cleverness, his admiration, the intensity of his interest in my anecdote; and without making too much of the divergence of our respective estimates mentioned that my friend was already of opinion that he saw much further into a certain affair than most people. He was quite as fired as I had been at Bridges. He was moreover in love with the young lady: perhaps the two together would puzzle something out.

Vereker seemed struck with this. 'Do you mean they're to be married?'

'I daresay that's what it will come to.'

'That may help them,' he conceded, 'but we must give them time!'

I spoke of my own renewed assault and confessed my difficulties; whereupon he repeated his former advice: 'Give it up, give it up!' He evidently didn't think me intellectually equipped for the adventure. I stayed half an hour, and he was most good-natured, but I couldn't help pronouncing him a man of shifting moods. He had been free with me in a mood, he had repented in a mood, and now in a mood he had turned indifferent. This general levity helped me to believe that, so far as the subject of the tip went, there wasn't much in it. I contrived however to make him answer a few more questions about it, though he did so with visible impatience. For himself, beyond doubt, the thing we were all so blank about was vividly there. It was something, I guessed, in the primal plan, something like a complex figure in a Persian carpet. He highly approved of this image when I used it, and he used another himself. 'It's the very string,' he said, 'that my pearls are strung on!' The reason of his note to me had been that he really didn't want to give us a grain of succour – our destiny was a thing too perfect in its way to touch. He had formed the habit of depending upon it, and if the spell was to break it must break by some force of its own. He comes back to me from that last occasion – for I was never to speak to him again – as a man with some safe secret for enjoyment. I wondered as I walked away where he had got *his* tip.

V

When I spoke to George Corvick of the caution I had received he made me feel that any doubt of his delicacy would be almost an insult. He had instantly told Gwendolen, but Gwendolen's ardent response was in itself a pledge of discretion. The question would now absorb them, and they would enjoy their fun too much to wish to share it with the crowd. They appeared to have caught instinctively Vereker's peculiar notion of fun. Their intellectual pride, however, was not such as to make them indifferent to any further light I might throw on the affair they had in hand. They were indeed of the 'artistic temperament', and I was freshly struck with my colleague's power to excite himself over a question of art. He called it letters, he called it life – it was all one thing. In what he said I now seemed to understand that he spoke equally for Gwendolen, to whom, as soon as Mrs Erme was sufficiently better to allow her a little leisure, he made a point of introducing me. I remember our calling together one Sunday in August at a huddled house in Chelsea, and my renewed envy of Corvick's possession of a friend who had some light to mingle with his own. He could say things to her that I could never say to him. She had indeed no sense of humour and, with her pretty way of holding her head on one side, was one of those persons whom you want, as the phrase is, to shake, but who have learnt Hungarian by themselves. She conversed perhaps in Hungarian with Corvick; she had remarkably little English for his friend. Corvick afterwards told me that I had chilled her by my apparent indisposition to oblige her with the detail of what Vereker had said to me. I admitted that I felt I had given thought enough to this exposure: hadn't I even made up my mind that it was hollow, wouldn't stand the test? The importance they attached to it was irritating – it rather envenomed my dissent.

That statement looks unamiable, and what probably happened was that I felt humiliated at seeing other persons derive a daily joy from an experiment which had brought me only chagrin. I was out in the cold while, by the evening fire, under the lamp, they followed the chase for which I myself had sounded the horn. They did as I had done, only more deliberately and sociably – they went over their author from the beginning. There was no hurry, Corvick said – the future was before them and the fascination could only grow; they would take him page by page, as they would take one of the classics, inhale him in slow draughts and let him sink deep in. I doubt whether they would have got so wound up if they had not been in love: poor Vereker's secret gave them endless occasion to put their young heads together. None the less it represented the kind of problem for which Corvick had a special aptitude, drew out the particular pointed patience of which, had he lived, he would have given more striking and, it is to be hoped, more fruitful examples. He at least was, in Vereker's words, a little demon of subtlety. We had begun by disputing, but I soon saw that without my stirring a finger his infatuation would have its bad hours. He would bound off on false scents as I had done – he would clap his hands over new lights and see them blown out by the wind of the turned page. He was like nothing, I told him, but the maniacs who embrace some bedlamitical theory of the cryptic character of Shakespeare.[5] To this he replied that if we had had Shakespeare's own word for his being cryptic he would immediately have accepted it. The case

there was altogether different – we had nothing but the word of
Mr Snooks. I rejoined that I was stupefied to see him attach
such importance even to the word of Mr Vereker. He inquired
thereupon whether I treated Mr Vereker's word as a lie. I
wasn't perhaps prepared, in my unhappy rebound, to go as far
as that, but I insisted that till the contrary was proved I should
view it as too fond an imagination. I didn't, I confess, say – I
didn't at that time quite know – all I felt. Deep down, as Miss
Erme would have said, I was uneasy, I was expectant. At the
core of my personal confusion – for my curiosity lived in its
ashes – was the sharpness of a sense that Corvick would at last
probably come out somewhere. He made, in defence of his credulity, a great point of the fact that from of old, in his study of
this genius, he had caught whiffs and hints of he didn't know
what, faint wandering notes of a hidden music. That was just
the rarity, that was the charm: it fitted so perfectly into what I
reported.

If I returned on several occasions to the little house in Chelsea I daresay it was as much for news of Vereker as for news of
Miss Erme's mamma. The hours spent there by Corvick were
present to my fancy as those of a chessplayer bent with a silent
scowl, all the lamplit winter, over his board and his moves. As
my imagination filled it out the picture held me fast. On the
other side of the table was a ghostlier form, the faint figure of
an antagonist good-humouredly but a little wearily secure – an
antagonist who leaned back in his chair with his hands in his
pockets and a smile on his fine clear face. Close to Corvick,
behind him, was a girl who had begun to strike me as pale and
wasted and even, on more familiar view, as rather handsome,
and who rested on his shoulder and hung upon his moves.
He would take up a chessman and hold it poised a while over
one of the little squares, and then he would put it back in
its place with a long sigh of disappointment. The young lady, at
this, would slightly but uneasily shift her position and look
across, very hard, very long, very strangely, at their dim partici-
pant. I had asked them at an early stage of the business if it
mightn't contribute to their success to have some closer communication with him. The special circumstances would surely

be held to have given me a right to introduce them. Corvick immediately replied that he had no wish to approach the altar before he had prepared the sacrifice. He quite agreed with our friend both as to the sport and as to the honour – he would bring down the animal with his own rifle. When I asked him if Miss Erme were as keen a shot he said after an hesitation: 'No; I'm ashamed to say she wants to set a trap. She'd give anything to see him; she says she requires another tip. She's really quite morbid about it. But she must play fair – she *shan't* see him!' he emphatically added. I had a suspicion that they had even quarrelled a little on the subject – a suspicion not corrected by the way he more than once exclaimed to me: 'She's quite incredibly literary, you know – quite fantastically!' I remember his saying of her that she felt in italics and thought in capitals. 'Oh, when I've run him to earth,' he also said, 'then, you know, I shall knock at his door. Rather – I beg you to believe. I'll have it from his own lips: "Right you are, my boy; you've done it this time!" He shall crown me victor – with the critical laurel.'

Meanwhile he really avoided the chances London life might have given him of meeting the distinguished novelist; a danger however that disappeared with Vereker's leaving England for an indefinite absence, as the newspapers announced – going to the south for motives connected with the health of his wife, which had long kept her in retirement. A year – more than a year – had elapsed since the incident at Bridges, but I had not encountered him again. I think at bottom I was rather ashamed – I hated to remind him that though I had irremediably missed his point a reputation for acuteness was rapidly overtaking me. This scruple led me a dance; kept me out of Lady Jane's house, made me even decline, when in spite of my bad manners she was a second time so good as to make me a sign, an invitation to her beautiful seat. I once saw her with Vereker at a concert and was sure I was seen by them, but I slipped out without being caught. I felt, as on that occasion I splashed along in the rain, that I couldn't have done anything else; and yet I remember saying to myself that it was hard, was even cruel. Not only had I lost the books, but I had lost the man himself: they and their author had been alike spoiled for

me. I knew too which was the loss I most regretted. I had liked
the man still better than I had liked the books.

VI

Six months after Vereker had left England George Corvick,
who made his living by his pen, contracted for a piece of work
which imposed on him an absence of some length and a journey of some difficulty, and his undertaking of which was much
of a surprise to me. His brother-in-law had become editor of a
great provincial paper, and the great provincial paper, in a fine
flight of fancy, had conceived the idea of sending a 'special
commissioner' to India. Special commissioners had begun, in
the 'metropolitan press', to be the fashion, and the journal in
question felt that it had passed too long for a mere country
cousin. Corvick had no hand, I knew, for the big brush of the
correspondent, but that was his brother-in-law's affair, and the
fact that a particular task was not in his line was apt to be with
himself exactly a reason for accepting it. He was prepared to
out-Herod the metropolitan press; he took solemn precautions
against priggishness, he exquisitely outraged taste. Nobody
ever knew it – the taste was all his own. In addition to his
expenses he was to be conveniently paid, and I found myself
able to help him, for the usual fat book, to a plausible arrangement with the usual fat publisher. I naturally inferred that his
obvious desire to make a little money was not unconnected
with the prospect of a union with Gwendolen Erme. I was
aware that her mother's opposition was largely addressed to
his want of means and of lucrative abilities, but it so happened
that, on my saying the last time I saw him something that bore
on the question of his separation from our young lady, he
exclaimed with an emphasis that startled me: 'Ah, I'm not a bit
engaged to her, you know!'

'Not overtly,' I answered, 'because her mother doesn't like
you. But I've always taken for granted a private understanding.'

'Well, there *was* one. But there isn't now.' That was all he
said, except something about Mrs Erme's having got on her

feet again in the most extraordinary way – a remark from which I gathered he wished me to think he meant that private understandings were of little use when the doctor didn't share them. What I took the liberty of really thinking was that the girl might in some way have estranged him. Well, if he had taken the turn of jealousy for instance it could scarcely be jealousy of me. In that case (besides the absurdity of it) he wouldn't have gone away to leave us together. For some time before his departure we had indulged in no allusion to the buried treasure, and from his silence, of which mine was the consequence, I had drawn a sharp conclusion. His courage had dropped, his ardour had gone the way of mine – this inference at least he left me to enjoy. More than that he couldn't do; he couldn't face the triumph with which I might have greeted an explicit admission. He needn't have been afraid, poor dear, for I had by this time lost all need to triumph. In fact I considered that I showed magnanimity in not reproaching him with his collapse, for the sense of his having thrown up the game made me feel more than ever how much I at last depended on him. If Corvick had broken down I should never know; no one would be of any use if *he* wasn't. It wasn't a bit true that I had ceased to care for knowledge; little by little my curiosity had not only begun to ache again, but had become the familiar torment of my consciousness. There are doubtless people to whom torments of such an order appear hardly more natural than the contortions of disease; but I don't know after all why I should in this connection so much as mention them. For the few persons, at any rate, abnormal or not, with whom my anecdote is concerned, literature was a game of skill, and skill meant courage, and courage meant honour, and honour meant passion, meant life. The stake on the table was of a different substance, and our roulette was the revolving mind, but we sat round the green board as intently as the grim gamblers at Monte Carlo. Gwendolen Erme, for that matter, with her white face and her fixed eyes, was of the very type of the lean ladies one had met in the temples of chance. I recognized in Corvick's absence that she made this analogy vivid. It was extravagant, I admit, the way she lived for the art of the pen. Her passion visibly preyed upon her, and in her presence I felt almost tepid. I got hold of 'Deep Down' again: it was a desert in which she had lost herself, but in which too she had dug a wonderful hole in the sand – a cavity out of which Corvick had still more remarkably pulled her.

Early in March I had a telegram from her, in consequence of which I repaired immediately to Chelsea, where the first thing she said to me was: 'He has got it, he has got it!'

She was moved, as I could see, to such depths that she must mean the great thing. 'Vereker's idea?'

'His general intention. George has cabled from Bombay.'

She had the missive open there; it was emphatic, but it was brief. 'Eureka. Immense.' That was all – he had saved the money of the signature. I shared her emotion, but I was disappointed. 'He doesn't say what it is.'

'How could he – in a telegram? He'll write it.'

'But how does he know?'

'Know it's the real thing? Oh, I'm sure when you see it you do know. *Vera incessu patuit dea!*'[6]

'It's you, Miss Erme, who are a dear for bringing me such news!' – I went all lengths in my high spirits. 'But fancy finding our goddess in the temple of Vishnu! How strange of George to have been able to go into the thing again in the midst of such different and such powerful solicitations!'

'He hasn't gone into it, I know; it's the thing itself, let severely alone for six months, that has simply sprung out at him like a tigress out of the jungle. He didn't take a book with him – on purpose; indeed he wouldn't have needed to – he knows every page, as I do, by heart. They all worked in him together, and some day somewhere, when he wasn't thinking, they fell, in all their superb intricacy, into the one right combination. The figure in the carpet came out. That's the way he knew it would come and the real reason – you didn't in the least understand, but I suppose I may tell you now – why he went and why I consented to his going. We knew the change would do it, the difference of thought, of scene, would give the needed touch, the magic shake. We had perfectly, we had admirably calculated. The elements were all in his mind, and in the *secousse*[7] of a new and intense experience they just struck

hurry to Rapallo, on the Genoese shore, where Vereker was making a stay. I wrote him a letter which was to await him at Aden[8] – I besought him to relieve my suspense. That he found my letter was indicated by a telegram which, reaching me after weary days and without my having received an answer to my laconic despatch at Bombay, was evidently intended as a reply to both communications. Those few words were in familiar French, the French of the day, which Corvick often made use of to show he wasn't a prig. It had for some persons the opposite effect, but his message may fairly be paraphrased. 'Have patience; I want to see, as it breaks on you, the face you'll make!' '*Tellement envie de voir ta tête!*'[9] – that was what I had to sit down with. I can certainly not be said to have sat down, for I seem to remember myself at this time as rushing constantly between the little house in Chelsea and my own. Our impatience, Gwendolen's and mine, was equal, but I kept hoping her light would be greater. We all spent during this episode, for people of our means, a great deal of money in telegrams, and I counted on the receipt of news from Rapallo immediately after the junction of the discoverer with the discovered. The interval seemed an age, but late one day I heard a hansom rattle up to my door with the crash engendered by a hint of liberality. I lived with my heart in my mouth and I bounded to the window – a movement which gave me a view of a young lady erect on the footboard of the vehicle and eagerly looking up at my house. At sight of me she flourished a paper with a movement that brought me straight down, the movement with which, in melodramas, handkerchiefs and reprieves are flourished at the foot of the scaffold.

'Just seen Vereker – not a note wrong. Pressed me to bosom – keeps me a month.' So much I read on her paper while the cabby dropped a grin from his perch. In my excitement I paid him profusely and in hers she suffered it; then as he drove away we started to walk about and talk. We had talked, heaven knows, enough before, but this was a wondrous lift. We pictured the whole scene at Rapallo, where he would have written, mentioning my name, for permission to call; that is *I* pictured it, having more material than my companion, whom I felt hang on my lips as we stopped on purpose before shop-windows we didn't look into. About one thing we were clear: if he was staying on for fuller communication we should at least have a letter from him that would help us through the dregs of delay. We understood his staying on, and yet each of us saw, I think, that the other hated it. The letter we were clear about arrived; it was for Gwendolen, and I called upon her in time to save her the trouble of bringing it to me. She didn't read it out, as was natural enough; but she repeated to me what it chiefly embodied. This consisted of the remarkable statement that he would tell her when they were married exactly what she wanted to know.

'Only when we're married – not before,' she explained. 'It's tantamount to saying – isn't it? – that I must marry him straight off!' She smiled at me while I flushed with disappointment, a vision of fresh delay that made me at first unconscious of my surprise. It seemed more than a hint that on me as well he would impose some tiresome condition. Suddenly, while she reported several more things from his letter, I remembered what he had told me before going away. He found Mr Vereker deliriously interesting and his own possession of the secret a kind of intoxication. The buried treasure was all gold and gems. Now that it was there it seemed to grow and grow before him; it was in all time, in all tongues, one of the most wonderful flowers of art. Nothing, above all, when once one was face to face with it, had been more consummately done. When once it came out it came out, was there with a splendour that made you ashamed; and there had not been, save in the bottomless vulgarity of the age, with every one tasteless and tainted, every sense stopped, the smallest reason why it should have been overlooked. It was immense, but it was simple – it was simple, but it was immense, and the final knowledge of it was an experience quite apart. He intimated that the charm of such an experience, the desire to drain it, in its freshness, to the last drop, was what kept him there close to the source. Gwendolen, frankly radiant as she tossed me these fragments, showed the elation of a prospect more assured than my own. That brought me back to the question of her marriage, prompted me to ask her if what she meant by what she had just surprised me with was that she was under an engagement.

'Of course I am!' she answered. 'Didn't you know it?' She appeared astonished; but I was still more so, for Corvick had told me the exact contrary. I didn't mention this, however; I only reminded her that I had not been to that degree in her confidence, or even in Corvick's, and that moreover I was not in ignorance of her mother's interdict. At bottom I was troubled by the disparity of the two assertions; but after a moment I felt that Corvick's was the one I least doubted. This simply reduced me to asking myself if the girl had on the spot improvised an engagement – vamped up an old one or dashed off a new – in order to arrive at the satisfaction she desired. I reflected that she had resources of which I was destitute; but she made her case slightly more intelligible by rejoining presently: 'What the state of things has been is that we felt of course bound to do nothing in mamma's lifetime.'

'But now you think you'll just dispense with your mother's consent?'

'Ah, it may not come to that!' I wondered what it might come to, and she went on: 'Poor dear, she may swallow the dose. In fact, you know,' she added with a laugh, 'she really *must*!' – a proposition of which, on behalf of every one concerned, I fully acknowledged the force.

VIII

Nothing more annoying had ever happened to me than to become aware before Corvick's arrival in England that I should not be there to put him through. I found myself abruptly called to Germany by the alarming illness of my younger brother, who, against my advice, had gone to Munich to study, at the feet indeed of a great master, the art of portraiture in oils. The near relative who made him an allowance had threatened to withdraw it if he should, under specious pretexts, turn for superior truth to Paris – Paris being somehow, for a Cheltenham[10] aunt, the school of evil, the abyss. I deplored this prejudice at the time, and the deep injury of it was now visible – first in the fact that it had not saved the poor boy, who was clever, frail and foolish, from congestion of the lungs, and second in the greater remoteness from London to which the event condemned me. I am afraid that what was uppermost in my mind during several anxious weeks was the sense that if we had only been in Paris I might have run over to see Corvick. This was actually out of the question from every point of view: my brother, whose recovery gave us both plenty to do, was ill for three months, during which I never left him and at the end of which we had to face the absolute prohibition of a return to England. The consideration of climate imposed itself, and he was in no state to meet it alone. I took him to Meran[11] and there spent the summer with him, trying to show him by example how to get back to work and nursing a rage of another sort that I tried not to show him.

The whole business proved the first of a series of phenomena so strangely combined that, taken together (which was how I had to take them) they form as good an illustration as I can recall of the manner in which, for the good of his soul doubtless, fate sometimes deals with a man's avidity. These incidents certainly had larger bearings than the comparatively meagre consequence we are here concerned with – though I feel that consequence also to be a thing to speak of with some respect. It's mainly in such a light, I confess, at any rate, that at this hour the ugly fruit of my exile is present to me. Even at first indeed the spirit in which my avidity, as I have called it, made me regard this term owed no element of ease to the fact that before coming back from Rapallo George Corvick addressed me in a way I didn't like. His letter had none of the sedative action that I must to-day profess myself sure he had wished to give it, and the march of occurrences was not so ordered as to make up for what it lacked. He had begun on the spot, for one of the quarterlies, a great last word on Vereker's writings, and this exhaustive study, the only one that would have counted, have existed, was to turn on the new light, to utter – oh, so quietly! – the unimagined truth. It was in other words to trace the figure in the carpet through every convolution, to reproduce it in every tint. The result, said Corvick, was to be the greatest literary portrait ever painted, and what he asked of me was just to be so good as not to trouble him with questions till he should hang up his masterpiece before me. He did me the honour to declare that, putting aside the great sitter himself, all aloft in his indifference, I was individually the connoisseur he was most working for. I was therefore to be a good boy and not try to peep under the curtain before the show was ready: I should enjoy it all the more if I sat very still.

I did my best to sit very still, but I couldn't help giving a jump on seeing in *The Times*, after I had been a week or two in Munich and before, as I knew, Corvick had reached London, the announcement of the sudden death of poor Mrs Erme. I instantly wrote to Gwendolen for particulars, and she replied that her mother had succumbed to long-threatened failure of the heart. She didn't say, but I took the liberty of reading into her words, that from the point of view of her marriage and also of her eagerness, which was quite a match for mine, this was a solution more prompt than could have been expected and more radical than waiting for the old lady to swallow the dose. I candidly admit indeed that at the time – for I heard from her repeatedly – I read some singular things into Gwendolen's words and some still more extraordinary ones into her silences. Pen in hand, this way, I live the time over, and it brings back the oddest sense of my having been for months and in spite of myself a kind of coerced spectator. All my life had taken refuge in my eyes, which the procession of events appeared to have committed itself to keep astare. There were days when I thought of writing to Hugh Vereker and simply throwing myself on his charity. But I felt more deeply that I hadn't fallen quite so low, besides which, quite properly, he would send me about my business. Mrs Erme's death brought Corvick straight home, and within the month he was united 'very quietly' – as quietly I suppose as he meant in his article to bring out his *trouvaille*[12] – to the young lady he had loved and quitted. I use this last term, I may parenthetically say, because I subsequently grew sure that at the time he went to India, at the time of his great news from Bombay, there was no engagement whatever. There was none at the moment she affirmed the opposite. On the other hand he certainly became engaged the day he returned. The happy pair went down to Torquay[13] for their honeymoon, and there, in a reckless hour, it occurred to poor Corvick to take his young bride out for a drive. He had no command of that business: this had been brought home to me of old in a little tour we had once made together in a dog-cart. In a dog-cart he perched his companion for a rattle over Devonshire hills, on one of the likeliest of which he brought his horse, who, it was true, had bolted, down with such violence that the occupants of the cart were hurled forward and that he fell horribly on his head. He was killed on the spot; Gwendolen escaped unhurt.

I pass rapidly over the question of this unmitigated tragedy, of what the loss of my best friend meant for me, and I complete my little history of my patience and my pain by the frank statement of my having, in a postscript to my very first letter to her after the receipt of the hideous news, asked Mrs Corvick whether her husband had not at least finished the great article on Vereker. Her answer was as prompt as my inquiry: the article, which had been barely begun, was a mere heartbreaking scrap. She explained that Corvick had just settled down to it when he was interrupted by her mother's death; then, on his return, he had been kept from work by the engrossments into which that calamity plunged them. The opening pages were all that existed; they were striking, they were promising, but they didn't unveil the idol. That great intellectual feat was obviously to have formed his climax. She said nothing more, nothing to enlighten me as to the state of her own knowledge – the knowledge for the acquisition of which I had conceived her doing prodigious things. This was above all what I wanted to know: had *she* seen the idol unveiled? Had there been a private ceremony for a palpitating audience of one? For what else but that ceremony had the previous ceremony been enacted? I didn't like as yet to press her, though when I thought of what had passed between us on the subject in Corvick's absence her reticence surprised me. It was therefore not till much later, from Meran, that I risked another appeal, risked it in some trepidation, for she continued to tell me nothing. 'Did you hear in those few days of your blighted bliss,' I wrote, 'what we desired so to hear?' I said, 'we' as a little hint; and she showed me she could take a little hint. 'I heard everything,' she replied, 'and I mean to keep it to myself!'

IX

It was impossible not to be moved with the strongest sympathy for her, and on my return to England I showed her every kindness in my power. Her mother's death had made her means sufficient, and she had gone to live in a more convenient quarter. But her loss had been great and her visitation cruel; it never would have occurred to me moreover to suppose she could come to regard the enjoyment of a technical tip, of a piece of literary experience, as a counterpoise to her grief. Strange to say, none the less, I couldn't help fancying after I had seen her a few times that I caught a glimpse of some such oddity. I hasten to add that there had been other things I couldn't help fancying; and as I never felt I was really clear about these, so, as to the point I here touch on, I give her memory the benefit of every doubt. Stricken and solitary, highly accomplished and now, in her deep mourning, her maturer grace and her uncomplaining sorrow incontestably handsome, she presented herself as leading a life of singular dignity and beauty. I had at first found a way to believe that I should soon get the better of the reserve formulated the week after the catastrophe in her reply to an appeal as to which I was not unconscious that it might strike her as mistimed. Certainly that reserve was something of a shock to me – certainly it puzzled me the more I thought of it, though I tried to explain it, with moments of success, by the supposition of exalted sentiments, of superstitious scruples, of a refinement of loyalty. Certainly it added at the same time hugely to the price of Vereker's secret, precious as that mystery already appeared. I may as well confess abjectly that Mrs Corvick's unexpected attitude was the final tap on the nail that was to fix, as they say, my luckless idea, convert it into the obsession of which I am for ever conscious.

But this only helped me the more to be artful, to be adroit, to allow time to elapse before renewing my suit. There were plenty of speculations for the interval, and one of them was deeply absorbing. Corvick had kept his information from his young friend till after the removal of the last barriers to their intimacy; then he had let the cat out of the bag. Was it Gwendolen's idea, taking a hint from him, to liberate this animal only on the basis of the renewal of such a relation? Was the figure in the carpet traceable or describable only for husbands and wives – for lovers supremely united? It came back to me in a mystifying manner that in Kensington Square, when I told him that Corvick would have told the girl he loved, some word had dropped from Vereker that gave colour to this possibility. There might be little in it, but there was enough to make me wonder if I should have to marry Mrs Corvick to get what I wanted. Was I prepared to offer her this price for the blessing of her knowledge? Ah! that way madness lay – so I said to myself at least in bewildered hours. I could see meanwhile the torch she refused to pass on flame away in her chamber of memory – pour through her eyes a light that made a glow in her lonely house. At the end of six months I was fully sure of what this warm presence made up to her for. We had talked again and again of the man who had brought us together, of his talent, his character, his personal charm, his certain career, his dreadful doom, and even of his clear purpose in that great study which was to have been a supreme literary portrait, a kind of critical Vandyke or Velasquez.[14] She had conveyed to me in abundance that she was tongue-tied by her perversity, by her piety, that she would never break the silence it had not been given to the 'right person', as she said, to break. The hour however finally arrived. One evening when I had been sitting with her longer than usual I laid my hand firmly on her arm.

'Now, at last, what *is* it?'

She had been expecting me; she was ready. She gave a long, slow, soundless headshake, merciful only in being inarticulate. This mercy didn't prevent its hurling at me the largest, finest, coldest 'Never!' I had yet, in the course of a life that had known denials, had to take full in the face. I took it and was aware that with the hard blow the tears had come into my eyes. So for a while we sat and looked at each other; after which I slowly rose. I was wondering if some day she would accept me; but this was not what I brought out. I said as I smoothed down my hat: 'I know what to think then; it's nothing!'

A remote, disdainful pity for me shone out of her dim smile; then she exclaimed in a voice that I hear at this moment: 'It's my *life*!' As I stood at the door she added: 'You've insulted him!'

'Do you mean Vereker?'

'I mean – the Dead!'

I recognized when I reached the street the justice of her charge. Yes, it was her life – I recognized that too; but her life none the less made room with the lapse of time for another interest. A year and a half after Corvick's death she published in a single volume her second novel, 'Overmastered', which I pounced on in the hope of finding in it some tell-tale echo or some peeping face. All I found was a much better book than her younger performance, showing I thought the better company she had kept. As a tissue tolerably intricate it was a carpet with a figure of its own; but the figure was not the figure I was looking for. On sending a review of it to *The Middle* I was surprised to learn from the office that a notice was already in type. When the paper came out I had no hesitation in attributing this article, which I thought rather vulgarly overdone, to Drayton Deane, who in the old days had been something of a friend of Corvick's, yet had only within a few weeks made the acquaintance of his widow. I had had an early copy of the book, but Deane had evidently had an earlier. He lacked all the same the light hand with which Corvick had gilded the gingerbread – he laid on the tinsel in splotches.

X

Six months later appeared 'The Right of Way', the last chance, though we didn't know it, that we were to have to redeem ourselves. Written wholly during Vereker's absence, the book had been heralded, in a hundred paragraphs, by the usual

ineptitudes. I carried it, as early a copy as any, I this time flattered myself, straightway to Mrs Corvick. This was the only
use I had for it; I left the inevitable tribute of *The Middle* to
some more ingenious mind and some less irritated temper. 'But
I already have it,' Gwendolen said. 'Drayton Deane was so
good as to bring it to me yesterday, and I've just finished it.'

'Yesterday? How did he get it so soon?'

'He gets everything soon. He's to review it in *The Middle*.'

'He – Drayton Deane – review Vereker?' I couldn't believe
my ears.

'Why not? One fine ignorance is as good as another.'

I winced, but I presently said: 'You ought to review him
yourself!'

'I don't "review",' she laughed. 'I'm reviewed!'

Just then the door was thrown open. 'Ah yes, here's your
reviewer!' Drayton Deane was there with his long legs and his
tall forehead: he had come to see what she thought of 'The
Right of Way', and to bring news which was singularly rele-
vant. The evening papers were just out with a telegram on the
author of that work, who, in Rome, had been ill for some days
with an attack of malarial fever. It had at first not been thought
grave, but had taken in consequence of complications a turn
that might give rise to anxiety. Anxiety had indeed at the latest
hour begun to be felt.

I was struck in the presence of these tidings with the funda-
mental detachment that Mrs Corvick's public regret quite
failed to conceal: it gave me the measure of her consummate
independence. That independence rested on her knowledge, the
knowledge which nothing now could destroy and which nothing could make different. The figure in the carpet might take on
another twist or two, but the sentence had virtually been written. The writer might go down to his grave: she was the person
in the world to whom – as if she had been his favoured heir –
his continued existence was least of a need. This reminded me
how I had observed at a particular moment – after Corvick's
death – the drop of her desire to see him face to face. She had
got what she wanted without that. I had been sure that if she
hadn't got it she wouldn't have been restrained from the

endeavour to sound him personally by those superior reflections, more conceivable on a man's part than on a woman's,
which in my case had served as a deterrent. It wasn't however, I
hasten to add, that my case, in spite of this invidious comparison, wasn't ambiguous enough. At the thought that Vereker
was perhaps at that moment dying there rolled over me a wave
of anguish – a poignant sense of how inconsistently I still
depended on him. A delicacy that it was my one compensation
to suffer to rule me had left the Alps and the Apennines between
us, but the vision of the waning opportunity made me feel as if
I might in my despair at last have gone to him. Of course I
would really have done nothing of the sort. I remained five
minutes, while my companions talked of the new book, and
when Drayton Deane appealed to me for my opinion of it I
replied, getting up, that I detested Hugh Vereker – simply
couldn't read him. I went away with the moral certainty that as
the door closed behind me Deane would remark that I was
awfully superficial. His hostess wouldn't contradict him.

I continue to trace with a briefer touch our intensely odd
concatenation. Three weeks after this came Vereker's death,
and before the year was out the death of his wife. That poor
lady I had never seen, but I had had a futile theory that, should
she survive him long enough to be decorously accessible, I
might approach her with the feeble flicker of my petition. Did
she know and if she knew would she speak? It was much to be
presumed that for more reasons than one she would have nothing to say; but when she passed out of all reach I felt that
renouncement was indeed my appointed lot. I was shut up in
my obsession for ever – my gaolers had gone off with the key.
I find myself quite as vague as a captive in a dungeon about the
time that further elapsed before Mrs Corvick became the wife
of Drayton Deane. I had foreseen, through my bars, this end of
the business, though there was no indecent haste and our
friendship had rather fallen off. They were both so 'awfully
intellectual' that it struck people as a suitable match, but I
knew better than any one the wealth of understanding the bride
would contribute to the partnership. Never, for a marriage in

literary circles – so the newspapers described the alliance – had
a bride been so handsomely dowered. I began with due promptness to look for the fruit of their union – that fruit, I mean, of
which the premonitory symptoms would be peculiarly visible
in the husband. Taking for granted the splendour of the lady's
nuptial gift, I expected to see him make a show commensurate
with his increase of means. I knew what his means had been –
his article on 'The Right of Way' had distinctly given one the
figure. As he was now exactly in the position in which still
more exactly I was not I watched from month to month, in the
likely periodicals, for the heavy message poor Corvick had
been unable to deliver and the responsibility of which would
have fallen on his successor. The widow and wife would have
broken by the rekindled hearth the silence that only a widow
and wife might break, and Deane would be as aflame with the
knowledge as Corvick in his own hour, as Gwendolen in hers
had been. Well, he was aflame doubtless, but the fire was
apparently not to become a public blaze. I scanned the periodicals in vain: Drayton Deane filled them with exuberant pages,
but he withheld the page I most feverishly sought. He wrote on
a thousand subjects, but never on the subject of Vereker. His
special line was to tell truths that other people either 'funked',
as he said, or overlooked, but he never told the only truth that
seemed to me in these days to signify. I met the couple in those
literary circles referred to in the papers: I have sufficiently intimated that it was only in such circles we were all constructed
to revolve. Gwendolen was more than ever committed to them
by the publication of her third novel, and I myself definitely
classed by holding the opinion that this work was inferior to its
immediate predecessor. Was it worse because she had been
keeping worse company? If her secret was, as she had told me,
her life – a fact discernible in her increasing bloom, an air of
conscious privilege that, cleverly corrected by pretty charities,
gave distinction to her appearance – it had yet not a direct
influence on her work. That only made – everything only
made – one yearn the more for it, rounded it off with a mystery
finer and subtler.

XI

It was therefore from her husband I could never remove my eyes: I hovered about him in a manner that might have made him uneasy. I went even so far as to engage him in conversation. *Didn't* he know, hadn't he come into it as a matter of course? – that question hummed in my brain. Of course he knew; otherwise he wouldn't return my stare so queerly. His wife had told him what I wanted, and he was amiably amused at my impotence. He didn't laugh – he was not a laugher: his system was to present to my irritation, so that I should crudely expose myself, a conversational blank as vast as his big bare brow. It always happened that I turned away with a settled conviction from these unpeopled expanses, which seemed to complete each other geographically and to symbolize together Drayton Deane's want of voice, want of form. He simply hadn't the art to use what he knew; he literally was incompetent to take up the duty where Corvick had left it. I went still further – it was the only glimpse of happiness I had. I made up my mind that the duty didn't appeal to him. He wasn't interested, he didn't care. Yes, it quite comforted me to believe him too stupid to have joy of the thing I lacked. He was as stupid after as before, and that deepened for me the golden glory in which the mystery was wrapped. I had of course however to recollect that his wife might have imposed her conditions and exactions. I had above all to recollect that with Vereker's death the major incentive dropped. He was still there to be honoured by what might be done – he was no longer there to give it his sanction. Who, alas, but he had the authority?

Two children were born to the pair, but the second cost the mother her life. After this calamity I seemed to see another ghost of a chance. I jumped at it in thought, but I waited a certain time for manners, and at last my opportunity arrived in a remunerative way. His wife had been dead a year when I met Drayton Deane in the smoking-room of a small club of which we both were members, but where for months – perhaps because I rarely entered it – I had not seen him. The room was empty and the occasion propitious. I deliberately offered him, to have done with the matter for ever, that advantage for which I felt he had long been looking.

'As an older acquaintance of your late wife's than even you were,' I began, 'you must let me say to you something I have on my mind. I shall be glad to make any terms with you that you see fit to name for the information she had from George Corvick – the information, you know, that he, poor fellow, in one of the happiest hours of his life, had straight from Hugh Vereker.'

He looked at me like a dim phrenological bust. 'The information—?'

'Vereker's secret, my dear man – the general intention of his books: the string the pearls were strung on, the buried treasure, the figure in the carpet.'

He began to flush – the numbers on his bumps[15] to come out. 'Vereker's books had a general intention?'

I stared in my turn. 'You don't mean to say you don't know it?' I thought for a moment he was playing with me. 'Mrs Deane knew it; she had it, as I say, straight from Corvick, who had, after infinite search and to Vereker's own delight, found the very mouth of the cave. Where *is* the mouth? He told after their marriage – and told alone – the person who, when the circumstances were reproduced, must have told you. Have I been wrong in taking for granted that she admitted you, as one of the highest privileges of the relation in which you stood to her, to the knowledge of which she was after Corvick's death the sole depositary? All *I* know is that that knowledge is infinitely precious, and what I want you to understand is that if you will in your turn admit *me* to it you will do me a kindness for which I shall be everlastingly grateful.'

He had turned at last very red; I daresay he had begun by thinking I had lost my wits. Little by little he followed me; on my own side I stared with a livelier surprise. 'I don't know what you're talking about,' he said.

He wasn't acting – it was the absurd truth. 'She *didn't* tell you—?'

'Nothing about Hugh Vereker.'

I was stupefied; the room went round. It had been too good even for that! 'Upon your honour?'

'Upon my honour. What the devil's the matter with you?' he demanded.

'I'm astounded – I'm disappointed. I wanted to get it out of you.'

'It isn't *in* me!' he awkwardly laughed. 'And even if it were—'

'If it were you'd let me have it – oh yes, in common humanity. But I believe you. I see – I see!' I went on, conscious, with the full turn of the wheel, of my great delusion, my false view of the poor man's attitude. What I saw, though I couldn't say it, was that his wife hadn't thought him worth enlightening. This struck me as strange for a woman who had thought him worth marrying. At last I explained it by the reflection that she couldn't possibly have married him for his understanding. She had married him for something else. He was to some extent enlightened now, but he was even more astonished, more disconcerted: he took a moment to compare my story with his quickened memories. The result of his meditation was his presently saying with a good deal of rather feeble form:

'This is the first I hear of what you allude to. I think you must be mistaken as to Mrs Drayton Deane's having had any unmentioned, and still less any unmentionable, knowledge about Hugh Vereker. She would certainly have wished it – if it bore on his literary character – to be used.'

'It *was* used. She used it herself. She told me with her own lips that she "lived" on it.'

I had no sooner spoken than I repented of my words; he grew so pale that I felt as if I had struck him. 'Ah, "lived"—!' he murmured, turning short away from me.

My compunction was real; I laid my hand on his shoulder. 'I beg you to forgive me – I've made a mistake. You *don't* know what I thought you knew. You could, if I had been right, have rendered me a service; and I had my reasons for assuming that you would be in a position to meet me.'

'Your reasons?' he asked. 'What were your reasons?'

I looked at him well; I hesitated; I considered. 'Come and sit down with me here, and I'll tell you.' I drew him to a sofa, I lighted another cigarette and, beginning with the anecdote of Vereker's one descent from the clouds, I gave him an account of the extraordinary chain of accidents that had in spite of it kept me till that hour in the dark. I told him in a word just what I've written out here. He listened with deepening attention, and I became aware, to my surprise, by his ejaculations, by his questions, that he would have been after all not unworthy to have been trusted by his wife. So abrupt an experience of her want of trust had an agitating effect on him, but I saw that immediate shock throb away little by little and then gather again into waves of wonder and curiosity – waves that promised, I could perfectly judge, to break in the end with the fury of my own highest tides. I may say that to-day as victims of unappeased desire there isn't a pin to choose between us. The poor man's state is almost my consolation; there are indeed moments when I feel it to be almost my revenge.

Appendix

Henry James on 'The Aspern Papers', from his Notebooks and the Preface to the New York Edition

FROM THE NOTEBOOKS

[*Florence, 12 January 1887*]

Same date. Hamilton (V.L.'s brother)[1] told me a curious thing of Capt. [Edward] Silsbee – the Boston art-critic and Shelley-worshipper; that is of a curious adventure of his. Miss Claremont, Byron's *ci-devant* mistress (the mother of Allegra) was living, until lately, here in Florence, at a great age, 80 or thereabouts, and with her lived her niece, a younger Miss Claremont – of about 50. Silsbee knew that they had interesting papers – letters of Shelley's and Byron's – he had known it for a long time and cherished the idea of getting hold of them. To this end he laid the plan of going to lodge with the Misses Claremont – hoping that the old lady in view of her great age and failing condition would die while he was there, so that he might then put his hand upon the documents, which she hugged close in life. He carried out this scheme – and things *se passèrent* as he had expected. The old woman *did* die – and then he approached the younger one – the old maid of 50 – on the subject of his desires. Her answer was – 'I will give you all the letters if you marry me!' H. says that Silsbee *court encore*. Certainly there is a little subject there: the picture of the two faded, queer, poor and discredited old English women – living on into a strange generation, in their musty corner of a foreign town – with these illustrious letters their most precious possession. Then the plot of the Shelley fanatic – his watchings and waitings – the way he *couvers*[2] the treasure. The denouement needn't be the one related of poor Silsbee; and at any rate the general situation is in itself a subject and a picture. It strikes me much. The interest would be in some price that the man has to pay – that the old woman – or the survivor – sets upon the papers. His hesitations – his struggle – for he really would give almost anything. – The Countess Gamba came in while I was there: her husband is a nephew of the Guiccioli[3] – and it was *à propos* of their having a lot of Byron's letters of which they are rather illiberal and dangerous guardians, that H. told me the above. They won't show them or publish any of them – and the Countess was very angry once on H.'s representing to her that it was her duty – especially to the English public! – to let them at least be seen. *Elle se fiche bien*[4] of the English public. She says the letters – addressed in Italian to the Guiccioli – are discreditable to Byron; and H. elicited from her that she had *burned* one of them.

FROM THE PREFACE TO
THE NEW YORK EDITION

I not only recover with ease, but I delight to recall, the first impulse given to the idea of 'The Aspern Papers'. It is at the same time true that my present mention of it may perhaps too effectually dispose of any complacent claim to my having 'found' the situation. Not that I quite know indeed what situations the seeking fabulist does 'find'; he seeks them enough assuredly, but his discoveries are, like those of the navigator, the chemist, the biologist, scarce more than alert recognitions. He *comes upon* the interesting thing as Columbus came upon the isle of San Salvador, because he had moved in the right direction for it – also because he knew, with the encounter, what 'making land' then and there represented. Nature had so placed it, to profit – if as profit we may measure the matter! – by his fine unrest, just as history, 'literary history' we in this connexion call it, had in an out-of-the-way corner of the great garden of life thrown off a curious flower that I was to feel worth gathering as soon as I saw it. I got wind of my positive fact, I

followed the scent. It was in Florence years ago; which is precisely, of the whole matter, what I like most to remember. The
air of the old-time Italy invests it, a mixture that on the faintest
invitation I rejoice again to inhale – and this in spite of the mere
cold renewal, ever, of the infirm side of that felicity, the sense,
in the whole element, of things too numerous, too deep, too
obscure, too strange, or even simply too beautiful, for any ease
of intellectual relation. One must pay one's self largely with
words, I think, one must induce almost any 'Italian subject' to
make believe it gives up its secret, in order to keep at all on
working – or call them perhaps rather playing – terms with the
general impression. We entertain it thus, the impression, by the
aid of a merciful convention which resembles the fashion of
our intercourse with Iberians or Orientals whose form of courtesy places everything they have at our disposal. We thank
them and call upon them, but without acting on their professions. The offer has been too large and our assurance is too
small; we peep at most into two or three of the chambers of
their hospitality, with the rest of the case stretching beyond our
ken and escaping our penetration. The pious fiction suffices;
we have entered, we have seen, we are charmed. So, right and
left, in Italy – before the great historic complexity at least –
penetration fails; we scratch at the extensive surface, we meet
the perfunctory smile, we hang about in the golden air. But we
exaggerate our gathered values only if we are eminently wit-
less. It is fortunately the exhibition in all the world before
which, as admirers, we can most remain superficial without
feeling silly.

   All of which I note, however, perhaps with too scant relevance to the inexhaustible charm of Roman and Florentine
memories. Off the ground, at a distance, our fond indifference
to being 'silly' grows fonder still; the working convention, as I
have called it – the convention of the real revelations and surrenders on one side and the real immersions and appreciations
on the other – has not only nothing to keep it down, but every
glimpse of contrast, every pang of exile and every nostalgic
twinge to keep it up. These latter haunting presences in fact, let
me note, almost reduce at first to a mere blurred, sad, scarcely

consolable vision this present revisiting, re-appropriating impulse. There are parts of one's past, evidently, that bask consentingly and serenely enough in the light of other days – which is but the intensity of thought; and there are other parts that take it as with agitation and pain, a troubled consciousness that heaves as with the disorder of drinking it deeply in. So it is at any rate, fairly in too thick and rich a retrospect, that I see my old Venice of 'The Aspern Papers', that I see the still earlier one of Jeffrey Aspern himself, and that I see even the comparatively recent Florence that was to drop into my ear the solicitation of these things. I would fain 'lay it on' thick for the very love of them – that at least I may profess; and, with the ground of this desire frankly admitted, something that somehow makes, in the whole story, for a romantic harmony. I have had occasion in the course of these remarks to define my sense of the romantic, and I am glad to encounter again here an instance of that virtue as I understand it. I shall presently say why this small case so ranges itself, but must first refer more exactly to the thrill of appreciation it was immediately to excite in me. I saw it somehow at the very first blush as romantic – for the use, of course I mean, I should certainly have had to make of it – that Jane Clairmont, the half-sister of Mary Godwin, Shelley's second wife and for a while the intimate friend of Byron and the mother of his daughter Allegra, should have been living on in Florence, where she had long lived, up to our own day, and that in fact, had I happened to hear of her but a little sooner, I might have seen her in the flesh. The question of whether I should have wished to do so was another matter – the question of whether I shouldn't have preferred to keep her preciously unseen, to run no risk, in other words, by too rude a choice, of depreciating that romance-value which, as I say, it was instantly inevitable to attach (through association above all, with another signal circumstance) to her long survival.

I had luckily not had to deal with the difficult option; difficult in such a case by reason of that odd law which somehow always makes the minimum of valid suggestion serve the man of imagination better than the maximum. The historian, essentially, wants more documents than he can really use; the dramatist only wants more liberties than he can really take. Nothing, fortunately, however, had, as the case stood, depended on my delicacy; I might have 'looked up' Miss Clairmont in previous years had I been earlier informed – the silence about her seemed full of the 'irony of fate'; but I felt myself more concerned with the mere strong fact of her having testified for the reality and the closeness of our relation to the past than with any question of the particular sort of person I might have flattered myself I 'found'. I had certainly at the very least been saved the undue simplicity of pretending to read meanings into things absolutely sealed and beyond test or proof – to tap a fount of waters that couldn't possibly not have run dry. The thrill of learning that she had 'overlapped', and by so much, and the wonder of my having doubtless at several earlier seasons passed again and again, all unknowing, the door of her house, where she sat above, within call and in her habit as she lived, these things gave me all I wanted; I seem to remember in fact that my more or less immediately recognizing that I positively oughtn't – 'for anything to come of it' – to have wanted more. I saw, quickly, how something might come of it *thus*; whereas a fine instinct told me that the effect of a nearer view of the case (the case of the overlapping) would probably have had to be quite differently calculable. It was really with another item of knowledge, however, that I measured the mistake I should have made in waking up sooner to the question of opportunity. That item consisted of the action taken on the premises by a person who *had* waked up in time, and the legend of whose consequent adventure, as a few spoken words put it before me, at once kindled a flame. This gentleman, an American of long ago, an ardent Shelleyite, a singularly marked figure and himself in the highest degree a subject for a free sketch – I had known him a little, but there is not a reflected glint of him in 'The Aspern Papers' – was named to me as having made interest with Miss Clairmont to be accepted as a lodger on the calculation that she would have Shelley documents for which, in the possibly not remote event of her death, he would thus enjoy priority of chance to treat with her representatives. He had at any rate, according to the legend, become, on earnest

Shelley grounds, her yearning, though also her highly diplomatic, *pensionnaire* – but without gathering, as was to befall, the fruit of his design.

Legend here dropped to another key; it remained in a manner interesting, but became to my ear a trifle coarse, or at least rather vague and obscure. It mentioned a younger female relative of the ancient woman as a person who, for a queer climax, had had to be dealt with; it flickered so for a moment and then, as a light, to my great relief, quite went out. It had flickered indeed but at the best – yet had flickered enough to give me my 'facts', bare facts of intimation; which, scant handful though they were, were more distinct and more numerous than I mostly *like* facts: like them, that is, as we say of an etcher's progressive subject, in an early 'state'. Nine tenths of the artist's interest in them is that of what he shall add to them and how he shall turn them. Mine, however, in the connexion I speak of, had fortunately got away from me, and quite of their own movement, in time not to crush me. So it was, at all events, that my imagination preserved power to react under the mere essential charm – that, I mean, of a final scene of the rich dim Shelley drama played out in the very theatre of our own 'modernity'. This was the beauty that appealed to me; there had been, so to speak, a forward continuity, from the actual man, the divine poet, on; and the curious, the ingenious, the admirable thing would be to throw it backward again, to compress – squeezing it hard! – the connexion that had drawn itself out, and convert so the stretched relation into a value of nearness on our own part. In short I saw my chance as admirable, and one reason, when the direction is right, may serve as well as fifty; but if I 'took over', as I say, everything that was of the essence, I stayed my hand for the rest. The Italian side of the legend closely clung; if only because the so possible terms of my Juliana's life in the Italy of other days could make conceivable for her the fortunate privacy, the long uninvaded and uninterviewed state on which I represent her situation as founded. Yes, a surviving unexploited unparagraphed Juliana was up to a quarter of a century since still supposeable – as much so as any such buried treasure, any such grave unprofaned, would defy probability

now. And then the case had the air of the past just in the degree
in which that air, I confess, most appeals to me – when the
region over which it hangs is far enough away without being
too far.

I delight in a palpable imaginable *visitable* past – in the
nearer distances and the clearer mysteries, the marks and signs
of a world we may reach over to as by making a long arm we
grasp an object at the other end of our own table. The table is
the one, the common expanse, and where we lean, so stretching, we find it firm and continuous. That, to my imagination, is
the past fragrant of all, or of almost all, the poetry of the thing
outlived and lost and gone, and yet in which the precious element of closeness, telling so of connexions but tasting so of
differences, remains appreciable. With more moves back the
element of the appreciable shrinks – just as the charm of looking over a garden-wall into another garden breaks down when
successions of walls appear. The other gardens, those still
beyond, may be there, but even by use of our longest ladder we
are baffled and bewildered – the view is mainly a view of barriers. The one partition makes the place we have wondered about
other, both richly and recognizeably so; but who shall pretend
to impute an effect of composition to the twenty? We are divided of course between liking to feel the past strange and liking
to feel it familiar; the difficulty is, for intensity, to catch it at the
moment when the scales of the balance hang with the right
evenness. I say for intensity, for we may profit by them in other
aspects enough if we are content to measure or to feel loosely.
It would take me too far, however, to tell why the particular
afternoon light that I thus call intense rests clearer to my sense
on the Byronic age, as I conveniently name it, than on periods
more protected by the 'dignity' of history. With the times
beyond, intrinsically more 'strange', the tender grace, for the
backward vision, has faded, the afternoon darkened; for any
time nearer to us the special effect hasn't begun. So there, to
put the matter crudely, is the appeal I fondly recognize, an
appeal residing doubtless more in the 'special effect', in some
deep associational force, than in a virtue more intrinsic. I am
afraid I must add, since I allow myself so much to fantasticate,

that the impulse had more than once taken me to project the Byronic age and the afternoon light across the great sea, to see in short whether association would carry so far and what the young century might pass for on that side of the modern world where it was not only itself so irremediably youngest, but was bound up with youth in everything else. There was a refinement of curiosity in this imputation of a golden strangeness to American social facts – though I cannot pretend, I fear, that there was any greater wisdom.

Since what it had come to then was, harmlessly enough, cultivating a sense of the past under that close protection, it was natural, it was fond and filial, to wonder if a few of the distilled drops mightn't be gathered from some vision of, say, 'old' New York. Would that human congeries, to aid obligingly in the production of a fable, be conceivable as 'taking' the afternoon light with the right happy slant? – or could a recognizeable reflexion of the Byronic age, in other words, be picked up on the banks of the Hudson? (Only just there, beyond the great sea, if anywhere: in no other connexion would the question so much as raise its head. I admit that Jeffrey Aspern isn't even feebly localized, but I *thought* New York as I projected him.) It was 'amusing', in any case, always, to try experiments; and the experiment for the right *transposition* of my Juliana would be to fit her out with an immortalizing poet as transposed as herself. Delicacy had demanded, I felt, that my appropriation of the Florentine legend should purge it, first of all, of references too obvious; so that, to begin with, I shifted the scene of the adventure. Juliana, as I saw her, was thinkable only in Byronic and more or less immediately post-Byronic Italy; but there were conditions in which she was ideally arrangeable, as happened, especially in respect to the later time and the long undetected survival; there being absolutely no refinement of the mouldy rococo, in human or whatever other form, that you may not disembark at the dislocated water-steps of almost any decayed monument of Venetian greatness in auspicious quest of. It was a question, in fine, of covering one's tracks – though with no great elaboration I am bound to admit; and I felt I couldn't cover mine more than in postulating a comparative American

Byron to match an American Miss Clairmont – she as absolute
as she would. I scarce know whether best to say for this device
to-day that it cost me little or that it cost me much; it was
'cheap' or expensive according to the degree of verisimilitude
artfully obtained. If that degree appears *nil* the 'art', such as it
was, is wasted, and my remembrance of the contention, on the
part of a highly critical friend who at that time and later on
often had my ear, that it had been simply foredoomed to be
wasted, puts before me the passage in the private history of
'The Aspern Papers' that I now find, I confess, most interesting.
I comfort myself for the needful brevity of a present glance at it
by the sense that the general question involved, under criticism,
can't but come up for us again at higher pressure.

My friend's argument bore then – at the time and afterward –
on my vicious practice, as he maintained, of postulating for the
purpose of my fable celebrities who not only *hadn't* existed in
the conditions I imputed to them, but who for the most part
(and in no case more markedly than in that of Jeffrey Aspern)
couldn't possibly have done so. The stricture was to apply itself
to a whole group of short fictions in which I had, with whatever ingenuity, assigned to several so-called eminent figures
positions absolutely unthinkable in our actual encompassing
air, an air definitely unfavourable to certain forms of eminence.
It was vicious, my critic contended, to flourish forth on one's
page 'great people', public persons, who shouldn't more or less
square with our quite definite and calculable array of such
notabilities; and by this rule I was heavily incriminated. The
rule demanded that the 'public person' portrayed should be
at least of the tradition, of the general complexion, of the face-
value, exactly, of some past or present producible counterfoil.
Mere private figures, under one's hand, might correspond with
nobody, it being of their essence to be but narrowly known; the
represented state of being conspicuous, on the other hand,
involved before anything else a recognition – and none of my
eminent folk were recognizeable. It was all very well for
instance to have put one's self at such pains for Miriam Rooth
in 'The Tragic Muse'; but *there* was misapplied zeal, there a
case of pitiful waste, crying aloud to be denounced. Miriam is

offered not as a young person passing unnoticed by her age –
like the Biddy Dormers and Julia Dallows, say, of the same
book, but as a high rarity, a time-figure of the scope inevitably
attended by other commemorations. Where on earth would be
then Miriam's inscribed 'counterfoil', and in what conditions
of the contemporary English theatre, in what conditions of
criticism, of appreciation, under what conceivable Anglo-Saxon
star, might we take an artistic value of this order either for produced or for recognized? We are, as a 'public', chalk-marked
by nothing, more unmistakeably, than by the truth that we
know nothing of such values – any more than, as my friend
was to impress on me, we are susceptible of consciousness of
such others (these in the sphere of literary eminence) as my Neil
Paraday in 'The Death of the Lion', as my Hugh Vereker in
'The Figure in the Carpet', as my Ralph Limbert, above all, in
'The Next Time',[5] as sundry unprecedented and unmatched
heroes and martyrs of the artistic ideal, in short, elsewhere
exemplified in my pages. We shall come to these objects of anim-
adversion in another hour, when I shall have no difficulty in
producing the defence I found for them – since, obviously, I
hadn't cast them into the world *all* naked and ashamed; and I
deal for the moment but with the stigma in general as Jeffrey
Aspern carries it.

The charge being that I foist upon our early American annals
a distinguished presence for which they yield me absolutely no
warrant – 'Where, within them, gracious heaven, were we to
look for so much as an approach to the social elements of habi-
tat and climate of birds of that note and plumage?' – I find his
link with reality then just in the tone of the picture wrought
round him. What was that tone but exactly, but exquisitely,
calculated, the harmless hocus-pocus under cover of which we
might suppose him to have existed? This tone is the tone, artistically speaking, of 'amusement', the current floating that
precious influence home quite as one of those high tides
watched by the smugglers of old might, in case of their boat's
being boarded, be trusted to wash far up the strand the cask of
foreign liquor expertly committed to it. If through our lean
prime Western period no dim and charming ghost of an

adventurous lyric genius might by a stretch of fancy flit, if the time was really too hard to 'take', in the light form proposed, the elegant reflexion, then so much the worse for the time – it was all one could say! The retort to that of course was that such a plea represented no 'link' with reality – which was what was under discussion – but only a link, and flimsy enough too, with the deepest depths of the artificial: the restrictive truth exactly contended for, which may embody my critic's last word rather of course than my own. My own, so far as I shall pretend in that especial connexion to report it, was that one's warrant, in such a case, hangs essentially on the question of whether or no the false element imputed would have borne that test of further development which so exposes the wrong and so consecrates the right. My last word was, heaven forgive me, that, occasion favouring, I could have perfectly 'worked out' Jeffrey Aspern. The boast remains indeed to be verified when we shall arrive at the other challenged cases . . .

Notes

Most of the notes below trace allusions, identify persons and places, and translate foreign words and phrases. In places I've touched on some of the issues in James's career, and defined social or artistic practices that are not clear from context, e.g. Miss Bordereau's desire, in 'The Aspern Papers', to be paid in French francs rather than Italian lira. I have not provided notes for foreign phrases that are regularly used in English, for words that James himself defines in the text, or for people and places the reader may be assumed to know, such as Dickens. Languages, except for French, are identified.

In preparing these notes I was greatly helped by the skill and persistence of my research assistant, Stephanie Friedman.

THE AUTHOR OF *BELTRAFFIO*

1. *Beltraffio*: Perhaps a reference to Giovanni Beltraffio or Boltraffio (1467–1516), a pupil of Leonardo da Vinci, who worked as a painter in Milan. Little is known about him, and most of his works now carry a disputed attribution; a suitably obscure figure for the subject of a novel affiliated with the aesthetic movement.

2. *Ambient*: The names James chooses for his characters are rarely as precise a guide to their characters as those of Dickens (e.g. Veneering) or Thackeray (Steyne or Sharpe). But many of them are vaguely and deliberately evocative. Temperature may be ambient, or music too, and the name suggests that Mark Ambient produces an atmosphere, an environment in which the people around him must live. Other similarly resonant examples in this volume are the ingenuous Paul Overt in 'The Lesson of the Master' and the stately Major and Mrs Monarch in 'The

Real Thing'. James's notebooks contain lists of possible names for characters, many of them drawn from odd bits in the newspapers.

3. *æsthetic war-cry ... art for art*: The aesthetic movement in England ran from the 1870s through the end of the century. Inspired by such French writers as Théophile Gautier (1811–72), who coined the phrase 'L'art pour l'art', it emphasized and indeed insisted upon art's appeal to the senses, while repudiating the conventional expectation that the artist should offer some explicit moral statement; the work of art in itself provided its own justification, and had no necessary relation to truth or wisdom. The writers most associated with the movement are the essayist and Oxford don Walter Pater (1839–94), and his former student Oscar Wilde (1854–1900): see also note 21. Gilbert and Sullivan satirized such attitudes in the opera *Patience* (1881), in which a character based on Wilde claims that 'you will rank as an apostle in the high aesthetic band / If you walk down Piccadilly with a poppy or a lily in your medieval hand'.

4. *London season*: Coinciding with the sitting of Parliament, the social season of London's upper classes began in May, peaked with the great horse races of the Derby and Ascot in June, and ended in early August.

5. *cet âge est sans pitié*: That age is pitiless.

6. *Waterloo*: Not the battle but the London train station named for it, on the south side of the Thames.

7. *wide-awake*: A soft, low-crowned, wide-brimmed felt hat.

8. *velvet jackets ... dishevelled*: Though he is not a model for Ambient's character or situation, the description matches that of James's friend the writer Robert Louis Stevenson (see also 'The Middle Years' note 1).

9. *thirty-eight ... published*: This was James's age when *The Portrait of a Lady* was published.

10. *pre-Raphaelites*: In context the term refers to such Italian painters of the period before Raphael (1483–1520) as Fra Lippo Lippi (1406–69) or Botticelli (1445–1510). But readers would also have heard an allusion to the Pre-Raphaelite Brotherhood, founded in 1848 by the poet and painter Dante Gabriel Rossetti (1828–82) and other young Victorian painters who admired the art of that earlier time. Their highly finished and minutely detailed work stands as a forerunner to the aesthetic movement. James's ambiguity here is deliberate.

11. *Dolcino*: From Italian *dolce*, or sweet.

12. *bornée*: Narrow-minded.

13. *impressions*: For James's initial readership the word was inextricably linked to Pater (see note 3), and especially his 'Conclusion' to *Studies in the History of the Renaissance* (1873), where he describes the way the human mind registers 'impressions unstable, flickering, inconsistent, which burn and are extinguished with our consciousness of them'.

14. *apple of discord*: In Greek mythology, the minor goddess Discord was not invited to the marriage of the sea-nymph Thetis and the mortal Peleus. In revenge she threw an apple labelled 'For the Fairest' into the midst of the party. Aphrodite, Athena and Hera argued over which of them should receive it, and eventually asked the shepherd-prince Paris to decide. His awarding it to Aphrodite led to the Trojan War.

15. *type*: James uses this word repeatedly; if Miss Ambient is of an extinct type, her sister-in-law is 'a type of the lady' (p. 26) and the Misses Bordereau in 'The Aspern Papers' are 'a new type of the American absentee' (p. 79). The word comes from the Latin *typus* – figure, image, form, kind – and when applied to a person it suggests someone who can be immediately recognized as conforming to an already existing pattern; a familiar model or kind of person. In James's day it was familiar term from physical anthropology, which classified people according to the colour of the skin or the shape of the head, thereby dividing them into presumably separate 'races'. Some pseudo-scientists, such as phrenologists, believed that human character could be read from such features (see 'The Figure in the Carpet' note 15), while the influential Italian quack Cesare Lombroso (1835–1909) argued that criminal 'types' could be immediately recognized by such facial features as the slope of their foreheads.

16. *Rossetti*: See note 10 and also 'The Aspern Papers' note 37.

17. *Gainsborough . . . Lawrence*: English portrait-painters: Thomas Gainsborough (1727–88); Sir Thomas Lawrence (1769–1830).

18. *Balzac and Browning*: Honoré de Balzac (1799–1850), French novelist whom James greatly admired, and to whom he devoted some of his most important critical essays (see also 'Greville Fane' and its note 5); Robert Browning (1812–89), English poet, often criticized for his obscurity, known especially for dramatic monologues that draw on the Italian Renaissance and a friend of James's.

19. *cinque-cento*: From Italian: the 1500s or sixteenth century.

20. *prémices*: Presages, first fruits.

21. *'purpose'*: Cf. Wilde's 'Preface' to *The Picture of Dorian Gray* (1891): 'No artist has ethical sympathies. An ethical sympathy in an artist is an unpardonable mannerism of style.'

22. *Observer*: English weekly newspaper, established 1791, and published on Sundays. Now in association with the *Guardian*.

23. *Ginistrella*: James also uses this as the title of Paul Overt's first novel in 'The Lesson of the Master'. Edoardo Ginistrelli was an Italian politician of James's day, and Ginistrella is the name of a local grape used for white wine in the region around Naples. James was not an oenophile and appears to have chosen the word for the sake of its generic Italian flavour.

24. *bonnes gens*: Good people, but with an ironic suggestion of worthy dullness.

25. *ideally hard*: Cf. Pater's dictum, in his 'Conclusion' to *Studies in the History of the Renaissance* (see note 13), that we should 'burn always' with the 'hard gemlike flame' of sensation.

26. *the best*: Cf. Gustave Flaubert's (1821–80) accounts in his letters of his pained struggle to find '*le mot juste*', the right word.

27. *hanged . . . best word*: From Boswell's *Life of Johnson* (1791): 'Depend upon it, Sir, when a man knows he is to be hanged in a fortnight, it concentrates his mind wonderfully.'

28. *arrière-pensée*: Afterthought.

29. *lock them up in a drawer . . . very bad, I am afraid, for the novel*: The discussion alludes to a debate, active throughout James's period, about the place of candour in English fiction, on sexual questions in particular. The prolific novelist Margaret Oliphant (1828–97), who often criticized James's work, argued that the special glory of the English novel lay in its purity. English books, unlike French ones, did not have to be kept away from the innocent but corruptible young. James himself, however, attacked what in 'The Art of Fiction' (1884) he called the difference between 'that which people know and that which they agree to admit that they know . . . what they talk of in conversation and what they talk of in print'. See also the symposium on 'Candour in Fiction', *New Review* (January 1890), to which Thomas Hardy, among others, contributed.

30. *Sir Joshua*: Sir Joshua Reynolds (1723–92), English painter and first president of the Royal Academy, whose grandly idealizing work established the canons of taste for English portraiture.

31. *Elle ne s'en doute que trop*: She's only too suspicious of it!

32. *fratello mio*: My brother (Italian).

33. *dog-cart*: A light two-wheeled carriage, drawn by a single horse. Early models had a seat for the driver and an open box behind for hunting dogs; most Victorian dog-carts added a second seat, with the passenger sitting back-to-back with the driver.

34. *Basta*: Enough; a favourite Italian interjection of James's.

35. *Mentone*: A resort on the Riviera, at the French-Italian border. James uses the Italian spelling; annexed by France, as Menton, from Monaco in 1861.

THE ASPERN PAPERS

1. *severed the Gordian knot*: A proverbial phrase for the best way to deal with an intractable problem. Legend held that whoever managed to undo a fiendishly difficult knot in the ancient Phrygian city of Gordium would go on to rule Asia; rather than attempt to untie it, Alexander the Great took out his sword and sliced through it.

2. *Mrs Siddons . . . extinct*: Famous, or indeed, notorious women of an earlier age. Sarah Siddons (1755–1831), leading actress on the London stage, member of the great Kemble clan of performers. Queen Caroline of Brunswick (1768–1821), estranged wife of Britain's George IV, who tried to divorce her and, when that failed, barred her from his coronation. Lady Hamilton (1765–1815), born Amy Lyon, famously beautiful former servant girl; model, dancer and mistress of several aristocrats before marrying her lover Sir William Hamilton, English ambassador in Naples; then mistress of Admiral Horatio, Lord Nelson.

3. *Orpheus and the Mænads*: In Greek mythology the musician Orpheus was ripped to shreds by these female devotees of Dionysus after he had switched his own allegiance to Apollo.

4. *old palace*: In a letter of 6 December 1906 to Alvin Langdon Coburn, who was taking photographs for the frontispieces of the New York Edition, James wrote that 'the old house I had more or less in mind for that of the Aspern Papers' was called Ca' Capello, on the Rio Marin in the Santa Croce district. It is near the train station and James described it as 'old faded pink-faced, battered-looking and quite homely and plain' (*Henry James: Letters*, ed. Leon Edel, vol. IV (Cambridge and London: The Belknap Press, 1984), p. 426).

5. *quartier perdu*: A lost or forgotten neighbourhood; back streets.

6. *felze*: The cabin (no longer in use) of a gondola (Italian).

7. *padrona*: Landlady (Italian).

8. *scagliola*: Plasterwork painted to imitate marble (Italian).

9. *C'est la moindre des choses*: It's the least of things – that is, no work at all.

10. *a thousand francs a month*: The Italian lira was not yet a hard currency and as many commercial transactions as possible, and especially those involving foreigners, were therefore conducted in French francs. The franc traded at twenty-five to the British pound, which was itself valued at a bit less than $5 (USA). The price Miss Bordereau asks is therefore £40 (or just under $200) per month at a time when, according to Baedeker (see note 19), good hotel rooms in Venice could be had for five francs – a dollar – a day.

11. *forestieri*: Foreigners (Italian).

12. *quartiere*: Quarter or district, but in this case his section of the house; his lodgings (Italian).

13. *locus standi*: Place to stand (Latin).

14. *parti pris*: A position or principle resolved upon in advance.

15. *stringer of beads*: The beads were made of glass, whose manufacture was one of Venice's chief industries. James's friend John Singer Sargent did two paintings of women at this work.

16. *contadina . . . pifferaro*: Peasant woman . . . fife player (Italian); conventional figures in picturesque paintings for the tourist trade.

17. *annihilated surprise*: See James's 1903 *William Wetmore Story and his Friends*, the biography of a Boston-born sculptor who settled in Rome, for a richly detailed account of what the novelist called his 'precursors', those Americans who went to Europe when the going was not yet easy.

18. *Piazza*: The Piazza San Marco is Venice's great central space, an oblong anchored at one end by what James called the 'strange old basilica' and enclosed on the other sides by arcades lined with shops and cafes. The most famous is Florian's cafe, founded in 1720; many of its customers sit outside, at tables in the Piazza itself, in a way that is said to have made Napoleon call it the 'best drawing room in Europe'. In front of the church, the Piazza throws off an arm, called the Piazzetta, that runs down to the Grand Canal and is bordered on one side by the ducal palace.

19. *Bädeker*: In English, more commonly Baedeker. The Leipzig publishing firm of Karl Baedeker produced a series of authoritative guidebooks, in several languages, with information about prices and routes, and lists of paintings and other works of art to

be seen in a city's museums and churches. Venice is included in Baedeker's volume for Northern Italy, and most visitors would have carried it or one of the rival guides produced by the English firm of John Murray.

20. *Carmelite nuns*: An especially strict Roman Catholic order, whose members spend their lives in solitary prayer; for Protestant writers in the nineteenth century, they often function as an image of removal from the world and submission to authority.

21. *arrière-pensée*: Afterthought.

22. *passeggio*: A walk or promenade (Italian).

23. *Lido*: A long low island across the Venetian lagoon from the city itself, and the site of its beach resorts.

24. *avvocato*: Lawyer (Italian).

25. *capo d'anno*: New Year's Day (Italian).

26. *Casanova*: Giacomo Girolamo Casanova (1725–98), Venetian-born adventurer – gambler, con man, cleric, lawyer, womanizer, diplomat, prisoner, spy, and many other things besides – who in his last performance became a great autobiographer.

27. *cicerone*: Guide (Italian).

28. *all sorts of changes*: Among them, the introduction of the steam-launches called *vaporetti* on the Grand Canal in 1881, the filling in of some canals to make new streets and some much-criticized attempts at the restoration of San Marco.

29. *giro*: Tour (Italian).

30. *parti*: Desirable match.

31. *Treviso, to Bassano, to Castelfranco*: Cities in the Veneto, the mainland region that surrounds and was long ruled by Venice.

32. *poste restante*: General delivery. A system in which the post office holds mail until called for, used often by travellers who might be unsure of their precise address or arrival date.

33. *la vecchia*: The old one (Italian).

34. *Poveretta*: Poor little one! (Italian).

35. *island of tombs . . . Murano*: Venice's cemetery is on the island of San Michele, in the lagoon to the north of the city itself; Murano is one of the lagoon's largest islands, and famous for the manufacture of coloured glass.

36. *Giorgione at Castelfranco*: Italian painter (1477/8–1510), born in Castelfranco, a determinative figure in the development of Venetian painting. The work in question is a Madonna and Child in the city's cathedral.

37. *violating a tomb*: In 1862 Elizabeth Siddal, the model, mistress and eventually wife of Dante Gabriel Rossetti (see 'The Author of

Beltraffio' note 10), died of an opium overdose after delivering a stillborn child. At her burial, Rossetti placed the manuscript of his poems in her coffin. Seven years later he had it exhumed by court order and retrieved the poems, which he then published.

38. *Dove commanda*: Where to? (Italian).

39. *tenda*: Awning (Italian).

40. *Malamocco*: A small town towards the southern end of the Lido.

41. *Bartolommeo Colleoni*: Venetian military leader (1400–1475); a *condottiere* is a mercenary warlord. Colleoni worked for a variety of Northern Italian princes, but ended his career in the service of his native city. His memorial statue, by the Florentine Andrea del Verrochio (*c.* 1435–88), does indeed make him look stern and terrible, and the narrator here shares in the conventional judgement of its aesthetic value.

42. *fondamentas*: Walkways alongside a canal (Italian).

43. *almost intolerable*: In his revision for the New York Edition, James changed the last sentence to read: 'When I look at it I can scarcely bear my loss – I mean of the precious papers.'

THE LESSON OF THE MASTER

1. *Ginistrella*: See 'The Author of *Beltraffio*' note 23.

2. *Manchester Square*: First laid out in the eighteenth century, London's Manchester Square lies in the Marylebone neighbourhood, just to the north-east of Hyde Park. In James's time it was a solid but not aristocratic address, and is best known today as the site of the Wallace Collection.

3. *confrère*: Colleague.

4. *Il s'attache à ses pas*: He follows her everywhere.

5. *fine frenzy*: From Shakespeare's *A Midsummer Night's Dream* (V.i.12–17):

> The poet's eye, in a fine frenzy rolling,
> Doth glance from heaven to earth, from earth to heaven;
> And, as imagination bodies forth
> The forms of things unknown, the poet's pen
> Turns them to shapes, and gives to airy nothing
> A local habitation and a name.

6. *modern reactionary nymph . . . her hair*: The description recalls the medieval dress of Mark Ambient's sister in 'The Author of

Beltraffio', as well as the paintings of James's friend, the second-generation Pre-Raphaelite Edward Burne-Jones (1833–98), e.g. *The Beguiling of Merlin*.

7. *à fleur de peau*: Sensitive; on the surface of the skin.

8. *mot*: Literally, word; a remark or witticism.

9. *Master*: With this story in mind, James's disciples began in the early years of the twentieth century to call him 'The Master', and the name has endured in the secondary literature about him. Even Joseph Conrad used the term, albeit in French, when writing to him.

10. *Adam ceiling*: After the Scottish architect and designer Robert Adam (1728–92) and his brothers. A style associated with elaborate plaster work and ceiling medallions, often painted in pastel; dominant in aristocratic households during the latter eighteenth century. (In the first edition 'Adam' is printed as 'Adams'.)

11. *Euston*: North London railway station.

12. *Cela s'est passé comme ça*: So that's how it happened?

13. *jamais de la vie*: Not on your life!

14. *between ten and one*: James's preferred working hours.

15. *victoria . . . brougham*: The first was an open carriage, with a collapsible hood and a single roomy passenger seat facing forward; most tourist carriages today are of this type. The brougham was a smallish vehicle with a closed compartment for two passengers, and the driver sitting on a box in front.

16. *père de famille*: Father of a family.

17. *mornes*: Dismal.

18. *moeurs*: Habits, manners, mores.

19. *Park . . . Row*: Rotten Row is a fashionable riding track in Hyde Park. From *Route du Roi*, the King's Road, and a place to look and be looked at.

20. *hansom*: A light one-horse cab, with a closed compartment for (usually) two passengers and with the driver sitting up and behind.

21. *C'est d'un trouvé*: He has such a gift (for finding resemblances and the words to express them).

22. *Comment donc*: Literally, 'How, though?', but here 'And so?'

23. *Marble Arch . . . Serpentine . . . Kensington Gardens*: The Marble Arch is exactly what its name suggests, and marks the north-east corner of Hyde Park; the Serpentine is an ornamental lake that runs north-west from the southern side of the park and on into the adjoining Kensington Gardens.

24. *linkmen's*: Torch-carriers who lit the way for pedestrians at night; in the gaslit London of James's day, an upper-class relic of earlier times.

25. *il ne manquerait plus que ça*: That's the last thing we need.

26. *carton-pierre . . . Lincrusta-Walton . . . brummagaem*: Carton-pierre is a papier-mâché made to imitate stone or bronze; Lincrusta-Walton is an embossed wallpaper that simulates carved plaster or wood; and 'brummagem' (the usual spelling) derives from Birmingham, and denotes a cheap and showy article of inferior manufacture.

27. *n'en parlons plus*: Let's drop it.

28. *Ennismore Gardens*: Small, chic square just south of Hyde Park in the London district of Knightsbridge.

29. *Chillon*: The Castle of Chillon, near Montreux on Lake Geneva, dates from the eleventh century and was a touristic landmark of the nineteenth century. It figured in 'The Prisoner of Chillon' (1816), a popular poem by Byron, and James used it as a setting in 'Daisy Miller'.

30. *Clarens*: A village on Lake Geneva, now part of Montreux.

THE REAL THING

1. *'sunk' piece of painting*: Oil paint put on to an inadequately prepared surface will sink in and lose its colour; a damp sponge will temporarily revive it.

2. *lappets*: A decorative fold or flap on a garment.

3. *Kilburn*: A then-suburban district in north-west London, and dingy.

4. *Philip Vincent*: The description suggests no one novelist of the time, but it does match James's own profile, as well as that of George Meredith (1828–1909), best known today for *The Egoist* (1879). James disliked the idea of having his novels illustrated, and explained why in his New York Edition preface to *The Golden Bowl*.

5. *Maida Vale*: Residential district to the west of Regent's Park.

6. *especially for the h*: Miss Churm drops her 'h's, and would say ''alf' for 'half' and ''Arry' for 'Harry', a mark that she belongs to the London-born working class known as Cockneys.

7. *Cheapside*: The name comes from an ancient and important street in the City of London, and recalls those of the actual monthly magazines of Victorian London, e.g. *Cornhill*, *St Paul's* and *Temple Bar*. James also uses the name in 'Greville Fane'.

8. *bêtement*: Stupidly.
9. *profils perdus*: Three-quarters views.
10. *lazzarone*: In Neapolitan dialect, a beggar or rogue.
11. *Ce sont des gens qu'il faut mettre à la porte*: They're the sort of people to whom you have to show the door.
12. *coloro che sanno*: James makes the meaning clear, but it may also be a glancing allusion to Dante (1265–1321); the words occur in *Inferno* IV.131, where the poet describes Aristotle in these terms as the 'maestro' of those who know.
13. *afflatus*: Inspiration (Latin).

GREVILLE FANE

1. *Primrose Hill*: A London park and neighbourhood lying to the north of Regent's Park; in James's time, a bit out of the way (now distinctly up-market).
2. *said to be by some one else*: The narrator's obituary essay has appeared, like much Victorian journalism, without a byline.
3. *Montpelier Square*: Just south of Hyde Park in Knightsbridge, this was in the 1890s a good address, but not as good as Henry St George's, a few streets away, in 'The Lesson of the Master'.
4. *Doncaster to Bucharest*: A Yorkshire town best known for its horse-racing track, and the capital of Romania, respectively.
5. *Balzac ... Lucien de Rubempré and the Vidame de Pamiers*: Balzac created Lucien de Rubempré in *Lost Illusions* (1837–43); the Vidame figures in several of his novels, especially *Ferragus* (1833) and *The Duchess of Langeais* (1834). See also 'The Author of *Beltraffio*' note 18.
6. *Desdemona*: From Shakespeare's *Othello*, I.iii.164–6. On hearing Othello's story, she swore "Twas pitiful, 'twas wondrous pitiful. / She wished she had not heard it, yet she wished / That heaven had made her such a man.'
7. *George Sand*: Pen-name of Aurore Dupin (1804–76), French novelist whose lovers included Chopin, and who for a time wore men's clothing in public. Mrs Stormer too uses a masculine pseudonym.
8. *gagne-pain*: Literally, win-bread; a livelihood.
9. *paid there*: There was no reciprocal copyright agreement between Great Britain and the United States until 1891, and many British writers had their work pirated by American publishers, earning little despite their popularity.

10. *femme du monde*: Woman of the world.
11. *Rhadamanthus*: In Greek mythology, the son of Zeus and Europa, a wise king whose inflexible integrity made him, in the afterlife, into one of the judges of the dead.
12. *Young Person*: See Dickens, *Our Mutual Friend* (1864–5), ch. 11; the character Podsnap will not allow anything into his house that might 'bring a blush into the cheek of the young person', i.e. anything that touches on sexual issues. See also 'The Author of *Beltraffio*' note 27.
13. *premiers frais*: Initial expenses.
14. *Cheapside*: See 'The Real Thing' note 7.
15. *great thing was to live*: Cf. Strether's speech in James's *The Ambassadors*, ch. 11 (Book V, ch. ii in the New York Edition): 'Live all you can; it's a mistake not to. It doesn't so much matter what you do in particular, so long as you have your life.'
16. *embonpoint*: Portliness.
17. *vieux jeu*: Old hat.
18. *feuilletons*: Serialized fiction in newspapers; often scandalous.
19. *Peckham and Hackney*: Impoverished inner London districts, the first well south of the Thames and the other north-east of the City of London.
20. *Brighton*: Resort town on the south coast of England. The railway had put this once-fashionable resort town on the south coast of England within the reach of London day-trippers. In an 1879 travel essay James described it as having 'a kind of cheerful, easy, more or less vulgar, foreign air.'
21. *trouvailles*: Discoveries.
22. *Academy*: The Royal Academy (founded 1768) at Burlington House in Piccadilly holds an exhibition each summer of contemporary art; in James's day, a major event in the London Season (see 'The Author of *Beltraffio*', note 4).

THE MIDDLE YEARS

1. *Bournemouth ... Island*: A popular Victorian resort, Bournemouth lies opposite the Isle of Wight in Dorset on England's south coast. James stayed there several times, most notably in 1884 when he became good friends with Robert Louis Stevenson, who, like Dencombe, had come there for his health. See also 'The Author of *Beltraffio*' note 8.

2. *catchpenny*: Cheap but noticeable; designed to sell without regard for quality.

3. *circulating library*: Very few Victorians bought their own copies of newly released books, fiction in particular. Most instead joined commercial circulating libraries – the best known was Mudie's – which bought up to half of the first edition of almost all new novels. Their power in the marketplace shaped the form of fiction itself. For an annual fee, normally 21 shillings, members could take out the first volume of as many novels as they wanted, but they then had to pay 1 shilling each for the second and third volumes. Most novels therefore appeared in three volumes, and sometimes had to be stretched out to the requisite length. Dencombe prefers to publish in a single volume, which suggests not only that his work is unusually tight and polished, but also that he has earned some independence from customary practices. See Guinevere L. Griest, *Mudie's Circulating Library and the Victorian Novel* (Bloomington: Indiana University Press, 1970), and also my own *Portrait of a Novel: Henry James and the Making of an American Masterpiece* (New York: Liveright, 2012), chs. 17 and 19 for an account of Victorian publishing.

4. 'The Middle Years': In taking the title of Dencombe's last book for a tale of his own, James anticipates not only his own later decision to use the phrase as the title for his own last and unfinished volume of autobiography, but also Leon Edel's choice of these words as the name for the third book (1962) in his five-volume biography.

5. *sponge over colour*: See 'The Real Thing' note 1. Evidently one of James's favourite images. But the meaning here is different, and suggests watercolour rather than the oil paint of 'The Real Thing'. Here the sponge serves to blur or muddle the details of an image, as Decombe's illness has his memory of the recent past.

6. *diligence vincit omnia*: Diligence (usually 'love' or in Latin *amor*) conquers all.

7. *Qui dort dine*: Whoever sleeps forgets his hunger!

8. *bergère*: Shepherdess.

9. *bath-chair*: An early form of wheelchair, usually with three wheels like a tricycle and a collapsible hood, and pushed from behind by an attendant.

THE FIGURE IN THE CARPET

1. *The Middle*: The context later makes clear that, like *The Cheapside* of 'The Real Thing' and 'Greville Fane', this journal too publishes its contributions anonymously.

2. *spotted jacket*: A smoking-jacket, probably in a printed silk foulard, hence the spots.

3. *element of form or an element of feeling*: Cf. James's critical manifesto, 'The Art of Fiction' (1884): 'a novel is a living thing, all one and continuous, like any other organism, and in proportion as it lives will it be found, I think, that in each of the parts there is something of each of the other parts . . . What is character but the determination of incident? What is incident but the illustration of character?'

4. *Kensington Square*: A fashionable address near Kensington Palace; laid out in 1681, it sits just south of Kensington High Street and still contains many of its original houses. At the time James wrote this story he lived a few streets away in De Vere Gardens.

5. *maniacs . . . Shakespeare*: The belief that Shakespeare was not Shakespeare, that his plays had been written by someone else, was widely held and debated in this period, and by some associated with deciphering coded messages in Shakespeare's texts. Despite its characterization here as 'bedlamitical' (after London's Bedlam or Bethlehem Royal Hospital, the first to specialize in the treatment of the mentally ill) James himself became a fellow traveller in this belief; not because he accepted the claims, e.g. of the Earl of Oxford, but because he thought no biographical explanation could offer a sufficient account of genius. See James Shapiro, *Contested Will* (New York: Simon & Schuster, 2010).

6. *Vera incessu patuit dea*: Virgil, *Aeneid*, I.405, where Aeneas recognizes his mother Venus, disguised as a Spartan huntress, only when she turns away: 'in her gait she was revealed to be a very goddess' (Latin).

7. *secousse*: Shock or jolt.

8. *Aden*: Seaport in Yemen, at the entrance to the Red Sea; a regular port of call for ships travelling to or from India.

9. *Tellement envie de voir ta tête*: I'd so love to see your face! ('Ta' is second-person singular, i.e. familiar.)

10. *Cheltenham*: Spa town in south-western England, known as a place of utterly conventional, well-heeled gentility.

11. *Meran*: In Italian Merano, a spa town in the Italian Alps, just below the Austrian border.

12. *trouvaille*: Discovery.

13. *Torquay*: Coastal resort on the Devon coast in southern England, known especially for its mild climate. James spent the summer and autumn of 1895 there, where he sketched this story out.

14. *Vandyke or Velasquez*: Anthony van Dyck (1599–1641), Flemish painter who in England became the court artist to Charles I, and whose portraits of the royal family determined English taste for generations to come. Diego Velasquez (1599–1660), greatest painter of the Spanish Golden Age, best known for his canvases of that royal family (*Las Meninas*), but who worked in many other genres besides; an influence on painters as different as Manet and Picasso.

15. *phrenological bust ... bumps*: Phrenology was a popular pseudo-science in James's period, and claimed to be able to define a person's character traits based on the dimensions and irregularities of the skull; demonstration busts showed a bald head marked with numbers to denote the particular bumps associated with specific traits.

APPENDIX

Henry James on 'The Aspern Papers'

1. *V.L.'s brother*: V.L. stands for Vernon Lee, the pen-name of the English writer Violet Paget (1856–1935), remembered today mostly for the ghost stories collected in *Hauntings* (1890), but known in her lifetime for her many essays on Italian history, art and places. She was a childhood friend of John Singer Sargent, spent much of her life in Florence and modelled a character in her 'Lady Tal' (1892) on James himself – after which he broke off their friendship. Her half-brother Eugene Lee-Hamilton (1845–1907) was a minor poet and one-time diplomat, but best known as a conversationalist. Edward Augustus Silsbee (1826–1900) was a former sea-captain, born in Salem, Massachusetts, and noted collector of Shelley memorabilia. In 1872 Silsbee began to visit the Florence home of Claire (Clara Mary Jane) Clairmont (1798–1879), Mary Shelley's stepsister and one of Byron's many mistresses, in the hopes of acquiring her papers (Claremont is James's early spelling of her surname; cf. the New

York Edition preface). Unlike Juliana Bordereau, she was quite willing to talk about her past, and Silsbee recorded their conversations in a series of notebooks; but he did not get the documents he craved. Allegra Byron died, aged five, in 1822 after being taken from her mother and left in the care of a convent.

2. *se passèrent ... court encore ... couvers*: Happened ... [is] running still ... covets.

3. *Guiccioli*: Family of minor Italian aristocrats. Teresa Gamba Guiccioli (1800–1873) was Byron's last mistress.

4. *Elle se fiche bien*: She doesn't much care about.

5. *Miriam Rooth ... 'The Next Time'*: These names and titles belong to James's works about the artistic life. Miriam Rooth, Biddy Dormer and Julia Dallow are all characters in *The Tragic Muse* (1890), a multi-plotted novel about the idea of artistic vocation. 'The Death of the Lion' (1894) concerns a missing manuscript by the celebrated but little-read Paraday. 'The Next Time' (1895) is about a novelist who hopes always to write a trashy best-seller, while instead producing one unremunerative masterpiece after another. 'The Figure in the Carpet' is reprinted in this volume.

Penguin Classics

DAISY MILLER
HENRY JAMES

'I'm a fearful, frightful flirt! Did you ever hear of a nice girl that was not?'

Travelling in Europe with her family, Daisy Miller, an exquisitely beautiful young American woman, presents her fellow-countryman Winterbourne with a dilemma he cannot resolve. Is she deliberately flouting social conventions in the way she talks and acts, or is she simply ignorant of them? When she strikes up an intimate friendship with an urbane young Italian, her flat refusal to observe the codes of respectable behaviour leaves her perilously exposed. In *Daisy Miller* Henry James brilliantly dramatized the conflict between old-world manners and nouveau riche tourists, and created his first great portrait of an enigmatic and independent American woman.

Part of a series of new Penguin Classics editions of Henry James's works, this edition contains a chronology, further reading, notes and a wide-ranging introduction by David Lodge discussing the genesis of the tale, its huge success and James's controversial revision of the text for his New York Edition. Appendices include Henry James's Preface from the New York Edition and a note on James's adaptation of his story as a play.

'A small masterpiece' Leon Edel

Edited with an introduction and notes by David Lodge
Series editor Philip Horne

PENGUIN CLASSICS

THE EUROPEANS
HENRY JAMES

'They are sober; they are even severe ... But we shall cheer them up'

Eugenia, an American expatriate brought up in Europe, arrives in rural New England with her charming brother Felix, hoping to find a wealthy second husband after the collapse of her marriage to a German prince. Their exotic, sophisticated airs cause quite a stir with their affluent, God-fearing American cousins, the Wentworths – and provoke the disapproval of their father, suspicious of foreign influences. To Gertrude Wentworth, struggling against her sombre puritan upbringing, the arrival of the handsome Felix is especially enchanting. One of Henry James's most optimistic novels, *The Europeans* is a subtle and gently ironic examination of manners and morals, deftly portraying the impact of experience upon innocence.

Part of a series of new Penguin Classics editions of Henry James's works, this edition contains a chronology, further reading, notes and an introduction by Andrew Taylor exploring the novel's shifting patterns of opposites and James's portrayal of personal and national identity.

'This small book, written so early in James's career, is a masterpiece of major quality' F. R. Leavis

Edited with an introduction and notes by Andrew Taylor
Series editor Philip Horne

THE STORY OF PENGUIN CLASSICS

Before 1946 ... 'Classics' are mainly the domain of academics and students; readable editions for everyone else are almost unheard of. This all changes when a little-known classicist, E. V. Rieu, presents Penguin founder Allen Lane with the translation of Homer's *Odyssey* that he has been working on in his spare time.

1946 Penguin Classics debuts with *The Odyssey*, which promptly sells three million copies. Suddenly, classics are no longer for the privileged few.

1950s Rieu, now series editor, turns to professional writers for the best modern, readable translations, including Dorothy L. Sayers's *Inferno* and Robert Graves's unexpurgated *Twelve Caesars*.

1960s The Classics are given the distinctive black covers that have remained a constant throughout the life of the series. Rieu retires in 1964, hailing the Penguin Classics list as 'the greatest educative force of the twentieth century.'

1970s A new generation of translators swells the Penguin Classics ranks, introducing readers of English to classics of world literature from more than twenty languages. The list grows to encompass more history, philosophy, science, religion and politics.

1980s The Penguin American Library launches with titles such as *Uncle Tom's Cabin*, and joins forces with Penguin Classics to provide the most comprehensive library of world literature available from any paperback publisher.

1990s The launch of Penguin Audiobooks brings the classics to a listening audience for the first time, and in 1999 the worldwide launch of the Penguin Classics website extends their reach to the global online community.

The 21st Century Penguin Classics are completely redesigned for the first time in nearly twenty years. This world-famous series now consists of more than 1300 titles, making the widest range of the best books ever written available to millions – and constantly redefining what makes a 'classic'.

The Odyssey continues ...

The best books ever written

PENGUIN CLASSICS

SINCE 1946

Find out more at www.penguinclassics.com